# THE
# BONES
# OF THE
# STORY

## ALSO BY CAROL GOODMAN

*The Lake of Dead Languages*
*The Seduction of Water*
*The Drowning Tree*
*The Ghost Orchid*
*The Sonnet Lover*
*The Night Villa*
*Arcadia Falls*
*River Road*
*The Widow's House*
*The Other Mother*
*The Night Visitors*
*The Sea of Lost Girls*
*The Stranger Behind You*
*The Disinvited Guest*

### CHILDREN'S AND YOUNG ADULT

*Blythewood*
*Ravencliffe*
*Hawthorn*
*The Metropolitans*

### AS JULIET DARK

*The Demon Lover*
*The Water Witch*
*The Angel Stone*

### AS LEE CARROLL (WITH LEE SLONIMSKY)

*Black Swan Rising*
*The Watchtower*
*The Shape Stealer*

# THE
# BONES
# OF THE
# STORY

*A NOVEL*

## CAROL GOODMAN

*wm*

WILLIAM MORROW

*An Imprint of HarperCollinsPublishers*

THE BONES OF THE STORY. Copyright © 2023 by Carol Goodman. All rights reserved. Printed in the United States of America. No part of this book may be used or reproduced in any manner whatsoever without written permission except in the case of brief quotations embodied in critical articles and reviews. For information, address HarperCollins Publishers, 195 Broadway, New York, NY 10007.

HarperCollins books may be purchased for educational, business, or sales promotional use. For information, please email the Special Markets Department at SPsales@harpercollins.com.

FIRST EDITION

Designed by Renata DiBiase
Illustration by Daria/AdobeStock

Library of Congress Cataloging-in-Publication Data has been applied for.

ISBN 978-0-06-326524-0 (paperback)
ISBN 978-0-06-332017-8 (library edition)

23 24 25 26 27  LBC  5 4 3 2 1

*For my old college friends,*
*forever young in my heart*

# THE
# BONES
# OF THE
# STORY

# CHAPTER ONE

*NOW*

"I'M JUST HAVING trouble getting back on track."

Nina Lawson isn't the first student this semester—or even the first today—to attribute their academic woes to a deviation from some metaphorical *track*. As Dean of Liberal Arts, I've heard every excuse, sob story, and tragedy over the course of the last two years. But the image, coming as it does at the end of a long day at the end of a very long year, jolts me as if we're both on a train that has suddenly jumped off the rails into an abyss.

To give myself time to craft a response I look down at Nina's folder. I see that she comes from Newburgh—a small city about an hour south of campus—that she did well in her public high school even after her classes went remote in March of her senior year, and that she'd earned the Raven Society writing scholarship to Briarwood on the basis of a short story she wrote in high school. There's a note in my assistant's meticulous handwriting that Nina had to defer admission for a year to help her single, out-of-work mother with the bills. She has a work-study job in the financial office and an off-campus job at a local restaurant. No wonder she looks tired, I think, gazing up at her. Her light brown skin is mottled with acne. She's slouched in a zippered sweatshirt, hood up, eyes swollen and bloodshot, lips raw and chapped. "I wish you had come to see me sooner," I say in my firm-but-gentle voice. "The withdrawal deadline passed six weeks ago."

"Someone told me it had been extended," she says, not looking up.

"During the earlier part of the pandemic it had been but not this year. We're all trying to get back to normal." The twitch of Nina's lips makes me flinch. What does *normal* even mean?

"Did you try speaking with your professor?"

She shakes her head, the irritation on her cheeks flaming red. "I just . . . I wasn't sure what President Hotchkiss wanted—and it's weird, you know, having the president as a teacher."

*It is weird,* I could say, but instead I clasp my hands together and put on my best dean's smile. "It's a Briarwood tradition that every professor and academic administrator takes a turn teaching the first-year seminar. I took my FYSem"—I use the college vernacular to show her that I've been where she is now—"with President Hotchkiss before he was president. I remember he could be demanding. Did you have trouble understanding the assignments?" I recall that when I took the class freshman year, Hotch had taught FYSem as a sort of Socratic ramble punctuated by off-the-cuff writing assignments (pensées, as he had called them) that would be graded according to some mysterious rubric known only to him. He'd given Nina a C, which lowered her average below the minimum she had to maintain to keep her scholarship. If I gave her the withdrawal Hotch would complain that I was undermining his authority. If I didn't—

Nina is staring out the window, as many students do when they sit on the opposite side of my desk. My office in the tower of Main has a spectacular view facing west toward the Catskill Mountains. Usually, the view seems to calm students, but on this bleak December day all that implacable stone has brought tears to Nina's eyes.

"It's been a rough semester for everyone—" I begin.

She shakes her head, splattering tears. "I shouldn't be here . . ." Her eyes flick around my office as if its heavy oak furnishings, which Ruth, my executive assistant, has tried to soften with needlepoint pillows and mugs depicting my favorite authors, is a hostile war zone. "I don't understand all these weird rules and rituals."

I smile despite her tears, remembering how those traditions had seemed like a code I hadn't been given the key to when I first came here. "Briarwood is a small old college"—getting smaller every day, I think, recalling a recent memo from Admissions that the enrollment had dropped below our usual two thousand—"with a lot of traditions, like the Raven Society, for instance, which gave you your scholarship. If you keep up your grades and make the society senior year you may get to take the senior seminar. It can take a while to get used to," I add, "but if you give it a chance you might find some of those traditions are fun. They're meant to bring us together." *Because once you are initiated into the Mysteries of Briarwood,* a voice from the past intrudes into my thoughts, *you're unfit for life anywhere else.* "Are you going to the Luminaria tonight?"

She shrugs. "I'm not sure I'm in the mood to carry a candle up a mountain in the freezing cold. I don't really see the point."

"It's supposed to honor the coming solstice," I say. "The idea is we carry candles up Briarwood Mountain and light a bonfire at the foot of High Tor"—I gesture toward a stone tower on the top of the nearest mountain—"as a pledge that the light will return, that there's hope even when things seem darkest." I grimace self-consciously at how corny it sounds. "There's also hot cocoa and apple cider doughnuts."

She shifts uneasily in her chair. "I heard some of the older students in my dorm talking about a girl who got lost at one of these things, like a million years ago. They said she still haunts the ridge and that anyone who dies in the caves comes back to avenge their death."

I can feel my lips stretching into the shape of a smile and hope it doesn't look as strained as it feels. *A million years ago.* There are a number of legends about girls going missing in the ice caves but only one about a girl who went missing during the Luminaria, and that happened twenty-five years ago, as I'd just been reminded this morning by an email from President Hotchkiss about some last-minute details for this weekend's Commemoration. What a terrible word, I'd thought, as if we could ever share something like memory. As if remembering wasn't always something done alone. "Old colleges like Briarwood always have these stories, urban legends—" I begin.

"You mean like Bloody Mary and Slender Man?"

"Sort of."

"Because they say this girl who got lost is still living up there in the ice caves and that if you get too close, she'll drag you in and eat you alive."

"The ice caves are off-limits," I tell Nina, looking down at her withdrawal form. "And no one could live in them." I quickly scrawl my name across the bottom of the form. Why shouldn't this girl get a second chance? She's been the victim of a disaster through no fault of her own. "That story of a girl haunting the ice caves was around when I was a student here. One of my professors said she was a remnant of an old tradition that we oust the old year in order to welcome in the new year." *Slaughter,* my professor, Hugo Moss, had said, not *oust.* "And goodness knows there have been some years lately that I've been only too glad to see the back of." I try a smile on again as I hand Nina her signed form. "Think of this as an opportunity to get back on track and make a fresh start."

*As if it's ever possible to walk away from the past.*

This voice from the past is borne on a gust of cold air that rattles the loose windowpanes and prickles the back of my neck. It feels like it's come directly from those mountains, from the caves hidden in their folds where ice remains even in summer. Nina snatches the withdrawal form as if I might change my mind and take it back from her. *That's all she wanted from you.* Another voice from the past—Dodie this time. That's who this girl reminds me of, with her cringing shrugs, poor hapless Dodie. It makes me want to take the paper back and rip it to shreds in front of her face.

Then Nina looks up at me and meets my eyes for the first time since she entered my office. I'm startled by how fearful she looks. "There's something else—" she begins, but before she can continue there's a knock on the door and Ruth sticks her head in.

"I'm sorry to interrupt," she says, "but President Hotchkiss just sent you an electronic funds request that needs to be initialed before four."

I sigh. It's just like Hotch to leave paperwork till late Friday afternoon and then make the rest of us scramble. "I'd better take care of it before he comes banging on my door," I tell Ruth.

When I turn back to Nina, I see she's gotten up and shouldered her backpack. "Wasn't there something else?"

"No, it wasn't anything," she says with a quick nervous smile that doesn't disguise the worried look in her eyes—no, more than worried. She looks afraid. Then she smiles again and the look vanishes. "Thank you for everything. I'll try to make a new start . . . and go to your Lumin-thingy." Then she blushes and heads toward the door.

"Wait," I say, getting to my feet.

She turns to me expectantly but I'm suddenly unsure what to say to her. I want to tell her that everything will work out all right but how can I possibly know that? Instead, I grab a book off my shelf and hand it to her. "Here," I say. "This memoir was written by one of my classmates, Lance Wiley. He had a hard time fitting in here, too. Maybe you'll find it helpful."

She attempts a smile then takes the book and opens the door to the outer office.

"If you change your mind and want to talk about what's bothering you, Nina," I tell her, "my door is always open."

"Thanks, Dean Portman," she says. Then she turns and leaves quickly, as if embarrassed by my gesture.

I consider calling her to come back to find out what she'd been about to say. Was it a complaint against Hotch? It wouldn't be the first. Hotch, who considered himself a defender of free speech, often managed to offend his students. He mocked their requests for trigger warnings, resisted efforts to diversify his reading list, and refused to use gender-neutral pronouns. Even as president, he would have been sacked years ago if he didn't also have a knack for fundraising. His crowning achievement has been to expand and promote the Wilder Writers House, which will reopen in the spring. Using an existing endowment earmarked for the creative writing program, Hotch has overseen the restoration of Wilder Hall, which will house students and a writer-in-residence each year and host writing conferences during the summer. His hope is that it will evolve into a high-profile writing institution that will attract prestigious authors, boost our sagging admissions, and drive donations for the college.

As a cotrustee of the endowment, I've approved the project because it provides scholarships for underserved students and will bring dynamic and diverse writers to the campus. But I've been against this weekend's event—which Hotch decided on having only a month ago—to commemorate the twenty-fifth anniversary of the death of Hugo Moss, our first writer-in-residence, and our last. All of Moss's former students, as well as wealthy alums and trustees, have been invited for a reception Saturday night—tomorrow night, I think with a shudder of nerves—and a ceremony in the chapel Sunday afternoon. In addition, Moss's last class of students have been invited to stay at Wilder House for the weekend. It's meant rushing the last renovations of Wilder Hall and tackling a host of eleventh-hour details, which have largely fallen to me and to Ruth. Hotch bulldozed through my objections, claiming we need the fund-raising push to cover some extra expenses that have cropped up during the renovation. I suspect he simply enjoys hobnobbing with the rich and famous—he's always dashing off to Manhattan to attend galas and fancy lunches and traveling to exclusive locales where the wealthy gather—and is oblivious to the extra work his last-minute whims have entailed for the rest of us . . . which reminds me to review that funds request.

Still troubled by Nina's quick exit, I open the electronic funds request. It's made out to a local catering company, Mes Amis, one of the town's fanciest restaurants and one of the lucky ones to survive the last few years. The amount *is* rather surprising. I imagine Hotch is trying to impress the potential donors attending this weekend's event.

I spend the next hour answering emails—students wanting last-minute incompletes, the financial office wanting more data for the coming January audit of the Wilder Writers House endowment, and then one from Kendra Martin, the head of the creative writing program, asking me again if I've reviewed her recommendations for the writer-in-residence position. I open the orange folder she left for me earlier in the week and read over the CVs—there's a Vietnamese memoirist whose scheduled campus visit was cancelled last year when the pandemic hit, an African American mystery writer who's won multiple awards, and a sixty-something nature writer. They're all excellent candidates, but when I sent their CVs to Hotch earlier in the week, he'd said he wanted an alum to fill the position. I've procrastinated telling Kendra that but it's not fair to let her go to the reception tomorrow without knowing, so I write and tell her.

She immediately emails me with the subject line "Why?"

I sigh and write back that Hotch wants an alum to honor Hugo Moss and while according to the endowment we have equal authority over hiring, it would be difficult to overrule him. Hotch is counting on getting contributions from alums who will see themselves in the running for the job while the alum he really wants, Laine Bishop, will never take the job. But I can't put any of that in writing. *See you at the reception tomorrow!* I end with false cheer.

I move on to reply to a few late RSVPs declining the invitation to this weekend's Commemoration. Some cite the weather—I check the forecast and see that the temperature is supposed to drop overnight and snow might develop late tomorrow—and some cite ongoing concerns about gathering in crowds even vaccinated. Most send a contribution to the Wilder Writers House, which is the purpose of the event anyway. I thank them and express a hope they'll come in the spring when the house will be officially open, secretly grateful that only a few dozen people are coming. Maybe it will snow and the whole thing will be cancelled.

When I close my laptop and look out the window, the mountains have grown dark against the purpling sky. It makes them look closer, as if they have been creeping forward while I wasn't paying attention. I shiver at the thought and get up to close the window, making a mental note to follow up with Nina after the break and refer her to the counseling center if she's still having trouble coping. I was probably reading into her affect, recalling the bad things that happened to me when I was her age. At least, though, I'd tried to use what I had learned to help someone not suffer the same consequences.

*And what use is art,* Hugo Moss had asked on our first day of the senior writing seminar (I knew he'd show up sooner rather than later for the Commemoration I'm holding in my head), *if not to take the horrible things that have happened to us and make something beautiful out of them?*

I'm not an artist, I think as I straighten the papers on my desk and add a colorful silk scarf Ruth had given me for my last birthday to brighten my drab winter coat, but I can still make something good from the horrible.

*There's no amount of good you can do that will ever make up for what you did.*

This time it's my own voice I hear, only it sounds distant, as if it's coming from the bottom of one of those ice caves within the folds of the mountains. From the past? Or maybe, I think, feeling suddenly very cold, from the future, to warn me that not all my mistakes are safely behind me.

# CHAPTER TWO

*NOW*

AS I COME out of my office into the anteroom between my and Hotch's offices where Ruth has her desk, she lifts the steel-grey helmet of her head and gazes at me through thick, teal-framed eyeglasses. I sometimes think that the owlish glasses, stiff grey hair, and heavy pasty makeup are armor against the world. When she interviewed for the executive assistant's job five years ago, she was reticent about her personal history. Hotch, newly appointed president, said he thought a woman in her mid-fifties was too old for the job. I'd told him that was ageism and that she came with excellent recommendations from a state college in Maine and had scored exceptionally high in her civil service clerical exams. She's a stellar assistant—efficient, tireless, and meticulous—and goes out of her way to help students, especially ones from underprivileged backgrounds and ones who have been victims of trauma.

Now she tells me she's processed Nina Lawson's withdrawal form.

"I suppose I should go tell Hotch," I say, grimacing.

"Too late," she says, shaking her head. "He left soon after Nina did to go to the Luminaria."

"I thought he wanted to confirm the details about this weekend."

Ruth's eyebrows lift above the rims of her glasses before vanishing beneath her bangs—her patented *Don't waste my time* look. "*I* have confirmed all the details," she says. "Wilder House is cleaned and stocked with food and fresh linens; transportation from the airport and train station has been arranged for tomorrow. Everyone has RSVP'd except for—"

"The famous Laine Bishop," I say before she has to. "President Hotchkiss keeps asking me if she's coming."

"Does he think you can do anything to change her mind?" Ruth asks as she snaps open a dustcover and fits it over her computer. "The woman's been a recluse for twenty-five years."

"I think Hotch is frustrated that the college's most well-known alum writer and biggest potential donor remains outside the orbit of his personal charms. And even with the endowment for the writing program, the center still needs more funding and he's nervous it will be cut from the college budget given our financial difficulties since the pandemic."

"He should be nervous," Ruth says, straightening already straight papers on her desk and getting to her feet. "Do you know that they've cancelled the repair contracts for our copy machine? I had to fix it myself today."

"How . . . ?"

She gives me a satisfied smile. "I watched a YouTube, just like the young people do. There's really nothing you can't figure out how to do on the internet if needs be."

I laugh, feeling lighter. "Too bad you can't watch a YouTube on how to balance an overstretched college budget," I say.

Ruth tsks as she wraps a red cashmere shawl—my Christmas present to her last year—over her head. "I wouldn't have squandered the endowment on fripperies, like waffle stations in the cafeteria and Jacuzzis in the gym," she says, taking me literally. She continues to list expenses that she considers extraneous as we go down the wide marble staircase, our footsteps echoing in the empty building. It's the last day of the semester so many of the students and faculty have already gone home for winter break and those remaining will be at the Luminaria already. "And I wouldn't have wasted all this money on a Commemoration for a dead professor while the college is in financial straits," Ruth concludes as she pushes open the heavy door at the bottom of the stairs.

"Absolutely," I concur as we set off briskly on a paved path beneath bare sycamore trees, their spotted white limbs bright in the last rays of the setting sun. "I agree a hundred percent, but Hotch wants a fancy writers center that attracts famous authors and for the trustees to see what he's done."

Ruth snorts. "If you ask me, those writers are more trouble than they're worth. This one we're commemorating—you were in his class, weren't you? Was he worth all the fuss?"

"Hugo Moss?" I ask, feeling that chill again, like a shard of ancient ice from the caves has lodged under my coat collar. "He was certainly . . . charismatic. And he made Laine Bishop's career. But . . ." *The man's a monster,* I hear Truman saying, his eyes wide with fear. The same look, I realize now, that I'd seen for a second in Nina's face when I'd joked about Hotch bursting into my office. Was she afraid of Hotch? Maybe I should have made her stay—

"He was a bully, wasn't he?" Ruth finishes my thought for me. We've reached the edge of Mirror Lake, now a perfect circle of ice that reflects our namesake mountain, Briarwood. The lawn is full of students, faculty, staff, and locals from town, bundled in coats and scarves and clutching cups full of cider and cocoa and candles in paper cones. Many of the students—and some of the faculty and townspeople—are wearing long green robes and crowns woven of holly and ivy, traditional Luminaria garb. Where do these students even dig up these old practices, I wonder, or come up with stories like the lost girl in the cave?

I look up at the mountain and see a bright gold snake made

by the procession of students bearing candles to the top. Each year since I came back to Briarwood fifteen years ago, I've watched this procession thinking that it won't just be the light that returns. *They say that anyone who dies in the caves comes back to avenge their death.* Even now, as the ribbon of light reaches the summit and flares from the battlements of High Tor, I feel an answering kindling in my heart, as if something is at last coming—

"Something's wrong," Ruth says. "They've set off a flare."

Of course, I realize, the light couldn't have come from the top of High Tor; no one's been allowed in the tower for twenty-five years. The crowds on the Great Lawn ooh and aah as if watching fireworks on the Fourth of July. But the flare is a message. For a moment I think it's a message from the past.

"It's a distress signal," Ruth says as another flare streaks across the sky. "Something must have happened."

She spots a security guard and pushes people out of the way to get to him. When I catch up, I hear the words *student* and *accident* come through the static of the guard's walkie-talkie.

"What's happened?" I ask.

"A student's fallen in one of the caves," the guard says.

"Do we know which student?" I ask, my skin prickling.

I hear the word *body* coming through the static but I can't make out the rest. Ruth says something but it's drowned out by a blast from the walkie-talkie.

"What did you say?" I ask Ruth, sure I must have misheard the name she said.

"They've brought up a student from the caves," Ruth says. "It's Nina Lawson."

The ice shard that has been lodged in my spine since Nina left my office spreads down my back and through my chest, crystallizing my blood. That look in her eyes—she'd been afraid of something.

*Why didn't you make her stay? Why didn't you stop her?*

All the voices that have been clamoring for attention today are talking at once, merging into a siren. It *is* a siren. Ruth turns to watch a police car drive onto the lawn, her glasses reflecting the blue and white lights as if she's the one who's been pulled out of the subterranean fissure sheathed in ice. That image of a woman sheathed in ice has haunted my nightmares for twenty-five years.

"Is she hurt?" I ask.

Ruth turns to me, her face unreadable behind her thick glasses. "No, thank God," she says, "she's okay. But they brought something up with her. Human remains. They're saying they've found bones in one of the caves." I turn away from her and push blindly through the crowd, which is buzzing now with conjecture and rumor, to the foot of the mountain, but I'm stopped there by campus security. "We're asking that no one else goes up," the young man says. "We're trying to evacuate the path so we can bring down the injured student."

"I know her," I say. "I should be with her."

The guard, hardly older than a student, looks unsure, but then Ruth catches up with me and barks at him, "This is Dean Portman. The administration will need to determine how this happened."

"I understand, ma'am," he says, "but the path is mobbed with people coming down the mountain."

He turns and points upward. The snake of light has doubled back on itself, as if eating its own tail, and is writhing downhill. As those returning get closer I see that most are still holding their candles, making their faces look ghoulish. EMTs have arrived with a stretcher and are regarding the crowd impatiently.

"There's another way up," Ruth whispers to me. "Behind Wilder Hall."

I nod and follow her through a grove of pine trees to a Tudor stone and half-timber building that looks like an old English manor out of a Gothic novel. It was originally a private home, then the dean's house, then a lecture hall, and then, when I was a student here, a residence house for a select group of seniors. It's had many other incarnations until five years ago when it was closed for renovations to turn it back into a writing center. Although I've signed off on all the renovations and preparations for its opening weekend, it still unnerves me to see two of its lead-glass windows glowing amber, like the eyes of an animal in its lair that's just woken up.

Ruth leads the way past the arched doorway and flagged terrace and the wrought iron gate that leads into the woods, her red shawl giving her the appearance of Little Red Riding Hood setting off through the woods to Grandmother's house. The path is steep, practically carved out of the rockface, the stone steps crumbling in places, but Ruth, despite being in her late fifties, navigates it like a mountain goat. I can barely keep up with her. I know she swims regularly at the campus pool, but I'm still impressed by her endurance. I imagine she's as eager as I am to make sure Nina's all right and to find out what she'd been doing near the caves, which were clearly off-limits. I keep thinking of how Nina talked about the story of the girl who'd been lost in the caves as if Nina were drawn to another girl who didn't fit in and went missing. Maybe she'd gone looking for her.

*Maybe she had found her.*

Ruth vanishes suddenly from the path up ahead and I am seized by the crazy, irrational fear that she's been swallowed by the mountain. But, of course, it's just that she's reached the top. The path ends so abruptly that it's like stepping out of a tunnel straight into the sky.

*Like being born,* Laine had said the first time we came up this path together.

Even now, with the light fading on the western ridges, the

sight takes my breath away. As far as the eye can see, wild grasses and dwarf pines glow purple in the twilight. The pine barrens, they're called, an alpine habitat sustained by the cold air that seeps out of the ice caves, hidden within the folds of the ridge along ancient fault lines. When people hear *cave* they think of something scooped out of a hill, but the ice caves are actually fissures in the rock—dozens of them folded into the ridge—some shallow, but others long and deep and leading to caverns that go on for miles beneath the earth. *Like the entrance to the Roman underworld,* I remember Laine saying when she looked down into one of the deeper caves. I turn toward the group gathered around High Tor and see that several are wearing robes and wreaths and antlers and medieval masks. They might be a band of ancient priests gathered to observe a pagan rite. One figure is lying on a stone slab as if she has been laid out for sacrifice.

My heartbeat quickens, and I pick up my pace. As I get closer, I see that the figure on the stone slab, who has been given a blanket by a "druid," is Nina. The other "druids" resolve into students wearing blankets cinched with belts, ivy wreaths, and papier-mâché raven masks.

"Dean Portman!" Nina sits up and cries as I approach.

"Oh, Nina," I say, kneeling beside her. "I'm so sorry! What happened?"

"I took your advice and went to the Luminaria. I saw some people gathered by the caves and was thinking about that girl who got lost . . ." Her voice falters and I realize she's shivering despite the blanket around her shoulders. Recalling how cold the caves are, I begin to shiver, too. "But when I got there, they were gone. I thought maybe they'd gone down in the cave so I looked over—"

"Which was very foolish."

The voice comes from behind me. I turn to find Prentiss

Hotchkiss in a tweed jacket, quilted vest, and brogues—the picture of an English country gentleman down to the red patches in his cheeks, as if he's been out stalking pheasants. "Those caves are dangerous," he scolds. "The slick ice makes it easy to fall in. That's why they're strictly off-limits." He turns toward the robed onlookers. "All of you who were there should be suspended for trespassing, especially those of you in the Raven Society. You should be setting a better example." The students in the circle exchange nervous glances with each other. One starts to volunteer that they'd only gone toward the caves because they'd heard Nina cry out.

"I suppose I can overlook the infraction *this time*," Hotch says grudgingly.

The students shift uneasily, mutter muted thanks, and then disperse quickly as the EMTs arrive from the other path.

"And as for you, young lady," Hotch continues, looking down at Nina, "I think you've already paid a high enough price for your folly. You won't be repeating your mistake, am I right?"

She nods tearfully.

"Good," Hotch says, already looking away from her. "I see a police officer has arrived with the EMTs. I'll have a word with him."

Hotch walks past the EMTs to intercept a uniformed officer while one of the medics kneels beside Nina to examine her ankle.

"It's okay," I say. "Hopefully it's just a sprain."

She nods and wipes her tears away. "It doesn't hurt that bad, it's just . . . it was so scary when I turned on my phone flashlight and saw . . . *her* . . . staring up at me from below. I could have gone down into that pit and died like her if I'd fallen a few inches over! Do you think it's the lost girl?

"Are you sure they were even human bones?" I ask. "They might belong to an animal—"

"They're human bones." The disembodied voice raises the hair on the back of my neck.

I turn and see a bulky figure silhouetted against the purple sky. It's impossible to make out his features. When he steps forward, the creak of a leather holster and the flash of a metal badge reveal him to be a police officer.

"Any investigation by the police needs to go through my office," Hotch says, a few steps behind the officer.

"We received a dispatch that there'd been an accident in the caves and human remains had been discovered," the officer says in an icy tone. "It was deemed expedient to secure the site before any further contamination could occur. My men are doing that now. We need to clear the area and bar access to both paths to the summit."

*Both paths? How does he know about the path behind Wilder?*

I rise to my feet so quickly my head spins, making me wobble. The police officer moves forward and puts a hand on my arm to steady me, bringing his face into the light. *Ben.* All my buried ghosts are coming home.

But he's not a ghost. His hand is so warm that when he takes it away my flesh feels instantly colder, as if he's stolen what little warmth I had left in my body. Or the temperature is dropping. I recall that the weather report forecast temperatures in the low teens overnight.

"We have to make sure no one else is up here," I blurt out. He looks as if I've slapped him, as if he's shocked that *these* are the words I've chosen to be my first to him after all these years of silence. "Nina said she saw some people near the caves before she fell," I add. "If they're still out here they could freeze overnight."

"Surely no one would be so foolish as to stay out here," Hotch says.

"I've learned not to underestimate the stupidity of college

students," Ben says, his eyes still locked on mine. Then he wrenches his gaze away and directs his wrath at Hotch. "You might want to reconsider the wisdom of holding a college event in a dangerous location where lives have been lost before."

Hotch bristles at the rebuke. "I don't know what stories get bandied about in *town*, Officer, but I can assure you that here at Briarwood the welfare of our students is our first concern."

The corner of Ben's mouth twitches into a sneer. You'd have to know him well to sense the injury of not being recognized. It would never occur to Hotch that the town police officer is an alum, even though Ben was included in the list of invitees to this weekend's event—and the first to decline. I can see in the way that Ben shifts his weight that he's getting ready to hit back, but then he breathes in and out and turns his attention to me.

"I've already got a team searching the area," he says. "We'll be sure to send any strays back to campus after we've questioned them. I just need to ask Ms. Lawson a few questions and then we can get her someplace warm."

"I think a representative of the college should be present at any questioning," Hotch says, drawing himself up the way he does at meetings when someone questions his authority.

"I'll stay with her," I tell Hotch, trying to disengage him from a standoff with Ben. "Someone should release a statement about what's happened before it gets out on social media." I look pointedly toward the "druids," who are tapping away on their phones. I notice that Ruth is talking to them, no doubt scolding them to stay away from the caves and dress more warmly. I hear a ping on my phone and when I look down I see that there's a tweet tagging the college. *Briarwood student finds body in caves* and another that reads *Ice Cave Mystery Resurfaces*. I try to open one of the tweets but it refuses to load; cell reception on the mountain is always dodgy. Hotch is holding up his phone,

moving away from us to get a better signal. Ben crouches next
to Nina and begins talking to her quietly. I can see her tensing
up. I sit on the other side of her, wincing at how cold the stone
is, and put my hand on her arm. She gives me a worried smile
and then looks back at Ben, who's talking so softly I can barely
hear his questions. They elicit from her a recounting of how she
thought she saw people near the caves.

"Did you recognize them?" he asks.

"No," she says, glancing at me uneasily. "They were wearing
hooded robes and masks. I thought they were in the Raven Society, performing some kind of ceremony for the lost girl."

Ben stares at me, a mix of horror and anger on his face. "The
Raven Society?" he echoes, his voice trembling. "A ceremony
for the lost girl? What the hell, Nell?"

"I don't know anything about a ceremony," I say stiffly, pulling my authority around me like an academic robe, "but I can
get their names and email them to you, Officer." Then I turn to
Nina and say, "If you could let me know who you saw, that'd be
really helpful," hoping Ben will follow my lead in reassuring her.
She's had enough men scolding her today.

"We'll track them down," he says, as if he's talking about
fugitives from the law. "And in the future think twice before
you hare off after people you don't really know." He gets to his
feet and moves off into the dusk, barking orders into his walkie-
talkie.

"I just wanted to feel like I *belonged*," Nina says softly.

"I know," I say, putting my arm around her and squeezing her
shoulders. *The problem*, I could add, but don't, *is what we might
find ourselves willing to do to avoid losing that sense of belonging.*

# CHAPTER THREE

*THEN*

I THOUGHT I'D finally found where I belonged when I received my acceptance letter to Briarwood. It had come as a surprise to everyone: my mother, my guidance counselor, even my English teacher, a Briarwood College alum who had urged me to apply. Grade-wise, I was an average student, my only distinction a poetry contest award junior year and a high verbal SAT score attributable to a lonely bookish childhood. During the summer before freshman year, spent working at a diner, I dreamed every night that the acceptance letter had been a mistake. I would arrive at the college gates—pictured in the brochure as black spikes silhouetted against a violet sky—and be told by an impossibly tall man dressed in black that the letter had been sent in error.

*Here,* he would say, pointing a long taloned finger to a smaller figure standing beside him, *is the true intended recipient, whose place you would have usurped.*

I would try to make out the figure through the camouflage of dappled shade, her face a soft blur of trapped sunlight amid the shadow leaves. As her face came slowly into focus her features would become sickeningly familiar.

*But that's me!* I would scream as the gatekeeper laughed and the gates closed with a shriek that pierced my sleep and woke me, half strangled in the clammy polyester sheets in my narrow twin bed.

"Are you sure you wouldn't rather go to Nassau Community for the first year?" my mother said the morning after I recounted my nightmare. "There's no shame in admitting you're anxious about going away."

"I'm sure," I said, looking away from the desperation in her eyes, the *Don't leave me here alone* look.

What I had to do, I decided, was go *early*. Because I would be doing a work-study job in the library, I was allowed to move into the dorms up to ten days before classes began.

"It's not required," my mother said, looking over the letter when I told her my plans.

"It will give me time to settle in and show them that I'm hardworking," I countered. "Aren't you always telling me that it's important to make a good impression in a new job?"

It was one of the homilies she'd recite as she unfurled a new pair of pantyhose up her varicose-veined legs to look profes-sional for the dentist's office receptionist job she took after my father left her for *his* receptionist, along with *Never depend on a man, Always watch your figure,* and *Never drink from a glass left unattended at a party.*

I can still see the hurt in her eyes when I told her I could ship my belongings and take the bus to campus, as if she knew I'd be embarrassed by her Long Island accent and brightly dyed hair in the posh old-money setting of Briarwood College. My mother was my first sacrifice on the altar of Briarwood. The first toll I paid to get through that gate.

Which I found locked when I arrived on a sweltering August day—my nightmare come true.

"They don't open those till next week," an overalled janitor told me. "Go around the back."

He directed a skinny boy, who I guessed from his identi-cal snub nose and ruddy complexion was his son, to show me the way. And so, I entered Briarwood College for the first time through the service entrance along with the janitors and house-keepers, who greeted my arrival as an unwelcome interruption to their floor waxing and radiator bleeding, and one disgruntled janitor's son who vanished into the basement with his father as soon as he could. I lugged my boxes up to the fourth floor, where I'd been assigned, and wandered the empty, echoing halls looking for Suite E-4, the numbers on the doors following no obvious order—or at least no order I had been initiated into. After two loops of the entire rectangular floor, no E-4 appeared. Here was another sign that I didn't belong: the room I'd been assigned didn't exist. Finally, one of the dorm matrons took pity on me. She must have heard my echoing steps and squeaky-wheeled suitcase circling the floor and reckoned if she didn't do something I'd become one of those campus legends: the fresh-man girl who never found her room.

"*E* for East Tower," she told me briskly, leading me down a narrow hall I hadn't noticed and opening a door to a sunlit room. "*Four* for four occupants, two singles and one double. That's the best room." She pointed to an open door through which I spied tall leaded glass windows looking out over the leafy quad and a view of the mountains.

"I don't want to seem greedy," I said, turning away from the spacious sunlit room and regarding the middle room with its two narrow beds, their bare mattresses a dingy yellow, only a few feet apart from each other. I couldn't imagine sleeping so close to a stranger. "You said there was another single?"

She jerked her chin to another door that I had thought must be a closet. It opened to a narrow room with a single window at the end facing the brick wall of the opposite tower. A monastic cell of a room suitable for a medieval nun. "It was the servant's room when the ladies brought their own maids," the matron said with a sniff.

I turned to express my amazement that former students had

come to college with their own maids, but she was already gone. I'd found my place at Briarwood College, someplace safe and hidden.

For the next ten days I felt invisible. When I reported to the library, a harried clerk pointed to a roomful of book-laden carts and told me to start reshelving without once glancing at me. I spent hours each day pushing a squeaky-wheeled cart through empty stacks, slotting each book into its Dewey decimal–appointed place. I ate in the cafeteria with the half dozen work-study students, who huddled to themselves, and the staff, who ignored me, including the janitor's son. He sat by himself with a brown bag lunch, his snub nose stuck in a book. On my third day I noticed it was a Latin grammar.

"I took Latin," I blurted out, mostly to see if I still had a voice. "Are you studying for an exam?"

He peered up out of deep brown eyes that looked like they belonged to a hunted animal and said, "I'm studying so I'll be ready for classes next week."

"Oh! You go here?" I asked, surprised both that he wasn't just the janitor's son and that anyone would take Latin in college. I couldn't wait to drop it in high school.

He turned pink. "They do let in janitors' sons," he told me. "They even have a scholarship for it."

"For janitors' sons?" I asked, realizing as I said it what a stupid question it was.

His milk-white skin turned even redder, the blush spreading to the tips of his ears. "For the children of faculty and staff," he bit out between clenched teeth.

"Cool," I said, desperately trying to backpedal to make up for my gaffe and hoping he'd ask me to sit down. He didn't. I fled from the staff dining room and out into the fog that swallowed the campus for that whole first week. *Ice fog,* I overheard the dorm matrons and janitors murmur as they went about their business, *come down from the ice caves. Don't go up into the mountains,* my dorm matron warned when I left in the morning, *people have disappeared in those caves.*

I followed the paths from dorm to library to cafeteria to the dorm again, peering into the grey fog for the sun-dappled campus from the brochure. Occasionally a building or tree would loom out of the mist, a specter of my dream campus. I would catch glimpses of approaching figures that would vanish before reaching me or hear voices that evaporated into the cries of mourning doves and foghorns from the river. After a few days I began to wonder if I were entirely solid. When I ran into someone I blurted out, "I thought you were a ghost!"

What I'd really thought, though, was that I'd run into the blur-girl I'd glimpsed through the gates in my nightmare, the one intended for my spot at Briarwood.

One night I heard a sound at the window. When I got up to see what it was, I saw *her* face in the glass—the blur-girl from my dream—*the intended*—come to take her rightful place, which I had stolen. A moment later I saw it was my own reflection in glass steamed over by fog. I stepped closer to the window to wipe away the condensation—and something banged hard against the glass. I screamed and stumbled back. She *was* coming for me. A shred of her black shroud had fallen through the open window. I knelt, my beating heart echoing the bang on the window, and lifted from the floor a black feather with a drop of blood at its tip. A crow must have gotten lost in the fog and slammed up against my window.

Or the blur-girl had turned into a crow, like a girl in a fairy tale, and this was her sign to me that she would return.

I somehow made my way back into a fitful sleep, and the next morning, I awoke to high-pitched shrieks—the intended come to tear me apart.

"I thought there were four singles," a girl's voice said. "What's the point of a suite if two of us have to share? We all know that Dodie snores."

"I'm happy to take the double, Chilton," another voice—rich and raspy with an undercurrent of strained amusement—said. "You know I sleep like the dead."

"I have enlarged adenoids," a third, nasal voice said defensively. "I suppose I could take the single and then no one will have to be bothered by me."

"We agreed Laine would have the large single," the first girl—*Chilton?*—said. "She's the reason we got the suite because her name came up first in the lottery. But I assumed I'd have the other. Do we even know who this other girl is? Or if she's even in there?"

"The matron said she's been here all week," Nasal Voice—*Dodie? What kind of a name was that anyway?*—said. "The girl is"—Dodie lowered her voice as if someone with ears, and feelings, might truly be behind the door—"*a work-study.*"

"It's not a crime," the rich voice—Laine—said. "And it doesn't mean the poor girl is deaf. She's probably listening to us squabbling this whole time. No doubt she's filling out a room transfer right now so she doesn't have to live with three bickering shrews. Halloo in there! Are you awake? Have we driven you out the window in disgust?"

What was I supposed to do? Reveal that I'd been listening? Pretend to have just woken up? Take Laine's obvious suggestion to exit through the window? Clearly, they wanted me gone. I could hear rustling outside the door, the sound of crinkling paper. Were they starting a bonfire to burn me out? Then something slid under the door. A heavy card with a gold embossed monogram of swirly initials and a hastily drawn sketch of three witches around a bubbling cauldron.

*Come on out,* it read, *we don't bite. Much.*

I made an involuntary half laugh, half snort and the one

called Laine cried, "Aha! It lives!," and there was nothing else to do but open the door.

They were crouched on the floor, around an open suitcase, for all the world like the three witches in *Macbeth*. A petite snub-nosed blonde in a polo shirt and culottes, a long-faced brunette in a khaki skirt and madras-print sleeveless blouse, and a striking raven-haired beauty in cutoff jeans and a white T-shirt that showed off a golden tan.

"You can have the single," I said, fighting back tears. "I only took it because it's so small I didn't think anyone else would want it."

The raven-haired beauty sat back on her heels and laughed. "Are you always so self-effacing?" she asked, unfolding her long bronzed legs and getting to her feet. "I'm Laine," she said, holding out a slim hand. "And these hoydens are Chilton and Dodie. I apologize for our bad manners. We've known each other for dog's ages and are used to scrapping for boarding school leftovers."

I stared at her, not sure if she was making fun of me. I'd never heard anyone speak like she did outside of books. But her smile seemed genuine and she was still holding out her hand. It seemed rude not to take it.

Her grip was surprisingly strong, and she used it to pull herself past me to look into my room. "Gad, you weren't exaggerating. Like a nun's cell—oh, is that the Waterhouse *Lady of Shalott*? I saw it at the Tate this summer." She looked around at the other reproductions of Pre-Raphaelite paintings I'd taped to the wall. I felt myself blushing at how childish they must seem to someone as sophisticated as this girl, but instead she seemed pleased. "Oh, you've got more of her. No wonder you like this room." She gestured to the view of brick wall reflected in the mirror and the notebook open below it on my desk. "'But in her web she still delights, to weave the mirror's magic sights,'" she quoted. I stared at her, still unsure if she was making fun of me or not, but compelled by the words of the poem, which so perfectly summed up how I'd felt this last week, to echo the end of the stanza. ""I am half sick of shadows'"—"

"'Said the Lady of Shalott,'" Laine finished for me, beaming. "I'm named for her, you know—Elaine, but everyone calls me Laine." She touched her throat where a gold locket rested in the deep well of her clavicle as if molten gold had pooled there. The locket was inscribed with the same fancy monogram that was on the card.

"Oh, that's funny," I said, "my name's Ellen, which is almost the same as Elaine, but everyone calls me Ellie."

For a moment I saw a shadow pass over her face, as if I had suggested that she could be a version of anyone else when clearly, she was an *original,* but then her face cleared and she leaned in and lowered her voice to a conspiratorial whisper that seemed to make a space just big enough for the two of us. "It's like we were meant to share the same suite. But . . ." She tilted her head, birdlike, and studied me. "You don't look like an Ellie; you look more like a Nell with an *e,* which is Ellen spelled backward."

"Nelle with an *e,*" I repeated, feeling like I'd been turned inside out like a sock in the dryer, but Laine looked so pleased with herself—and by association, me—that I said, "I like it."

"I had a cocker spaniel named Nellie," Dodie said brightly. Chilton rolled her eyes.

"Perhaps you should spell it without the *e,*" Laine suggested.

"Yes," Chilton agreed, "we wouldn't want to confuse you with Dodie's cocker spaniel."

"No, you're right. Nell without an *e* is much better."

"That's settled, then," she said with finality. "I can tell that you and I are going to be great friends." Then she shouted to the other two, "You girls will have to bunk together. The Lady of Shalott needs her bower."

Dodie and Chilton exchanged a disgruntled look; they were going to hate me for this.

"Look," I said, "I really don't mind sharing with either of you. Maybe Dodie should take this room because . . . er . . ."

"Because of my snoring?" Dodie asked with a forced smile. "I can use nose strips and Chilton can use earplugs. If Laine thinks you should have the single—"

"Then the single you shall have," Chilton chimed in with a smile even faker than Dodie's. "What are some nose strips and earplugs compared to a medieval curse?"

"Exactly," Laine said, either ignoring or not hearing the thick sarcasm and resentment in Chilton's voice. "Now that's settled, let's go over to Wilder Hall. We have to be early for registration so we get the best classes."

"Oh," I said, "I didn't know you had to do that. I'm not dressed—"

"And besides, there's the whole curse thing," Chilton said sweetly.

"Nonsense," Laine said. "I hereby decree the curse lifted. Come, Nell, I know the perfect class for a romantic such as yourself."

I scrambled into clothes and joined my new suitemates hurtling down four flights of stairs, Laine's laugh filling the dormitory. Suddenly there were other students climbing the stairs, hauling boxes, shouting out to one another, as if Laine's good spirits had shaped them out of the fog—

Which was gone, I discovered, as we burst outside. The sun was shining, the shade-dappled paths, ivy-covered brick buildings, and ancient trees as bright and promising as those pictures in the brochure. I felt as if Laine really *had* lifted a curse from me, although, of course, as I remembered later, the curse isn't lifted when the lady leaves her tower, it's just beginning.

# CHAPTER FOUR

*NOW*

I WAIT TO make sure that Nina has been brought to the infirmary, and then I stand on the ridge looking west as the police team, outlined in black against the last embers of the dying sunset, trudge across the purpling pine barrens. They look like figures in a Bruegel painting returning from some rustic hunt.

I shiver at the image and feel the warmth of a blanket settling over my shoulders. For a moment I think it's Ben, that despite the coldness in his eyes and voice he's relented and come back to make sure I'm all right.

But, of course, it's only Ruth. She's even got a thermos of hot chocolate, which she pulls from her capacious tote bag. Ruth always comes prepared. "You should go home," I tell her. "It's been a long day and the temperature's dropping."

"Low teens by dawn," she says with satisfaction, her glasses reflecting the last orange light like the glass doors of a wood-burning stove. "And snow on the way tomorrow."

"I'll email Hotch and tell him we'll really have to cancel the Commemoration. He'll have to see reason. I'll let you know as soon as I get his okay—"

"And I'll have emails to all the guests ready to go. You should go home and get some rest."

"You, too," I say.

When we part at the base of the mountain, though, I suspect that she's heading back to the office. She prefers to work on the office computer, she once told me, rather than her old computer at home. Even during the earlier days of the pandemic lockdown, she would come in, using her spare key that gave her access to the janitors' tunnels. That way she could evade the sensors on the card-swipe entrances so she wouldn't have to do the mandatory testing required for anyone coming to campus. *I'm the only one here,* she replied when I asked if she wasn't worried about getting the virus, *and someone's got to keep an eye on things.* Usually it reassures me, knowing she's up in Main "keeping an eye on things." Like the Lady of Shalott, I told her once, inviting a blank stare that I'd interpreted as her failure to get the reference. But then she'd said, *She was under a curse, you know, and she dies in the end.*

I'd learned after that never to underestimate Ruth's encyclopedic knowledge.

Before walking home I take out my phone and with freezing fingers I type out a short email to Hotch saying that we need to cancel the Commemoration both because of the weather forecast and because it will look callous to go ahead with it while the police are removing human remains from the cave. Then I walkthrough the college gates, which had seemed so imposing when I first arrived at Briarwood all those years ago, as if they'd never open to let me in. Tonight, I have a momentary fear that they won't let me out, but they swing open easily and then clang with a finality as if they'll never open for me again.

Although I'm not particularly hungry I stop at the Acropolis Diner on my walk home. I got into the habit during the pandemic of going there for takeout, worried that they wouldn't survive the shutdown. Places like the Acropolis barely made it. Because I helped the owner fill out the paperwork for a small business loan, I know that they're barely making it now. I'd tried to get Hotch to hire them for this weekend's catering but he'd said we needed something more upscale for our donors, hence the pricey bill from Mes Amis.

It's probably just as well. That order will have to be cancelled now. We can't possibly go through with the event after what's happened today.

As Photini, the owner's daughter, lifts her head from her iPad to greet me, I realize that I'll have to tell her that the breakfast pastry basket I'd convinced Hotch to order for Sunday morning would have to be cancelled, too.

"Dean Portman, I was wondering if you were going to make it in tonight after what happened at the college."

I shouldn't be surprised that news has traveled so fast. Photini is in her second year at the local community college and applying to finish her degree at Briarwood. She's friends with Briarwood students and no doubt follows them on social media.

"Is that girl who fell in the cave okay?" she asks. "Is it true that she found a skeleton? Do you think it's the ice cave girl?"

So, stories about the ice cave girl circulated even in town. "She's fine," I say, regarding the display of pastries in the revolving glass case and feeling as if I'm spinning with them. "Just some bruises and a twisted ankle. What are people saying?"

"Well . . ." Photini leans forward, elbows propped on the counter, her olive-toned skin glowing gold in the light from the pastry case. "You know there's that legend that the ice cave girl walks the ridge on the night of the winter solstice? People are posting stories about her—a podcast did an episode on her last year—saying she's returned because it's been twenty-five years since she took her last victim and that there's a cycle, like cicadas." She takes a breath and then adds, "I saved the last of the spanakopita. Do you want that with a salad?"

I say yes to the food, more to gain a moment to myself to process Photini's story than because I think I'll be eating it. I know how rumors spread, how legends and ghost stories spring up like mushrooms, perhaps most of all when the truth has been hidden or suppressed, but I'm still startled by the underground life the legend has acquired, especially the idea that the ice cave girl follows some sort of *cycle*.

*Like cicadas.* I shudder, picturing the bulbous insects pushing up from beneath the earth.

"I added some of Mama's homemade yogurt and honey because I know how much you and Earl like it." Photini startles me out of a vision of subterranean creatures by holding out a brown paper bag. I hand her my credit card in exchange as she goes on about the legend of the ice cave girl. She was a witch, according to some, banished from one of the first settlements in the valley, or a remnant of a prehistoric race that lived in the mountains before the valley was settled by Europeans, or the ghost of a girl from one of the towns drowned when the reservoir was built.

"You know they moved the graves when they built the reservoir," she says, giving me my receipt. "And a spirit is restless when it's not buried properly—oh, Mama will want to know if you'll still need the pastries on Sunday."

I take a moment to sign the receipt, adding a 25 percent tip as I had throughout the lockdown.

"Tell your mother we still need them," I say, figuring that even if the event is cancelled Ruth can bring the basket to the food pantry where she volunteers. If Hotch can shell out a fortune to Mes Amis, the college can buy some baked goods from the local diner. "And would you mind stopping by my house to feed Earl Sunday morning?"

"I'll do it on the way to deliver the pastries," Photini says, her almond-shaped eyes lighting with mischief. "I've always wanted to see the inside of Wilder Hall. I hear it's haunted."

PAST THE ACROPOLIS the neighborhood changes from the stately Colonials belonging to professors to the ramshackle subdivided

Victorians of student housing and smaller bungalows where the town's working class used to dwell. Since the pandemic even these have gotten pricier as New Yorkers fled the city for the open lands of upstate. The migration probably saved the town when Briarwood's enrollment dropped by half last year and all those students weren't here to order pizza and go for 4 A.M. pancakes at the Acropolis. Still, it's a little unsettling to walk through my modest neighborhood past brand-new hybrid Jeeps, newly expanded houses, and labradoodles being taken for their evening walks. I can't help but feel a little invaded, as if I've been rooted out of my foxhole.

My own house is one of the smallest on the block, a Sears, Roebuck & Co. model delivered to the village of Briarwood on a railroad flat in 1929. It's tiny: twenty-eight by twenty-two feet containing two bedrooms, one of which I use as a study; a parlor; a galley kitchen; and one bathroom. Photini, on her cat-sitting visits, says it's like the new tiny houses that ecologically minded hipsters favor. It has always reminded me of the humble cottages where disgraced or diminished heroines go at the end of their stories—Ferndean, where Jane Eyre finds blind Rochester, or the seaside cottage where Hester Prynne takes shelter at the end of *The Scarlet Letter*.

Tonight, closing the door behind me, I feel as if I've gone to earth. Earl, my grey tabby, bestirs himself from the embroidered cushion on the Morris chair and rubs up against my leg, mewing for the yogurt he knows is in the takeout bag. In the kitchen, I spoon some into a saucer, set it on the floor for Earl, then turn on the kettle. I put the rest of the food in the fridge and wait for the water to boil.

*You don't even know it's her,* I tell myself as I take my teacup to my desk and open my laptop. A dozen notifications pop up in the corner of my screen like a flock of crows alighting on something dead.

A *murder of crows,* Laine, who loved the terms of venery, corrects in my head, *an unkindness of ravens.*

I open my Briarwood email account and look for a reply from Hotch. I'm expecting an angry response but there's no response at all. I check to make sure my email to him went through—it did—and then send him a follow-up message urging him to see how bad it will look if we go ahead with the event. Then, before I write something I will regret, I close my laptop.

I make another cup of tea to warm myself up and bring it into my bedroom, then crawl under the covers, which feel as heavy as that blanket Ruth laid on my shoulders as I stood on the ridge—

Which is where I go as soon as I close my eyes, the bruised purple waiting behind my eyelids turning into the western sky at dusk, the weight on my shoulders not Ruth's blanket but a hand—

Laine's hand. It is Laine, not Ruth, standing beside me looking toward the west. We are on the ridge just above one of the ice caves, a fissure in the stone that gapes black beneath our feet, an otherworldly cold rising up out of it. I can hear the tick and crack of ice breaking and re-forming, aftershocks of that one dreadful crack.

*Should we go down and make sure?* I ask.

*Chilton already did. She said her head was broken open like a cracked egg—*

*We have to go,* I say to Laine, my eyes still locked on the gaping mouth of the cave, *we'll leave this in our past.*

*As if it's ever possible to walk away from the past,* Laine says, her voice cracking.

I turn and see that *she* is cracking. The fault lines opening up beneath our feet have worked their way into her flesh, the way a trickle of water will break open stone when it freezes.

Fine cracks spread across her face like the crazing in an old china teacup, so beautiful I reach out my hand to touch her—

I wake up to the sound of something shattering, my heart thumping so hard I think that it's my chest that has cracked open. But it's only the teacup that I left on my nightstand last night, now a scattering of shards in the wedge of light from the bathroom door.

*Like splinters of bone.*

I must have flailed out my arm and knocked it over. I sit up, shaking my head to shed the vestiges of the dream, and check the time on my phone. I'm relieved to see it's six-thirty so I don't have to lie here alone in the dark or try to go back to sleep where Laine's shattered face might be waiting for me. I'll walk to campus and make sure that both paths up the mountain are blocked.

After I get dressed and feed Earl, I open my email. Still no reply from Hotch. Instead, there are three emails from Chilton with subject lines full of all caps and multiple question marks. I don't feel up to dealing with Chilton yet so I leave her emails unopened. I text Ruth instead, asking if she's heard from Hotch, then dress in warm clothes. According to my phone it's eleven degrees out. When I step outside the cold freezes the hairs in my nostrils, but there's no wind and the sky is light enough to see by. I consider taking my car but there's a layer of ice on the windshield that will take ten minutes to chip off and it's only a fifteen-minute walk to campus.

I walk briskly, the clean, sharp cold waking me up and dissipating the remnants of that awful dream. *It's natural that the finding of the bones would bring this all up,* I tell myself as I walk through the gates, *it doesn't mean anything. A girl vanished twenty-five years ago during the Luminaria and now her bones have been found,* I recite as I walk around Wilder Hall and head up the path (which is *not* blocked off, I notice). The medical examiner will see the crack in her skull (*cracked open like an egg*) and determine that the cause of death was blunt force trauma consistent with a fall from a height onto hard stone. Any traces of clothes—*would there still be any?*—will confirm her identity. Her next of kin (a cousin in Ohio) will be notified and her remains will be interred. There will be a flurry of articles about the case but the girl (*you can't say her name, can you?*) hadn't had any siblings, few friends, and her parents died years ago. By the time school reopens for the spring semester the students will have moved on to their usual occupations—complaining about the cutbacks to the meal plan, increased class sizes, and the endowment's investments in fossil fuels.

When I reach the summit my leg muscles are warm and my heart is thumping like an engine. The sun is rising across the river, turning the ancient rock of the ridge gold. The huckleberry bushes and snowberries, rimmed with frost, glow like amethysts and garnets and the ground crunches under my feet like broken glass as I wind my way through the maze of deer trails that traverse the pine barrens.

Yellow police tape flutters in the wind like medieval banners at a joust. A lone figure stands on the ridge just where Laine stood in my dream. Ben. Of course he would be here at first light to see the bones brought up. *To bear witness.* Would he say anything? He almost did back then. He was the one who argued that we should go to the police. But then Laine said that it would ruin all of us, him most of all because he wouldn't be able to become a lawyer. That's what he wanted back then. I suppose the same argument would apply to becoming a cop. I wonder if he was thinking that when he turned to me and asked, *What about you, Nell, what do you want me to do?*

One thing is for sure, he isn't going to ask me that now.

He doesn't turn when I reach him, but he knows it's me. "I knew you would be here, too," he says, "when they bring her up."

Does that mean he doesn't think so badly of me that he believes I, too, am compelled to bear witness? But then he adds, "To see if I plan to say something."

I flinch at the rancor in his voice, but when he turns to me, I see the pain carved into every line of his face. He looks like Laine in my dream—cracked open by guilt and grief. "Do you?" I say, the words slipping out. The wrong words—just as I said the wrong words twenty-five years ago. I want to take them back. I want to take it *all* back, everything I did and said back then. But how far back would I have to go to undo the wrong I did? Before I walked through the gates of Briarwood? Or even further, back to the time before the glaciers moved across this earth and scooped out the caves below us—

Which are, even now, giving up their secrets. A ghostly shape is rising out of the cave, white cloth reflecting the light of the rising sun. Her ghost preceding her bones, I think before I realize it's a crime investigator in white coveralls holding something out in a plastic bag to Ben. Ben steps away from me to take the bag and holds it up to the light. The sun strikes two metal objects inside, one a slim piece of silver that might be part of a buckle or clasp, the other a locket engraved with intertwining loops and curlicues. As I step closer for a better look, I feel those lines like a net tightening around my heart as if their pattern is already etched there—the pattern I first saw on Laine's locket.

# CHAPTER FIVE

*NOW*

I WANT TO snatch the locket from Ben's hands. I want to shout that it didn't mean anything. That girl could have stolen Laine's locket. It doesn't mean Laine was here when she died.

"That could have fallen in anytime," I blurt before he says anything. "We don't even know the bones are hers. They searched for her and didn't find her. Why would Nina find her now?"

"The searchers couldn't look until the spring," he reminds me. "By then the ice could have cracked rocks and moved the bones. Nina just happened to fall in the right place to see them."

Or the wrong place, I think, but before I can say it my phone pings an email notification. There's only one person whose emails get through my Do Not Disturb setting. Still, when I look down at the screen, I have to read the message twice before I believe it. As if summoned by the appearance of her locket, Laine has responded to the invitation I sent out a month ago.

*I'd be delighted to attend the Commemoration. There's so much to commemorate. I'm driving down from the island. See you tonight.*

I look up from my phone into Ben's eyes, which have the same disappointed look they had when last we stood here. "I have to go—"

"That was her, wasn't it?" he asks.

"How . . ." Heat flames in my cheeks. How could he know?

"You have the same look on your face you always got when she summoned you. She's decided to come this weekend, hasn't she?"

I nod, amazed into silence that he still knows me so well after all these years.

"Good," he says, holding up the bagged locket. "Maybe she can explain what her locket is doing next to the body of a dead girl."

I GO DOWN the main trail, not wanting to risk the precarious footing of the steeper, back trail in my current state. A thick meniscus of clouds lies over the campus, making the voices of students shouting their goodbyes to each other echo strangely. It's Leaving Day, the last day to get out of the dorms. I remember at the end of my first semester Laine and I sat on top of Rowan Hall watching all the activity, Laine mocking the repeated cries of *Drive safely! Merry Christmas! Don't forget to write!*

I'm so lost in thought that I don't realize I've stopped walking to gaze at the rooftops until someone lurches into me from behind.

"I'm s-s-o s-sorry I ran into you, Dean Portman," Nina stammers, sniffing back tears from a pink and raw-looking nose.

"My fault," I say, "I was lost in thought. How are you? How's the ankle?"

"Yeah, my ankle's not so bad and if I don't get these books back to the library I'll have to pay a fine." She gestures to a stack of books in her arms.

"That's very conscientious of you," I say. "Considering what you went through yesterday I'm sure the library would have understood. You should get going home before the storm."

"Yeah, no, I've got a catering job on campus tonight. I need the money."

"Of course," I say, beginning to tell her that the catered event may be cancelled, but I stop. There's no sense disappointing her until I know for sure. "I worked over break when I went here. The pay was good." And it meant I didn't have to go home.

That's what I'd been remembering when I stopped abruptly on the path: Laine and I sitting up on top of Rowan Hall at the end of the first semester and her turning to me and saying, *You don't want to go home either.*

"But it can get a little lonely. I'll be here over break, too. Email me if you need anything . . . or want to talk. Finding those bones must have been upsetting. I can give you a referral to a counselor—"

"Thanks, Dean," Nina says abruptly. Some students get defensive at the thought of counseling.

I say goodbye and head into Main Hall. As I climb the four flights of stairs, I think about Nina's decision to stay on campus over break. Sure, it's probably about money—that's what I told my mother when I decided to stay over winter break during freshman year—but the *real* reason I'd stayed was that Laine wanted me to. When she said to me, *You don't want to go home either,* I realized I didn't. I didn't want to spend the break watching my mother try to be cheerful without my father (who was going skiing in Colorado with his new wife), or answering her questions about classes and what I planned to do after college and trying to convince me I should major in business. But I hadn't realized any of that until Laine said it. She had that power. When she said a thing, it happened, and now I see, as I reach the outer office, her announcement that she's coming has produced Hotch. He's perched on the edge of Ruth's desk—which I know Ruth *hates*—looking over her shoulder at her computer screen.

"The Van Ettens are coming, too," he's saying with an approving nod as I walk in, "they hardly ever go anywhere."

"They say a window opened in their schedule," Ruth says. I can see that every muscle in her back is tensed, her hands flexed over the keyboard like talons. Hotch appears oblivious to her irritation. When I step forward, trying to think of a way to get him away from Ruth, he glances at me with a manic gleam in his eyes. He looks as if he hasn't slept. In fact, he's wearing the same tweed jacket and shirt, now rumpled, he was wearing yesterday.

"What did you do?" he demands.

As if we have gone twenty-five years back in time and I am a miscreant student and he's the dean. Before I can answer he says, "Did you ask Laine Bishop to come? Is that why she changed her mind?"

Again, I'm dumbfounded. Hotch has been after me for weeks to wield my "influence" to get my friend Laine Bishop to come to the Commemoration but now that she is coming, he's behaving as if I've gone against his wishes.

"I don't know why she's changed her mind," I say as calmly as I can. "Laine was always . . . mercurial. But regardless, I think it's a bad idea to go ahead with the event. The forecast says snow—a blizzard—"

"The media always exaggerate these forecasts to drive up ratings and we can't cancel now. Since *your friend* Laine RSVP'd we've gotten a flurry of last-minute acceptances on the invitation message board, haven't we, Ruth?"

I try to catch Ruth's eye, but she's resolutely scrolling through a spreadsheet, her glasses reflecting blue light. "Darla Sokolovsky has discovered an *opening* in her calendar," Ruth confirms. "And Miranda Gardner says her publisher has sprung for a car service. My aunt always said it was rude to base your RSVP on who else was coming to an event," she says primly.

"And that *rock musician*"—Hotch pronounces the words distastefully; he only listens to classical music—"says he can squeeze us into his show schedule."

"Truman wouldn't miss a chance to see Laine," I say, pleased in spite of myself to think of seeing him again. "And I think Darla and Miranda may be hoping that showing up will increase their chances of getting the writer-in-residence position."

"We'll see about that," Hotch says. "Perhaps Laine will want it now. Imagine the attention that will draw to the program— 'Reclusive author comes out of isolation to teach at Briarwood College.'"

I can't tell if Hotch is glad Laine is coming or not, but then Laine always did provoke conflicting emotions. "I hope they all won't be too disappointed if Laine changes her mind or gets stuck in weather," I say. "It's a long drive from Maine."

Hotch scowls at me and gets to his feet. "Let's try to think positively, shall we? I'm going to pop over to Wilder Hall and check that everything is in order. The caterers are due at three. Can I count on you both to be there then so we can go over the agenda for the evening?"

Ruth raises her eyes from the screen to exchange a barbed look with me.

"Of course," I say before Ruth can reply. She looks like she'd like to tell Hotch to stuff his agenda. "I'll be there. I can hardly wait."

AS SOON AS Hotch leaves the office I roll my eyes at Ruth and gesture for her to join me in my office. I sink onto the couch by the window while she closes the door behind her. "What was that?" I ask. "Why is Hotch so hyped up?"

Ruth stands stiffly, declining to sit, hands clasped in front of the neat waistband of her plaid skirt. "When I got to the office last night President Hotchkiss was already here—in my office, at my desk, using my computer."

"What?" I know how angry it makes Ruth when anyone uses her computer or sits at her desk. "Why was he on *your* computer?"

"He *said* his wasn't working properly. I offered to call IT but he said he didn't have time, that he needed to 'get ahead' of the situation. I assumed he meant the news of the remains being found and I asked if he wanted me to look up the contact information for the next of kin of the girl who went missing twenty-five years ago to send the college's condolences. But he said"—Ruth takes a deep breath, gathering strength to suffer the foolishness of others—"'I doubt any of them are still alive and besides, we have bigger fish to fry.'"

"'*Bigger fish to fry*'? He said that?"

Ruth purses her lips and nods. "He said the important thing was to 'get ahead' of the story and 'control the narrative so it wouldn't adversely affect the reputation of Writers House.' He wanted me to prepare a press release saying that it was fitting that this weekend's Commemoration is dedicated to the valiant bravery of Hugo Moss, who died looking for that poor lost girl whose remains had at last come home."

"Oh," I say, looking out the window. Curdled grey clouds are pressing down on the ridge like a ghost memory of the glacier that shaped the mountains millennia ago. "*That* story."

Ruth's eyebrows rise above the rim of her glasses. "Isn't that what happened? He was found dead on the ridge near the ice caves and some of his students said he'd gone looking for the girl and must have slipped on the ice and hit his head."

"Yes, that's what happened," I reply, not adding that I was one of those students. Ruth must know that although we've never talked about it. "But the nerve of Hotch using it now to promote Writers House as if he *planned* to find the bones as part of his *Commemoration*. And the nerve of him to commandeer your computer and make you prepare a press release after hours. Did you mention that I'd asked you to cancel the event?"

"I did," she said, "but he wouldn't hear of it. I came in early this morning hoping he'd changed his mind, but then we got the email from Ms. Bishop and additional acceptances started coming in. Are you excited?"

The question takes me by surprise. "About the Commemoration? God, no! I think it's a disaster in the making. What are we going to do with all these people if we get snowed in?"

"I meant," Ruth says patiently, "about Laine Bishop coming. She was your friend, wasn't she? And you haven't seen her in a long time."

"Not since college," I say, looking back out the window. The cloud cover has lowered over the mountains, obliterating High Tor and most of Briarwood from sight. It feels like something is coming toward us, something more ominous than a winter storm. "Yes, I'll be glad to see her. I just hope she knows what she's doing . . . I mean, driving all the way from Maine with a snowstorm on the way."

"From what I've heard about Laine Bishop," Ruth says, "she doesn't let much get in her way."

# CHAPTER SIX

*THEN*

WHEN WE ARRIVED at Wilder Hall for freshman registration, we found the door locked and posted with a small card that read: *Registration will begin at twelve noon. No one is admitted until then.* Carved into the front door above the card was a design of interlocking *W*'s.

"It's the same as your locket," I remarked with awe. It felt as if it had been cast there by the force of Laine's will.

Chilton sniggered. "Of course. Laine's a Wilder," she said as if stating a fact as obvious as the rising of the sun.

"One of my ancestors was a founder of the college," Laine conceded with a shrug that made the locket wink. "And it's my middle name. All the Wilder women have a big *W* right smack in the middle of our monograms so we'll match the family silver. And we all go to Briarwood."

"Your mother went here?" I asked.

"*All* our mothers went here," Chilton said, giving me a once-over that made me conscious of my Gap jeans and rumpled T-shirt. "I don't suppose yours did."

I smiled weakly. My mother had gone to Queens College for two years and then quit when she got pregnant with me. She was taking night classes at Nassau Community to get a business degree now, but I didn't tell Chilton that.

"I imagine you know which teachers are best," I said. "And whose English 101 I should take."

"No one's," Laine replied coolly. "It's bad enough we have to take FYSem but that's tradition, and Art History 101 is a classic survey everyone takes. The rest of the intro classes are lame."

"Oh," I said, crestfallen. My plan for freshman year, as far as I had one, was to take intro everything—English 101, World History 101, Philosophy 101, and, of course, the mysterious freshman seminar—a smorgasbord of the world's knowledge that would turn me into the sort of cultivated person who knew everything. I assumed I'd major in English. It had been my high school English teacher who had recommended me to Briarwood because English was my favorite subject and Briarwood was known for its English department. But according to the catalog I had to take the intro class before I could take any of the literature classes, so I figured I'd sample the other disciplines. "How can I get out of English 101?" I asked. "Isn't that a prerequisite?"

"Did you take any APs?" Laine asked.

"Well . . . yes . . . AP English and AP History . . ."

"Perfect," Laine pronounced with a smile that made me feel warm inside. "And how did you do on your SATs?"

"Not great in math but pretty good on the verbal."

"Pretty good?" Chilton asked with a lifted eyebrow.

"Seven-eighty," I admitted.

"Seven-eighty? That's better than these two."

"I have test anxiety," Dodie said, chewing her bottom lip.

"And dyslexia," Chilton said, rolling her eyes. "We know. And I'll remind you that my scores—verbal *and* math—were perfectly respectable. I'll place out of English 101 because I spent the summer at Choate doing precollege classes."

"I think I'll have to take remedial English because of my dyslexia," Dodie said with a sigh.

"That's fine for you, Dorothy Ann." Laine smiled sweetly (Of course Dodie is a nickname, I realized). "But some of us want to get into the Raven Society, and there's a very particular path for that."

"The Raven Society?" I asked, thinking uneasily of the bird that had flown into my window the night before.

"It's the literary honor society," Laine explained. "Named for Edgar Allan Poe's poem, of course. If you get into it you get to take senior seminar with Hugo Moss."

"The famous writer?" I asked, remembering my English teacher mentioning that he taught at Briarwood.

"The *brilliant* writer. He's why *I'm* here. Having Moss as your mentor could make your career as a writer. He's too busy to read submissions, though, so Dean Haviland is the one who decides who gets into senior seminar. That's why we have to take her Romantics class, then her Gothic Novel and Nineteenth Century Lit, and *then* you submit a short story junior year, which she reads and decides who gets into the Raven Society and takes senior seminar with Moss."

"But I thought the stories were submitted anonymously," Dodie said, "so Dean Haviland wouldn't know whose story she was reading."

Laine sighed and rolled her eyes indulgently at her friend's naivete. "It's *supposed* to be a blind submission, but if you've been in Dean Haviland's classes for three years she's sure to recognize your style. That's why we have to take *all* her classes—plus she's the best teacher, second only to Moss, at Briarwood. So, what about it, 780?" she asked, abruptly turning to me. "Are you a writer?"

No one had ever asked me that question before and I wasn't

sure what the right answer was. Mostly I was a reader who loved books so much I wanted to be a part of them. I had been writing poems and stories since the fourth grade—I'd even won that contest—but was I a writer? Didn't you have to be published to be a writer? Wouldn't it sound presumptuous to lay claim to the title, especially while caught in the spotlight of Laine's attention? What had made me feel warm before now made me feel cold, as if I were standing on a frozen lake that might shatter beneath my feet if I didn't answer the question correctly.

"I-I write some poetry," I admitted, suppressing an urge to add *badly*.

"Well, then," Laine said with a smug look as if I'd proved her right about something, "you're a writer so you'll want to get into the Raven Society and take Hugo Moss's senior seminar. And I'm going to show you how to get there." She laid her hand on the bronze door pull, and although it had been locked a moment ago, and there were still fifteen minutes to go before noon, it opened for her and she strode through like a knight returning home from the Crusades to claim her ancestral lands.

"Right answer," Chilton said. "If you had said that you wrote fiction Laine might have smelled competition. And trust me," she added, walking past me and letting her words float behind her like a casually tossed scarf, "you don't want to compete with Laine."

INSIDE THE DIM foyer was a sign directing freshmen to wait in the antechamber until their group was called. Laine ignored the sign and turned right into a long, vaulted hall with oak tables lined up under oak beams—all emblazoned with the Wilder *W*—antler chandeliers, and ornate tapestries. The staff and student aides who were setting up looked up from their tables as if caught in the act of stealing the family silver—all except a grey-haired woman who stood up from the front table and tapped the watch on her left wrist, her blunt unpolished fingernail chiming on the watch crystal.

"Registration does not begin for another fifteen minutes. You are to wait in the foyer."

"Oh!" Laine said, her face a mask of innocent surprise. "My mother told me *she* always came early to make sure she got her classes. Are you Miss Higgins, by any chance? I think my mother took chemistry with you. Laurel Wilder Bishop?" The emphasis she placed on *Wilder* echoed in the vaulted hall.

The woman pursed her lips, revealing red cracks where her lipstick had bled into the creases around her mouth. She looked so sour I thought she was going to tell us to go wait with the rest of the freshmen, who were now filing into the foyer. I was already backing out of the hall when she said, "You can line up but you'll have to wait until noon to begin registration."

"Thank you, Miss Higgins, I'll send your regards to my mother. I'm sure she'll be in touch about the fundraising auction . . ." Laine was already moving past her, scanning the tables, Dodie and Chilton close at her heels.

"Your friends will, of course, have to wait with their *class*." Her gaze fell on me as she said *class,* as if she were questioning if I belonged to the same one she did.

"Oh, dear," Laine said, "I wouldn't think of going without them. I'll wait with them. I'm just afraid Dean Haviland's Romantics class will be full and Mother *particularly* wanted me to take that."

"Very well," Miss Higgins said with a defeated sigh. "Your friends can queue up. But again, you may not register—"

"Until the stroke of noon," Laine sang, adding under her breath as she pulled me into the hall, "or you'll turn back into a shrew. Mother says Miss Higgins always smelled like she'd been chewing alfalfa pellets. Now let's find Dean Haviland's Romantics."

"I think I'll get on the line for econ," Chilton said. "Daddy wants me to major in business."

"But then you'll never get into senior seminar, Chill, and I *need* you there. Can't you double major in business and English?"

"I suppose," Chilton said with a sigh and a haughty look aimed at me, as if to say, *See? She needs* me.

"You can get on line for astronomy, Dodie. It's the easiest of the sciences and I know you don't care about senior seminar."

"I do write poetry—"

"And very pretty poems, too, but remember you need to take remedial English."

Dodie frowned, but at me, not Laine, as if I had given her dyslexia, and sidled off to a table bearing a placard that read "Stargazing for Poets." There were printed cards, like table settings at a wedding, placed at three-foot intervals. A student aide sat behind each one with a legal pad and pen. We passed several sections of English 101 and then a few 200-level English courses that all sounded heady and alluring: American Pastoral: Hawthorne, Poe, and Emerson; Madwomen in the Attic: Nineteenth Century Women Writers; Fairy Tales and Enchantment: A History of Children's Literature. Laine was right; these classes sounded far more exciting than bland English 101. Then we came to a handwritten card that read *The Romantics*. No subtitle, only the professor's name written in a beautiful, sloping hand: *E. Haviland*.

"Romantics—does that mean like Keats and Shelley?" I asked Laine. "Because I haven't actually read much of them." The truth was I hadn't read any Keats or Shelley and I had only the vaguest idea of what "the Romantic period" meant.

"There's some Keats and Shelley, of course," Laine replied.

"But really it's more about a certain . . . *mood*. Don't worry. You'll love it."

She positioned herself in front of the card and smiled at the girl sitting behind it, who ignored her. She was sharpening pencils and lining them up in front of her like a picket fence meant to keep us out.

"We'd like to register for Dean Haviland's class," Laine announced in a clear, forceful voice.

"Registration begins at noon," Pencil Girl said without looking up. "It's not noon. At noon the bell will ring and registration will begin. I can take your name then. At noon. After the bell rings."

Laine cut her eyes sideways at Chilton and me and leaned in closer to the girl. "So let me get this straight. You can't write my name down now because it's not noon. But at noon, after the bell rings, you will be released from the spell of dysgraphia and magically be able to write down my name?"

"Yes," the girl said, realigning her row of pencils. "That's what I said. I can't take down your name until registration begins. At noon. After the bell rings."

"This is just like a fairy tale," Laine said to Chilton and me but loud enough that the girl behind the pencils could hear her. "When the troll under the bridge won't let the hero pass." She leaned down closer to the girl. "I bet you have three questions."

The girl looked up then. Beneath choppily cut bangs, she was wearing thick glasses that magnified her eyes. She was one of the work-studies I had glimpsed over the last week scurrying through the fog—in fact, she was the one I'd bumped into and accused of being a ghost. When her gaze settled on me, she scowled. "I'm supposed to check that each student signing up has the right prerequisites."

"Which are?"

The girl licked her cracked, chapped lips. "English 101."

"You said prerequisite*sss*," Laine hissed, emphasizing the plural. "That's just one."

"That's the only one I can accept. If you have any others, you have to talk to the professor and get permission."

"Maybe I should get on one of the 101 lines," I said, looking over at the next table, where the lines for all the 101 classes were forming.

"Nonsense," Laine said to me, and then to the girl: "My friend here took AP English in high school and she's an expert on Tennyson's 'Lady of Shalott,' which I happen to know is one of Dean Haviland's favorite poems. The Romantics class is tailor-made for her. In fact"—she leaned so close to the girl that their noses almost touched—"I happen to know, since my mother and Dean Haviland are good friends, that Dean Haviland would be quite angry if Nell here was not in the class."

"Then *your friend* should have gotten a note from the professor," the girl said and then, looking at me, added, "since *your friend* has been here all week."

I flinched as if the phantom crow from my dream had flown into my face. I had felt so invisible all week it had never occurred to me that I'd been observed.

Laine smiled sweetly. "But Dean Haviland wasn't. I know because she was with my family on our island off the coast of Maine. We talked about her class over cocktails and spent the whole week sailing while reciting Keats and Shelley." Laine spun such a persuasive tale that I could almost picture myself on her family's island drinking cocktails on the beach and playing rounds of pinochle (or whatever rich people played) on a screened porch on rainy days. Perhaps that's what my double—the blur-girl of my nightmare—had been doing while I was trapped here in the fog. Pencil Girl, though, wasn't buying it.

"I need proof of having taken 101 or the equivalent before writing a name on the list," she said. "And as it's almost noon—"

She was cut off by the blat of the noon bell. "I have to begin registration *now*. If you don't have the proper paperwork, please step aside."

"You stay right here," Laine told me. "I see Dean Haviland. I'll be back with a note for all of us."

"I don't need a note," Chilton said, shouldering past me and plastering a pink sheet onto the table in front of Pencil Girl. "I have my Choate transcript."

Why hadn't I thought to bring my high school transcript? It was one more thing I hadn't known I was supposed to know, like which class unlocked the door to the next right class and the next right one, like stepping stones on the Yellow Brick Road to Oz.

While Pencil Girl wrote Chilton's name down in painstakingly slow motion, the lines for English 101 moved briskly forward, halting only when the student aide at the head of one of the lines shouted, "Full!" and turned the card around to say "Closed." One after another the other English 101 sections filled and closed while Pencil Girl registered the student after Chilton and the one after her. Should I bolt and try to get one of the 101s? But what would Laine say if she came back and I had abandoned our spots? She would know then that I wasn't special. I wasn't the Lady of Shalott. I was only Ellen Portman from Massapequa. And who was that? Just an invisible girl swallowed up by the fog.

Pencil Girl filled in twelve of the sixteen spots on her page. I looked around for Laine but didn't see her anywhere.

"Are you still here?" Chilton asked, fanning herself with a full registration card. "You're going to get stuck with all the worst classes."

"I know!" I wailed. "But Laine said—"

"Laine says a lot of things and rarely means any of them.

It's not her fault; it's how she grew up. Her mother broke every drunken promise by the next morning and moved them all over the country wherever her new husband or whim took her. Laine means well, but if you follow her, you'll end up going over a cliff and breaking to pieces on the rocks while Laine's caught by a safety net."

I stared at her, shocked at this cool assessment of her friend, as a skinny boy in black jeans, a black leather jacket, and messy hair slouched up to the front of the line. "Truman Davis," he said, sticking his hand in his front pocket. "I've got my transcript in here—"

I watched as if mesmerized as he attempted to retrieve the folded paper from the pocket of his too-tight jeans. When I looked up our eyes met and he winked. I felt a flicker of warmth go through me. Was he purposefully delaying to give me more time? After a minute, Pencil Girl told him if he didn't "present his credentials" he'd have to step aside. He retrieved the paper and became number thirteen on the list of chosen ones. Number fourteen had a long Russian name that she had to spell out letter by letter for Pencil Girl, who pressed so hard her pencil broke and she had to reach for a new one. I found myself tempted to sweep the remaining pencils from the table. That's what Laine would do; she would sweep away all obstacles as she was now sweeping across the floor, a tall elegant blond woman at her side, parting the crowds of students like the prow of an icebreaker. They were coming straight toward us.

"Look," I said, "there's Laine now and I bet that's Dean Haviland. Can you please wait—"

But number fifteen was standing at the front of the line, unfolding a pink permission slip. "Excuse me," I said, "but I'm holding this spot for my friend and she's here now."

"So am I," the boy said. It was the annoying boy from the

staff cafeteria, the janitor's son, the one who'd been so sensitive about my little mistake. Well, he didn't like me already; I had nothing to lose.

"But she's *with the teacher*," I explained, "and she's right here."

Only she wasn't. Laine and Dean Haviland had stopped to talk to a tall man with a white mane of hair and leonine features. He looked as I had imagined Gandalf would look when I read *The Lord of the Rings*. Laine said something that made him throw his head back and laugh.

"That's the great Hugo Moss," Chilton said. "There's a rumor that he and Dean Haviland were lovers when she was his student here."

"*Nice*," the janitor's son said. "Can you put down my name, please? It's Ben Breen."

"Does Breen have an *e* at the end?" Pencil Girl asked, picking up a new pencil.

"No, they ran out of *e*'s by the time they got through Benedict Edwin Breen."

"Do you want me to put down Benedict Edwin Breen?"

"Knock yourself out," he said. "If you take your time this girl's friend will get in—or do you think she'll give *you* the spot?"

"That wouldn't be fair," I said. "She's the one who knows the teacher. I guess all the good classes are already full."

"They're begging for students over in the classics department," Ben Breen told me. "And you did say you'd taken Latin."

"There are still a few spots in Art History 101, too," Chilton said. "It's in the big lecture hall. And there's room in Professor Hotchkiss's FYSem—though no one likes him very much."

"I guess that's all right, then," I said, seeing my college career whittled down to dead languages, overcrowded lecture halls, and unpopular professors.

Pencil Girl finished writing down Ben Breen's full name just as Laine arrived. Chilton was right. There would always be a safety net to catch Laine Bishop while the rest of us plunged over the side of the cliff to the rocks below. "Hey," I said, as she reached the table, "there's only one spot left. I'm going over to the classics department to sign up for Latin."

"Oh, that's a good idea," Laine said vaguely as she took her place at the head of the line.

There was a murmur of complaint from the students left on the line, but one look from the regal Dean Haviland sent them scurrying. Laine reached past me and swiveled the yellow legal pad around so it was facing her.

"Hey!" Pencil Girl squawked. "You can't do that!"

But Laine clearly could do whatever she wanted. Although I should have been heading to the Latin line, I watched mesmerized as she wrote in large flowing letters *Nell Portman*. She had written in my brand-new name—Nell without an *e*—instead of hers.

"But—"

"It's only fair," she said with a wave of her hand. Turning to Dean Haviland, she added, "I can take your class next year."

"Don't be ridiculous, Lainie, write yourself in."

"But—" Pencil Girl began but was silenced by a glance from Dean Haviland's icy blue eyes. She looked meekly away but when Dean Haviland left and Laine bent down to add her name to the list, Pencil Girl glared at me as if I were to blame for ruining her meticulous management of the registration. I might have gotten saved this time by Laine Bishop's safety net but I'd still taken a blow.

# CHAPTER SEVEN

*NOW*

EVEN THOUGH I know I should get some rest before the guests begin arriving tonight, I'm too on edge when I get home. Instead, I answer emails and put out the usual end-of-semester fires as well as respond to some last-minute requests from the CFO concerning next month's audit. Around three, I shower and dress, choosing a black velvet skirt and a burgundy silk blouse I bought for a conference two years ago that had been cancelled when we all went on lockdown. They still have the price tags on them. I haven't dressed up like this since . . . I can't really recall how long. As I coil my hair into a French twist and pull on knee-high boots, I feel like I'm a medieval knight girding myself for battle, although I'm not sure who it is I think I'll have to fight.

Hotch, I remind myself, with his insistence we hire one of the alums as the first writer-in-residence. He's thinking about fundraising, hoping for a commercial name like Miranda Gardner or Laine Bishop to impress the donors and trustees instead of thinking about the students. And it's turned this event into a circus. I'm sure it's why some of the alums are coming; they see it as the first round of a job interview.

I don't really care if Miranda Gardner is disappointed—she was opportunistic in college and has barely done anything to help Briarwood since becoming a bestselling mystery author. Besides, there's a very good reason why she'd be a poor choice for the position, which I'll have to tell Hotch if it looks like he's seriously considering her.

I do feel bad, though, if Lance Wiley has gotten his hopes up. He was emotionally fragile in college and sounded like he was having a hard time in lockdown the last time I spoke with him. As for Darla Sokolovsky, I know from her social media posts that she's always flitting from one writers' retreat to another. I doubt one residency more or less will make much of a difference to her. At least I hope not. She would be quite vocal if it did.

I toss an overnight bag into the back of my car and drive to campus, using the service entrance on the west end by the old gym, and then park behind Wilder Hall between Hotch's red Jaguar and a moss-green Mercedes with a vanity plate that reads "Chill-AX." *My girls gave it to me,* Chilton had explained when I saw her a few months ago for a planning committee meeting for this event. *Isn't that sweet? They think I'm chill.* Emma, her older daughter, who has just been admitted early decision to Briarwood, had rolled her eyes and told me later that what they meant was that Chilton took an ax to anything remotely *chill.*

I find Chilton and Hotch in the kitchen unloading insulated carriers from Mes Amis—or at least Chilton is unloading; Hotch seems to be sampling caviar and imported pâté. "Thank Gawd!" Chilton brays in the exaggerated lockjaw I'm never sure is supposed to be a joke or not. "Someone with a modicum of sense. Back me up on this, Nell: Shouldn't we have our old rooms? I'm sure Laine will expect it. Remember how she came early senior year to lay claim to the one in the tower?"

"Laine had a thing for towers," I say, remembering very well that Laine had convinced me to come to campus early senior year because with my work-study permit, I could get a key to Wilder Hall. "But I doubt she cares very much now."

A vein on Chilton's forehead throbs, the only thing that

moves on her perfectly composed face. Ruth once asked me
if I thought Chilton used "that Botox thing" and I responded
that I thought Chilton had learned to control her face muscles
in the womb and so had no need for it. Chilton looks now as
if she's just emerged from a spa, her chin-length hair the exact
blond hue of her youth, her wool slacks, houndstooth blazer,
and cream silk blouse tailored precisely to her trim figure. I
remind myself that even though she looks like a Connecticut
matron who golfs daily at the country club, she's a hardworking
book editor who spent the lockdown working remotely while
homeschooling her two teenage daughters and running virtual
fundraising events for the Briarwood development office. All
while working on her core, she'd told me a few months ago.

"Well, yes, of course," Chilton says now as if repeating a
disclaimer her lawyer husband had prepared, "we have all reas-
sessed our priorities during these trying times, but still, I think
that makes it all the more paramount to make the most of our
time together. Laine will want her old room." She pronounces the
last sentence as if daring me to claim I know Laine's preferences better. Is that what this is all about? Chilton's old jealousy
that I—a brash nobody from Long Island—had taken her place
as Laine's best friend?

Hotch cuts in. "I thought Ms. Bishop would want the Fellow's Suite. It's the nicest and it's where our writer-in-residence
will live. I thought it might encourage her to accept our offer of
being the first guest author at Wilder Writers House."

Chilton cuts her eyes over to me and I see what the problem
is. "You mean Hugo Moss's old apartment?" I ask, although I
know the answer. "Laine might feel . . ." I falter and Chilton's
eyes widen slightly, which for her is tantamount to a panicked
scream. "*Presumptuous*," I manage, "taking her mentor's place."

Hotch throws up his hands. "Whatever you two think is

best—you girls sort it out." As if we're bickering over the last sourdough at the local bakery. "I have to drive to the Pough-keepsie train station to pick up Darla Sokolovsky because the student who was supposed to do it had a family emergency and had to cancel." He rolls his eyes as if he doesn't believe the student's excuse.

"Yes, why don't we *girls* sort it out," Chilton says. "You'd best be going, Hotch. Darla hates being kept waiting."

As soon as Hotch is gone, Chilton signals for me to follow her down a narrow corridor. We pass the row of wooden cubbies, originally the butler's pantry when the house was a residence, but used for mail and messages when it was a dorm. I automatically glance at the one that was mine senior year, as if expecting a message or assignment will be waiting in it for me, but of course they are all empty. Past the cubbies is the resident's apartment when Wilder Hall was a dorm and a faculty member was assigned to live on the premises. Hugo Moss lived there our senior year. *My college digs,* as he referred to them, making sure we all knew that he had a pied-à-terre in the city and a summer place in Maine.

As Chilton pauses at the open doorway, I can see over her shoulder that the sitting room has been refurbished since I last saw it five years ago, when the renovations began. The high-backed couch (the chesterfield, Moss called it) has been reupholstered in green velvet, the old-fashioned Mission-style tables and chairs polished to a honey-gold sheen, birch logs laid in the fireplace, a cashmere throw tossed over the Morris chair angled toward the hearth. The room retains its old-world charm (what my students would call a Dark Academia aesthetic) down to the stuffed stag's head mounted over the fireplace. Hotch has spared no expense (I know because I've cosigned all the work orders) to court Laine Bishop to accept the fellowship but he's gone about it the wrong way. Laine won't want to stay in these rooms; even Chilton hesitates on the threshold. "Do you think," she says, "she's coming because they found the body?"

I pat the air to caution Chilton to keep her voice down. "There could still be cleaning staff upstairs," I whisper.

Chilton rolls her eyes. "I checked on that. Your assistant, Ruth, sent them all home because of the snow. But if you want to make sure, let's go upstairs." She turns and heads back down the corridor and begins climbing the back stairs without pausing to see if I'm following her. Of course I am. We both want to get away from Moss's rooms. The back stairs are narrow and steep, the treads worn in the center from years of housekeepers carrying trays up and dirty laundry down when Wilder Hall was a private home—the ancestral estate of Laine's blue-blood family—and of students sneaking out at night when it was a dorm and Briarwood still had curfews. We didn't have a curfew in our time, but it was still a good idea to know which creaky treads to avoid if you didn't want the rest of your housemates knowing when you were stealing out in the middle of the night.

Chilton doesn't bother to avoid the creaky treads. "God damn these stairs, they're a deathtrap. They should have been closed off—or at least carpeted."

I seem to remember signing a work order for carpeting for the stairs, I think as I follow Chilton; they must not have come yet in the rush to get the house ready for this weekend. When I arrive at the top I take a deep breath, catching the faint, fleeting scent of roses and Shalimar, Laine's signature scent. *Is she already here?* But the scent dissipates as I walk down the hall, looking into each room that Chilton has opened. The beds are made up with pristine white sheets and plump duvets, the walls decorated with tasteful framed prints featuring Hudson River School landscapes and botanical studies. Gone are the touches that made each room different—the posters and art prints we hung up, the tasseled scarves tossed over lamps, Indian tapestries draped over bedposts, the stag skull Truman hung from his door, the orange and black crepe paper streamers left over from our Halloween party. The hallway, where we had thumbtacked literary quotes—Hemingway's "Write drunk, edit sober," Dorothy Parker's "I hate writing; I love having written"—has been papered over in a toile de Jouy print featuring bucolic shepherds and shepherdesses. Chilton has stopped to inspect a section of the wall.

"This wasn't done right," she says, clucking her tongue.

"I suspect Hotch rushed the contractors at the end," I say. "I wonder if they got to the tower room."

We both look back down the hall to the one unopened door. Chilton takes a deep breath and heads down the hall and I follow her, but she steps aside to let me open the door. As I put my hand on the doorknob, I recall standing here with Laine the week before our senior year began. *This is it, Nell, everything we've worked for and dreamed about has led to this moment.*

I turn the brass knob, which feels slick under my hand, brace—

Light floods out into the hall, over Chilton and me, as if it had been trapped there all these years, just waiting for someone to let it out: the last rays of the setting sun cascading down the stone slope of the mountain and flowing through the floor-to-ceiling lead glass windows like an amber wave. The first time I'd seen that view, I'd thought, Who would want to live here under the weight of all that stone? It would be like living in the path of an avalanche.

"Do you think it's because they found the body?"

Chilton is only repeating the question she asked downstairs but for a moment I think she's asking if all this light—which has turned crimson in the seconds since I opened the door—is spilling down the mountain because the body has been found.

I notice, too, that her eyes, like mine, are on the rafters of the high-ceilinged room.

"It must be," I say. "She only said yes after the news came out about the bones being found. Why else would she come after all these years?"

"Maybe she wants to see us," Chilton says, jutting out her chin defiantly. "I sent her an email last week saying how much I was looking forward to seeing her and how the pandemic had taught me to value the people in my life so much more. Maybe Laine feels the same."

"I doubt the pandemic made much of a difference to Laine's life at all. She's been isolated on that island since college."

"How do you know she hasn't left sometimes or had people visit her?" Chilton asks.

"Have you been to visit her?" I ask. "Or seen her *anywhere* since college? Has anyone? We'd have heard about it if she'd been spotted." For a moment Chilton's chin crumples just a little and I'm sorry I've exposed the naked truth—that her *best friend* in all the world walked away from her twenty-five years ago. "You *know* why she's stayed away," I say, a little more gently. "Only the body showing up would make her come now. Remember, it was part of the pact."

*If they find her body we'll all come back to Briarwood and face it together.*

Chilton's carefully controlled facial muscles can't hide the blood leaving her face. Even her lips turn white. "We've kept the pact. So a body has been found. Everyone knows a girl went missing during the Luminaria twenty-five years ago. There's no reason for any of us to panic."

"They found something else," I say, keeping my voice low despite knowing the house is empty. "Laine's locket. It was with the body."

Chilton's eyes widen. "How do you know?"

"I was there this morning when the forensics crew brought it up out of the cave and handed it to Ben Breen."

"Ben Breen? *He's* in charge?"

"He *is* deputy chief." I immediately leap to Ben's defense as if Chilton were impugning Ben's credentials, but she impatiently waves away the niceties of police hierarchies.

"That's good. He has a vested interest to keep us out of this."

"I don't think Ben sees it that way."

She narrows her eyes. "You always thought Ben was such a Boy Scout, but I notice he's made the most of his opportunities since college. I hear he's running for county legislature. I wouldn't be surprised if he has higher political ambitions, which is all the more reason to keep this quiet. And besides, Laine's locket being in the cave proves nothing. She was crazy about those caves. Remember how she wanted us to go with her at the beginning of senior year? I refused to go in them, of course, but you and Truman and Ben went with her. That's when she thought she'd discovered Merlin's Crystal Cave. She could have lost her locket in the cave then."

Chilton takes a deep breath and blows it out through pursed lips—a breathing technique I imagine she learned from her mindfulness coach. "It will be fine. When Laine gets here, we can talk it through—"

The sound of tires crunching on gravel draws her to the window, which overlooks the parking lot. I can see by her eagerness that she hopes it will be Laine, here to swoop in and tell us all what to do like a maestro conducting a symphony. Like she did the last time. But I can tell by the slump in her shoulders that it's not Laine. I look past her and see a woman in a fur-trimmed parka, tight leggings, and sherpa-topped boots getting out of a limousine.

"Randy," Chilton drawls, her voice dripping with disdain. "She's dressed to go skiing in Aspen."

"She only goes by Miranda now," I say automatically. "She's sent me several emails asking me to remind everyone of that, all signed *Miranda Leigh Gardner, Bestselling Author,* with all her awards listed underneath."

Chilton snorts. "She'll always be Randy Lee Gardner from Doylestown, Pennsylvania, to me. I wonder if she got her publisher to pay for that limo in the hopes that she'll get a blurb from Laine . . ."

Her voice falters as someone else gets out of the car. All I can make out at first are long thin legs in skinny black jeans and black motorcycle boots but it's enough to make my heart skip a beat.

"Truman," Chilton says, trying to affect the same dismissal she'd injected into Miranda's name and failing. "What's he doing with her? He couldn't stand her."

"Maybe she offered him a ride from the city," I say, disliking the nervous edge in my voice. "It would be like him not to make any travel arrangements and then count on someone giving him a lift." Like the time I'd run into him on the train coming back to campus after spring break our freshman year with nothing but a leather satchel and his guitar. He'd told me he'd spent his last "tenner" on a nickel bag in Grand Central and didn't have cab fare but he was sure something would turn up. And it had, in the person of Laine waiting in a yellow 1968 Mustang convertible she'd driven all the way from Maine with the top down. She said she'd just stopped at the Poughkeepsie station on the off chance she'd run into me. He had that in common with Laine. There was always a net waiting to catch him, too.

"Or Randy finally got her hooks in him after all these years," Chilton says. "She always liked him, you know, since freshman year. We'd better get down there and rescue him."

Chilton brushes past me on the way out the door, but I stay for a moment at the window, watching Truman stretch his arms up over his head and turn toward the mountains, the last light burnishing his sharp features. I can see that the twenty-five years that have passed since I saw him have etched lines in his face, but instead of making him look old the light seems to burn away the years and restore him to the boy I remember. I step closer to the window, as if I could bridge the gap of those years and join him on the other side, my breath misting the glass. When I raise my hand to wipe it clear the motion must draw his attention to me. He looks up, the light still sparking in his eyes and kindling an answering spark in me. Then he frowns and the light drains from his face. He turns to walk inside, and I'm left standing alone in the dark tower room. *Laine's room.* That's what had lit the spark in Truman's eyes. He had thought I was Laine. When he realized his mistake, that light had died. Of course he was disappointed. It was only a trick of the light that had made him look for a moment as if he was scared. As if he'd seen a ghost.

CHAPTER EIGHT

*NOW*

WHEN I COME down the front stairs into the foyer, the same oak-paneled room where I waited freshman year for registration, there's enough light and noise to drive away the gloomiest thoughts. Hotch has arrived from the train station, bringing not just Darla, dramatic in a long black cloak, but Lance, too, who stands nervously next to the Van Ettens, the elderly couple from Rhinebeck who RSVP'd at the last minute. Carl Van Etten is no doubt regaling Lance with the same speech he gives at every college function—how he met his wife, Betty, at Spring Fling freshman year, got his first job on Wall Street from his room-mate's uncle, and his daughter made partner in a law firm run by Betty's freshman roommate. *All the most important connections of my life were made at Briarwood,* he will conclude. It would be a mercy to rescue Lance, but I'm not sure I can paste on the appropriate smile for the Van Ettens right now. I slip past the group and into the Great Hall, which has been decked in pine and holly. The long tables that held registration cards twenty-five years ago have been pushed along the walls and covered with forest-green tablecloths. The catering staff is laying out cheese boards, canapés, crystal decanters, and punch bowls. I see Miranda ensconced in the best chair by the fireplace—the one Moss always took—and Truman bending over the hearth. Before I can reach them, though, I run into Emily Dawes, who was in Moss's senior seminar two years before me. I ask her how the pandemic has been for her and she tells me it's been rough. Her wife is an emergency-room doctor and Emily had been stuck at home with a nine- and eleven-year-old trying to make deadlines at her newspaper while supervising remote learning and preparing food for her family.

"Honestly, I don't know how I got through it," she says.

Then she shows me pictures of her wife and children and I see how she got through it. She's in love with her wife and family. I can see it despite the few grey strands in her red hair and the stress lines beside her mouth and eyes.

"I'm sorry it's been so hard on you, but it's good to see you looking well. You have a beautiful family," I tell her.

She leans forward, touching my hand. "Thank you, Nell. Sometimes I think I got out of here just in time, before Moss—"

Before she can finish what she's about to say, Adam Scanlon, a theater arts teacher who was hired two years ago, appears with a glass of sherry for me. "The dry stuff," he says, sniffing the amber liquid appreciatively.

"I didn't know people still served sherry," Kendra Martin says, joining us. She's wearing an embroidered shawl in jewel tones that smolder in the candlelight. I feel warmer just standing next to her.

"Briarwood College tradition," I say, feeling suddenly ancient although I'm not much older than the two teachers. It's just that I've been here so long I've become the repository of Briarwood lore and tradition.

"They had to do away with stonings and all-male dining clubs," a deep voice says behind me. "So, this is all they have left to remind us of the patriarchy."

Adam snickers—as if he's too young to be part of the patriarchy, gender and race notwithstanding—and then does a double take as he turns to find Truman behind him. "Hey, you're Truman Davis, aren't you? Didn't you play bass for the Ravens?"

"For my sins, yeah," Truman says, his eyes on me. He hangs back a moment, as if gauging my mood, and then he moves in for a hug, his arms hard as steel. *You think it's easy banging away at a bass for hours?* he'd retorted once when Ben accused him of being soft.

"Nellie," he growls into my ear, a nickname only he ever used for me.

"That's Dean Nellie to you," I say, instantly falling into the teasing banter we'd engaged in for four years of college. I glance uneasily over my shoulder at Kendra and Adam, and see them exchanging a look that I imagine is a reassessment of my age and street cred.

"Oh, man," Truman says, his eyes flicking toward Adam and Kendra. He's playing to the audience. "Is she a hard-ass?"

Kendra nods. "Yeah, she really had my back when a student complained about their grade in my class last semester. Told her that she was lucky I hadn't failed her."

"The students waiting outside her office to beg for incompletes always look like they're waiting for an audition," Adam says. "Or an execution."

I laugh, hoping no one can see the blood rise in my face. "I think you're being a little *dramatic,* Adam. I just don't want to see students becoming dependent on extensions and incompletes. It can become a bad habit—"

"Actually," Hotch says, coming over to us, "she's become quite the soft touch. Only yesterday she gave a student a withdrawal weeks after the deadline."

"It's been a rough semester," I say, my face even hotter when I realize he's referring to Nina Lawson. He *had* noticed her withdrawal. "Some of these students hadn't been in live classes for over a year and have gone through a lot of stress—"

"Tell me about it," Miranda says from her chair. "I *almost* missed my deadline for my last book."

I look down at Miranda, thinking about my students who lost their last year of high school, their proms and senior year trips and graduations gone up in smoke. "You were always good at making deadlines," I say diplomatically, remembering that Miranda has donated generously to Writers House and Hotch will expect me to be cordial. "You always got your workshop submissions in first."

"That's right," Truman says, snapping his fingers as if trying to remember something. "Didn't Moss have a nickname for you? What was it?"

"Handy Randy," Chilton, who has arrived with two glasses of red wine, says. "He predicted you would produce bestsellers and look at how right he was!" She hands one of the glasses to Miranda and then holds up the other as if toasting her. What I am remembering is that Moss had phrased it a little differently; he'd said, *You'll churn out potboilers.*

"Moss sounds a bit . . . *authoritarian,*" Kendra says. "I would never presume to tell a student what kind of books I think they'll write."

"He could be quite draconian," Miranda says. "Remember the ghost story assignment?"

"I'd rather not," Chilton says, her hand shaking as she lifts her wineglass to her lips.

"What was that?" Adam asks.

"Oh, this was Moss's favorite assignment," Miranda says. "'Write about the thing that scares you the most.' He had this theory that the greatest writers drew from their deepest fears."

"Or he just wanted to scare the fuck out of us," Truman says. "Moss was an asshole." He's edged back toward the fireplace and stretched one arm out over the mantel—a pose Moss would often strike. "Remind me why we're commemorating him?"

I can feel Hotch bristling three feet away. Before he can muster a defense of Hugo Moss, Miranda does. "Actually, I owe my career to Hugo. He was a ruthless critic, but he made me a better writer and gave me a thicker skin." She laughs. "No editor has ever been as demanding, no reviewer so scathing. Nothing could have prepared me better for the world of publishing."

"I agree," Darla says as she joins us. "Moss used to cross out half the words in my poems and stories. It was through him that I became an erasure poet."

Darla, in her long black cloak, black tights, and ballet flats, looks like she's working at erasing herself. She'd always been thin in college, but now she's grown cadaverous.

"I suppose I owe him my career as well," Lance says as he joins us, finally released from the Van Ettens. "I was so traumatized by his senior seminar and then what happened to him that I spent the spring semester in a psychiatric hospital, thus giving me the material for my memoir."

"I recommend your memoir to many of our students who are struggling with stress and mental health issues," I tell him. "I gave it to a student just yesterday."

He turns his round face toward me. Whereas Darla has grown thinner, Lance has plumped up. With his receding hairline and pink lips, he looks babyish—and grateful for my remark. "You do?"

"Yes. You should come here and give a talk at the Writers House when it opens in the spring."

I look toward Hotch, hoping he'll second the invitation, but he has become preoccupied by activity at the buffet tables where the caterers are lining up champagne flutes. "I should go tell them that we're not ready for the toast," he says, walking toward the buffet. "We're not all here yet."

"I suppose he means Laine Bishop," Miranda says as soon as Adam and Kendra drift off together. I look over and see that

Adam has been cornered by a couple of theater-loving alums. It's just *us*, I realize, looking around the circle—Lance, Darla, Truman, Chilton, Miranda, and me—drawn close around the fire, as if huddling together for warmth. And yet I don't feel warm at all.

A tap on my arm startles me. I turn to find Ruth holding out a highball full of ice and amber liquid. As I take it from her, I smell the peaty aroma of aged whiskey. "You're a mind reader," I say. "I couldn't stand another sherry." Then, turning to the circle: "I know you know Chilton; have you met the rest of my classmates?" I go around the circle naming each one, Ruth nodding stiffly at each introduction, the reflection of firelight turning her glasses into a mask.

"I know all your names from the invitations and your very generous donations," she says formally when I'm done. "Please let me know if there's anything you need."

"Some of that scotch you just gave Nell?" Truman suggests with an impish grin. "I can smell from here it's the good stuff."

"The restoration crew came across a case of it in the basement," Ruth says. "It was Hugo Moss's favorite. Dean Hotchkiss left instructions to save it—"

"For special guests," I finish for Ruth. "And that certainly includes all of you. I'll go get it, Ruth. Is it still in the basement?"

Ruth turns to me but doesn't answer right away and I'm afraid I've offended her by interfering, but then she nods and says, "Yes. But the basement's locked. Guests aren't allowed down there. Someone might slip on the uneven steps and our insurance wouldn't cover it—"

"I've got the keys, Ruth," I interrupt, trying to forestall a litany of potential dangers in the basement. "And I'll take full responsibility." She nods, but she still looks dissatisfied. "Is there anything else you wanted to see me about?" I ask.

"It's begun to snow heavily," she says. "I'd like to tell the caterers from town that they can leave. President Hotchkiss has said they should stay, but the roads will be treacherous before long."

I look toward the windows and see that several inches of snow have accumulated on the sills. The rest of the pane reflects back my image along with the group gathered around the fire. For a moment I feel as if I am standing outside in the cold and dark looking in on the festive scene. "I'll take care of Hotch," I say, shaking off that old chill of being the outsider. "You can tell anyone who has a long drive to leave—including you, Ruth. I know you don't live far but still—"

"I can always stay in one of the dorm rooms," she says curtly, "but I will tell the women who live in town that they can go. The student workers who live on campus can stay on." Ruth looks at Miranda, Lance, Chilton, Truman, and Darla. "You don't have to worry about the snow because you're staying for the memorial tomorrow. You should be aware, though, that if the snow keeps up, the memorial may be cancelled and you may not be able to leave tomorrow. I hope no one had planned on leaving early."

With that pronouncement Ruth turns to go. She's only a few feet away when Miranda mockingly repeats Ruth's words. "'I hope no one had planned on leaving—ever!' What a strange little person. Does she always talk like the housekeeper in a Shirley Jackson novel?"

Darla titters, but Lance looks uncomfortable, and Truman only smirks. "If we're going to be stuck here," he says, linking his arm in mine, "I say we go get that scotch." Both the grin and the warmth of his arm chase away the chilly feeling of not belonging. It's Miranda and her cliquishness, I think, as we wend our way across the Great Hall, which is now populated with a few dozen guests—not the crowd Hotch was hoping for, but a respectable turnout considering the short notice and the weather. I notice looks of recognition dawn on the faces of the guests as Truman passes by. With his unruly shock of jet-black hair, lanky frame, and black motorcycle boots, Truman looks every bit the rock star. Even the older guests—board members like the Van Ettens and the Morris Wrayburns, and the gaggle of professors emeriti surrounding the punch bowl—who don't recognize him know that he is *someone*. He smiles and waves at all of them as if he is used to the attention and an expert at dodging it. His arm tightens on mine and I can feel the glow of his celebrity reflecting on me. When we reach the kitchen, the median age plummets. Several of the young catering staff in their black uniforms stop what they're doing to gawk. As I'm unlocking the door to the basement, a young guy with a man bun and lip piercings looks up from a tray of ceviche. "Hey, man, you're Truman Davis. I saw you at Burning Man a couple years ago."

"Hey, *man,* don't remind me, I'm still picking sand out of my ass." He pushes me through the door and closes it behind him before finishing with: "Aston Martin." We're instantly plunged into darkness.

"Hey," I say, quickly turning on the light switch on the wall, "people will talk."

He smirks and heads down the stairs in front of me. "My reputation is pretty tanked already."

"I was talking about mine," I say, joining him at the bottom of the stairs and scanning the basement. There's only one bare light bulb dangling from the ceiling, affording a small circle of illumination in the dank, dark space. I take out my cell phone and turn on its flashlight to explore the metal shelves against the walls. There are boxes labeled "Archives" along with cleaning supplies and canned goods. There are also some boxes shoved against a wall. I make a mental note to send over some maintenance staff to shelve them before they end up water damaged on the damp basement floor.

Truman laughs as he joins me in looking for the scotch. "Heavens forfend! Dean of Liberal Arts caught canoodling in the basement with disgraced musician."

"*Canoodling?*" I echo. "What are we, the class of forty-seven?"

"That's how old I feel seeing those kids outside. Did we ever look that young when we were here?"

"Younger," I say, recalling Truman leaping onto a table during freshman caroling.

"How can you stand being surrounded by the callow youth all the time?"

"Aren't you?" I counter. "Or are your fans older these days?"

"My fans are a blur in the footlights," he says. "Ah, here's the stash." He's found the case of scotch beside a box labeled "Assignments 1996–7" and hands me two bottles. "Good ole Moss, how he loved this stuff. Hard to believe it just sat all these years gathering dust."

"Ruth said it was camouflaged in a box labeled 'Dead Matter' awaiting the archivist."

"Why has it taken so long to catalog his papers?" Truman asks, surveying the wall of boxes.

"Budget cuts. The college ran into financial trouble after 2008. It was finally back on its feet when the pandemic hit and our admissions numbers plummeted."

"I thought Laine donated a shitload of money."

"She did, but in the original endowment she made when we were in college she earmarked money for scholarships, teachers, and building renovations—not archivists. Mind you, Hotch has used her name to attract donors. That's how he got the Writers House off the ground, but we're still awaiting funds to hire a full-time archivist and make Moss's papers available to scholars."

"I'm not surprised she didn't want to shell out to preserve Moss's *ephemera*. I *am* surprised she'd want to have anything to do with this house at all. I was shocked when I got her email—"

"She emailed you? When?"

"Last night," he says, taking out another bottle from the box. "Do you think she's really coming?" When he turns to me, my phone flashlight catches a gleam in his eye, the one he'd get when something—a line of poetry, a slant of light, the sound of Laine's laugh—moved him.

"I don't know," I say. "I didn't think so, but then the bones were found . . ."

"She'd want to be here," he says. "If it all came out, she wouldn't leave us to deal with it on our own."

"She did last time," I say.

"Only because she knew you would manage everything." He gives me a look that feels too fierce for the close, dark space we're in. I feel suddenly warm and breathless, aware of the heat of his body so close to mine. "And you have," he adds, moving closer. For a moment I think he's going to hug me again, but he's got those bottles in his hands. "She won't leave us on our own this time. She said if it ever came out—if *she* were found—we'd all come back. She made us make that pact. That's what the email from her said: *Remember your promise.*"

I try to smile. "Laine and her pacts," I say. "We must have made a dozen."

"She'll keep this one," he says. "I'm sure."

"Well, then," I say. "We'd better get back in case she's already here."

He doesn't wait for me to finish. He bounds up the stairs and pushes the door open with his shoulder. I hear him fending off some of the students in the kitchen, his voice growing faint as he makes his way back to the Great Hall. I stand for a moment at the foot of the basement stairs, schooling my disappointment. *Of course he came for her,* I tell myself. She always came first with him since she claimed him for her own freshman year.

# CHAPTER NINE

*THEN*

WHEN I'D SUBMITTED my course card at the end of registration Miss Higgins frowned, checked a list, and told me there was a hold on my account and that I had to go to the financial office. My face turned red as I turned to my suitemates but they were too far away to have overheard. "I'll catch up with you later," I called. "I've got to take care of something . . ." My voice trailed off but they were already out the door before I had to come up with an excuse.

I spent most of the rest of the day waiting on lines and going from one office to another trying to find out why there was a hold on my account—*Had my mother not paid a bill? Had the college decided to revoke my financial aid?*—only to find that it was because I'd forgotten to sign a form. Relieved it wasn't anything worse, I headed to the bookstore and waited on more lines. I was shocked to find out how many books there were for Haviland's class: hardcover collections of Wordsworth, Blake, Keats, Shelley, and Byron; thick novels by Sir Walter Scott and Thomas Hardy; dense tomes by Edmund Burke and Mary Wollstonecraft; and a slim monograph by Dean Haviland herself entitled *The Romantic Spirit.* I was grateful that Latin only required a single text (the same Wheelock I'd used in high school) and that the classic civ textbook was available to rent, but the art history textbook—what my mother would call "a doorstop cat squasher"—exhausted all the credit I'd earned in ten days of working at the library.

I lugged the heavy bags of books back to my dorm. There was a chill in the air that seemed to come down from the mountains, and a violet tinge to the sky that matched the purple Briarcliff College sweatshirts so many of the students I passed wore. As I approached the dorm, though, the air filled with the deep-throated crooning of Ella Fitzgerald singing about summertime with such longing that my heart clenched and the backs of my eyes burned. It was as if the loneliness of the waning afternoon had been given voice. I looked up and saw that the music was coming from East Tower, where someone had placed a stereo speaker facing outward on a windowsill.

Not someone. *Laine.* The music was coming from Laine's single. It felt as if she had cast a net out—*Out flew the web and floated wide*—to reel me back in.

When I came into the suite, I saw the central room had been transformed into an oriental seraglio with painted bamboo screens and silk scarves wafting in the incensed air. Embroidered throw pillows littered the carpeted floor. Tapestries hung from the walls.

I dropped my bags and peered into my tiny single to make sure I was in the right place. Yes, there was my nunlike cell and the crow feather that had drifted in through the window last night. Perhaps it had been a harbinger of future enchantments. Then I walked through the seraglio to the other single from where the music—and voices—were coming.

If the central room looked like a seraglio, Laine's room looked like the inner sanctum of the Pasha: candles burning, deep red cloth covering the bed and the wall behind it, old books lined up on shelves. Laine, wearing a silk kimono over her shorts and T-shirt, was sitting in the window seat, drinking something from a china teacup that smelled more like bourbon than tea. Dodie and Chilton were on the bed, backs against the wall, Chilton cross-legged, Dodie's legs sticking out straight in front of her like a rag doll's.

"There you are," Laine said when she spied me hovering in the doorway. "We were afraid you'd miss cocktail hour." She pointed to a bottle of Southern Comfort, a box of Triscuits, and a can of Cheez Whiz on her desk. "Get yourself a drinking vessel and come join us."

I retrieved the college mug I'd received with my acceptance letter and hurried back, still fearful that my three suitemates would vanish into the shadows in the seconds that I was away. *They waited for me,* my heart sang. So what if the bourbon burned my empty stomach; I gulped it down like communion wine.

"Thatta girl," Laine said approvingly. "Sustenance for the night ahead. There's freshman caroling and the bonfire."

I thought she was kidding. "Isn't that all . . . kind of corny?"

The truth was that big, organized events—like pep rallies and football games and school dances—terrified me. It had been easiest to affect a bored, superior attitude during high school. I'd expected Laine to exhibit the same disdain but instead she widened her eyes at me and gravely pronounced, "It's tradition. And tradition matters. Come on, there's a caroling meeting downstairs in the East Parlor right now. We have to make up a song about our dorm and outsing all the other dorms. If we're late we'll be stuck with lame lyrics."

I bolted down the rest of my bourbon and followed them into the central room. Dodie ducked behind one of the screens to get a sweatshirt. "You'd better get one, too," Laine said to me, plucking a faded Briarwood sweatshirt off the back of a chair and exchanging it for her kimono. It was so old that the purple had faded to lavender and the gold thread in the insignia had unraveled. They all had vintage sweatshirts, from their mothers and aunts and great-aunts and grandmothers, no doubt. "Here," Laine said, handing me a brand-new sweatshirt. "My advisor sent this to me when I got into Briarwood, but I have one so you can have it."

I zipped it up, the heavy fleece warm and soft on my bare arms, mumbling thanks as we raced down the stairs. The lounge was crowded, the dorm meeting in full swing when we arrived. I tried to squeeze into the back but Laine grabbed my hand, raised it in the air, and began to sing in a loud and unexpectedly sweet, high voice.

"Row-Row-Rowan, my heart belongs to you—"

The dorm matron looked up from her clipboard and called for order, but she was drowned out by the other girls joining in. I followed along as best I could through a dozen refrains. Some of it must have been old bits from previous years—corny lines like *Bright college years, with pleasure rife, the shortest gladdest years of life*—and some which Laine seemed to be making up as she went along. A few other students shouted new lines that Laine repeated and made part of the song. The skinny boy in black, whom I recognized from registration, jumped up on a table and belted out a refrain to the tune of the Talking Heads' "Psycho Killer."

*"Rowan Fresher, Qu'est-ce que c'est*
*Fa-fa-fa-fa-fa-fa-fa-fa-fa-fa better*
*Row row row row row row row away."*

I thought Laine might object, but instead she jumped up on the table and began belting out our dorm fight song to the tune along with him. The whole room was bouncing up and down, pogoing to the beat like eighties punks. When we reached the last stanza, Laine and the skinny boy pumped their fists in the air and jumped into the crowd holding hands as if they were kids jumping off a pier into an icy lake. I saw them look at each other and felt a stab of envy at the sizzling energy between them. How did Laine do it, I wondered, how did she draw people to her like moths to a flame? I felt sure she hadn't met this boy until today and just as sure that he was *hers* now—if she wanted him.

I could feel myself separating from the seething crowd, like a drop of oil bubbling to the top of a vinegar cruet, but Laine, as she passed me, grabbed my hand and pulled me along. Then we were all running from the dorm, singing at the top of our lungs, on our way to the next dorm, where we shouted our song to them and they shouted theirs to us. Apparently, the object was to get the opposing dorm to adopt our song and join our ranks. Our dorm won each time until we were hundreds strong, streaming into the quad, where an enormous bonfire stood waiting to be lit. Upper classmen were already there, drinking beer from kegs and singing their class songs. Ours, with its driving beat, was indomitable. We roared into the quad, singing, shouting, pumping our fists, our hearts beating as one. That sense of being separate was gone. I'd never felt so much a part of something, the part of myself that always stood to one side, observing and critiquing, for once silenced—

Until I turned and saw *him*—Ben Breen, standing off to the side, hands in his pockets, *not* singing, just watching.

For a moment I felt taken out of the group again—and then I felt angry. Who was he to stand there looking so smug and judgmental? Did he think he was better than the rest of us? I sang louder and pumped my fist harder and roared with the rest of my class when the upper classmen took up our song and one of the seniors handed Laine a torch to lead the procession up the mountain to High Tor. As I followed I had a thought: Ben Breen probably didn't live on campus. He didn't have a dorm, so of course he hadn't been able to participate. A feeling of regret and shame swept through me as the procession began winding its way up the mountain. I turned to find him in the crowd but he was gone, vanished into the night like the embers that floated up into the sky and melted into the dark.

# CHAPTER TEN

*NOW*

WHEN I COME out of the basement, the kitchen is, thankfully, empty. It may have been a joke to him but I didn't relish the idea of being teased about "canoodling" with Truman Davis, rock star. He probably thought it would improve my "street cred," but I knew it would only become a reminder of what I didn't have and what I wasn't. I refresh my drink, steeling myself to face the party, and go back to the Great Hall.

I needn't have worried that people were talking about me. My absence has gone as unremarked as my reappearance. Everyone has settled into their own conversational bubble. At a table by the fireplace, Miranda commands a group of silver-haired bookish women who have brought copies of her latest novel to be signed. She looks in her element, wielding a gold fountain pen with an elegant flip of the wrist, splaying manicured fingers over her right breast to show she is touched by a compliment, leaning into an upheld phone for the most flattering selfie angle. Chilton sits beside her, a polite smile on her lips as she hands her another book open to the title page for her to sign, the picture of a supportive editor even though she isn't Miranda's editor.

I look around the room and find Lance with Truman, who is leaning against a bookcase, surrounded by a few of the younger professors and most of the student catering staff. Darla is by the buffet gesticulating in front of the Van Ettens. With her pale face framed by slicked-back black hair and a black turtleneck she looks like a mime performing a silent interpretation of one of her erasure poems.

Hotch should be pleased, I think, finding him in a group of older alums and trustees. Moss's last students are putting on a show for the donors, demonstrating the value of Moss's legacy and the worth of continuing it with the Writers House. But he doesn't look pleased. He looks tense, his eyes swiveling every few seconds between his watch and the foyer. I notice now that he's not the only one who's distracted. I see the Van Ettens exchange a practiced marital signal of raised eyebrows while Darla turns to freshen her drink; two women in Miranda's book circle lean their heads together to whisper and then glance at the window, where the snow has climbed higher on the sill. As I start walking toward Hotch I pass a smartly dressed woman checking her phone, who looks up at me and demands, "Why won't my weather app load?"

*As if I'm IT.*

"Service this close to the mountain is a bit dodgy," I say with my most patient smile. "You can log into the Wi-Fi, Wilder Writers House, password: *Wilder.*"

"Could you also remind Hotch that my staff has to go? He's made them wait until after the toast, which was supposed to happen half an hour ago."

I recognize her now—Margot Dubreus, owner of Mes Amis. "I thought Ruth had told all the staff to go except for the students who live on campus."

"She tried to and Hotch stopped her. Honestly—" She leans in closer and lowers her voice. "I love Hotch and we appreciate the business, but I can't get snowed in here. I've got a baby shower to cater tomorrow morning."

"Of course," I say, thinking that if it keeps snowing like this her baby shower's going to be cancelled. "I'll talk to him."

I make my way toward Hotch, scanning the room for Ruth. It isn't like her to back down from an argument with Hotch even if he is president. She should have at least come to me . . . but then, I remember guiltily, I'd been in the basement with Truman. Maybe she didn't want to disturb us. I insert myself into the group next to Hotch and gently touch his arm. He flinches so hard his drink spills. He *is* wound up.

"I think some of our guests are becoming anxious about the weather," I say, deciding not to blame the restaurant owner. "Perhaps it's time to give the toast . . . and make a statement encouraging people to drive safely."

"I would have thirty minutes ago," he says, squeezing the words past a rictus, "*if* your friend had arrived on time. Have you heard from her?"

"I imagine Laine's been delayed by the weather." *If she had ever intended to come at all.* "Let's hope she hasn't been in an accident and that everyone else gets home safely."

"*Very well,*" he snaps. "Tell the caterers to pass around the champagne. And please tell your rock star friend to ease up on the scotch. That stuff's expensive."

I signal Margot to alert her staff by miming a toast and then make my way over to Truman, who's been abandoned by his coterie at their boss's summons.

"Hotch looks like he's going to have a stroke," he says, refilling his glass from the scotch bottle stashed on the bookshelf behind him. I see it's nearly empty and hope it's because he's been sharing it with his fans.

"He's disappointed Laine isn't here," I say, and then because I've also had too much to drink, I add, "Are you?"

He shrugs, studiously casual. "This is so like her—staging it so everyone's talking about her and waiting for her appearance, like Gatsby at his own party—that I feel like she's already here. Like we're in a play she's directing and she's just offstage." He waves his glass toward the window and I can feel Laine's presence, too, hovering outside in the snow, waiting for just the right moment to make her entrance.

A waiter appears with a tray of champagne flutes. As I take one, I recognize Nina Lawson. "Thank you, Nina. How's your ankle doing?" I look down and see she has an ACE bandage wrapped around it.

"It's okay," she says, shifting her weight and wincing.

"I bet you're anxious to get back to your dorm," I say.

She shakes her head. "Not really. There's no one else staying on my floor and it's kind of creepy." She angles her tray toward Truman so he can take a glass but he declines, holding his highball up.

"Never mix my poisons," he says suavely. Nina smiles nervously as if he were accusing her of poisoning his drink.

"Don't pay him any attention," I say. "He gets like this when he's had too much to drink."

She looks back and forth between me and Truman. "Were you two friends in college?"

Truman answers before I can. "The best," he says, saluting me with his scotch.

"You were lucky," Nina says shyly. Then she intercepts a glare from her boss and hurries away with a slight limp.

I turn to Truman to ask if he really meant that, but a chime draws both of our glances to the front of the room where Hotch is standing on a raised platform, striking a knife to the edge of his champagne flute. He strikes it again and the clear musical note shivers in the air.

"Ladies and gentlemen," Hotch begins and then, mocking contrition, "and nonbinary friends and anyone betwixt, thank you for venturing out on this snowy winter's eve. Although I regret the weather has kept some of us away, I think Hugo Moss would have approved of the atmosphere. I don't think he would have been daunted by the weather. Twenty-five years ago, nearly to the night, Hugo Moss went out in a storm like this to search for a missing student. Because that's the kind of man he was." He says *man* with a defiant glint in his eye as if daring anyone to call him on gender stereotyping. I look around and catch Kendra Martin's gaze; she rolls her eyes at me. I suppress a laugh and make a mental note to set up a lunch date with her after the holidays. "And that's the kind of teacher he was. Demanding, I'm sure, but look at the writers and artists he nurtured."

He aims his glass at no one in particular, but Miranda sits up straighter and lifts her chin higher as if he's been speaking about her. Beside me I hear Truman snort.

"That is the tradition we hope to carry on here at Wilder Writers House. That is the tradition you are supporting by your presence here tonight. That is the tradition—"

I hear Truman softly humming the song "Tradition" from *Fiddler on the Roof.*

"—we raise a glass to tonight. To Hugo Moss and those like him . . ." He pauses for a moment and I can hear Moss finishing the toast. *To us and those like us,* he used to say at the end of each class, *damn few!* I must be drunker than I realized because when Hotch finishes the toast I think I hear *damned few* instead. Glasses are raised, some are clinked, someone calls, "*Hear! Hear!*" Truman echoes the end of the toast and then he grins at me. "Getting fewer every day."

THE EXITS COME quickly after the toast, the Van Ettens leading the pack, followed by the trustees and board members and the older professors. The wide oak doors yawn open, letting in snow gusts and cold air and the sounds of car doors slamming and voices calling holiday greetings and admonitions to get home safe. A burst of laughter and shouting accompanies the student caterers, who leave in a pack, pushing each other into the knee-high drifts and throwing snowballs, and talking loudly to make up for their hours of compulsory good behavior. Watching them go, I find myself longing for the same release. Then I notice that Nina isn't with them.

Inside the Great Hall those remaining have huddled closer to the fire. In addition to my classmates who are staying the night, Kendra and Adam, both of whom have apartments in faculty housing, have joined the group. Hotch has commandeered the big chair beside Miranda. He's telling a story I've heard before about running into Moss wandering the ridge during a lightning storm. He was so well known for such nocturnal rambles that when he died on one of them no one was all that surprised.

Truman nudges an empty chair and beckons me to join the circle. *I am not an outcast watching from outside,* I remind myself. But then I think of that pack of students that doesn't include Nina. "I just need to check on some things in the kitchen," I say. "I'll be right back."

As I open the kitchen door, I hear a soft murmur of voices, which halts as I enter. Ruth and Nina look up from a Tupperware container of mini quiches. "There's enough here to feed an army," Ruth says disapprovingly. "I was just telling Nina that she should bring some back to the dorm."

"I'm lactose intolerant," Nina says apologetically, "and it's too much to carry all the way back to the dorm."

"Shouldn't the rest of the crew have stayed to help?" I ask, surveying the containers and trays heaped with food. Hotch must have ordered expecting twice the number of guests. Nina cringe-shrugs and Ruth purses her lips.

"That Dubreus woman said she couldn't pay overtime and it was Hotch's fault for keeping them late," Ruth says, briskly pulling out a length of plastic wrap and swaddling a ham with it. "Nina was the only one to offer to stay over without pay, but I told her she was free to leave."

"I really don't mind helping," Nina says, wringing a dish towel in her hands.

Ruth and I exchange a look. Nina's clearly nervous about something, probably about going back to her dorm alone.

"Why don't I walk you back to your dorm?" I suggest. "You're in Rowan Hall, right?"

Nina nods, biting her lip and looking like she's about to cry.

"You go on," Ruth urges. "I can handle the rest of this on my own."

"Won't you miss hanging out with your friends?" Nina asks me as we head to the coatrack near the back door to get our coats. "Ruth's been telling me that you haven't seen them in a long time. I can't believe you were really friends with Truman Davis in college."

"Old friends now," I say as I put on my coat.

"That's so cool," Nina says, pulling on a bright orange puffer jacket and a pink pom-pom hat. "He was like my favorite singer in middle school. My mom has all his albums."

I smile as I pull on my snow boots, thinking how much Truman would hate this damning praise.

"And you knew Laine Bishop, too? I read *The Intended* when I got in here. It made this place seem magical. Was it really like that?"

"Magical?" I echo, stepping out the back door into the falling snow. The porch light illumines a wedge of glittering white snowdrift, but beyond that all I can see is the dim cloak of snow mantled over shrubs and benches. "Yes," I say, "it was. I'm sorry it hasn't been that way for you."

"I think I'm beginning to see what you meant about traditions and rituals bringing people together," she says as we walk on the barely distinguishable path. It hasn't been shoveled and I worry that Nina's thin shoes will soon be soaked and the walk will be too much for her injured ankle. "Since I fell into the cave yesterday, I've been getting messages."

"What do you mean?" I ask, the skin on the back of my neck prickling. "What kind of messages?"

"You know, on Instagram and Twitter."

"Oh," I say, relieved. But then the next thing she says turns those prickles to icy needles.

"Because I found the girl lost in the ice caves people have asked me how I knew she was there."

"But you didn't!" I say so fiercely that Nina shrinks away from me on the path. "I mean, you said you went there because you thought you saw some people near the cave."

Nina looks sideways at me through eyelashes matted with snowflakes. Thanks to all my years of dealing with students I can tell there's something she doesn't want to tell me. "I-I did think I saw some students but that wasn't the only reason I walked toward the cave. I was trying to avoid President Hotch-kiss."

"Because you were afraid he was going to ask you about withdrawing from his class?" I ask.

"Sort of . . ."

"I'm so sorry, Nina," I say, noticing that she's shivering. I take off my scarf and wrap it around her shoulders. "You shouldn't have had to worry about that. It must have been awful falling in that cave—" I shiver myself, recalling how cold those caves are. "But you didn't know the bones were there. How could you?"

"Maybe I was led there," she says, "by the girl's ghost."

I take a deep breath, filling my lungs with cold air and counting to three, letting it out in a steamy plume that hovers in the air around us like the ghost of Nina's story. "Well, then," I say, summoning every ounce of authority I possess. "I don't believe in ghosts, but if I did I would say that you've done your job.

You found the bones. The forensic team will soon identify them and that poor girl's family"—*she had no family*—"will know what happened to her. She'll have a proper burial. Her grave will bear her name"—*you can't even say her name to yourself, can you?*—"and she'll be at rest and so should you be."

"But that's not what they're saying online," she blurts out. "They're saying that now that her bones have been found the ice cave girl is loose and seeking vengeance for her murder."

"Who says it's murder?" I demand. "She fell. Just like you did. It was an accident."

"Maybe . . ." she says. "But then earlier tonight when I checked my phone in my coat pocket I found this." She draws something out of her pocket. I can't see anything in the dark and I wonder if she isn't more troubled than I'd realized. She's hallucinating, holding up invisible evidence. But then she hands it to me and I feel it, as if the dark air between us had sprouted wings, and I know what it is that I hold in my hands.

## CHAPTER ELEVEN

*NOW*

I TELL NINA that there are a million ways that feather could have gotten in her pocket—there are crows all over the campus; one of the catering staff could have been playing a prank on her—and then say goodbye, urging her to get inside before she freezes to death. I watch her swipe her ID card to unlock the dorm door, taking solace in the security systems that weren't in place when I lived in the dorms—

*Not that they would have helped.*

—and then I stand there in the falling snow staring up at the tower of Rowan Hall like the fool that I am. What am I waiting for? For a light to come on in Laine's old room? For strains of jazz to waft out and turn the wintry air to summer breezes? For Laine to come tripping out the front door filling the night with laughter and life?

*I feel like she's already here,* Truman had said.

A light does come on, on the fourth floor, but it's not in the tower, it's one of the rooms on the hall. That must be Nina, I think, glad now that I remained long enough to see her get safely to her room, as if that's what I had been waiting for. I turn and start back toward Wilder Hall. I walk slowly, thinking about how that feather could have gotten into Nina's pocket. I shiver. I'm headed straight into a strong wind that blows snow in my face, stinging my eyes. It's as though something doesn't want me to go back—

I pick my head up and realize I'm not quite sure where I am. I appear to be on a dark windswept plain, the contours of my familiar campus altered by the snow and dark. There's no light to guide my way. Where are the lampposts that were installed ten years ago to prevent campus assaults? A group of students had objected to them last year because they weren't eco-friendly so they were put on motion detector timers. I must have wandered off the path or—

I have become invisible to the motion detectors: a ghost wandering the campus like one of those urban legends we used to scare ourselves with—the freshman suicide who prowled the rooftops, the ice cave girl.

A gust of wind sweeps over the field and clears a gap in the curtain of snow, enough to reveal a light in the distance. It's too far away to have been triggered by me; someone else must be out on this wild night. The comfort the light gave me quickly shifts to fear. Why would anyone else be out in this? And why aren't they moving? Are they watching me?

Then I realize where I am. I'm in the open bowl below the mountain, beside the frozen lake. I could have wandered out onto the ice and fallen through. The light I see is coming through the woods surrounding Wilder House. It's a beacon leading me home. I take off across the snowy field, through the stand of ancient pines. The snow isn't as deep here and it comes down more gently, sifting through the pine boughs like flour through a sieve. I feel a burst of excitement as I grow closer—a traveler finding home after a long journey. Then I realize that I've become the girl standing outside looking in at the brightly lit scene, only as I come closer, I see that the Great Hall is deserted. Have they all gone to bed already?

But no, here are Miranda and Hotch, entering from the back

hallway like characters on a stage. I can tell by the anger in Hotch's face that they're arguing about something, but for once he isn't the one delivering the tirade; Miranda is leaning toward him, talking in what I imagine is a low but persistent voice. She must be saying something disagreeable because Hotch's face is growing steadily congested. He looks like he is about to have a heart attack. Miranda must think so, too, because she touches his arm. He pulls it away abruptly, raising it as if he means to strike her.

Instead, he spits out something that makes Miranda flinch and then turns and leaves the room. A moment later a wedge of light appears at the front door and I see Hotch come out, coat-tails flapping, hatless, striding so fast he slips and curses—sound restored to the pantomime I've been watching. He recovers himself and disappears around the back of the hall to the parking lot. As he vanishes, something moves in the shadows. For a moment it looks like one of the robed figures from yesterday's Luminaria, but then it's gone, resolved into pixels of blowing snow. I turn to go in but am startled to find Miranda at the window, disconcertingly close, looking out as if she is watching me. Most surprising is the expression on her face. She is smiling.

THE FRONT DOOR gapes open when I reach it, snow drifted over the flagstone entry. The Great Hall is empty, the fire burnt down to embers, candles guttering in pools of wax, empty glasses and bottles scattered on the buffet. It looks like the abandoned castle in "Sleeping Beauty" after the curse has fallen on it. I imagine my classmates slumbering upstairs—

Then I make out the sound of voices coming from the rear of the house. I follow them through the back hall until I reach Moss's apartment and pause outside the door, feeling as though I'm late for class, that when I open the door, I'll find Moss seated in his big chair by the fire holding my story in his meaty hands, and he'll say, *How good of you to join us, Miss Portman.* Laine will look up from her seat, always to the right of Moss, and wink at me. Instead, the only eyes winking at me are the glass ones in the stuffed stag's head. Below it, Miranda is seated in the big chair by the fire holding a book in her lap, flanked by Lance and Chilton. Truman is stretched out on the couch; Darla is standing at the open window, smoking.

"There you are," Truman says, moving his legs to make room for me on the couch. "You've missed Miranda's big announcement . . . or maybe you already knew Hotch was making her the first writer-in-residence at Wilder Writers House."

I stare at Miranda and notice that it's not a book in her lap, it's a framed photograph. "No, I didn't think it had been decided." I did know Hotch had been holding out in the hope he'd get Laine to take the position, counting on her cult appeal to boost admissions and alumni donations. Had he changed his mind? But why give it to Miranda? She was well known, but she didn't have the literary clout to enhance the program's prestige. Was this what Miranda and Hotch had been fighting about? "Congratulations," I say a beat too late. "Our students will be lucky to have you."

"Aren't you worried this will get in the way of your demanding writing schedule?" Darla asks, tossing her cigarette out the window and turning toward the group. Her face is even paler than before, her lips bloodless.

Miranda shrugs. "Not really, I mean, how hard could it be? I don't remember Hugo breaking a sweat over our writing." She looks down at the picture in her lap and I see that it's one of Hugo with all of us from senior seminar—Laine, Truman, Chilton, Dodie, Ben, Darla, Lance, Miranda, and me—gathered in front of High Tor at the Luminaria. We're all holding candles and wearing long robes. Behind us the sky is violet and orange—a violent sunset over snowcapped peaks.

"Students expect more these days," I say, thinking of all

the worthy applicants for the residency inside Kendra's orange folder. I look down at the photograph, at all our impossibly young faces. "They're not as complacent as we were."

Truman snorts. "Not all of us were so complacent; Laine wasn't."

"Laine worshipped Moss," Chilton says. "At least she did until the end."

"He treated us like shit," Lance says suddenly, his face turning pink. "The things he said were abusive. He called my writing fey."

"But he didn't know it was your writing," Miranda says. "We all submitted anonymously."

Truman makes another dismissive noise and refills his glass. "That was the biggest fiction of them all. It was obvious whose work was whose. The lyrical poetic prose was always Darla, the stories with hideous parents disguised as Lovecraftian monsters were Lance's—"

"The gritty noir stuff was always Truman's," Lance adds, seemingly unoffended at Truman's characterization of his college writing.

Truman nods. "Yeah, I thought I was the next Raymond Chandler. And Chilton always wrote something Cheever-esque set in Maine, while Dodie wrote those twee fantasy stories about talking squirrels—the only ones I couldn't always tell apart were Laine's and Nell's."

"Laine's were better," I say. "That's how you could tell us apart." Before Truman can argue I add, "Ben always wrote something where the bad guys were punished. Moss called them Old Testament morality tales. Truman's right. We all knew whose work we were talking about but because it was all supposed to be anonymous no one held back in their critiques."

"Moss egged us on," Truman says. "Remember that smile he got when someone said something really harsh."

"He was a monster," Lance cries. "Why in the world are we honoring him?"

"Because it will bring in money," I say. "I'm sure you'll do a better job, Miranda." Though I'm not at all sure. Truman says what I'm really thinking.

"You can hardly do worse." And then, slamming his empty glass down on the table, Truman adds, "And clearly Laine doesn't want it. I don't suppose she'll show up now. The roads are probably impassable."

He gets to his feet unsteadily. A sound from the doorway snaps his head in that direction, his expression giving away his lie; he's still hoping Laine will show up. The disappointment on his face tells me it's not Laine. I look to the door and see Ruth standing on the threshold, wiping her hands dry on a dishcloth.

"Ruth!" I say, surprised. "I thought you would have gone by now!"

"I was putting all the food away so it doesn't go to waste," she says, sniffing the cigarette smoke in the air and gazing askance at the glass rings on the coaster-less coffee table. "I'm leaving now, but I just wanted to check to see if anyone needed anything before I go."

"You can't mean to go home in this. Why don't you stay in one of the spare rooms?"

She shakes her head. "Charlie from Grounds is taking me on his snowplow. I'll be fine and he'll bring me back in the morning with shovels to dig out your cars, although—"

Before she can go on, Miranda finishes for her. "We know, we shouldn't plan on leaving. I certainly won't. I'm heading up to bed now, although, really, I should take one of these rooms since they'll be mine in the spring." She places the photograph back on the mantel as if she's already in charge of decorating.

"They're not made up," Ruth says abruptly. "Your room is at the top of the front stairs on the right—it's your old room."

She looks pointedly at Chilton. "I made sure you all had your old rooms as Ms. Prior requested. Your luggage was brought up earlier."

"I'm sure it's lovely," Miranda says, getting to her feet. "And I wouldn't want to be presumptuous. There are a few things I'd like to discuss with you about the arrangements in the spring . . ."

"Can't that wait?" I ask, but Miranda has already taken Ruth's arm and is steering her down the hall, murmuring to her about air filters and dietary preferences. Ruth's back is rigid with indignity. Miranda is acting as if Ruth were the house-keeper of Wilder Hall instead of a skilled, experienced executive assistant.

"Good Gawd," Chilton says, "Hotch has created a monster. Why on earth would he pick Miranda for the job? Did you know?" she asks, turning to me.

"No," I reply. "I thought he wanted Laine—"

"I have ten times the number of awards," Darla says. "*Literary* awards. What's Miranda going to teach them? How to plot a murder? How to pose for an author's photograph?"

"What does she need it for?" Lance asks. "Surely those books of hers make enough money."

"She complained on the drive up that no one takes her writing seriously," Truman says. "She wants literary credibility."

"She wants to be Laine," I say. "She always did. Taking Laine's place here is as close as she'll get."

"As if *anyone* could ever take Laine's place," Truman says.

"No, I don't suppose anyone could ever do that," I say, surprising myself with the bitterness in my voice. "I'd better go make sure Miranda isn't haranguing Ruth to death." I hurry out of the room before I can say what had been on the tip of my tongue—that no one would ever replace Laine for Truman either. What had I been hoping for? I demand of myself as I hurry toward the Great Hall. That Laine would come back? Or that when she didn't Truman would finally give up on her and turn to me? I don't know which is the more deluded hope.

I find Ruth in the front foyer putting her coat on.

"Has she gone up?" I whisper.

Ruth nods. "She wanted me to come with her to make sure everything was in order but I told her Charlie was waiting."

"I'm so sorry, Ruth. I'll explain to her that it's not your job to cater to her."

"I don't mind," she says, "I just worry she won't be good for our students. I don't think she's serious about the job."

I glance up the stairs to make sure that Miranda isn't lurking on the landing, eavesdropping, and then lean close to whisper in Ruth's ear. "I agree. I'll talk to Hotch over the break. Maybe he'll change his mind."

"The only way he'll change his mind is if Laine Bishop comes back and agrees to take the job herself and we both know—"

A shriek cuts her off. The sound freezes me to the floor, taking me back to another moment when I stood in this same spot and heard a scream from upstairs. Truman, who has emerged from the Great Hall followed by Chilton, bolts up the stairs, taking them two at a time.

"What now?" Chilton mutters as she passes me. "Is she offended by the thread count? Has she found a spider?"

The joke doesn't disguise the fear in her eyes. She was here, too, the last time we heard a scream like that. If she can face it, I figure, so can I. I follow her up the stairs where we find Miranda screeching and pointing to the open door of her room. Truman is standing at the foot of the four-poster bed, his body blocking my view. I have a sudden urge to flee the room before seeing whatever is there. There are some things you can never *unsee*.

But before I can make my escape Truman steps aside, and

I see what caused Miranda's panic. The pure white duvet is splattered with blood and black feathers. It takes me a moment to make sense of the carnage and realize what I'm looking at. A dead crow lies in the middle of the bed, neck crooked at an unnatural angle, jet-black eye staring straight up at me.

"How did that get here?" Chilton demands as she comes in behind me.

"The window." Truman points to the broken pane. "It must have gotten lost in the storm."

His voice is so forlorn he might be talking about a lost child, but then he suddenly laughs. He lifts one black feather from the bed and turns to Miranda, who's still cowering in the doorway.

"Look, Randy," he says, holding up the blood-tipped feather. "You've been chosen."

# CHAPTER TWELVE

*THEN*

THE FIRST TIME I saw the black feather ceremony was in the last week of the spring semester of our freshman year. Laine must have known it was coming because she was up at the crack of dawn declaring that we were all going to have breakfast in the Student Commons at the Nook.

At 8 A.M. Dean Haviland walked in, regal in a spring green linen suit, platinum hair perfectly swept back in her usual chignon, a sprig of lilac pinned to her lapel. She carried in her hands a strange bouquet of what I thought were black flowers, but which I made out as black feathers. She looked like a bride in a fairy-tale wedding, perhaps one in which the bride was marrying the evil erl-king.

I'd become versed in such strange lore in Dean Haviland's Romantics class, where she'd favored the folkloric elements of the Romantic tradition: Keats's "The Eve of St. Agnes," Goethe's "The Erl-King," Coleridge's "Christabel," E. T. A. Hoffmann's "The Sandman," and the superstition-tinged novels of the Brontës and the macabre stories of Edgar Allan Poe. She seemed to have an almost religious ardor while reciting from these works, or listening to the Mozart and Beethoven she played for us, or standing in the wild places the Hudson River School painters Thomas Cole and Frederic Edwin Church had painted.

"They always do the Selection on May Day," Laine whispered, as if reading my thoughts, as she often seemed able to do by spring semester.

I noticed that more students were gathering in front of the mailboxes than would usually be up at this hour on a day with no classes. I recognized a few from the theater productions, dance recitals, and art shows Laine always insisted we all attend in school spirit. They were all upperclassmen. Juniors, I thought. There were also underclassmen sitting in the Commons. I recognized Darla from the Romantics class and Randy Gardner, who often came to the literary club readings, and Lance Wiley, a shy freshman I'd met in FYSem who'd confessed to me that he wrote "little stories." Even Ben was there, although he lived off campus, casually lounging against a wall, but with his eyes locked on the mailboxes. Laine waved him over, whispering to me, "There's your Latin Lover."

"What's the Selection?" I asked, blushing at the term Laine had come up with for Ben because we often studied Latin together in the library. "It sounds like something from that Shirley Jackson story."

"It's how you find out if you're in the Raven Society," Laine said, "which also means you'll be in Moss's senior seminar. Everyone submits their stories anonymously—the winning stories are in that box. Dean Haviland has a list that tells who they are. The winners get a black feather in their mailbox—oh, look who's carrying the box," Laine said, tilting her chin toward the student walking behind Dean Haviland. "It's the Bridge Troll. The one who didn't want to let poor Nell into Dean Haviland's class. How many campus jobs does she have? No wonder she's always in a bad mood."

The girl, whom I recognized now as the same work-study who had monitored the registration for Haviland's class, the one I'd accused of being a ghost that time in the fog, did indeed look to be in a bad mood. The box must have been heavy. She followed Dean Haviland into the back of the college post office with her head down as if she were heading into the bowels of the earth.

"Her name is Bridget," Dodie said, returning with our coffees and English muffins. "Bridget Feeley."

"Really? *Bridget?*" Laine asked, raising her eyebrows the way she did when something amused her. "See, she was born to be a bridge troll . . . Where's the strawberry jam, Dodie, go back and get some . . . Look," she added as Dodie went back for the jam, "there's Emily Dawes." She nodded to a tall, freckled redhead in slouchy khakis and a wrinkled linen blouse. "And Stephanie Chang," she added as an athletic-looking girl in a short tennis skirt and a pink polo shirt joined Emily. I recognized both of them from the readings sponsored by the literary club.

"I bet they're both chosen for the Raven Society," Chilton said.

"Stephanie, yes," Laine said slowly, "but Emily . . . I don't know . . ."

"She's editor of *The Raven,*" Chilton said, naming the college's literary magazine.

"*Exactly,*" Laine said. "She's a bit too . . . *strivey*. Dean Haviland doesn't like that."

"Aren't the submissions anonymous?" Dodie, back with the jam, asked.

"Yes," Laine said, "but Dean Haviland recognizes her students. Why else do you think I made sure we were in her Romantics class?"

I *had* wondered. Although I'd enjoyed the class—loved it, really—I'd never been sure what reading Keats and Shelley and Byron had to do with learning how to write. Dean Haviland always spoke of the artists we studied as if they had been divinely inspired, rarified beings upon whom genius was visited, destined to dedicate their often short and doomed lives to the Muses and then expire of some Victorian malady—consumption, madness, drink—or all three at the same time.

*Who'd choose to be an artist?* Ben had said once during the study group Laine invited him to under the mistaken impression he was my boyfriend. *They all had such miserable lives and were mostly miserable people.*

*You don't choose, man,* Truman had replied. *If you are one you just have to make art.*

"*I am just going to write because I cannot help it,*" I said, quoting Charlotte Brontë and earning a smile from Laine.

"You mean," I asked on that May morning in the Student Commons as I absorbed this new lesson, "Dean Haviland chooses because of who you are and not the writing you submit?"

But Laine shushed me. Dean Haviland had come out from the post office—the sign that the black feathers had been delivered. Stephanie and Emily were approaching their mailboxes as if they'd made a pact to do it at the same time. I'd seen them together on campus, sitting side by side at the literary club meetings, skating on the pond with linked arms, studying together in the library, dark head bent beside red, and envied the purity of their friendship. It was just the two of them, no hangers-on like Dodie or Chilton, no boyfriends like Truman and Ben (not that Ben was *my* boyfriend; we were strictly study partners). Chilton had said once that they were lesbians and Laine had said that was "reductive." What they were, she said, were kindred spirits. What would happen now, I wondered, if one of them got into the senior seminar and the other didn't?

The Commons was filling with the sounds of disappointed sighs and a few gleeful shouts. I watched one girl reach her hand gingerly into the narrow mailbox as if into a badger's den and then let out a bloodcurdling scream. I pictured a live raven trapped inside, pecking at her fingers.

"Is it . . . ?" another girl asked, hand to heart.

The first girl drew out a black feather and waved it trium-phantly over her head. Soon, the air was full of black feathers, as if a flock of ravens had descended on the Commons. Some students were fleeing as if afraid of being pecked alive; a girl burst into tears, a boy slammed his mailbox and kicked the wall. How cruel, I thought, to make this such a public display.

Emily Dawes and Stephanie Chang still stood in front of their boxes as if frozen. We weren't the only ones in the Com-mons watching them now. The girls who had gotten their feath-ers had gathered in a clutch—an *unkindness,* I remembered the collective noun for ravens from our discussion on Poe's poem "The Raven." I heard Laine softly counting, "One, two, three . . ."

Emily glanced at Stephanie, whose mailbox was in the row next to hers—because Dawes and Chang were close in the alpha-bet, I realized. I wondered if that was how they'd met, whether the friends you made were as randomly sorted as that, like me ending up in the same suite with Laine.

Both girls turned back to their boxes and spun the combi-nation locks at the same time. Right, then left, then right again. In the sudden hush of the Commons every click was audible like the timer of a bomb. On the last click they looked at each other again, nodded, and then turned back to their boxes.

"Four, five, six . . ." Laine murmured.

Stephanie reached in her box and drew out a long black feather and turned to Emily . . . who shook her head and then shrugged. Stephanie uttered a cry that sounded as hoarse and guttural as a crow's caw. I looked at Laine to see how she was taking the scene. Her eyes were flicking rapidly around the Commons, counting again from one to eight. "There are only eight feathers," she said. "There are always nine in the seminar, the number of the Muses."

Stephanie had burst into tears and wrapped her arms around her friend. I could see her face over Emily's shoulder before she buried it in Emily's long red hair. "It doesn't matter, Em, it doesn't matter," she kept saying. Then she turned her face toward Emily's mailbox and her expression changed. She pushed Emily away, shoved her hand into the box, and brought out a black feather that trembled in the air as if alive. Emily tilted back her head and laughed.

"What nerve!" Chilton said with grudging admiration.

"She really had me fooled," Dodie said with a nervous laugh. "Why do you suppose she pulled a prank like that?"

"To find out what Stephanie would do," Laine said. "To find out how true a friend she really is."

"Well, she got what she wanted," Chilton said. "Promise you'll never pull a stunt like that."

Laine didn't say anything. Instead, she looked at me and I saw from her expression—the way she narrowed her eyes and her cheekbones sharpened when she was genuinely taken by surprise—that she had seen what I had: when Stephanie hugged her friend and thought no one could see her face she had smiled. In the moment when she thought she had succeeded where her friend had not, she had been secretly pleased that *she* was the one who had won.

# CHAPTER THIRTEEN

*NOW*

"IS THIS SOMEONE'S idea of a joke?" Miranda demands. "Did *you* do it?" she asks me. "Or"—she turns to Darla—"it was you, wasn't it? Because you're jealous that you didn't get the Writers House residency."

Darla gasps, her mouth open in a perfect circle, making her already gaunt face into a Kabuki mask. "I've had plenty of residencies," she says. "I don't need this one."

"No?" Miranda asks coyly. "I heard about the assault, how you were asked to leave the University of Kansas. Who will take you now? And it's really all you've got, fellowships and grants and residencies. You roam from one retreat to another. It's not like your little books make any money."

Darla flinches as if she has been struck. "I didn't hit that student. She was all up in my face about a grade and I was just trying to get past her . . . I may have pushed her a little." She turns to me. "You know what it's like. These students are so entitled and demanding."

"They can be . . ." I begin. "But I've never pushed one. That's not the point, though, is it?" I turn to Miranda. "How could Darla have done this? Wasn't she downstairs with you all night?"

"She went to the bathroom," Miranda replies. "*Several* times. I thought she might be purging like she used to in college, but she could have been planting *that*." She points a shaky finger at the dead crow.

"There's no reason to think that," I say in the reasonable voice I use for hysterical students, the ones I might *like* to push, but don't. "This is clearly an accident."

"That's what you all said about what happened to Moss and that girl," Miranda says, her tone low and threatening.

"There's no need to rehash all that now," I say, looking around the room. "We'll get this cleaned up and—"

"*You* were gone a long time," Miranda says, stepping closer to me and aiming her finger at my chest. "You could have found this—*thing*—outside and put it in my bed."

"Why in the world—"

"Because I'm taking your precious Laine's place and you can't stand it."

"No one can take Laine's place."

The voice is so deep and hoarse, I think it's Truman's at first, but then I turn and see it's Chilton, standing at my side, her eyes glinting. She looks nothing like the well-groomed Connecticut matron and professional editor she has worked so hard to become.

"And certainly not you," Truman says, coming to stand at my other side.

Miranda's eyes rove over the three of us. "Of course you three would stand together. It was you three and Laine, wasn't it? The core group. You three were the ones alone with Moss at the end—"

Chilton shoots a warning look toward the door where Ruth has appeared, snowflakes melting in her grey hair, staring aghast at the dead crow on the bed. Of course she didn't leave, I think. "Ms. Gardner can sleep in the tower room tonight," Ruth says. "It was all made up for Ms. Bishop."

"Maybe Nell won't want me to take Laine's room," Miranda says snippily.

"You're welcome to it," I say, turning to Ruth. "Thank you for thinking of it, Ruth. I'm sorry you've been delayed yet again. Is Charlie still here?"

Ruth shakes her head no. "I told him to go on without me. I'll stay here tonight. The room will be fine once I clean up this mess."

"But the window's broken—" I begin.

"I don't mind a little fresh air," Ruth says, drawing the heavy drapes over the broken window.

"If you're sure," I say. "Perhaps someone can help Miranda move her luggage to the tower room. It *is* the best room. Remember how we all decided Dodie should have it when Laine didn't come back for the spring semester?"

Miranda blanches. "I'd forgotten."

"You forgot about Dodie?" I ask innocently. "Poor Dodie. People often did forget about her. The morning of graduation we were all gathered downstairs in our robes ready to leave without her until . . . Who noticed she wasn't with us?" I look around the circle of faces, all blanched now with the memory of that morning.

"It was me," Chilton says, her lips barely moving in her frozen face. "I said, 'Where's Dodie?'"

"And Miranda said, 'She's going to make us late,'" Lance adds, his lips quivering. "And Chilton went up to get her and we heard her calling her name at the door—"

"So, I went up and Chilton asked me to break down the door since she wasn't answering," Truman says.

"Then we heard Chilton scream," Lance says, "and we all ran up to see—"

Truman puts his hand on Lance's shoulder and we all stand, hushed by the memory—in commemoration at last—all of us picturing Dodie hanging from the rafters of the tower room on the day we were all supposed to graduate.

LANCE CARRIES MIRANDA'S bags to the tower room, Truman volunteers to dispose of the crow in the bucket Ruth brought up—"I may take a selfie with it for my Instagram feed," he quips to no one's amusement—and Chilton strips the bed while I retrieve a broom and a dustpan from the hall closet. When I get back to the room Chilton is carrying away the bundle of used sheets—holding it away from her body as far as she can—and Ruth has begun putting fresh sheets on the bed.

"Are you sure you don't mind sleeping in here?" I ask, grabbing a corner of the bottom sheet. "After . . ." I study the mattress for any telltale sign of the dead crow but it doesn't look as if any of the blood soaked through the sheets.

"It was just a poor bird," Ruth says, clucking her tongue, "lost in the storm. I pity any living thing out on a night like tonight."

"Yes," I agree, "I'm glad you're staying. Can I lend you a nightgown?"

"I had an overnight bag in my car," she says, nodding to a quilted floral bag on the floor. "I always keep one in the trunk in case I get an inkling to take off."

I try not to smile at the unlikely image of Ruth as an adventurer, ready to take to the road on a moment's whim. "Very practical of you, Ruth. I'm sorry for the behavior of some of our guests. They shouldn't treat you like . . ."

"The maid?" she finishes for me, snapping the top sheet over the bed. The floating cloth shrouds her face. By the time it settles to the surface, like a swan alighting on a pond, her expression is carefully neutral, her thick glasses masking whatever she truly feels about our guests' behavior. "It doesn't matter. I learned a long time ago that no one sees you for what you really are."

"I do," I say, smoothing the sheet and tucking it under the mattress. (Ruth strikes me as the type who'd want her bedding tucked.) "You're good at your job and kind to the students. You're smarter than most of the professors and you could run the college better than Hotch."

I note the look of discomfort on her face and decide to drop the subject. Ruth doesn't like to be praised, a trait I admire in her. I grab the broom and dustpan to sweep up the glass under the window but when I get there, there's no glass to sweep.

I OPEN THE door to my own room—the last one on the hall before the tower room—with trepidation, steeled for nasty surprises. But there's no broken window, no dead crow on the bed. The only surprise is in how orderly and sedate the room is. When I lived here it was a scene of barely controlled chaos: books and stacks of papers piled on every surface, including the bed; walls covered with Post-it notes and index cards outlining my senior writing project, the novel I was writing for Moss's class; and the revision notes I'd gotten from workshops. So much paper it was like I'd papered a nest for myself, a secure cocoon that shut out the rest of the world. When I was inside it, I could tune out the voice of my mother asking me what I planned to do after college. *Writing isn't an option for people like us,* she would remind me on the weekly calls I made from the hall phone booth (people had begun to have cell phones by then, but I couldn't afford one). *You don't have an independent income like your rich friends at college. You should be getting a business degree—or if you like school so much, your teacher's certification.*

*Aim higher,* Laine said when I told her the options my mother considered reasonable, *excelsior!*

I cross the room to the window seat beneath the eaves and run my hands down the molding. Was it still here? Surely in all the remodeling . . . But I see right away that the wood hasn't been refinished. In fact, none of the moldings have been. Chilton was right—the renovations appear to have been shoddily done in places. At least it means my carving has survived, the letters etched so finely—I didn't want to lose the room cleaning deposit—they're invisible, but my fingertips can still make them out. *Excelsior!* Tracing the letters, I remember the prick of the pin I had used to etch them and imagine that a bit of my blood has soaked into the wood from when the pin slipped and sank into my finger. Blood to seal a pact, I had thought.

And it had sealed a pact of sorts, I think now. After all, I had aimed higher. I'd gotten my doctorate and college professorship and risen to Dean of Liberal Arts. If my mother had had her way I'd be teaching high school on Long Island. Sometimes I wonder if I wouldn't have been happier.

A knock at the door startles me out of the thought. I cross the room and open it without asking who it is. I'm pretty sure I know. And, of course, I'm right. Truman and Chilton are standing in the doorway, looking as guilty as they did the last time they knocked on this door.

"We should talk," Chilton says without preamble, entering my room and taking the only chair. Truman perches on the window seat. I close the door behind me and sit on the edge of the bed facing them. I point to the wall adjoining the tower room and mouth, *Miranda's right next door.*

"She's taking the world's longest shower in the hall bathroom," Chilton says. "Listen, you can hear the pipes."

I notice the knocking now, a sound familiar from when we lived here senior year.

"Apparently Hotch's expensive renovation didn't include revamping the ancient plumbing either," Chilton says. "But at least we'll know when she's done."

"What about Darla?" I ask.

"Raiding the kitchen for sweets. Lance is in his room wearing noise-cancelling headphones while doing some complicated meditation practice."

Her eyes flick from me to Truman as if wondering how she has ended up with the two of us as her comrades in arms. No Laine, no Dodie. We are the ones remaining who were there that night at the end, linked forever by what happened.

"Did either of you plant that crow in Miranda's bed?" she asks.

"I certainly didn't," Truman says.

"Why in the world would *I* do such a thing?" I ask.

Chilton shakes her head. "It's the type of thing Laine would do," she says, almost wistfully, as if a propensity for planting dead birds were an endearing trait.

"What are you saying?" Truman asks.

"Remember that time she got mad at something Darla said in a workshop and she left a decapitated chocolate reindeer on her bed?"

"A chocolate reindeer—decapitated or not—is not the same as a dead bloody crow," I say.

Ignoring me, Chilton turns to Truman. "Remember the time you broke up with Laine sophomore year and she unstrung all your guitar strings?"

"You broke up with her sophomore year?" I ask at the same time Truman says, "You think she's here, too, don't you? But why would she hide from us if she were here?"

"Maybe she wants to know what we're going to do now that they've found *her*." Chilton, I notice, can't say her name either.

"Why should any of us do anything?" Truman asks. "All we have to do is do nothing."

"They found Laine's locket with the bones," Chilton says, looking at me. "Or didn't Nell tell you? She was there when they brought it up from the cave. Maybe Laine wants to know if we're going to break the pact and tell what really happened."

Truman shakes his head. "Laine knows we'd never do that. Besides, it wouldn't just be giving *her* up; it would be giving ourselves up, too."

"The first one to talk could make a deal," Chilton says. "Nell's already talked to Ben—"

"Not about making a deal!" I cry. "He's in charge of the investigation. Of course we spoke."

"Do you think he'll confess?" Truman asks. "He's always had that Catholic choirboy mentality."

I'm startled by the hostility in Truman's voice. He and Ben had had a bit of a contentious relationship. Ben made no secret of his disapproval of Truman's wild behavior—of all our wild behavior—but Truman had always shrugged it off and acted like it didn't bother him. Had that been an act?

"I don't know," I say honestly. "I don't really know Ben anymore but he did say that Laine would have to explain what her locket was doing in the cave. I pointed out that there were lots of ways it could have ended up there. It's the cave we went into senior year—Merlin's Crystal Cave."

"Yeah, I remember she got separated from the rest of us . . ." He pauses as if he's remembering something else and then shakes himself and says, "Laine will tell them what happened. That's why she'll come back—"

The sound of a door opening down the hall cuts him short.

"That's Miranda now," Chilton says. "She's coming out of the bathroom."

We all listen to her footsteps coming down the hall, clearly audible on the bare floorboards. I should tell Hotch to get them carpeted. You could always hear everyone coming back at night; there were no secrets on this hall.

We wait until she goes into the tower room and closes the

door. Chilton starts to speak, but Truman places a finger to his lips to stop her. In the silence we hear every move Miranda makes. The wall between these two rooms is thinner than the others in Wilder Hall. Laine hypothesized that my room had been a sitting room or baby's nursery attached to the tower room and that the college had skimped when it put up the dividing wall.

*Good thing there are no secrets between us,* she'd said.

When we hear the sigh of bedsprings, Truman motions to Chilton that it's safe to go out. He follows her, walking in time with her steps so if Miranda hears anything she'll think it's a single person—presumably me—walking to the door. A trick that Truman remembers from our college days.

# CHAPTER FOURTEEN

*NOW*

IN MY ROOM I change into my Briarwood sweatshirt and sweatpants instead of the nightgown I brought. Better to be ready in case there are any more disruptions. I'm just getting into bed when I hear footsteps coming up the hall. Someone else wanting to discuss the probability of Laine's arrival, no doubt. I wait, but the footsteps pass my room and I hear someone knock on the door of the tower room, and then the soft murmur of Ruth's voice. When I open my door, I see Ruth standing in front of the closed door holding a tray with a full tea service.

"Ruth, you don't have to—" I begin.

"She *asked* me to," Ruth hisses.

Miranda swings her door open. She's changed into a flowy tunic and yoga pants that look like they were woven from organic bamboo and hemp. "Were you able to find organic chamomile?" she asks, looking down at the tea tray in Ruth's hands without offering to take it.

I see the corner of Ruth's mouth twitch so I answer for her. "We always order from that little tea company across the river and all their tea is organic. How thoughtful of you, Ruth, to bring this up for Miranda. I'll take it in. You should get some sleep now."

I carry the tray into the tower room as Ruth shuts the door behind her. Miranda has sunk into one of the two chairs set beneath the window. I glance at the night table and see that it's crowded with an assortment of bottles and tubes—vitamins, mineral supplements, night creams, and prescription bottles of Ambien and Xanax. Yoga must not always do the trick, I assume. I push the bottles over to make room for the tray and then pour the tea into two Briarwood mugs. "Mind if I join you?" I ask, sitting down in the other chair without waiting for an answer.

"Why not?" she says as I hand her a mug. "I'm not likely to get any sleep after my *unpleasant* experience—or with all of you creeping in and out of each other's rooms like a French bedroom farce," she adds slyly. "I heard Truman sneaking out of your room earlier."

"What good ears you have," I say. "You must have heard Chilton with him."

She shrugs and takes a sip of her tea. "Did I? I recall that Truman was in and out of your room a lot in college. I always wondered if the two of you . . ." She twirls her hand in the air to suggest, I suppose, illicit sex—or maybe she's just showing off the big emerald on her right hand (I recall that she wrote a blog last year about buying herself a right-hand ring).

"Truman was Laine's boyfriend," I say. "You know that."

She shrugs again and takes another sip of tea. "And yet, he was in your room an awful lot. I'd hear your door open and shut and then hear him walking by. Those big motorcycle boots he wore in college made a distinctive jingle."

"We were friends," I say. "He'd come by to talk when Laine was busy writing."

"Oh, yes, she was always writing. Remember the cartoon she drew and put up on her door—what was it? A drawing of Virginia Woolf sitting at her desk with a speech bubble that said, 'I'm writing, back the fuck away' . . ."

"It was Mary Shelley, and it was 'Back off, Percy.'"

"Whatever. So pretentious, I thought at the time, but now I'd like to make it my away message. Poor Truman, though, it must have been hard being Laine's boyfriend and getting shown the door by Mary Shelley. I can see why he'd seek solace with you. Of course, you must have been writing, too. Hugo kept us busy with revisions, didn't he? Didn't you mind being interrupted by Tru Davis . . . and being his *second choice*?"

"I don't know, Miranda, do you mind being Hotch's second choice for the residency?" I ask sweetly. "You must know that Laine was his first choice."

"We all know that Laine wasn't coming, let alone going to take that job. I think Hotch was genuinely relieved when I offered to."

"Funny," I say, "I happened to see the two of you in the Great Hall when I was coming back. He didn't look relieved; he looked angry."

She's sufficiently rattled that she has to take another sip of tea to give herself time to reply. "Oh, that. I did have to negotiate for better terms and Hotch was a little . . . *tetchy* about it. Overall, though, I think he was relieved and I think you are, too."

"Me? Why's that?"

"Because if Laine did come back, you'd have to live in her shadow again and I think you've gotten used to standing on your own. It was a shame how you let yourself be overshadowed by her in college. And not just with Truman. I always thought you were the better writer but you were afraid to let yourself shine because Laine couldn't stand competition. That's why she and I never got along. But you—I remember that story you wrote for the *Raven* contest sophomore year and the rumors that went around that Laine had actually written it."

"People talk," I say shortly, "as you well know."

"Yes," she says, grimacing, "but in this case I think it was Laine who started the rumor. I remember Emily Dawes called you both in?"

"That's right," I say, getting to my feet. "There were a few images and phrases in common between the two stories. It was embarrassing, but we were lucky Emily saw the similarities before either story was printed or Laine and I might have both been brought before the dean for plagiarism. Laine very generously withdrew her story. I'm sure you wish you'd been so lucky last year."

"Last year?" she asks, the smile slipping from her face.

"Last year when your publisher had to cancel your book because you'd lifted whole passages from another writer who you'd mentored for a conference. That's why you need this job, isn't it? No publisher wants you after that incident."

"How—?" she begins.

"One of our graduates works at your publisher—or should I say, your former publisher? In fact, I helped him get his first internship using our career services program. A bright young man. We keep in touch. He mentioned the, er, incident at lunch this past summer. I hadn't thought it necessary to mention it to Hotch before but I will now. Whatever leverage you used to get him to give you this job won't be sufficient for him to overlook this. Briarwood College has a zero-tolerance policy for plagiarism. We certainly can't have a writer-in-residence who committed plagiarism."

Miranda doesn't have anything to say to that, so I bid her good night. When I reach the door, though, she does think of something to say. "That story you wrote, it was called 'The Intended,' right? I remember because it was the same name as Laine's big novel."

# CHAPTER FIFTEEN

*THEN*

THE NEXT RUNG on the cursus honorum to get into the Raven Society and Moss's senior seminar was Dean Haviland's Gothic Novel class sophomore year. We read *The Castle of Otranto* and *The Mysteries of Udolpho*, which gave me nightmares about secret passageways and black-veiled horrors, and then *Frankenstein* by Mary Shelley. On a stormy day in October, Dean Haviland introduced the book by telling us its origin story, how young Mary Shelley—eighteen years old, just a year younger than most of us were then—had traveled to Switzerland with her lover, Percy Bysshe Shelley, and stepsister Claire Clairmont, where they joined up with Byron and his friend John Polidori at a villa on Lake Geneva.

"Imagine it as a spring break road trip, only by carriage and the road was over treacherous mountains—" As if in sync with her description, lightning flashed over Briarwood Mountain through the floor-to-ceiling windows of our classroom in Main. "And there is no spring or summer this year because a volcanic eruption in Indonesia has blotted out the sun . . . oh, and imagine that you're the daughter of two of the most important thinkers in Europe and your lover is one of the most promising poets of his generation and his friend Byron is already a rock star of a poet, an eighteenth-century Mick Jagger. Since you're stuck inside there's not much to do but read German ghost stories to each other, drink, flirt, and have long philosophical debates. One stormy night"—again the weather obliged with a crack of thunder—"Lord Byron proposes a contest: Who could write the scariest story? They all sat down to write—well, except for Claire, whom no one really expected much of—and Mary, who, according to her preface to the 1831 edition, couldn't come up with an idea. Later that night, though, she had what she described as a 'waking dream' in which her 'imagination, unbidden, possessed and guided' her, gifting her 'images of a pale student of unhallowed acts, a hideous phantasm of a man, a horrid thing,' which she imagined standing at her bedside regarding her with yellow eyes. This," Dean Haviland concluded, her face green-tinged by the lightning, "is where inspiration comes from—bad weather, doomed love, and nightmares."

When I looked over at Laine, I saw that she, too, was lit up as if she had been struck by lightning. She didn't speak for the rest of the hour and when class was done, she didn't, as she usually did, stay after to ask Dean Haviland some question. She wandered down the marble steps out of Main, not stopping at the Nook for lunch as we normally did, without an umbrella or raincoat. She walked through the pouring rain, not to the shelter of our dorm, but to the edge of Mirror Lake, where she stood staring up at the lightning crackling over High Tor.

"She's going to get struck by lightning," Dodie said.

"Or catch her death," Chilton added.

We'd followed her, of course, Chilton and Dodie in their sturdy L.L. Bean anoraks and gum boots, Truman in the caped Australian rancher's coat and wide-brimmed hat he affected sophomore year, me in sodden sneakers and sweatshirt. Even Ben had joined us, although he stood a little to the side, hunched in his yellow rain slicker, looking on with disapproval as we tried to reason with Laine to come inside. She only shook her head and said she had to soak up the energy from the lightning. Finally, I thought of something.

""'Run mad as often as you chuse; but do not faint,'"" I said.

And she, turning to me with a glint in her eyes, quoted, ""'take warning from my unhappy End . . . Beware of fainting-fits . . . Beware of swoons . . .'"""

""'Run mad as often as you chuse; but do not faint,'"" we both concluded together.

"You're the only one else who's read *that* Jane Austen," she said, linking her arm in mine. "I suppose Jane would tell me to get out of the rain."

"Absolutely," I agreed, leading her in the direction of the dorm, "and to have some hot tea."

Back in our suite in Rowan—Laine had pulled some strings to get us the same suite sophomore year—Dodie made tea, then Truman brought out his flask of whiskey and passed it around. We turned out the lights and lit candles and took turns reading from *Frankenstein* while thunder rolled down the mountains. Truman quoted, ""'When younger," said he, "I felt as if I were destined for some great enterprise.'"" And Ben read the lines that came after: ""'But this feeling, which supported me in the commencement of my career, now serves only to plunge me lower in the dust.'""

"Does that mean it's better not to be ambitious?" Dodie asked.

To which Laine replied, "'Better to reign in Hell than serve in Heaven.'"

Ben shook his head. "The story is a warning not to overreach . . ."

We argued on like that, as if it were within our power to choose one way or another—the perilous climb to greatness or the narrow path to a quiet life—all while the storm raged on outside. It felt as if we were in that villa on Lake Geneva.

"We should do it," Laine said, eyes glowing in the candle-light. "The *Raven* is holding a contest. Let's each write a scary story and submit it and see if anyone wins. I hear Moss always assigns a ghost story. It'll be good preparation for those of us who make it into his class."

"I don't like scary stories," Dodie said. "They scare me."

"You're excused," Laine said curtly. "Who's in?"

"Sure," Truman said, "I can think of a few horrors."

Chilton shrugged. "I listened to enough ghost stories around the fire at Camp Wa-No-Sakee. I'm sure I can come up with something."

Laine went straight to her room to begin. Dodie and Chilton said they were going to the cafeteria for dinner. "I have to get to the library to finish tomorrow's translation," Ben said. "Are you coming, Nell?"

I knew Ben hated any disruption in our study routine, but suddenly I felt as if I were just one more Latin noun that he had to slot into the right declension. "I've already done it," I lied. "I'll see you in class tomorrow."

Ben lingered for a moment, waiting for Truman to leave with him, but Truman stretched himself out on the floor, staring at Laine's door, and Ben left. I thought Truman would leave as he usually did when Laine shut him out, but instead he lit up a joint.

"That was fucking brilliant," he said on the inhale, adding on the exhale, "coming up with that Jane Austen crap."

I shrugged as he handed me the joint. I took a hit, holding it in to hide my pleasure at his compliment and replying only after I'd exhaled. "*Love and Freindship* is Laine's favorite. I think because hardly anyone knows it."

"I feel sometimes like there's a code I'm supposed to know with her, like she came with instructions, only they're all in Greek."

So, this was why he stayed; he thought I held the key to Laine's secret code. But Laine wouldn't like us talking about her behind her back. My eyes flicked to her closed door.

"You can't hear shit in there," he said, leaning toward me. When I looked back his face was suddenly very close. He took the joint and put the lit end in his mouth and leaned even closer. I kept myself very still, not moving away or toward him, my lips parted more in surprise than consent. I'd seen him doing this with Laine—shotgunning, they called it—but I'd assumed it was something intimate. And it *was* intimate. His lips almost touched mine as he blew a stream of smoke into my mouth. I almost forgot to inhale, but my lungs remembered. They took the smoke in as if hungry for it and held it so long that my vision swam and darkened.

When my vision cleared, he had moved back and I wondered if I'd imagined what had just happened. He was on his feet, sweeping that ridiculous coat on, donning his hat. He tilted the brim over his left eye and then winked, like we'd shared a secret, and was gone. I sat perfectly still, my fingers on my lips, which felt hot. I sat there until I heard Dodie's and Chilton's voices in the hall and then I got up and hurried to my room so I wouldn't have to talk to them. I tried to study—I had that translation due for Latin that I'd told Ben I'd already done and *Frankenstein* to finish reading for Gothic Novel—but the words were all jumbled. I lay on my bed and closed my eyes, quickly drifting off to sleep, but even my dreams were blurry.

I was standing in front of the gates of the college but when I looked up the metal spikes melted into the sky. My own hands, when I grasped the iron bars to get in, were a blur. Beyond the gates I could make out an indistinct figure standing with its back to me. As it turned, I knew what it was—the blur-girl, the *intended,* whose place I had taken here at Briarwood. She had come to reclaim her rightful place. She turned—and what I saw

was awful. She was me, but stitched together, a monster created out of spare parts. Some of those parts, I saw with horror,
belonged to Laine.

When I startled awake, I thought I saw her standing over
me, yellow eyes watching me, teeth bared. Even when I realized that the phantom was cobbled together from my sweatshirt
draped over a chair, the illuminated numbers on my clock radio,
and a string of beads discarded on the chair, the simulacrum
seemed ominous.

I turned on the lamp to dispel the illusion, but it remained
in my head. The only way to banish it was to take out my notebook and start writing. I barely saw the words that flew beneath
my pen, stringing together a story of a girl who is haunted by
her double—the blur-girl intended for her place. Each time she
sees it, a part of it—a leg, a hand, one eye—comes into focus
and the corresponding part on her own body loses function and
feeling. A hand goes numb, an ear grows deaf, her hair and fingernails fall out, until in her last glimpse of the blur-girl she sees
it has become her. Then her vision blurs and she realizes that
she has become the blur-girl and *it* has taken her place.

When I was done, light was pouring in through the window
and the rain had passed. I felt like I'd written myself out of the
storm. I collapsed into bed and slept through my 8 A.M. Latin
class and breakfast. When I woke up there was someone sitting
in my desk chair. For a moment I thought I had written the blur-
girl into life, but it was only Laine, flipping through the pages of
my story. A Styrofoam cup of coffee and an English muffin sat
on my night table.

"I thought you might be sick," Laine said without turning
around, "but I see you've been busy. Funny—" She turned to
me. "I thought you were a poet, not a fiction writer."

"You inspired me with your challenge," I said, blinking away the illusion of yellow eyes. It was just that the sun was in her eyes. Then I added, "It's probably not much good."

"Now you sound like Dodie," Laine said, aping the downcast expression—her Eeyore look, Laine called it—Dodie made when she diminished herself. "It's actually quite good . . . only, the idea of the blur-girl as double . . . is that something I told you?"

"I-I don't think so," I said. I recalled telling Laine about my blur-girl nightmare freshman year, but I didn't mention that.

Laine shrugged. "I guess it's one of those ideas floating around in the mythic sea. Are you going to type it up and submit it to *The Raven* for their story contest?"

"I—"

"You should," she said, tossing my sweatshirt at me. "Now get up. You're supposed to meet Ben at the library. He cornered me in the cafeteria and grilled me on your health and whereabouts, since you missed Latin, as if it would be my fault if you'd caught a cold from being out in the rain." At the door she turned and added, "It's adorable how sweet he is on you."

I wasn't sure about that. Sometimes it seemed as if Ben was my personal critic, and although we spent hours together in the library and he always walked me back to the dorm (because he didn't think the campus was safe), he'd never kissed me or asked me to go anywhere but the library or the Nook.

I got up and dressed but before I went to the library, I typed up my story. I was expecting that in the light of day it would be awful, and it *was* rough, but there was something satisfying about pounding it out in black-and-white type, pinning my elusive blur-girl onto the page. Maybe now she'd stop haunting my dreams.

When I was done, I stuck the pages in a large envelope and walked across campus to deliver it to the offices of *The Raven* on the third floor of Main. There was a metal grille set in the closed door with instructions posted above it to drop submissions through the slot. As I slid my story through it, I had the feeling that I was sliding it beneath the ironwork gates of the college, sending the blur-girl on her way. It didn't really matter, I told myself, whether I won the contest or not; the important thing was that I had exorcised the blur-girl.

Three days later I got a note in my mailbox to come to the *Raven* offices. I couldn't help thinking as I climbed the two flights of stairs that they were going to tell me I had won the contest. Why else would they ask me to come in? I had to school the smile from my face when I opened the door.

Laine was there, seated in front of a desk, behind which sat Emily Dawes. Miranda Gardner sat to one side with a notebook balanced on her knee. She'd gotten the job of assistant editor, much to Chilton's chagrin. Laine and Emily were laughing over some shared reminiscence of their days at Choate while Miranda looked on with an impatient expression. I could hear someone typing in a connecting room.

"Here's Nell now," Laine said, "I'm sure she'll clear this all up."

"Clear what up?" I asked, suppressing the strange, irrational thought that I'd been called in to sweep up the dust balls that floated in the corners.

"Just a little question of plagiarism," Miranda said crisply.

Emily sighed. "Randy is being dramatic," she said, shooting a reproving look at her. "It's just that I noticed some similarities between these two submissions, both of which are very good—"

"One is very good," Miranda corrected. "One is a plagiarism."

Emily pursed her lips and slid a sheaf of papers across the desk toward me. "Is this your story, Nell?"

I looked down to see the story I'd written, "The Intended," in front of me.

"Yes," I said. "I wrote it just a few days ago."

"And did you take any words or phrases from any other piece of writing?" Miranda asked.

"Noooo," I said, only the word came out strangely elongated as if I wasn't sure. Hadn't some of the words come from my dream? Hadn't some of them come from the blur-girl herself?

"You don't sound sure," Miranda said archly. "Did you or didn't you steal parts of this?"

"No!" I said, this time too stridently. "I didn't . . . at least not that I realized. The story came from a dream, after we read *Frankenstein* and Laine proposed we write stories like the ones the Shelleys and Byron had . . . Did I . . . Is there anything from *Frankenstein* in it?"

I could feel my face growing hot. Had I unconsciously borrowed phrases from *Frankenstein*? I knew that Briarwood had a zero-tolerance policy on plagiarism. I could lose my scholarship . . . I could be *expelled*.

"Not from *Frankenstein*—at least not that I could see." Emily looked to Miranda.

"There are some allusions," Miranda said, "but that's not the real problem. The problem is that some of the language matches passages in the piece Laine Bishop submitted. Here." She placed another sheaf of papers in front of me, this one marked with yellow highlighter.

I recognized some phrases I had written floating amid words I had not, as if bits of my story had broken off and stolen into someone else's story. They stared up at me, as accusing as the dead yellow eyes of Frankenstein's creature. "I don't understand . . ." I began.

"Are these your words?" Miranda demanded, tapping her finger on the highlighted parts.

"Yes, but . . ."

"Are you saying that Laine Bishop took your words and put them in her story?"

I froze. *This was Laine's story?* I looked toward Laine but she remained staring straight ahead.

"I—no—Laine would never—"

"Then you stole them from her?" Miranda asked. There was something almost gleeful in her voice and a smile was threatening to creep onto her lips.

"I—" I glanced again toward Laine but she still wouldn't look at me. "I might have borrowed some things she told me without realizing," I said, and then added, "We share the same suite and we're always talking . . ."

Laine sighed. "That's what I was telling Emily before you came in, Nell." She finally turned to me, her face soft and compassionate. "I told her that we're best friends and we talk about everything and share everything—why, I think that's my sweatshirt you've got on!"

I looked down and saw with horror that she was right. The Briarwood sweatshirt I was wearing was the old, faded vintage one she'd inherited from her mother. How had I come to be wearing it? "I-I didn't mean—"

"Of course you didn't," Laine said, grabbing my hand and squeezing it. "I'm sure it was completely unconscious. In fact, I really don't think we can say that one of us borrowed from the other. We probably just came up with similar ideas and phrases because we're so close. Really, there's no need to involve the dean."

*The dean?* Had there been talk before I got there of going to the dean?

Emily and Miranda exchanged a glance. "I think we can let it go—" Emily began.

"One of you will have to withdraw your story," Miranda said.

"I will—" I said, but then I felt Laine's cold hand on mine.

"No, I will," Laine said firmly.

In the silence that followed I noticed that whoever had been typing in the next room had stopped.

"Are you sure?" Emily asked.

"Yes," Laine said. "Nell deserves to win; she worked so hard for this."

"Well, in that case," Emily said, "congratulations, Nell, you're the winner of the *Raven* short story contest—"

"Once Nell certifies that the work is original," Miranda interrupted, shoving a form across the desk at me. "Can you do that, Nell?"

My mouth felt dry but I nodded and looked down at the form. The words blurred in front of me and my hand shook as I signed my name. I had a horrible moment when I began writing *Ellen* but then crossed it out and wrote *Nell,* as if I wasn't even sure of my own name.

When I looked up, I saw someone standing in the doorway to the inner office holding a sheaf of papers. "I finished typing these letters for you," the girl said.

"Not now, Bridget," Miranda snapped. "Can you not see I'm in a meeting?"

I was surprised to hear Miranda talk to another student that way but when I tried to send Bridget a look of commiseration—we'd both been raked over the coals by Miranda Gardner—she smirked at me as if to say that at least *she* hadn't been accused of plagiarism. She must have overhead everything.

By the next day the rumor had spread across the campus that I had stolen my story from Laine but that she'd withdrawn her own story because she felt sorry for me.

## CHAPTER SIXTEEN

*NOW*

WHEN I GET back to my room, I realize I'm shaking. Why? I chide myself; I've confronted students with plagiarism and dealt with irate parents. Why should I let Miranda Gardner get to me?

*Because she's good at figuring out people's weaknesses.* I remember in college how she insinuated herself in groups and clubs, always watching, alert to alliances and rivalries, collecting information to use later. I suspected she was the one who spread the rumor that Laine had withdrawn her story out of pity for me. Miranda had a calculating mind, which served her well as a mystery writer. She'd clearly gained leverage over Hotch to get the residency. The question was, what else was she up to?

I climb into bed, still in my Briarwood sweats, the heavy fleece welcome in the cold room. As I try to relax, I listen to the sounds of night, different from the ones at home. The knocking pipes and steaming radiator are making more noise than heat. Outside the wind is keening and flinging snow against the windows like something trying to get in.

When I close my eyes, I picture the dead crow, its head lolling to one side—

*Poor thing, lost in the storm.*

As I am in my dream.

I'm wandering across an arctic wasteland, a world engulfed in ice and blowing snow, the only distinguishable feature on the horizon a dark figure that fades in and out of view between snow gusts. It's the blur-girl and I am pursuing it across the wastes, as Victor Frankenstein pursued his creation across the arctic ice. I am as determined as he was to end the thing I made so that it can't do any more harm. As I trudge after it, my legs numb with cold, my face stinging with frostbite, I know that I am not pursuing it so much as *it* is luring me on, always staying just close enough to be seen, just far enough to elude capture, enticing me deeper and deeper into the arctic waste until the ice shatters and shifts beneath my feet, and I am stranded on an ice floe drifting out to sea. Only then does it turn to me, revealing its face, cracked and seamed as Frankenstein's creature—

*Cracked open like an egg.*

I startle awake to a sound like breaking glass. For a moment I think I'm on one of the ice floes from my dream, but of course I'm in bed, freezing because the window's open—

Did I leave it open?

I get up to close it but then pause halfway there, listening . . . Somewhere down below on the first floor a door opens and closes. Has someone gone out—or come in? Outside the wind wails and snow drifts in through the open window. Who would go out in this? Unless there was some emergency . . .

Conjuring images of campus disasters, I put my slippers on, grab my phone from the nightstand, and open my door. I pause, listening, but the only sound I hear is the wind—then I hear a door bang downstairs. The front door.

I pick up my phone, noticing that it's almost 6 A.M., turn on the flashlight, and head down the front stairs. I make a mental note to tell Hotch that there really ought to be some lighting on these stairs and a nonslip carpet runner. There's a lamp in the foyer, at least, on the heavy oak sideboard beneath the coat-rack. It illuminates a partially open front door banging in the wind. I hurry across the cold, wet floor—no carpet here either,

I see—grab hold of the door, and swing it open as if to surprise
an intruder. But I only see snow blowing across the threshold.
I step out onto the porch and make out indentations in the
drifted snow—footsteps maybe, but it's hard to tell in the shifting, windblown snow. Then, as I stand there, a security light is
triggered at the end of the front path. The snow is blowing too
hard to tell who—or what—set it off; then another lamp lights
farther along the path, and then another, marking the retreat
of an invisible intruder until the lights are swallowed by the
woods. I stand there another minute, watching, but whoever it
was is gone.

I go back inside and hear something from the back of the
house—a thump. It's probably Truman, I tell myself, looking for
more scotch in the study.

But Truman isn't in the study. Someone has been there,
though. A picture frame is lying on the floor, broken glass scattered around it. Maybe that was the sound I heard?

I pick it up and turn it over. It's the photograph Miranda had
taken down last night, the one of all of us from senior seminar
gathered in front of High Tor at the Luminaria. I hold it closer
to my phone, peering into each of our faces—all of us so young,
our skin pink in the cold, eyes not yet haunted—well, except for
Truman's. He's wearing dark sunglasses that hide his eyes and
reflect back twin figures of the photographer. As I peer closer, I
hear footsteps behind me.

I turn quickly, the light from my phone strafing a tall figure,
arm flung across his eyes like Frankenstein's creature threatened
by a torch. "Okay, okay," Truman says in mock surrender, "you
caught me scavenging for the last of the scotch. Put down your
weapon. I'm unarmed."

I lower the phone and the beam catches the glint of a half-
full scotch bottle. Truman sinks down on the couch in front of
it. "You couldn't sleep either?"

I direct the phone's flashlight onto the floor so I can navigate around the broken glass and make my way to the couch. "I heard someone opening the front door," I say, "then I heard a sound back here and found this." I lay the broken frame down on the table and shine the light on it so Truman can see. "Was it you? Did you go out?"

"Nah," Truman says, looking down at the photograph. "I heard you in the hall and followed you down the front stairs. Maybe the sound you heard was the shattering of our youthful dreams."

"You haven't done so badly for yourself," I say, sitting down beside him and pouring myself a finger of scotch into one of the glasses we'd left here. "You're a bona fide rock star. All those students couldn't get enough of you last night."

"One of them wanted an autograph for his *mother*," he says, grimacing. "Another had me mixed up with John Darnielle of the Mountain Goats. The worst was this nerd boy who knew all my stats like I was a category on *Jeopardy!*" He turns and catches me looking at him. "Shit, the *worst* is me sitting here whining like a prima donna that I didn't get a Grammy and my sales are down."

"I imagine it was hard for a performer during the lockdown," I say.

"What was hard was looking at all my mates' Instagram feeds with filtered pics of their studios and #findinspirationwithin and #artredeems and everyone coming out of lockdown with a new album or at least a couple new songs. Like a global disaster was a creative opportunity."

"Chilton worked on her core," I say.

He chokes on a mouthful of scotch.

"It's not too late," I say softly. "Maybe now is the time to write that novel you started in college."

"I tried," he says. "After college—and after *everything* that went down—I went out west and holed up in a little cabin in the woods and tried to write the Great American Novel and . . . nothing, zilch, nada. The only story I could tell was the only one I never could."

"At least you tried," I say, "and then you started playing the clubs in Seattle and San Francisco. It sounded so romantic—"

"It would have been," he says, "if you had come when I asked you."

I reach for the bottle and pour another finger of scotch. "I thought you only asked," I say, "because you asked Laine first and she said no."

He stares at me. "Why would you think that—" he begins, but his question, which I don't want to answer, is cut short by a loud scream.

"What the hell," he says, wobbling to his feet.

Truman bolts out of the study and heads to the back stairs. I follow him. When I turn the corner, I see Truman fall to his knees at the foot of the stairs. His body is blocking whatever—or whoever—he is looking at. Darla is crouched halfway up the stairs, one hand clasped over her mouth, one hanging onto the banister. She's rocking rhythmically and keening. Lance joins her on the landing, looking down through the rails of the banister like a child spying on the grown-ups. When Truman gets up, he exposes a body sprawled headfirst at the bottom of the stairs, legs splayed at unnatural angles, head lolling over the bottom step. It's Miranda, her neck broken just like the crow's she found earlier in her bed.

# CHAPTER SEVENTEEN

*NOW*

"IS SHE DEAD?" I ask, taking a step forward.

"I think so," Truman says. "She's not breathing."

Darla's keening goes up a decibel.

"Darla," I say tightly, as I move forward to place my fingers on Miranda's neck. I can't find a pulse. "What happened?"

Her wide, startled eyes swivel from Miranda's body to me. "I don't know!" she wails. "Why are you asking me? I was just heading downstairs and I found Miranda like this."

She starts keening again. I look up at Lance. "What about you?"

"I came when I heard Darla screaming."

As would anyone. So where are Chilton and Ruth?

"Okay," I say, taking out my phone and then realizing there's no reception. "I'm going to use the landline in the kitchen to call the police and campus security. Tru—" He looks up at me, his pupils dilated, his face drained of blood. "Can you stay here with the—with Miranda? Make sure no one touches her or moves anything."

He nods and sinks back against the wall, a few feet from Miranda's ghastly face.

"Shouldn't we cover her face? Or at least close her eyes?" Darla asks, getting shakily to her feet.

"No," I say sharply. "The police will want us to leave everything as is. And if you go back upstairs to get dressed or anything, be *careful*. We don't want anyone else falling down these . . ." Death trap stairs, Chilton had called them. Where *is* Chilton? And Ruth? Darla's scream could have raised the dead.

I dial 911 on the kitchen landline. The operator asks me what my emergency is, and I tell her my name and location, and that a woman has fallen down the stairs and appears not to be breathing and has no pulse. She tells me a police officer and ambulance will be on the scene as soon as they can get through the snow; the plows have just gone out and there are a lot of downed trees. "Sit tight," she tells me, "and don't move the body."

I need to call campus security and Hotch but I want to check on Chilton and Ruth first. Crossing the Great Hall, I see through the windows that it has stopped snowing and a thin line of orange has appeared on the horizon. I'm momentarily distracted by how beautiful it is, the light spreading a tangerine glaze over the sculpted snowdrifts and icicles, transforming the campus into the magical place it had seemed when I first came here. It feels almost as if something has been restored. I shake the thought away as I climb the stairs.

When I knock on Chilton's door, there's no response. I wait a full minute then open the door slightly. I see Chilton is lying in bed on her side, her back to the door. I walk over and put my hand on her shoulder and she flinches and rolls over, presenting me with the face of my nightmares—the blank, eyeless face of the blur-girl. Then she pushes away the peach satin sleep mask and plucks earplugs out of her ears. "What?" she demands.

"There's been a horrible accident," I say. "Miranda fell down the back stairs."

"Is she—?"

"She's dead," I say. With anyone else I might be tempted to

say it more gently, but I know from experience that Chilton is a lot tougher than people think and that the harsh reality will galvanize her into usefulness. And I need her to be useful right now. "The police will be here soon."

She clenches her jaw to still a tremor and then nods and tosses back the duvet, revealing a pink flannel nightgown. The innocence of its lace smocking and tiny rosebud print sweeps me straight back to college when all the former boarding school girls wore the same brand of old-fashioned flannel nightgown, as if it were part of an issued uniform. Dodie was wearing one with a hearts-and-teddy-bears print when we found her hanging from the tower room rafters.

I leave Chilton getting dressed and go to knock on Ruth's door. I'm expecting to find her as I found Chilton, muffled and blinkered to explain why she didn't hear Miranda's fall and Darla's scream, but the room is empty, bed neatly made, the only sign of Ruth's occupancy the aroma of chamomile tea rising from the half-full teacup on the night table and her quilted overnight bag sitting zippered at the foot of the made bed like a faithful pet waiting for its owner. Did she get up early? Had she been the one who went out the front door? I wonder as I head down the front stairs.

When I get to the foyer, I find her peeling off her overcoat, scarf, hat, mittens, and winter boots.

"There you are!" I cry, relieved to see her. "Where were you?"

"I went out to meet Charlie on the road and make sure he got us dug out. What's wrong? I didn't think anyone would be up so early after the late night you all had."

I could point out that she had a late night, too, but there isn't time. "Something terrible has happened," I say. "Miranda Gardner fell down the back stairs and broke her neck. She's . . . dead."

Ruth goes very still, breathing so hard her glasses fog. "Oh, the poor woman!" she says at last. "I wonder if it was because of all those sleeping pills? Did you see them on her night table? I've heard they can make you sleepwalk. Perhaps she wandered out onto the back stairs in her sleep."

"I suppose that's possible," I say. "The police will determine the cause of death. I've called them but I haven't called campus security yet."

"I'll take care of that," she says, pulling her cell phone from her pants pocket.

"Do you have a signal?" I ask, staring at her phone.

"No, but you can get one outside by the generator. I think it's best you call President Hotchkiss. He'll be . . ."

I know she wants to say the expected thing: *President Hotchkiss will be devastated* or at least *Hotch will be upset,* but we both know—and would never say—that given the pressure Miranda had exerted to get the residency, Hotch may well be relieved.

I CALL HOTCH from the kitchen landline but the call goes straight to voicemail. Then I go upstairs to shower and dress in fleece leggings, a warm sweater, and a quilted vest. It feels good to be suited up for a quick exit should one be called for. I go down the front stairs and open the door. The snow, drifted into peaked waves like a frozen ocean, lies undisturbed up to the tree line. There are no tracks leading out, I note, recalling the cascade of lights I saw earlier. If someone fled this way their tracks have been swept away by drifting snow.

Everyone is gathered in the Great Hall, an urn of coffee steaming on the buffet table along with an assortment of muffins, pastries, rolls, fruit, and individual yogurt containers. Ruth is arranging the baked goods in a basket.

"That sweet girl Photini sent these with Charlie from the Acropolis," she says when I come up beside her. "I assume the police will want us to stay out of the kitchen as it's close to where poor Ms. Gardner died. I just quickly popped in there and got what I thought we needed. For breakfast, that is, I don't know what we'll do about lunch. Charlie says we got over three feet and there's more snow on the way tonight. Do you think the police will be able to conduct their investigation and remove Ms. Gardner's body before the next storm comes?"

"I don't know," I tell her truthfully, taking a muffin and a cup of coffee. "I suppose it depends on whether they think it was an accident."

"What else could it have been?" Ruth demands. "You'll tell the police about all those pill bottles on her nightstand, right? She probably took too many because she was upset about the crow and then she wandered out onto the landing—I told Hotch those back stairs were treacherous and we ought to lock them off—"

"It will be all right," I tell Ruth, laying my hand on her arm. I've never seen her this agitated. "Could you call Charlie and see if he could go by Hotch's house and bring him here? I haven't been able to reach him. I've tried calling."

"I'm not surprised after how much he drank last night," Ruth says, pursing her mouth. "I'll talk to Charlie and make sure he gets him."

Truman has built up the fire, but everyone around it still looks like they've dressed for an arctic expedition. Chilton is wearing a Fair Isle sweater and a quilted vest over a turtleneck and heavy corduroy slacks—a preppy outfit nearly identical to what she wore every winter day in college. Darla is wrapped in layers of dark shawls and sweaters, cuffs hiding her hands, leg warmers pulled over tights. Lance is wearing a sweater so bulky and fuzzy it looks like the sheep it was shorn and knit from is still inside it. Even Truman, whom I've seen walk through a blizzard in a denim jacket, is wearing two flannel shirts. I'm not the only one dressed to break out of here, by dogsled if need be.

"How long are they going to make us stay here?" Lance demands as I sit down. "With poor Miranda's body rotting on the back stairs."

"I don't know what the police are going to ask us to do, but I doubt they'll leave Miranda here for long, and it's not like you were going anywhere in this snow. Hadn't you planned to stay today anyway for the memorial service?" As I say it, I realize the service will have to be cancelled, but I don't have the energy to start sending out emails and I don't want to add anything else to Ruth's responsibilities right now.

"It was one thing to spend a weekend with old friends," Chilton says dryly, "another to expect us to spend it with a *dead* friend."

"I don't know," Truman says, poking the fire, "it seems only right to sit vigil with Miranda until the police take her away. I don't think she has any family. She told me on the way up here that both her parents are dead and she's estranged from her sister. She said she thought of her readers as family."

That seems so unbearably sad that no one says anything for several minutes. Then Lance blurts out, "Do you think the police will grill us like last time? We were just kids, but they treated us like criminals. They gave me the third degree even though I wasn't even there when Moss went after that poor girl. I've had a phobia about the police ever since."

"This isn't like last time," Chilton says. "This was clearly an accident."

"It was an accident *last time*," Lance wails.

His cry is broken by the sound of a car pulling into the back parking lot.

"That will be the police now," I say, getting to my feet.

I head into the kitchen, glancing uneasily toward the back stairs. Someone has closed the door at the bottom of them. I'm not sure if the police will approve of that but I'm relieved not to have to see Miranda's broken body. I open the back door and watch three figures in bulky police jackets getting out of a patrol car. I'm taken so forcibly back to *last time* that when one of them looks up and I recognize Ben I want to laugh and ask him what he's doing in that getup, playing grown-up. *Why aren't you here inside with us, jittering with nerves by the fire?* But then I take in his grim expression and I realize that he's never really been one of us and we're all grown-ups now, whether some of us act like it or not, and no one, Ben least of all, is going to go easy on us because we're *just kids.*

# CHAPTER EIGHTEEN

*THEN*

"WHY DO YOU let her get away with it?" Ben asked when I told him what had happened in the *Raven* office. We were in the library, working on our Gothic Novel essays. He was writing his on *Dr. Jekyll and Mr. Hyde,* his favorite from the class. I was writing mine on *The Portrait of Dorian Gray.* "Don't you see what she's done? She's deliberately made it seem as if she's the injured party."

"It's not her fault," I said.

"You can't be serious." He put down his pen. "Clearly Laine stole your story idea and then convinced you it was her idea all along."

"How do you know it's not the other way around, that I stole her idea?"

"Because you never would," he said bluntly. "You're a good person and Laine is not. She uses people to get what she wants, and she wanted that prize because it's a step toward getting into that ridiculous senior seminar."

"But if her aim was to win the contest, why did she withdraw her story?" I pointed out.

"Don't you see?" Ben asked. "She has it both ways now. People will think her story should have won *and* that you're a plagiarizer. She's removing you from the competition."

"You don't understand her," I said, secretly pleased that he'd called me a good person even though I wasn't sure he was right. "She had a really messed-up childhood. Her father abandoned them and her mother's an alcoholic. She told me she used to make up an imaginary friend so she wouldn't be so alone."

"Poor little rich girl," he mocked.

"That's mean, Ben. Just because a person comes from money doesn't mean they can't have problems, too."

Ben snorted so loudly someone at the next table glared at us. He leaned across our table and whispered, "Yes, it does, because they will always have someone who can make their problems go away, like an impressionable, naive roommate who will let everyone believe she plagiarized her own story."

"I am not impressionable and naive," I said, although this time, unlike when he had said I was good, I was pretty sure he was right.

His verdict stung and haunted me through study week and finals. I found myself watching Laine while we stayed up in the twenty-four-hour study room, where she corralled us into a precision study team, allocating roles for each of us: flash cards for me because my handwriting was the best; timelines for Chilton because she was good with figures; and snacks for Dodie because Laine didn't trust her with anything else. Truman was deputized to score coke and uppers to keep us awake. Why did we all jump to her orders? I wondered.

Sometimes I would look over at other groups and pairings. Emily Dawes and Stephanie Chang always studied together, their heads bent over the same book. Randy Gardner presided over a group of girls who drank diet sodas and color-coded their notes. There were three shy girls from my Greek class—Kara, Jocelyn, and Toby—who quizzed each other and giggled whenever anyone said "I dunno; it's all Greek to me."

I could join them, I thought. They were moving off campus next semester and had asked if I wanted to be their fourth. We'd take turns cooking and stay up late drinking cocoa and eating popcorn. I could double major in classics and education and forget about trying so hard to get into Moss's senior seminar. I wasn't going to anyway if everyone thought I had plagiarized Laine's story.

I went so far as to register for an education class in the spring and tell Kara I was thinking of joining them but just had to check with my mother about money since my scholarship didn't cover off-campus housing. I made the call to my mother from the dorm phone booth the day of the Luminaria, closing the wooden accordion door even though it made me feel like I was trapped in a coffin. I didn't want anyone to overhear me asking if we could afford off-campus housing or for Laine to know yet that I was thinking of not sharing the suite next semester.

My mom picked up on the sixth ring, out of breath because she'd just gotten in from after-work drinks with friends. This wasn't my usual time to call, was something wrong? she asked. Was I still coming home tomorrow for the winter break?

I told her first that I had signed up for the education class because I knew she'd be pleased. When I told her, though, about the girls asking me to live with them she said, "That's great you're making new friends, sweetie, but there's definitely not enough money for off-campus housing. In fact, I was waiting until you got home to talk about this, but . . ."

She proceeded to tell me that she was finding it really hard to make the part of the tuition not covered by my scholarship. She'd checked with the admissions office at Queens College, where I'd been offered a full scholarship, and I could still register there for next fall.

"We'd save so much, sweetie, and you'd be closer . . ." She went on for so long, building the case she had clearly prepared, that I had to open the door to get some air. Even then I felt like

I was sinking into the ground, the narrow wooden booth with its decades' worth of initials and graffiti my final resting place.

When I got off the phone, agreeing with my mother that we'd talk about it more over break even though it was clear her mind was made up, I felt like I had become part of the wood. Like one of those girls in Ovid who become trees. Only I hadn't been chased by some lecherous god; I'd just been brought down to earth by mundane financial reality. It wasn't even a big tragedy. I'd go to Queens College and get certified to teach high school Latin and English. I'd be better off, I told myself, walking (woodenly) up the stairs to our suite, outside the orbit of Laine Bishop.

As if to demonstrate the celestial orbit I'd be leaving, our suite was decked out in fairy lights and pendant stars. Laine had made us holly wreaths and blanket robes for the Luminaria, and heated spiced wine.

"There you are!" she shouted when I came in. "I was afraid we'd have to go without you. Here's your robe."

"I don't think I should go," I said, "I have a sore throat."

"Nonsense," Laine said. "Have some glogg and put this on. We're going to have a bonfire on the ridge. That will keep you warm."

She was like a steamroller. Ben was right: she really didn't care about anyone but herself. I could argue but then we'd just go around in circles until I gave in. Besides, this might be my last Luminaria. Laine led the way, singing "O Come, All Ye Faithful" at the top of her voice and waving a wand made out of birch wrapped with holly and glitter. I followed glumly, weighed down by the heavy robe and financial reality, feeling as if I were going to be the sacrifice in this year's rite. We'd watched *The Wicker Man* a few weeks earlier and Laine had been talking about pagan sacrifices and folk horror ever since. She said the whole idea of the Luminaria was to oust the old year in a sacrificial bonfire and then light the beacon in High Tor as a symbol of the new year. Maybe, I thought, feeling sorry for myself, it would be better to go out in a blaze of glory on Solstice Eve. I would go down in Briarwood lore as the solstice sacrifice girl, haunting the ridge to scare future Briarwood students—the ones who could afford to go here, the ones whose mothers and grandmothers had gone here, the ones who belonged.

By the time we made it up the mountain I'd worked myself into a lather of self-pity. I tossed my birch wand into the fire, then turned away and walked into the dark. Even when I realized I wasn't heading toward the path back down to the campus, I kept going: through the pine barrens, over rough ground, toward the ice caves that gaped like so many hungry mouths waiting to swallow me up.

I tripped over a rock and landed hard on my knees. I yelped in pain. How much more painful would it be to fall into the cave and break my neck?

I sobbed then, on my knees, letting all my sorrow and anger out in a long, low wail that came back at me from the cave sounding inhuman, as if the rocks were shrieking in despair. Even after the echo of my cry had faded, I heard another— softer, sadder, wilder—cry wrenched from the very bowels of the earth. I crawled closer until the ground beneath my hands crumbled. Cold air gusted against my face like the breath of an ice-breathing dragon. Something in it called to me and I stood up to face it—as I should have faced Laine and my mother and Ben. But it was too late. My legs buckled and I teetered on the edge of the pit, the cold pulling me—

Only it was a human hand that grabbed me from behind, a hand that steadied me.

"Whoa," said a voice in the dark, "easy."

It was Laine, pulling me back. "What are you doing here at the caves? You could have fallen in."

"I got lost," I said, feeling that it sounded true enough. "How did you know where I was?"

"I followed you when you left the fire," she said. "I saw that you looked unhappy and then I heard you cry out. What's wrong? Did something happen?"

I could have told her then that I was angry about the story, but instead I told her what my mother had said and that I'd be leaving Briarwood and going to Queens College, which was a perfectly good school, and getting certified to teach high school, which was a perfectly good career. When I finished, I was surprised to hear her laugh.

"You idiot," she said, putting her arm around my shoulder and leading me away from the edge. "I'll pay the rest of your tuition out of my trust. You're not going anywhere."

# CHAPTER NINETEEN

*NOW*

BEN IS ACCOMPANIED by a young female police officer and a gruff grey-haired woman in a white jumpsuit who immediately demands to be shown to the body. Ben asks his partner to make sure everyone in the house is gathered in the Great Hall. She glances at me as she passes and I realize she once stopped me for speeding but let me go with a warning when I told her I was late for a class. Now she looks at me sternly as if she's sorry for her earlier leniency. Ben introduces the older woman to me as Dr. Suseelan, the Ulster County assistant medical examiner. I open the door to the back stairs, looking quickly away from Miranda's face, which has grown more purple since I saw her last.

"Has anyone touched the body?" Dr. Suseelan asks.

"Just me," I say, "I checked her pulse. No one's touched her since then."

"Were you and Mr. Davis the first two on the scene?" she asks.

"No," I tell her. "Darla Sokolovsky found her first, then Truman and I came from the study when we heard her scream."

"And what were you and Truman doing in the study?" Ben asks.

"We both couldn't sleep . . ." I close my mouth to keep from blabbering on, mad at myself for letting Ben's cold stare make me feel like I owe him an explanation.

The ME glances between me and Ben. "Did Marla see the victim fall?"

"Darla," I say, "and no, I don't think so. She says not."

"I'll take her testimony," Ben says, "and leave you to your work, Dr. Suseelan. Do you have any preliminary thoughts?"

"She most likely died of injuries from the fall, a fractured vertebra or cerebral hemorrhage . . . The interesting question"— she sits back on her heels and views the position of Miranda's body—"is why did she fall backwards? It looks as if she turned on the landing to face someone and was either startled enough to fall backwards or—"

Ben finishes the sentence for her: "Or she was pushed."

AS WE WALK into the Great Hall, Ruth is talking to Ben's partner, who's smiling at her. "Oh, Officer Breen," Ruth says, "I was just telling Officer Vegas that I know her mother from volunteering at the animal shelter and I was explaining why I took some food out of the kitchen. I know it's important not to disturb a crime scene—I watch all the mysteries on PBS and BritBox—but I didn't want everyone to go hungry."

"That's fine, Ms.—"

"Please call me Ruth. We've met, you know. I come to your public safety talk at the Rotary Club every year."

"Yes, I thought you looked familiar—"

"Of course, I also saw you Friday when that poor student fell in the cave. Who would have thought you'd be called back so quickly."

"Ruth has done a great job keeping everyone calmly gathered here in the Great Hall," I say, as much to rescue Ben as to soothe Ruth's frayed nerves.

"That's what the detective always wants, isn't it, for all the witnesses to gather in one place? Or do you want to speak to us all separately? You can use the study. I've got a fire going so it's warm." Ben sighs and I catch a glimpse of Ruth's eyes darting nervously behind her thick lenses. "Oh! Is that part of the crime scene, too? I didn't think! But I really didn't touch anything except for some glasses that were sitting on the table making water rings." She leans closer to Ben and whispers conspiratorially, "Someone—or *two* someones—were having a nightcap in there and a picture frame's been broken."

"Thank you for the heads-up, Ruth," Ben says. "If you'll have a seat, I'll talk to the group now, and then individually as needed."

Ruth, satisfied by these clear directions, sits in a straight-backed chair a little outside the circle.

"Hey, man," Truman says as Ben approaches them, "glad you could finally make the reunion."

All the color goes out of Ben's face, bringing out his freckles and making him look years younger. When he tightens his jaw and shifts his weight, though, revealing the holster on his hip, he suddenly looks like the only grown-up in the room, turning the rest of us into kids cowering under the glare of the law.

"It doesn't look like it's going too well," he says, sitting in another straight-backed chair. "Which I can't say surprises me."

"Shouldn't you, like, recuse yourself," Darla asks, "because we're friends?"

"Well, Darla," Ben says, taking out a notepad, "I'm not sure we were ever really friends." He looks at me, making it clear he's including me in this assessment. "And besides, we're a bit short-staffed at the moment, what with the blizzard and all, so I'm afraid you're stuck with me. Rest assured, I won't let our past history get in the way of finding out what happened to Miranda."

"She fell," Chilton says. "Isn't that obvious? I always said those stairs were a death trap."

"Homicide can't be ruled out," Ben says. "Why don't we start with Darla telling me how she came upon the body."

Darla blanches. "It's just that I was getting up to go downstairs for a glass of water—"

"I left several bottles in each room," Ruth begins, but is silenced by a glance from Ben.

"I wanted some with lemon," Darla clarifies. "It's part of a regimen I'm on. I set an alarm to wake up at six-thirty every morning and immediately drink a glass of lemon water. I was coming down the stairs and I saw Miranda—" She breaks off in a choking gasp.

"And you, Lance," Ben says, turning from Darla without commenting on her story. "You were close on Darla's heels, I hear."

"I'm a light sleeper," he says. "When I heard the scream, I woke up thinking I was back to that time in college, you know . . . when we found poor Dodie. I don't think that moment is ever really far from my consciousness."

"No," Ben says, giving Lance the first look of compassion that he's spared for any of us. "I don't suppose it is. And you, Chilton?"

"I slept through the whole thing. I wear earplugs to bed. Once you've had children your hearing is finely calibrated to the slightest noise." She smiles smugly at the rest of us. "Do you have children, Ben?"

"No," he says shortly, turning to Truman. "And you, Truman. How do you sleep?"

"Like a baby, which is to say I wake every couple of hours thirsty and cranky. I was in Moss's old study raising a reunion glass with Nell."

Ben's glance comes around to me. "And what brought you downstairs, Nell?"

"I heard the front door open and I came downstairs to check.

I suppose that was Ruth," I say, looking toward her. She smiles and explains to Ben that she'd gone out to see if the plows were on the way.

"And did you find the plows?"

"Yes," she says, "Charlie—that's Charlie Grandin—promised me he'd dig us out first and he was as good as his word. He even brought us our bakery order from the Acropolis. I thought everyone would need a treat after the upset last night."

"The upset?" Ben asks.

I begin to explain but Ben holds up his hand. "Why don't you take me to Miranda's room now, Nell," he says to me. "You can explain on the way."

BEN LEAVES OFFICER Vegas taking statements from the others and I tell him about the crow in Miranda's bed as we go up the stairs.

"Do you think someone put it there deliberately?" he asks, as we reach the room that had been Miranda's in college.

"I think that's more likely than it just happening to fly in," I say, opening the door. A cold breeze stirs the drapes over the broken window. "It seemed like a message."

"Conveying what?" he asks, following me into the room and to the window.

"Since the black feather was how we found out that we'd gotten into the Raven Society, maybe a dead crow means you've been chosen for something . . . *bad*."

"You think it was some kind of sign that she was going to die?" he asks skeptically.

"I don't know," I admit, following him out into the hallway. As we head toward the tower room I tell him about Ruth bringing the tea tray and me taking it from her.

"Is serving tea in an executive assistant's job description? I wouldn't dare ask any of the staff at the station to bring me coffee."

"Not everyone's as progressive as you," I say. "Or as considerate. But no, it's not Ruth's job. She's just very attentive about things like that and she's been involved in all the details of the event. Ruth probably did it to smooth—"

"Ruffled feathers?" he says, guessing what I'd been about to say.

"Sorry, I pun when nervous."

He stops in front of the door to the tower room and gives me a sharp stare. "What do you have to be nervous about, Nell?"

I laugh. "Someone has died on our inaugural weekend of Wilder Writers House and, as your medical examiner has pointed out, it looks like she was pushed."

"Who do *you* think would push Miranda?" he asks.

"No one was very happy about Miranda's announcement that she'd gotten the residency," I say. "Darla and Lance had both applied for it. Ruth didn't think much of Miranda's application. Hotch wanted Laine."

"Then why would he give it to Miranda?"

"I don't think he wanted to." I tell him about seeing Hotch and Miranda arguing through the window. "It looked like she had something incriminating that she was holding over his head."

"And what could that be?" he asks as he opens the door. The room is in disarray, the duvet crumpled on the floor next to scattered pill bottles. He kneels down to get a closer look.

"I noticed those bottles on the nightstand when I brought in the tea tray. They were full." I point at another bottle lying sideways on the night table. "They're both empty now. Someone could have given Miranda an overdose."

"We'll know when we get the tox screen back, but if she

took—or was given—that much Ambien and Xanax she'd never make it to the stairs."

He gets up and approaches the bed. A Louis Vuitton tote bag lies on its side, its contents spilling out across the sheets. "It looks like she was looking for something she lost," I say.

"Or someone was looking for something she had," he says, taking out a pair of blue latex gloves from his pocket and putting them on. He opens one of the folders splayed across the bed. There's a spreadsheet with columns of figures. I peer over Ben's shoulder and recognize the document.

"That's an expense report for the renovations done on Wilder House," I say.

"How would Miranda Gardner have access to this information?"

"I have no idea," I say. "All of the budget requests go through the financial office so I suppose if you knew someone in that office—an assistant or a work-study maybe. Miranda was good at finding out stuff like that in college."

He moves on to another folder. This one has receipts. He holds up one in a gloved hand. It's from a local construction company we'd used to retile the foyer. Another one is for carpeting, which I notice includes runners for both the front and back stairs and the second-floor hallway.

"She'd have to get these receipts from local vendors and I can't see them just handing them over." He looks closely at them and then back at the expense report. "The amounts are different," he says, eyeing me suspiciously. "Have you noticed anything irregular in the accounting?"

"Of course not," I say, offended. "But," I add, "if I had, I would have reported it. I have noticed some irregularities since we've been here this weekend—some carpets that were ordered but aren't here, and Chilton noticed that the papering in the hall looks shoddy."

"Chilton's an expert on wallpaper?" he asks mockingly.

"The point is that someone might have skimped on the cost of the renovations."

"And you think that someone could be your college president?"

"I hate to make an accusation without more evidence, but . . ." I wave my hand at the papers spread across the bed. "It looks like *Miranda* might have thought so, and if she had evidence that Hotch was embezzling funds from the endowment, she could have used it as leverage to get the job."

"Which would also give Hotch a motive to kill her. If I were him I wouldn't trust Miranda Gardner to be satisfied with a little teaching job."

"No," I agree. "She'd never stop blackmailing him."

"So where is your illustrious president?"

"I don't know. He's not answering his phone. Ruth sent the groundskeeper to go check for him at his house. But I think that if he's worried about Miranda exposing him, he'd go to the office to get rid of any incriminating evidence."

"I'll send a patrol car there," he says.

"We could get there quicker on foot," I point out, getting to my feet. I feel a jolt of adrenaline—and an overwhelming urge to get outside. "I have the keys."

"Okay," Ben says after only a moment's hesitation. "Let's go."

# CHAPTER TWENTY

*NOW*

WHEN WE GET downstairs Ben explains what we're doing to Officer Vegas and asks about the medical examiner's progress. I head to the foyer to put on my coat and boots.

"Where are you going?"

I look up to find Truman hovering over me, his silhouette in the arched doorway scarecrow-like. I can feel nervous energy emanating from him like heat off a woodstove.

"I need to open an office in Main for Ben," I say.

"Can I come with you?" he asks. "If I have to sit here listening to Chilton talking about her children and Darla about her last residency and Lance about the benefits of meditation, I may throw *myself* down the back stairs."

"Those are closed off," Ben says, shoving past Truman into the foyer. "You'd have to use the front ones, but I'll thank you to take your destructive tendencies into someone else's precinct. Our resources are a bit overtaxed at the moment."

"Why don't I come with you two instead?" Truman suggests. "Don't you need, like, backup?"

"Another officer is meeting us there," Ben says. "What would you do to help anyway, sing to the perpetrator?"

"Perpetrator? So you think Miranda was killed and whoever killed her is in Main?" Truman asks, ignoring Ben's jab. "Is it Hotch? I can't imagine him putting up much of a fight."

Ben throws a disgusted look at Truman and swings open the front door. "I don't have time for this," he says. "Are you coming, Nell?"

It feels like college all over again, Ben peeling himself away from late-night revels and dangerous exploits while suggesting I do the same, testing the bounds of my allegiance and sobriety. I can't help but think of how things might have been different if I'd followed him more often. "You're not really dressed for the snow," I tell Truman as I follow Ben.

But Truman grabs a parka from the coatrack—Lance's, I think—and follows me out the door.

"Fine," Ben says when he sees Truman attaching himself to us. "I have a couple of questions you can answer on the way."

Truman falters, whether from the slippery footing or Ben's pronouncement, I can't tell. "I told you I was with Nell last night," he says. "She can vouch for me."

"You could have had a nightcap with Miranda earlier and drugged her," Ben says.

"Why would I want to do in Miranda?" Truman asked. "I mean, she could be annoying but I had nothing against her. In fact"—he ducks his head and glances sideways at me—"I suspect she had a bit of a crush on me. She called me yesterday morning and offered me a lift up here. And I took it."

"Did you?" Ben asks in a flat monotone that suggests he already knew this. "And what did you two talk about on the drive up?"

"Miranda did most of the talking," Truman says, picking his way through the snow like a long-legged crane. His boots don't offer much traction in the deep snow and his skinny jeans are already soaked. The snow isn't as deep over the paths, which the college repaved a few years ago with snow-melting concrete, but Ben has piloted us away from them and into the bowl below the mountains as if to deliberately make the trek more difficult for Truman, while Ben's own snow boots and gaiters make it easy for him. "She complained about her publisher and Amazon's algorithms and the literary establishment that refuses to give her the credit she deserves. You know Miranda . . ."

He hesitates, recalling that he's speaking of the dead. Ben is quick to pick up the thread. "I can't say I ever really knew her that well, but I do remember that she liked to collect information about people. I wonder what she had on you."

"On me?" Truman laughs nervously. "Man, it's not like my life's a secret. I'm kind of in the public eye, so yeah, she teased me a bit about the drug bust in Sydney and the paparazzo I punched in Seattle—"

"And the girl you killed in Oakland?"

This time Truman full-on skids and nearly face-plants in the snow. I look around and see that Ben has led us to the edge of Mirror Lake and let Truman step onto the ice. I reach out my hand to steady him and he meets my eye.

"It was an accident," he tells me, "and a long time ago."

"And yet she's still dead," Ben says. "I believe the charge was gross vehicular manslaughter. You were over the limit when you hit her." Ben turns to me. "A seventeen-year-old girl, AnnMarie Morrow, on her way to school early because she had band practice."

"I was on my way home from a gig," Truman says, still looking at me. "It was dark—"

"And you were drunk."

"I don't remember this being in the papers," I say, thinking of those first years after college when I looked hungrily for any mention of Truman in the press. "Did you do time, Truman?"

Ben laughs. "Nah, he got off. He'd just signed a big deal with a record company and their lawyers got him off with a fine and some community service. Made sure it didn't make the papers, hushed it up."

"I think about that girl every day," Truman says, looking away from me toward the frozen lake. "I see her face in my dreams."

"Poor tortured artist," Ben says with a sneer. "I notice you never went public with the story. Did Miranda threaten to leak it? I imagine it wouldn't help your floundering career."

Truman turns toward Ben, a puzzled look on his face. "I've never understood why you hate me so much, man. What did I ever do to you?"

A gust of snow whips against Ben's face, tearing away any semblance of civility and leaving only fury. I suddenly become aware that Ben has a gun and that he's backed Truman up against the edge of thin ice. I reach out a hand to touch Ben's arm but he steps away before I can.

"Ask Nell," he says, walking away from us. "Ask her what you did to me."

"What's he talking about?" Truman asks.

"Never mind," I say, reaching my hand out to Truman. "Let's leave it in the past."

The haunted look in his eyes suggests that's not going to be possible, but then he stares down at my hand and allows himself the faintest smile. "Why aren't you running away in horror now that you know I'm a monster?"

"I'm hardly in a position to judge," I say. "Come on. The college has a strict rule against skating on Mirror Lake. I could lose my job if I was seen allowing it."

He looks around the deserted snow-swept campus and laughs. "I wouldn't want that on my conscience," he says as he takes my hand. We both look away from each other at the same time, neither of us willing to acknowledge all the other crimes already on our consciences, as I lead us away from the ice.

BEN IS STANDING in front of Main, chuffing steam into his gloved hands and pounding his feet to get the snow off his boots. "My sergeant is having trouble getting here through the snow," he says, eyeing our linked arms.

"Do you want to wait?" I ask.

He shakes his head. "Just let me in. You two can wait here."

"No fucking way," Truman says. "I'm not waiting out here in the cold."

"I'll need to open the office for you," I say, swiping my ID in the lock sensor. "And that door takes a key that can be tricky. Truman can wait in the Rose Parlor—"

"Like some nineteenth-century suitor? I'm going with you two. I want to see Hotch's face when he sees the gig's up."

"Just stay behind me," Ben says reluctantly, pushing open the door. "And don't get in my way."

Coming in from the snow, it feels as if we're entering an ice palace, the fanlights and windows letting in only a dim alabaster glow. I was here yesterday morning but already the building feels as if it's been abandoned for years, cold and drafty—

"Wait," I say as Ben starts up the stairs, "something's wrong. Where's that draft coming from?"

"Now's not the time to worry about the college's heating bills," Ben says, turning back to the stairs.

Ignoring him, I head toward the back of the building where I find the source of the draft. The basement door has been propped open. I stand still for a second looking down the dark stairs, cold, dank air wafting against my face.

"A janitor must have propped it open," Ben says, reaching around to close the door. "My dad used to do that because sometimes the doors locked and were hard to open even with a key. Come on, I need to get into Hotch's office."

As I turn to follow him, I remember that the janitorial staff have off this weekend and this door was closed yesterday morning.

When we reach the fourth floor, Ben waits outside the suite that houses the offices of the president and the dean and knocks on the door.

"President Hotchkiss?" he calls. "Are you in there? It's the police."

"Remember when we got called in to the dean's office for letting out those lab mice in the biology building?" Truman asks. I start to smile back at him but the look in his eyes is so forlorn, so full of longing for a time when our biggest mistakes were redeemable, that I feel an answering ache in my chest and have to stop for a moment to catch my breath. Ben, impatient, holds out his hand for my ID card, but I shake my head and dig out my keys. Hotch insisted two years ago that we keep the physical locks instead of electronic ones for these offices. My hand is shaking as I slot the key in the keyhole and I'm overcome with a feeling of dread, the metallic smell of the key in my hand setting my nerves on edge.

The outer office, where Ruth has her desk, looks like it's been raided by the FBI. The computer monitor is on, folders and loose papers are strewn across the usually pristine desk surface, file drawers gape open. Ruth will be furious.

The door to my office is closed; Hotch's is open. Ben has shouldered past me and drawn his gun. I can smell the cold metal of it as he passes by me. The whole room reeks of it.

"President Hotchkiss," Ben calls through the open door in a loud authoritative voice, "if you're in there I need you to come out with your hands up."

I feel a swelling of pride for Ben—he's come so far from the shy janitor's son I knew in college!—but also a ripple of fear. When he gets no answer, Ben sidesteps through the door, gun held out rigidly in his right hand, his left waving us to stay behind him. Then he lowers both arms, as if in surrender, and disappears into the room. I follow, fighting back the waves of nausea from that metallic smell. As I step through the doorway, I see the source of the odor: a pool of blood spreading across Hotch's desk, seeping from Hotch's shattered skull.

# CHAPTER TWENTY-ONE

*THEN*

I COULDN'T TELL my mother that my roommate was going to pay my tuition—she would have been too proud to take charity—so Laine came up with another plan.

"I come into my inheritance in February on my twenty-first birthday and my accountant has been on me about making charitable donations to avoid taxes. All the Wilders donate to Briarwood. I could endow a scholarship and arrange for you to win it."

I listened to her machinate as we walked to the cafeteria and classes through the snow, dazzled as much by the pristine, sparkling winter campus as by Laine's talk of lawyers and taxes and endowments. It wasn't just that she was a year older than the rest of us (she'd lost a year due to how much her mother moved her around), but that she possessed the gravitas of property and old money. She took seriously the weight of being the last of the Wilders—she had no siblings or cousins and her grandmother had bypassed Laine's mother in the line of inheritance to leave Laine the Wilder fortune.

"I'm just like Roderick Usher," she was fond of saying, "living in a cracked house waiting for the roof to fall in. I might as well spread the wealth."

Still, I was doubtful that she'd be able to pull off her plan. Why would anyone let a twenty-one-year-old dictate the rules of a scholarship? Would her lawyer even allow such a thing? My only knowledge of bequests and wills and codicils came from *Bleak House,* which we were reading in our Victorian Novel class, and which suggested being an heir to a fortune never seemed to do anyone any good. But Laine was no shrinking Victorian heroine. On the day after her twenty-first birthday, which we celebrated with martinis at Alumni House, Laine and I met in the Rose Parlor with Dean Haviland, Associate Dean Hotchkiss, and Laine's lawyer, Mr. Humphreys, a white-haired older man in a tweed suit with an accent that reminded me of Thurston Howell on *Gilligan's Island.* Over a pot of Darjeeling, Laine outlined her plan for an endowment that would fund a center for creative writing to be called the Moss Writers House, including money for a writer-in-residence, funds to maintain Wilder Hall, and a full scholarship for a creative writing student. As she described it, drawing loops in the air with her long, slim fingers, I could see Dean Hotchkiss's eyes light up at the idea.

"What an asset to the college that would be!" he exclaimed, the delicate china teacup shivering in its saucer as he set it down. "And a boon to admissions and fundraising . . . but do we really want to call it *Moss* Writers House?"

"I wanted to honor Hugo Moss," Laine replied. "Although I haven't taken his class yet I've read his books and heard what an amazing teacher he is."

"Admirable," Dean Hotchkiss said, pursing his lips as if the word tasted bad, "but why not honor your own family and call it the Wilder Writers House?"

Rose Parlor was filling with students searching for afternoon tea and cookies. I noticed Lance and Darla, who were in Victorian Novel, and Randy, who sat as close as she could to our party. Mr. Humphreys whispered something to Dean Haviland, who nodded and suggested we move to the president's office, delicately indicating that perhaps I would find the rest of the discussion tedious.

"Oh no," Laine said immediately, "Nell is involved in this. I need her with me."

I had no choice but to go along, even though I felt awkward. I'd only ever seen Briarwood's president, Buck Ainsley, giving speeches at formal occasions, teeing off at the golf course, and walking his Cavalier King Charles Spaniels on campus. He greeted Mr. Humphreys like an old friend—they, and Dean Hotchkiss, were all wearing nearly identical tweed suits—and asked him how the fishing had been at "the club" this summer. Then he beamed at Laine, barely glancing at me when I was introduced as Laine's roommate.

"Nell's a marvelous writer," Laine said as we sat down in deep upholstered chairs. "She won the *Raven* short story contest."

I blushed as scarlet as the oxblood leather blotter on the president's desk, terrified that the rumor of "plagiarism" might have reached the ears of the president, but instead, Dean Haviland turned to me with a rare beatific smile, one usually reserved for verses of poetry or a Turner seascape. "I'm not surprised, Nell, you've shown an aptitude in your literary studies that reveals a refined aesthetic sensibility."

And yet the highest grade I'd received in her classes had been a B+. I muttered a strangled thank-you and took another sip of tea even though I suddenly realized I needed to use the bathroom. How long would we be in here? I wondered as Laine chatted as casually with President Ainsley as she did with me. When the conversation turned back to the particulars of the scholarship bequest, Dean Hotchkiss shouted into the outer office for "Babs," and a white-haired woman wearing a plum tweed suit appeared with a steno pad.

(Beatrice Ann Betelmans was her name. I still come across her initials—*bab*—at the bottom of letters.)

More tea was poured, every splash increasing the discomfort in my bladder, as Babs took down the particulars of the bequest. The trustees of the endowment would be Laine and two officials at the college. "I'd like Dean Haviland, of course," Laine said.

"I'd be honored," Dean Haviland said, "but what about when I'm gone? I suggest you name the office of the Dean of Liberal Arts instead of me in particular. That way when I've retired, the next dean will hold the position in the endowment. If you don't mind me suggesting, I think you should also name the president of the college as well; that way there will be oversight between the two offices."

"Yes," Dean Hotchkiss seconded, "we wouldn't want any one person to be in a position to take advantage of the situation. And about the name . . ."

"I'm sure Hugo won't mind if it's the Wilder Writers House," Dean Haviland said to Laine. And then, turning to Dean Hotchkiss, "He really doesn't care about such things."

As Ms. Betelmans left to type the contract up, I glanced over at Laine, wishing I could ask her why Dean Hotchkiss was against naming the writing center for Hugo Moss—and then I remembered how easy it had been to enroll in Dean Hotchkiss's FYSem while all the others filled up. Hugo Moss was an immensely popular teacher and Dean Hotchkiss was not. He was jealous; it was as simple as that, but it struck me as a revelation that my elders were as prone to insecurity and jealousy as I was.

After what felt like an interminable interval to my bladder, the secretary brought a sheaf of papers back and presented them to Laine, who read through them slowly and carefully, the whole room lapsing into silence. I would have been tempted to rush while everyone waited on me, but Laine took her time, making notes in the margins, using a Mont Blanc fountain pen her lawyer had lent her, striking out words and phrases. All I could think watching her was how Babs was going to have to completely retype the whole thing. When she got to the end, she looked up, the snowy white mountain peak on the tip of the pen pressed to her lips, the very picture of "girl author at work."

"I have one more codicil that I'd like to draft," she said. "Shall I scribble it down myself or dictate it?"

Beatrice Ann Betelmans looked down at the scrawl covering her meticulous typescript and said, "I'd be happy to take it down, Miss Bishop."

She flipped to a new page in her steno pad and Laine dictated: "'As benefactor of the Wilder Writer's Scholarship, I, Elaine Wilder Bishop, do hereby reserve the right to choose the first recipient of the scholarship' . . . How's that, Mr. Humphreys?" she asked, turning to her lawyer. "Is that legalese enough for you?"

"You'd make a fine lawyer, Miss Bishop," Mr. Humphreys said, "but if you don't mind, I'll make a few alterations to make sure your intentions are clear—if that's all right with everyone here?" He looked around the room. Dean Hotchkiss shifted in his chair and opened his mouth but Dean Haviland silenced him with a sharp glare. No matter what anyone thought of Laine's bequest, she was offering too much money to quibble over details.

"How do you propose to choose the recipient for the scholarship?" President Ainsley asked when Mr. Humphreys had finished whispering his alterations to the secretary. "Blind submissions? A contest?"

"We can do that next time," Laine said. "For this time, it's Nell, of course. Who else could it possibly be?"

There was a long moment of silence during which I was sure

someone would object. Laine's motives had been laid bare. One of these tweed-suited men would point out how it would look to endow a scholarship and then give it to your roommate. I could feel their eyes on me. Would they suspect that I had pressured Laine into giving me the scholarship? I saw President Ainsley exchange a look with Dean Hotchkiss and both men looked toward Mr. Humphreys.

"Er," President Ainsley began, "perhaps Miss Portman could wait in the anteroom for a moment while we discuss some of the, er, financial details."

I rose to my feet as if levitated there by an external force.

"I don't think that's necessary," Laine said.

But I wanted nothing more than to get out of there. Let Laine deal with the white-haired men. I didn't even care now if I got the scholarship. The last hour had shown me how little I belonged in this world of bequests and codicils. I'd be better off back on Long Island going to Queens College. When I got out into the anteroom, where Beatrice Ann Betelmans had her desk, I might have kept going out into the hallway, down three flights of stairs, straight to the Trailways station, down the Thruway, across the Throgs Neck Bridge, and home. But someone was blocking the way—a girl in a pink sweater and corduroy skirt bent over a file drawer pulled all the way out. I couldn't get around her.

"Excuse me," I said.

The girl looked up and I recognized Bridget Feeley. Of course, I thought, she'd be here now. I'd probably have to pay a toll to get *out* of Briarwood as well as to get in.

"Excuse me," I said again. "Can I get by?"

"They asked you to wait in the anteroom," she said, going back to her filing.

I noticed then that she had positioned herself next to a vent against the wall that led to the president's office. I could hear a

murmur of voices coming from it even from where I was standing. Crouched low beside it, she could no doubt hear everything
that was said inside. I was about to tell her that it was rude to
eavesdrop but she spoke first.

"It must be nice having a rich roommate. Aren't you afraid,
though, that she'll take advantage of you being in her debt?"

"Laine wouldn't do that," I said. "She's not like that."

She gave me a look of withering pity. "You mean she's only
awful to nobodies like me? I know what she calls me. Bridge
Troll. How clever. How long do you think you'll stay in her favor? What will you let her steal from you next—oh," she added
when she saw the look of shock on my face, "I know all about
your story. I was helping with submissions at *The Raven* last
semester and I saw your story come in the day before Laine's.
I recognized that description of being on the empty campus in
the fog from that week before classes freshman year. You even
include that time you bumped into me and screamed because
you thought I was a ghost. Laine stole your idea and whole
passages verbatim."

"She withdrew her story," I said.

"In a way that made it seem like a *favor* to you, leaving everyone still believing that *she* wrote the story. It was clever, really,"
she added with a grudging hint of admiration. "Did it ever occur
to you that she's giving you this scholarship so she can go on
stealing from you?"

"That's ridiculous—" I began, but the door to President
Ainsley's office opened then and they were all coming out on
a tide of laughter as if they were an audience spilling out of a
hit Broadway show. I turned guiltily toward Laine, aware that it
would look like *I* had been eavesdropping. Bridget Feeley had
already closed the filing cabinet and pushed her rolling stool
back to her desk, where she was innocently typing a letter.

"You'll be happy to know your scholarship has been approved," Dean Hotchkiss pronounced. "You're a very lucky young lady."

"I know." It came out sounding petulant. "I mean, yes, I am." I tried to catch Laine's eye to signal that I wanted to go, but she was laughing at something with Dean Haviland while Mr. Humphreys and President Ainsley hung on her every word. Only Dean Hotchkiss was focused on me. "I know how lucky I am," I said to him. "Laine's amazing—"

"Isn't she, though," he said, and then lowering his lips to my ear, he added in a whisper meant only for me, "You have a lot to live up to, Miss Portman. Try not to screw it up."

# CHAPTER TWENTY-TWO

*NOW*

BEN TURNS AND yells at Truman, who is retching. "Get out of here before you contaminate my crime scene!"

Truman stumbles out into the hall, but I stay nailed to the floor, in shock, staring at the gruesome scene before me.

Ben takes out his phone, dials, and barks instructions to get the medical examiner to the fourth floor of Main Hall. When he's done, I ask him, unable to keep my voice from trembling, if he thinks Hotch has killed himself.

"Either that or someone has tried to make it look like that," he says, pointing to a gun lying on the desk. "I've seen Hotch at the local shooting range with this model gun. Do you know if he kept it here in his office?"

I nod and then realize that Ben, his eyes raking over the desk, can't see me. "Yes. After the Virginia Tech shootings he applied for a license and took lessons. When he became president he made a big deal of installing a gun safe in his office. I think he thought he'd be the hero of the hour if we ever had an active shooter. He thought it should make me and Ruth feel safer but, frankly, it scared me."

"You were right to be scared," Ben says in a rare moment of sympathy. "He was a terrible shot; he'd probably have shot an innocent bystander—or provided a weapon for a shooter."

"Do you think someone else did this?"

"I don't know," he says. "From the blood splatter it's clear these files were on the desk when he was shot. Can you tell me—without touching any of this—what these papers are?"

I take a step closer, clenching my teeth to keep the smell of blood from making me sick, and look at the bloodstained files. "Most of these are related to Writers House—the proposal, fundraising, prospectus, renovations—"

"So he might have been looking at the files that would implicate him in embezzling," Ben says.

"Why not just destroy them?" I ask.

He shakes his head and takes a pencil out of his pocket. Using the tip of it, he gingerly opens one of the purple folders on top of a pile of documents. There's a typed letter to a local contractor approving their bid for the roof repair to Wilder Hall. I crane forward to see it better, holding my breath against the stench of blood. Ben uses the tip of the pencil eraser to carefully move the paper over so I can see the one beneath it: fund allocation requests for fundraising events, many catered by Mes Amis, and for carpet for Wilder Hall.

"I notice all these fund requests are cosigned by you," Ben says.

"Yes, as Dean of Liberal Arts I'm coexecutor of the trust along with the president and Laine—" I freeze in the middle of this formal recitation. "You don't think . . ." I meet Ben's gaze across the carnage. Has his opinion of me sunk so far that he'd suspect me of embezzling?

He holds my gaze for an agonizing moment and then shakes his head. "I've seen that pint-size house you live in," he says, coloring at the admission. "It's not the house of an embezzler."

I look away, relieved he doesn't suspect me and surprised to learn he knows where I live. "These are the same invoices

Miranda had in her folder," I say, "only she had the invoices that were billed to the college and the original ones from the vendors."

"Proving that Hotch was indeed billing the college more than he was paying the vendors and pocketing the difference."

"So, he *was* embezzling," I say. "But why in the world? I always thought Hotch had plenty of money."

"He certainly lives like he does," Ben says. "The flashy cars, the big house . . . Maybe his lifestyle outpaced his salary."

"I remember he was upset when our salaries were frozen during the pandemic; he'd been expecting a raise," I say. "But why would he be looking through all this now, early on a Sunday morning—or late Saturday night if he came here straight from Wilder House?"

"Maybe he was trying to figure out how Miranda got ahold of them." Ben looks back at the folder containing the funds requests. "Look at this," he says, pointing to a letter from the financial office confirming receipt of the requests. He jabs his pencil eraser at a row of initials at the bottom. *JRW* is typed in capital letters. "That's Janice Wells," I say, "our CFO."

"And *nml*?" he asks, pointing to the lowercase initials.

"That would be the initials of whoever typed it—oh!" I cry. "That's Nina. Nina Marie Lawson. She works in the financial office."

"The girl who fell in the cave?"

"Yes, and she told me she'd been trying to avoid Hotch when she walked toward the caves. I thought because she was embarrassed about withdrawing from his class. But—" I turn around to face the door that leads to the anteroom. Had his door been open when Nina left my office? Then I look down at the brass grate in the wall and I recall Bridget Feeley crouched on the other side, listening. Could Hotch have heard what I said to Nina as she was leaving? What had I said?

*If you change your mind and want to talk about what's bother-*
*ing you, Nina, my door is always open.*

"I thought Nina was uncomfortable about something Hotch said in class but maybe it was something she saw in her jobs. She was a work-study in the financial office during the fall semester, and she worked at Mes Amis."

"So, she could have noticed a discrepancy between an original invoice and what Hotch submitted to the financial office."

"Maybe," I say, noticing a green file under the purple ones on the desk. The green files are for students. I reach for it but Ben gets to it first and opens it with his pencil. I immediately recognize it. "It's Nina's file—I had it on my desk two days ago." I look down at the first page. It lists her student ID number, contact information, and dorm room at the very top. "If Hotch thought that Nina was the informant, that she was the one who gave Miranda all that information, he might have gone to her dorm to confront her."

I think of Nina all alone in Rowan Hall. I scan the sheet, find Nina's cell number, and enter it into my phone. It rings and is picked up by voicemail—Nina's voice saying, "Hey, text me, I never listen to these." Swearing, I hang up and text Nina.

*It's Dean Portman,* I type, *please call or text me as soon as you get this.* I send the message and then add, *You're not in trouble, I just want to make sure you're okay.* I add a worried face emoji.

"I'm concerned about her," I say, looking back at Ben. He's at the desk looking at Hotch's computer screen.

"Do you happen to know Hotch's password?"

"MrPresident2016," I say without hesitation. "He gave it to Ruth so she could answer his emails and she couldn't resist sharing it with me." *What a narcissist,* she'd said. "I think I should go check on Nina. What if he went to her dorm room last night? What if he's upset her? Or even hurt her?" I picture the dark deserted building and Nina's drawn face last night. Why didn't I make her come back and stay at Wilder Hall?

"I'll send an officer . . ." The uncertainty of his voice tells me the local force is already spread thin and that the road conditions will make it hard to get backup from the state. "You shouldn't go alone."

"She won't be alone." Truman appears in the doorway. "I can go with her."

"A fat lot of good you'll do her," Ben says as Truman walks toward us.

"I'm heading to Rowan Hall," I interject before he can say more, then turn to leave the office. Before I reach the door Ben calls me back—to talk me into not going, I think. But instead, he hands me a business card.

"That's my direct line," he says, "and I've written Officer Vegas's on the back. If anything goes wrong—"

"Your *business* card?" Truman says with heavy sarcasm. "Shall we follow each other on LinkedIn as well?"

I open the door and start toward the stairs, not wanting to listen to any more bickering between Truman and Ben. I hear footsteps behind me and turn to see Truman. I explain my fear about Nina and what Hotch may have been up to while we head down the stairs. Truman listens without comment until we get to the bottom of the stairs and then he turns to me, a question in his eyes. But it's not a question about Hotch or Nina.

"What did Ben mean before about what I did to him?"

I sigh with exaggerated impatience and push through the doors into the cold. It's grown greyer while we were inside, curdled dirty clouds pressing down as if the sky has lowered, sealing us inside a bubble. The snow-trimmed trees and buildings look like two-dimensional sets, a miniature model of a quaint college campus inside a cheap souvenir snow globe. I set off fast on the path where the snow isn't as deep, hoping that by the time Truman catches up with me he'll move on from the question.

He doesn't.

"What did Ben mean?" he repeats when he pulls alongside me. "He said to ask *you* what I did to him."

"Beginning of senior year," I say, giving in, "Ben wanted me to . . . well . . . he wanted our relationship to be less . . . platonic." I wince at how awkwardly it comes out, like a scripted line from one of the harassment training videos we all have to watch.

"Wait," Truman says, grabbing my arm so suddenly I nearly skid on the slippery snow. "You and Ben . . . you weren't . . . you never . . ."

"We weren't and we never," I say. "I'm not sure why everyone assumed we were."

"Laine," Truman says decisively. "She always called you the little married couple."

"Laine liked the idea of us being a couple. She thought we were well matched."

"You never said you weren't—"

"You never asked," I say.

That silences him for a few minutes. We pass Mirror Lake, invisible now under a blanket of snow. I look up toward the mountains but they, too, are invisible, erased by the heavy grey clouds. It feels as if the rest of the world has vanished and nothing exists beyond the campus, which is how it sometimes felt in college.

"So, what did you say," Truman asks as we reach Rowan Hall, "when Ben asked you to be . . . less platonic?"

"I told him I didn't feel that way about him and that I wanted to remain as we were—friends. And he said"—I keep my eyes on the façade of Rowan Hall as I speak—"he said it was because I was in love with you and holding out the hope that you and I would be together once Laine got tired of you."

I can feel Truman staring at me even as I keep my eyes on the building. I would say, if asked, that I am trying to remember which room's light went on last night so I can lead us to Nina's room, but the truth is that I'm staring at the tower room, daring the light in Laine's old room to come on and accuse me of giving up this secret at last.

"And what did you tell him when he said that?" Truman asks, his voice husky, as if the clouds have seeped into his lungs.

"I didn't tell him anything," I say, "because he was right." Then, before Truman can react, I say, "I saw Nina's light on, on the fourth floor last night, a few windows in from the east end, I think. I'm going up."

I swipe my card in the electronic lock to get in. I don't look back to see if he's following but when I let the door go, I hear him catch it before it closes. Then I race up the stairs as fast as I can, as if someone—or something—is at my heels.

WHEN I REACH the fourth floor, I knock on the third door on the hall but get no answer. I look down the hall and notice that many of the doors are propped open. The floor smells like beeswax and lemon oil. I can hear the hiss of radiators. The air feels heavy and moist as if the clouds over the mountain have seeped into the building. Ben explained to me once that when the maintenance staff bled the radiators over winter break, they had to turn the heating system on full blast. When Laine and I stayed in our suite over break it was like living in a sauna.

Maybe Nina had left the dorm because it was too hot—but where would she go?

"Nina!" I shout, knocking again. "It's Dean Portman. I just want to make sure you're all right."

I hear a faint stirring from inside and then the door eases open.

Nina stands before me in sweatpants and a T-shirt, hair tousled, eyes squinting in the hall light. "Dean Portman?"

"Thank God," I say. "You're all right."

She stares at me, puzzled. "Why wouldn't I be? Is something wrong? Has something happened?"

The agitation in her voice makes me want to comfort her and tell her everything's all right, but how can I when two people have died? "There's been an accident . . . with Ms. Gardner and President Hotchkiss. You're not in trouble, Nina, but I need to know if President Hotchkiss tried to talk to you last night."

She looks concerned and clearly uncomfortable. "Not last night, but he did at the Luminaria," she admits. "I told you he was trying to talk to me."

"Yes," I say, "but I thought you meant he was bothering you about withdrawing from his class. But that wasn't it, was it?"

She shakes her head, tears filling her eyes. "No, he asked me if I'd been sending college records to someone outside the college and said that if I had it was a serious offense and I could be expelled."

"Why would he think you had sent records to someone?" I ask.

"Because a couple of weeks ago he dropped off a funds request at the financial office. I happened to look down at it and notice that it was for an event that Mes Amis had catered and I said, like an idiot, 'Oh, I remember that event. I was one of the catering staff.' Then he looked at me funny, like he wasn't really sure who I was even though I was in his FYSem, and he asked, 'You mean you work at Mes Amis and this office?' I started to tell him yeah, I need both salaries to get by, but he said, 'No wonder you're not doing well in my class.'"

I suck in a breath, conditioned not to comment negatively on a fellow administrator's behavior, but then I remember this administrator is dead. "Oh, Nina, that's awful. I'm so sorry. You should have told me."

"I was afraid no one would believe me!" she wails. "Or they would think I was making excuses for doing badly in the class and then I started doing *worse* because I was too nervous to go to class, especially after I noticed that there was a big difference between the receipt I saw at Mes Amis and the fund request President Hotchkiss submitted."

"Is that why you wanted to withdraw from his class?" I ask, remembering how nervous she'd been at the idea of Hotch barging into the office.

Nina nods.

"Why didn't you tell me?" I ask, the question coming out angry, even though it's myself I'm angry at.

"I-I thought it would sound . . . paranoid? Like I was making excuses for not doing the work . . ."

"Oh, Nina," I say, sighing. "I'm so sorry. I saw you were scared. I should have tried harder to—" I cut myself off. Nina doesn't need my self-pity. "You have nothing to be afraid of now. President Hotchkiss . . ." I hesitate to tell her that Hotch is dead, afraid it will scare her even more, but I've already gone too far. "I'm afraid President Hotchkiss is dead."

"Oh my God, what? How?" she gasps.

"We're not sure but we found him in his office with a gun wound."

"That's horrible!" she wails.

"I know," I say, putting my arm around her shoulder. "I don't think it's a good idea for you to stay here alone. Come back to Wilder Hall with me. You can sleep there tonight."

"Okay," she says. "It *is* kind of creepy here. Last night I thought I heard someone out in the hallway. It sounded like . . ."

"Like what?" I prod when she pauses.

"Oh, it's stupid. The seniors in the tower suite told all the freshmen that the dorm was haunted by a girl dragging her suit-case around the halls because she couldn't find her room."

She must take my startled look for disbelief that anyone would be scared of a silly story. "Pack some things," I tell her curtly, too shocked by what Nina said to know how to respond. "I'll be right back."

I walk away quickly, my hand over my mouth as if to keep something inside. I find Truman in our old suite, where I sus-pected he might be, standing in the common room staring at Laine's door, the way he would when she'd shut him out.

"Tru," I begin. I want to tell him that he can stop waiting, that she's never coming back, but before I can he turns on me.

"You should have told me," he says. "You should have told me how you felt."

I'm shaken by the anger in his voice but when I see tears in his eyes, I understand that just as when I'd snapped at Nina a moment ago, it's not me he's angry at—it's himself.

He brushes past me and I follow, covering my mouth again to keep a hysterical wail from spilling out. The girl dragging her suitcase around the halls because she couldn't find her room could be me that first day freshman year. I've become my own ghost, dragging my past behind me like a cheap suitcase.

# CHAPTER TWENTY-THREE

*NOW*

OUTSIDE THE CLOUDS have darkened and lowered even further. I check my watch and see that it's only a little after 11 A.M. but it feels like a perpetual twilight has settled over the campus. As the air fills with snow, I realize the storm has arrived. I haven't been thinking about the weather. What else, I wonder, have I lost track of?

When we get to Wilder Hall, I take us in through the back door to the kitchen, where we find Ruth standing over a stove full of steaming pots. I glance toward the back stairs and am relieved to see that Miranda's body has been removed.

"The catering company called to say they couldn't come," she says with a sniff to indicate what she thinks of lightweights held up by a little snow (*she* always makes it in even on days when classes are cancelled). "And that group in there—no offense to your friends, Dean Portman—but they don't look like they would know how to boil an egg."

"Are they still all in the Great Hall? Is the police officer still here?"

"Yes, and no," Ruth answers. "The police officer, Alina Vegas, got a call saying that she was needed at Main Hall." She vigorously stirs a pot of fragrant stew. "I told her I'd make sure nobody left." She taps her wooden spoon against the rim of the pot and looks up, her glasses steamed over.

I look over to the kitchen table, where Truman and Nina are helping themselves to a tray of cheese and crackers. "Why don't you take those out to the others," I say to Truman. "I'll be there in a minute."

Truman grabs the tray and Nina pushes through the swinging kitchen door. Truman looks back at me. "Do you want me to tell them about—"

"Wait for me," I say. "I'll be right there." Then I turn to Ruth, who's lifting a wooden spoon to her mouth to taste the stew. "I'm afraid I have bad news, Ruth. Hotch . . . Hotch is dead."

She drops the spoon and hot stew splatters across the stovetop. She covers her mouth with her hand. "Oh! What happened?"

"We found him at his desk, shot in the head."

"How horrible," Ruth says, shaking her head. "I never liked him having that gun in the office." She grabs a dish towel to wipe up the splatter. "It makes it too easy to give in to a moment of despair."

"The police don't know for sure that it was suicide," I say.

"What else could it be?" Ruth asks, stirring the stew again. "If it's not"—she looks up, her glasses opaque with steam— "someone on this campus is a murderer."

Nina comes back at that moment with an empty tray. "They scarfed it down and want to know if there's more and when's lunch."

Ruth's lips turn white. "I couldn't even get in here until the police removed the body from the stairs."

"That's all right, Ruth, I'll bring some more crackers to keep the wolves at bay." I grab a box and a wheel of Brie left on the cutting board. "Nina, would you mind helping Ruth in the kitchen?" I give Ruth a pointed look meant to convey that she should keep Nina in the kitchen.

When I go out the door, I can hear that the group has moved

from the Great Hall to Moss's study. I can see why when I get there; it's by far the warmest room in the house, the fireplace amply able to heat the snugger space, the floor-to-ceiling bookcases providing insulation against the outside. As I sit down in the Morris chair by the fire, I remember that when I first sat in this room I felt as if the books were standing guard against the outside world. Here I didn't have to worry about what kind of job I'd get with this "frivolous" (as my mother had put it) degree or wonder if Laine would still be my friend after college or that I'd be the person I wanted to be.

As I glance around at Chilton, Lance, Darla, and Truman I wonder if they, too, are thinking about the selves they left behind in this room twenty-five years ago.

"I have some shocking news to share with you," I say with no preamble (sitting in Moss's chair gives me an extra dose of authority). "Hotch is dead. Ben, Truman, and I found him shot in the head at his desk."

"Oh my God!" Darla wails. "Someone shot him?"

"Or did he kill himself?" Chilton demands.

"We don't know for sure—" I begin.

"You should have prepared us!" Lance cries. "You know suicide is a trigger for me."

I look at Lance, his plump face pink in the firelight. "I'm sorry, Lance. I'm not sure how I could have prepared you for this. And it's not certain it *is* suicide."

"What else could it be?" Chilton demands, echoing Ruth's question. "A *murder*? Who would kill him? I didn't agree with many of his decisions, like hiring Miranda, for instance . . . oh . . ." Chilton covers her mouth. "Do you think this had something to do with Hotch giving Miranda the writing job?"

"What?" Truman asks with a derisive snort. "You think someone killed Hotch because they were angry they weren't named writer-in-residence and then they killed Miranda?"

"We don't actually know who died first—" I begin.

"It was the ghost," Darla interrupts in a sepulchral voice.

Chilton clucks her tongue and Truman snorts again. Lance asks in a hushed whisper, "What ghost?"

"Of the lost girl," Darla says, "the one who went missing twenty-five years ago at the Luminaria. Now that her bones have been found she's haunting us."

"That's ridiculous," Chilton says. I notice, though, that she takes a long gulp of her drink and refills her glass from a bottle of cognac. "There's no such thing as ghosts."

"Moss believed in them," Darla says, pointing to a shelf beside the fireplace. I glance at the shelf—one that would have been within Moss's reach when he held court in this chair—and see collections of his favorite ghost story writers—M. R. James, Sheridan Le Fanu, Mary Wilkins Freeman, Algernon Blackwood, Edith Wharton—all bequeathed to the college at his death.

"I always thought Moss was screwing with us," Truman says.

"He did make us write those ghost stories," Chilton says.

"Only because he said they were the hardest kind of story to pull off," Lance says. "What was that thing he read us?"

I reach over and take a collection of ghost stories down from the shelf, the gesture feeling so similar to Moss's that for a moment I feel that *his* ghost is inhabiting my body, and read from the introduction by L. P. Hartley. "'The ghost story is certainly the most exacting form of literary art, and perhaps the only one in which there is almost no intermediate step between success and failure. Either it comes off or it is a flop.'"

"Like no pressure, man," Truman says. "What kind of a teacher tells his students there's no grade between F and A plus?"

"And what kind of a sadist orders you to write about the one thing you're most afraid of," Lance asks, "and then mercilessly teases you about it for the rest of the semester?"

There's an uncomfortable silence as we all, I imagine, remember Lance's story about the son of a hunter who ends up killing and stuffing his father.

*Mr. Wiley has confused what he fears most with what he most desires,* Moss had pompously decreed. He'd called Lance "Oedipus" for the rest of the semester.

"Moss was an asshole," Truman says.

"I think the ghost story was the best thing I ever wrote," Darla says. "And I wanted to burn it after. It felt as if I had conjured a ghost. And that's what this feels like now. That girl— the one who went missing—"

"Bridget Feeley," I say. "She had a name."

There's a hushed pause as if I've said Bloody Mary's name and conjured a vengeful spirit.

"Yes, *her*," Darla says. "She's back now to haunt us and take her vengeance."

"Why?" Lance wails. "What does she have against us? I never did anything to her."

It occurs to me that this isn't strictly true, but I don't want to get Lance any more agitated than he already is.

"She was jealous of all of us, of course," Chilton says. "Everybody was. We were the chosen ones, the Raven Society chosen for Moss's senior seminar."

"Not everybody wanted to be in Moss's senior seminar," I point out. "Not everybody wants to be a writer."

Chilton laughs. "I didn't want to be a writer."

"You wanted it, Chilton," Truman says, almost gently, "because Laine wanted it and you wanted to be with her."

"Speak for yourself," Chilton says, jerking her chin up. "I wanted it because I thought Hugo Moss would help me get a job in publishing."

"We all had our reasons," Truman says. "The way they staged the Selection was designed to provoke envy, but why would that girl in particular—"

"Bridget Feeley." I say her name again as if daring fate.

"Why would she be especially jealous of us?"

"Because she wanted it," Darla says. "She wanted it so much she tried to steal it."

"What do you mean?" Chilton asks, sitting up straighter.

Darla's eyes flick around the group. She pulls the cuffs of her sweater over her hands. She looks both excited to finally have our attention and scared that someone might be listening. "I saw her go into Dean Haviland's office where the chosen submissions were kept until the morning when the dean would take them to the mail room and an assistant would read off the names on the master list to identify whose names corresponded to the chosen stories."

"Bridget helped with the Selection our freshman and sophomore years," Chilton says. "I think it was part of her work-study job for the dean's office."

"Yes, but she didn't help junior year," I say, recalling that it had been Beatrice Ann Betelmans who had accompanied Dean Haviland into the post office the morning of our selection. "Maybe Dean Haviland thought it was a conflict of interest for Bridget to do it because it was her cohort being judged."

"So, she would have to switch the stories before morning if she wanted to get in," Darla says. "I saw her go into the office just after midnight."

"What were *you* doing outside the dean's office after midnight, Darla?" Truman asks.

"I lived in Main, remember? I liked studying in the Rose Parlor." She tilts her chin up as if defying anyone to mention that the cookies for the afternoon tea were kept in a cabinet in the Rose Parlor. "I was in there studying and I saw her go by . . ."

She pauses, eyes flicking among us. "I knew Bridget didn't live in Main. I watched her let herself into the dean's office and then, through the window in the door, I saw her looking at the story submissions. There was a big pile, which I figured were the rejections, and a small one, which had to be the acceptances. She took one of the stapled packets from the big stack and put it in the shorter pile and then took one from the short stack and put it in the tall stack. Don't you see? She moved her own paper into the accepted pile. No one would have known! The stories didn't have our names on them, just a number that correlated to a list with the names on the master list. The next morning that old secretary—"

"Beatrice Ann Betelmans," I say, since I have become the namer of names.

"Whoever," Darla says. "She would have given Dean Haviland the names that corresponded to the chosen stories. If Bridget put her story in the accepted pile she'd get in the class."

"I don't know about that," Chilton says. "That whole anonymity thing . . . I never believed it. Laine believed that Dean Haviland knew whose story she was reading and took your whole record into consideration when she chose the nine winners. That's why we took all those classes with her."

"They were also good classes," I say.

"Another problem with your theory," Truman says, "is that I don't recall Bridget Feeley being in our senior seminar."

Darla smirks at him. "Because someone must have switched the papers back. I was standing right next to her when she opened her mailbox. She was shocked that it was empty. When I pulled out my feather, she glared at me as if I'd stolen hers."

"Why would she think that?" I ask.

Darla's cheeks flame pink. "How should I know?" she asks shrilly. "Maybe she saw me when I was looking through the window of the office and she suspected *I* had gone in and taken hers out of the accepted pile, which I *hadn't*, by the way." I glance at Chilton as she goes on and realize she's thinking the same thing I am—that Darla *did* go into the office and made sure her story was in the accepted pile. "I told her she shouldn't be up-set because not everybody was cut out to be a writer. She just about bit my head off. She said something very mean to me and I reported her to Dean Hotchkiss and she had to write me an apology. I'd always catch her glaring at me after that . . ." She shivers and tugs her sweater cuffs over her bitten fingernails. "I've felt her presence since I got here—look at that picture." She crooks one finger out of her cuff. "How did it get broken?"

"I found it like that," I say reluctantly, afraid that this will add fire to Darla's theory. "It must have fallen off the mantel."

"See!" Darla cries triumphantly. "*She* broke it. She didn't want us to see her."

"She's not even in it," Chilton says.

"But she is." Darla picks up the photo and jabs her finger at it.

"Darla, honey," Chilton says, "that's Truman you're point-ing at."

"No, look inside his sunglasses."

All of us lean forward to study the photograph, casting it in shadow so it's impossible to make out what's in Truman's sun-glasses. Chilton snatches it up impatiently and holds it under the light. "There's a reflection of someone there," she concedes, "but you can't see a face because they're holding the camera up—jeez, do you remember when we used cameras instead of phones?"

I take the photo from her and examine it. There are, indeed, twin images in the lenses of Truman's sunglasses of a figure framed against the backdrop of the stone wall at the edge of the ridge where the path goes down the mountain. The figure has a large bulky camera held up to its face, making it look like it's wearing a mask. I recognize, though, the boxy red duffle coat.

"I think that *is* Bridget Feeley," I say. "She had a coat like that. Remember she came up to High Tor during the Luminaria to deliver a message to Moss, and Laine asked her to take our picture?"

I look down at the picture, unsettled by the twin masked images, as if there had been two Bridget Feeleys there—and then I notice something else. Laine is smiling for the camera, her face lit up by a flash of gold as if she'd been caught in a spotlight.

"What I've never understood," Truman says, "is why Hotch sent that poor girl with the message. He must have known how angry Moss would be. Why subject her to his fury?"

"I think he wanted to humiliate Moss," I say. "And let someone else take the brunt of Moss's anger. Or maybe . . ." I pick up the photograph and study it again. There's something about it that's bothering me.

"She certainly took the brunt," Lance says. "She ran, right? After Darla and Miranda and I left? And got lost on the ridge? So, in a way, it was Hotch's fault she died. And now he's dead . . ."

"Now that her bones have been found she's taking her vengeance on everyone she blames for her death," Darla says. "Hotch for sending her with that message that made Moss angry. The rest of us for standing by and doing nothing. It's like that ghost story about the girl who died in the ice cave because no one looked for her and then her ghost came back and killed everyone."

"I remember that story," Lance says, "but I don't remember who wrote it."

"I thought it might be Dodie's," Truman says.

"It wasn't Dodie's," Chilton says.

"Whoever's it was," Truman says, slapping his knees, "the ghost has had her revenge. That should be it, then. She's done."

"No," Darla says, splaying her fingers wide. "She's not done. She's angry at everyone. Don't you see? She's coming for all of us."

# CHAPTER TWENTY-FOUR

*THEN*

ON THE NIGHT before the Selection junior year Laine had asked me to go to Main and find out if she was in the accepted pile.

"I just need to know," she said. "I can't wait until tomorrow and have everyone watching me as I check my mailbox. You don't have to change anything, but I just need you to go and find out."

What could I do? Without the scholarship she had given me I wouldn't even be at Briarwood. And so I went to Main, using the keys I had for my new work-study job in the dean's office, which I'd gotten along with the scholarship.

"Such a good friend of the Wilders," Beatrice Betelmans had said, "you ought to have a better campus job."

*The Wilders.*

I'd spent the summer before junior year with *the Wilders* at their summer cottage in Jonesport, Maine, and I knew that they consisted of two nonagenarian second cousins in Hartford, Laine's in-and-out-of-rehab mother, and Laine. Laine may have joked about living in an Edgar Allan Poe story, but the old cedar-shingled house at the end of a causeway off the coast had more cracks in it than the House of Usher. Rain seeped in through the cedar shingles and spread Rorschach test shapes over the carpets; wallpaper peeled away in strips like sunburned skin; and mold bloomed on the plaster coffered ceilings. Even the

Minton teacups, brought from England by the wife of the sea captain who built the house, were covered with tiny cracks, which Laine called crazing.

*The Wilders have been crazing for a couple centuries now,* she'd say, pouring out the smoky Lapsang Souchong that was delivered from the general store once a week, along with saltines and canned sardines, Pepperidge Farm white bread and slabs of English cheddar, celery sticks, and bottles of gin and Schweppes tonic water—the diet the Wilder women subsisted on. The deliveries appeared in crates at the end of the causeway as if left there by invisible servants. Days would pass without us seeing anyone from the mainland, which is how Laine liked it.

"Isn't it wonderful not to have to *see* anyone," she would say at the end of a long day of swimming and sunning on the rocks or, when it rained, reading and writing on the screened porch. "Sometimes I think I'd like to stay here where no one can bother me for the rest of my life. We could come up here after college and write our books together."

"What about Truman?" I asked. "Would he come, too? And Chilton and Dodie?"

She shrugged. "Sometimes Truman gets on my nerves. He's so . . . *loud.* So are Chilton and Dodie," she said, although the only time Dodie was loud was when she snored. "Not like you. You know how to be quiet."

Being quiet seemed to be a Wilder family trait, like having a long nose or a widow's peak. Laine's mother—*Call me Laurel; Mrs. Bishop makes me sound like the vicar's wife in a Barbara Pym novel*—stole in and out of the house as stealthily as a housecat. We never were really sure if she was there or not. She'd pick her way like a sandpiper across the causeway on high heels to go to the local bars and then miss the tides to come back. *God knows where she puts up,* Laine would say. *Some fishermen found her passed out in their nets one morning like a dipsomaniac mermaid.*

When she did make it back, she would sleep until late afternoon, emerging for cocktails on the poop deck at sunset, which had to be watched in reverential silence, drink in hand, until it sank below the cannery on the mainland. Then Laurel would bolt the last of her drink and say, *Toodle-loo, ladies, don't wait up.*

*As if,* Laine would mutter under her breath as her mother swanned past us on a cloud of Shalimar and gin.

But Laine did wait up, I learned one night when I went downstairs for a glass of water (*All that gin!*) and saw her sitting out on the deck, wrapped in a beach towel, eyes on the causeway. She always left a light on outside for her mother to see and she slipped copies of the tide schedule into her mother's handbag.

But she never said don't go. That, apparently, would be breaking the Wilder code of silence. Nor did they talk about Laine's grandmother, who had died only the year before, nor the fact that Laine had inherited the estate instead of her mother, nor the repairs that should be done to maintain the decaying house. Even I could see that the seawall was crumbling and that if nothing was done the house would eventually fall into the sea. When I mentioned it to Laine, though, she said, *Let it. Who would I be saving it for?*

*For us,* I replied. *Aren't we going to come here after college and write our novels? We won't get very far if we're underwater.*

That seemed to reach her. We drove up to Bangor one day to talk to an architectural firm about doing some repairs on the house and a contractor came out the next week. He took pictures and wrote notes in a little notebook and shook his head a lot.

"Gloomy little undertaker," Laurel called him, refusing to join us in the dining room to go over the estimate.

So it was just Laine and me—and the sea captain glaring down at us from his portrait above the mantel—in our damp sandy bathing suits beneath sundresses. Laine listened to it all, seeming to understand the arcane details of groundwater and shifting tectonics and seepage and subsidence. The figures he quoted for the "very most basic repairs" were more than what my mother made in a year, more than my entire college tuition, more than anything I could measure them against. Laine seemed unfazed. She thanked him and said she'd be in touch. When he left, she gathered up all the papers and stuffed them in an antique rosewood rolltop in the study.

"Well, that was illuminating," she said. "I don't know about you but I'm ready for cocktails."

"How does it feel," her mother asked when we joined her on the poop deck, "to be Lady Muck of the Manor? Did you think you'd magically heal all the Wilder woes with a bit of plaster and cement?"

"If we sold the other properties—" Laine began.

"All mortgaged to the eyeballs," Laurel replied, rattling her gin and tonic at Laine. "Maybe you'd like me to pawn my diamond rings or sell the family silver."

"Maybe," I said, "if you didn't have to fund the scholarship—"

"What scholarship?" Laurel asked, which is how I learned that Laine hadn't told her mother about endowing the Wilder Writers scholarship.

Laine explained tersely about the endowment and scholarship. Laurel listened with a tight smile, her diamond-beringed hands clenching her glass so hard I was afraid she'd shatter it. But she only smiled at Laine and then at me. "Well, heavens," she said, putting down her drink, "let your poor mother subsist on a pauper's allowance, but by all means, don't let your little friend get kicked out of Briarwood."

"Don't be so dramatic, Laurel," Laine said. "Nana made sure you'd have everything you need and you have only to ask me."

"I'll be sure to do that," she said, rising shakily to her feet. "I'll ask my own daughter for money . . . when hell freezes over." She lurched unsteadily down the deck stairs and onto the causeway.

"Don't you think we should go after her?" I asked Laine.

She shook her head. "She'll be fine. She always turns up again like a bad penny."

"I'm sorry I said anything about the scholarship—" I began, but Laine waved my apology away.

"She'd have heard about it eventually and I'd far rather the Wilder money be used for your education than poured down my mother's gullet."

And that was that. We spent the rest of the evening playing Yahtzee and went to bed early. That night, the sound of foghorns followed me into my dreams and I was back on the Briarwood campus wandering through the fog in pursuit of the blur-girl.

Or she was pursuing me.

I startled awake with her hair falling in my face, her coppery breath filling the room with vapor.

"Get up." It was Laine, shaking me. "Some fishermen saw my mother heading for the causeway an hour ago and the tide's coming in."

Downstairs, I stuffed my feet into a pair of rubber boots by the door. I half felt as if I were in a dream as I followed Laine out into the fog. She was carrying a kerosene lantern, which she held up, making her look like a figure out of a nineteenth-century illustration. Its light did little to dispel the fog, though, and as we stepped onto the causeway I could hear waves crashing on either side of us and feel their spray on my bare legs.

"Laurel!" Laine shouted, and then "Mother!," and finally "Mom-my!," the two syllables dragged out like the cry of a plaintive seabird. I pictured us all transformed into seabirds, like in a story by Ovid: spirits trapped in the fog, haunting the causeway forever. We walked to the mainland and back, water lapping over our ankles by the time we returned to the house.

"She'll have turned back," I said, leading Laine up to the house, "and found somewhere in town to stay."

I dragged her up to her room and peeled from her icy flesh her soaked nightgown, which came off like wallpaper from damp plaster, changed it with a fresh one—there were dozens crammed in the bureaus—and put her to bed. When I tried to leave, she grabbed my hand and demanded I stay with her. I exchanged my wet nightgown for a yellow floral one that smelled like mildew and talcum powder and lay down, pressing the length of my body against her long rigid back, the knobs of her spine rattling as if they would burst out of her skin if I didn't hold her tightly enough. I held her until she stopped shaking and her breathing eased and the foghorns ceased their mournful dirge. When we woke, the afternoon sun was pouring through the west-facing windows and the foghorns had been replaced by a tinkling sound like ice in a glass. Laurel would be out on the poop deck toasting the sunset, I thought, but when I walked onto the deck, I saw the sound came from the wind chimes. Two coast guard officers were marching across the causeway like a funeral procession.

"Can you go see?" I heard Laine say from behind me. "I just don't think I can bear it."

She used the same words nine months later when she asked me to break into the dean's office to find out if she had gotten into Moss's senior seminar. And just as I went down to meet the coast guard officers and let them think I was Elaine Bishop while they told me Laurel's body had washed up in the harbor, so I stole into the dean's office and stood in front of the two stacks—one high, one low—like a minor Greek deity allotting fates. The top story on the reject pile was Laine's story and the top one on the accepted was Miranda's. I knew them both because we'd all been in a writing class together that spring. I was almost positive that Laine's had been chosen by Dean Haviland

and that someone had already switched their story with Laine's.
I could just switch Laine's story with Miranda's . . . but when
I lifted Miranda's paper, my eye was drawn to a phrase on the
first page of the next submission. I picked it up and started
reading—*The thousand injuries of Blaine Bartlett I had borne as
best I could but when she ventured upon the insult of calling me
"Bridge Troll" I vowed revenge.*

I nearly laughed out loud at the bald appropriation of Edgar
Allan Poe. This must be Bridget's story. I read the rest quickly—it
wasn't very long—about a girl persecuted by a mean queen bee
named Blaine and her friends Ashton and Helen. Good for you,
Bridget Feeley, I thought, way to own your destiny. How surprised everyone would be when she pulled out a black feather
from her mailbox.

No one would be very surprised if she didn't.

Miranda, though, would kick up a fuss if she wasn't picked.

I stood like that for a moment, a sheaf of paper in each hand,
as if I were weighing our destinies. Then I picked up Bridget
Feeley's story and switched it with Laine's.

As I did, I saw that my story, "The Blur-Girl," was in the accepted pile. At least I hadn't ruined Bridget Feeley's chances for
my own gain, I told myself, but it didn't make me feel any better
about what I'd done. I looked through the rest of the accepted
pile and was able to pick out Chilton's submission as well as
Ben's and Truman's. Astonishingly, I found Dodie's story about
a changeling she'd asked me to read a few weeks ago. Wouldn't
she be surprised to see a black feather in her mailbox!

But not more surprised than Bridget Feeley was when she
*didn't* see one. I saw the look on her face when she opened her
empty mailbox and then saw her glaring at Darla. I understand
now from what Darla just revealed that Bridget must have gone
to the office before me and moved her story to the winning stack
and then she must have seen Darla go into the office afterward.

So she blamed Darla for not getting into senior seminar. Bridget had no way of knowing that *I'd* gone in afterward and switched her story with Laine's. That it was my fault she didn't get into senior seminar, which means that if the ghost of Bridget Feeley is coming for anyone, she's coming for me.

# CHAPTER TWENTY-FIVE

*NOW*

"WHO'S COMING?"

Ruth is standing in the doorway, scanning our faces. How long, I wonder, has she been standing there?

"Ben Breen," I say quickly before anyone can say Bridget Feeley's name. "He said he'd come back here after the medical examiner is done with Hotch."

"Oh, okay," Ruth says. "I was going to say, I couldn't imagine that anyone would be able to make it here in this weather. Can you hear it?" She cocks her head and looks upward. I'm not sure what she's talking about but then I make out a dry patter like dozens of fingers drumming against the roof and windows. "The snow has turned to ice. The Weather Channel says we're in for an ice storm. We'll probably lose power."

"Good thing we have a generator," I say, recalling the paperwork I'd signed for its purchase and hoping that it hasn't fallen victim to Hotch's embezzling.

"Yes, good thing," Ruth repeats, "but just in case I've cooked up a big stew. It's ready now if you'd like to eat. I know you didn't have much for breakfast." She says the last pointedly, as if preempting any complaints.

"That's a good idea. Thank you, Ruth, for doing all this." Chilton, Lance, and Truman all murmur their thanks; Darla, however, looks offended.

"I don't know how any one of you can even *think* of eating," she says. "I'd rather stay in here and have something simple. Tea and toast, with a little of that jam—"

"I think it would be better if you came and sat with us," I say, "instead of sitting in here and brooding."

"Yeah, Dar," Truman says, getting to his feet.

"I thought you would like the stew," Ruth says, "since you were asking for protein earlier."

Darla gets reluctantly to her feet and allows herself to be cajoled into the dining room. The coaxing feels familiar. When we all lived here senior year, we had dinner together each night as part of the "communal experience" that was supposed to bring us closer together as a group. As we take our seats now, all of us avoiding the chair at the end of the table that Moss always took, I recall how fraught and tense those dinners felt. Moss would go around the table asking each of us how much we'd written that day and what we were working on. When Darla began skipping dinners, we all thought she was trying to avoid the stress of those questions, but as the semester progressed, we began to notice that she'd stopped eating real food entirely. Dodie reported that she'd seen her buying bags of candy and bottles of soda at the campus store.

*Should we talk to someone?* I asked Laine once. *Like at the clinic?* We didn't know as much about eating disorders back then.

*She just likes the attention,* I can hear Laine say as Darla sits down and begins to pick at the threads of her napkin.

I don't think the attention did her any good, though, and I search now for a change of topic that will take the focus off her. Before I can, Ruth comes out with a steaming tureen and begins to ladle the heavy meat stew into Darla's bowl.

"We can serve ourselves, Ruth," I say, "you've already done so much."

"I feel better having something to do with myself," she says, continuing to ladle the stew. "I'm not like you writers, who can keep your minds busy making up stories; I have to have something to do with my hands."

"My mother is the same way," Nina says, coming in with a basket of rolls and taking the seat next to Lance. "When she's bothered about something she scrubs the whole house top to bottom but when something upsets me, I like to make up a story about it where things turn out better."

As she talks, I notice Darla's hand steal into her lap and then she lifts the napkin to her mouth, releasing a sweet, citrusy odor. She's got some kind of candy—gumdrops and gummy worms had been her favorite in college—which she's eating instead of the stew.

"Oh no," Truman says, helping himself to a roll, "I hate to break it to you, Nina, but that means you're a writer. God help you."

Nina laughs as if Truman is joking and nervously butters a roll. "You make it sound like a bad thing. It seems to have worked out for you all," she says, looking toward Lance. "Dean Portman gave me a copy of your memoir, Mr. Wiley. I haven't gotten far, but I really like it. The things you say about not feeling like you belonged here are just like how I've been feeling and it made me feel less alone to hear someone else say those things—especially someone who was able to publish a book and be so successful."

Lance's face has turned so pink and full that it looks like a balloon ready to burst. "That's very kind of you to say, but I'm hardly a big success."

"Sure you are, Lance," Truman says. "You won a PEN award."

"And your poetry, Miss Sokolovsky." Nina turns to Darla, who looks guiltily as if she's been caught eating candy from her lap. "I looked it up online and it's really good. I think it's important to talk about eating disorders the way that you do."

"Thank you," Darla says, licking her lips, which are tinted lime green, and looking down at her untouched stew, "but I'm not really comfortable talking—"

"And that story you wrote about the girl who gets erased was really amazing."

Darla's eyes snap up. "What do you mean?" she demands. "I've never published any short stories."

Nina frowns. "I-I think it's yours. It came up when I googled you. It's about a girl who doesn't like parts of herself. It begins . . . oh, let me remember . . . something like this . . . 'Daria Bennett hated her own nose so much that when her mother told her not to bite it off to spite her face, she thought doing so sounded like a good idea.'"

The whole table falls silent, even the chime of cutlery fading like the echo of the last toll of a bell. The only sound left is the whiskery patter of sleet against the shuttered windows. Everyone remembers the line from the story Darla wrote for Moss's class. Although it was supposed to be anonymous, we'd all known immediately it was hers.

"How—?" Darla begins. "I never published that."

"No?" Nina asks. "Why not? It's really good, although I have to admit it gave me the creeps." She turns to me and asks, "Did you read it when you were all in class together?"

"That was a long time ago," I say.

"Oh, you wouldn't forget this story." She turns to Ruth. "The girl who hates her nose buys a concealer stick from this old woman who tells her that it will make her nose look thinner. In fact, it will erase anything that she doesn't like about herself. The only hitch is that once you use the concealer to remove something, you can never get that thing back. Of course, the girl doesn't care about that—"

I can hear that Nina is warming to the retelling of the story.

Even if I could think of a way to stop her, I don't know if I could bring myself to; I've never seen her so animated.

"—why would she want that quarter inch of nose back? Or that mole on her chin or the flab under her arms or the dimpled flesh on the tops of her thighs? But even as she erases herself into perfection, she still feels ugly. One day she wrote in her journal how jealous she was of her best friend. Then she was so ashamed of what she'd written that she erased it, using her concealer stick because it was all she had with her—and presto! She didn't feel jealous anymore. She began writing down all her worst feelings and guilty desires—like that she sometimes wished her mother was dead or that she wanted her best friend's boyfriend—and then erasing her confessions, sure that she would become a better person once she had gotten rid of her worst thoughts and that once she wasn't ugly on the inside, she would no longer be ugly on the outside. Only she found that she also began forgetting those people—her best friend and her boyfriend, the teachers she'd resented for giving her bad grades, her little sister for stealing her clothes, even her mother. When she looked at those people it was as if their faces had been rubbed clean by an eraser. Then one day she looked in the mirror—"

"Stop!" Darla yells, getting to her feet. "I don't—" Whatever else Darla is going to say is drowned out in a gargled croak. Her mouth opens but no words come out, only a dribble of lime green that oozes over her lips and drips onto the table. Darla's eyes widen and she doubles over, as if she's been punched in the gut and she's collapsing in on herself.

"She's choking," I cry, leaping to my feet and circling the table to reach her, but Ruth, who was coming in from the kitchen, drops the pitcher she was carrying and gets to her first. She comes up behind her and wraps her arms around her waist, knotting her hands under her sternum, and jerks up hard. Something flies out of Darla's mouth and lands with a wet splat on the middle of the table. Lance screams and pushes his chair away from the table so hard he topples over backward and hits the floor.

Darla is hanging from Ruth's arms, her hair falling in front of her face so I can't see if she's breathing. I pull her hair back, horribly reminded of holding Dodie's hair back while she threw up green beer at a St. Patrick's Day frat party. Darla isn't throwing up; her eyes are bulging, her mouth open in a silent scream, green and yellow foam dribbling down her chin.

"I think her airway is still obstructed," I say, panicked. "Can you try again, Ruth?"

Ruth regrips her hands and jerks them up hard. I hear a rib crack and Darla flops limply forward like a rag doll. "Lay her down," I say, "on her side—maybe we can see what's in her throat."

Truman turns on his phone's flashlight and shines it in her mouth while Chilton takes hers out, swearing when she remembers there's no signal. I turn to Nina and tell her to go to the landline in the kitchen and call 911 for an ambulance. With the light shining from Truman's phone, I can see something lodged at the back of Darla's mouth. I swipe two fingers in and pull out a gumdrop. It doesn't look big enough to have choked her.

"She's still not breathing," Truman shouts. He presses his hands to her chest and begins CPR compressions, panic etched across his face, which is wet with tears.

I look down at Darla. Her lips are rimmed with green foam; her eyes stare glassily up at the ceiling. Then I look at the gumdrop and hold it up to my nose and sniff. It smells like burnt almonds.

Truman is bending down to press his mouth to Darla's. "Wait," I say, grabbing him by the arm. "This gumdrop doesn't seem right. I think it smells like almonds, which means she might have been given cyanide. It's possible she's been poisoned, Truman. If you put your mouth on hers you might be poisoned, too."

Truman sits back on his heels and stares down at Darla. "I think it might be too late anyway."

I grab the bag of gumdrops that had been in Darla's lap and scatter them on the ground. They're dusted with a white powder.

"They look like erasers," Lance says, rubbing his head where he hit it when he fell. "It's almost as if she was killed like the girl in her story."

# CHAPTER TWENTY-SIX

*NOW*

"WHO COULD HAVE done that?" Chilton asks. "Who had access to her candy or knew she'd be eating it at the table?"

"Any one of us could have gotten into her room and put poison in one of her bags of candy," I say, getting up. I'm still holding the gumdrop; my palm is stained lime green. "And any of us who knew Darla knew she ate candy at meals. I'm going to go put this—*evidence*—into a plastic bag and then wash my hands."

I walk toward the kitchen and see Nina in the doorway, her arms wrapped around her chest. "Were you able to reach 911?"

"Yes, but they said the roads are impassable. They may be a while."

I nod. "Ben's still on campus. I can try calling him—"

"And what are we supposed to do until then?" Lance moans. He's still on the floor, rubbing his head. I can see a knot bulging through his thinning hair. "Someone is trying to kill us! Someone who knew about those horrible ghost stories we wrote."

"Miranda didn't die like her story—" Chilton begins but then stops herself, her eyes widening. "Wait, wasn't her story about the ghost of Edna St. Vincent Millay?"

"Who died falling down the stairs!" Lance cries. "And her ghost pushes down the writer who's come to collect her letters."

"I'd forgotten about that," Truman says. "Moss loved to talk about the way authors died. Remember he said the reason he lived on the first floor was so he didn't go out like poor Saint Edna."

"I don't want to die like the man in my story," Lance wails. "I'm leaving."

"You can't go," Chilton says. "Didn't you hear Nina? The roads are impassable."

"I'll walk," he says. "I'll walk into town and sleep in the bus station."

"You'll freeze to death," I say and then regret it as I see Lance wince. "Look, let's get out of this room. We'll leave everything as it is until Ben comes back."

"Even the food?" Ruth asks, appalled.

I hesitate. "We should leave it in case Darla was poisoned by something else."

"She didn't touch my food!" Ruth snaps. "I watched her. There was nothing wrong with my stew. You all ate it and you're all fine."

"I feel a little sick," Lance says.

"I don't think any of us even had time to eat any of the stew," I say. "And Darla definitely didn't. Lance, you probably feel sick from your fall. Let's get you into the study."

Truman helps Lance to his feet and leads him out of the dining room. Chilton says she's going to go outside to find a cell signal to call her daughters and to get something from her car. I leave Ruth and Nina clearing up the mostly uneaten food, and poor Darla . . . Ruth has spread a spare tablecloth over her, covering her face. The tablecloth is the same color as the carpeting, so looking from the door it's almost possible not to see her. Darla has been erased like her character was in her story.

AFTER I BAG the gumdrops and wash my hands, I take out the card Ben gave me and call him from the landline, but it goes straight to voicemail. Then I try Alina Vegas's number. She answers on the first ring, but her voice is faint and the connection is poor. I tell her what happened to Darla.

"We'll get someone . . . as soon as . . . do you . . . poison?" Her voice is coming in and out.

"Yes!" I shout. "Tell Ben . . ." I hesitate, wondering if this will make me sound crazy. "Tell Ben that it's all happening like our ghost stories. He'll know what I mean."

There's such a long silence that I think the connection's been broken—or she's summoning psychiatric help for me—but then her voice crackles over the line. ". . . not with you? He said . . . going back to Wilder forty . . . ago."

"No," I say, "he's not and he didn't pick up his phone."

The line crackles and I hear a weird echo as if she's stepped into a large space. ". . . strange . . . I'm looking out the door of Main . . . no sign . . ."

"What?"

"I don't see any footprints leaving Main," she shouts, her voice suddenly loud and clear in my ear. "It's like he just vanished."

I HANG UP the phone after promising Alina Vegas that I'll call if Ben arrives at Wilder and then go into the study. Lance is stretched out on the chesterfield, an embroidered cushion perched on the top of his head, eyes closed and softly snoring.

"Lance has quite the bump from his fall," Truman explains. "I stuck the rest of the ice from the ice bucket in a cushion cover for him." He holds up a glass of neat bourbon as if to demonstrate the sacrifice he's making on Lance's behalf, even though Truman always takes his bourbon neat. The floppy cushion looks like a medieval hat, similar to the one I received when I got my doctorate, and it makes Lance look like a drunken court jester.

"I'm sure there are ice packs in the freezer," I say, sitting down in the Morris chair.

"I didn't want to get in the way of Ruth's cleaning. She's quite the dynamo, your Ruth."

"She gets more done at this college than the entire administration put together," I say, and then add in a lower voice, "Should we let Lance sleep? If he has a concussion—"

"I think he needs the rest," Truman says. "Darla's death came as a pretty big shock for him."

"For all of us," I say, "but you're right; it's worse for Lance with his history. Do you remember his ghost story?"

Truman shudders and looks up at the mounted deer head hanging over the mantel. "Yeah," he says, "who could forget it."

We're both silent for a few moments, recalling "The Museum of Curiosities," about a boy whose stepfather is an avid hunter. When the boy refuses to shoot any animals, he's assigned the job of preserving them. He stuffs each of his stepfather's trophies with his own rage along with sawdust and cotton, saving up the money he earns selling them at the family's roadside museum to make his escape. When the stepfather learns he's been selling the animals to save up for college, he flies into a drunken rage and chases the boy into the museum, where the animals come to life and attack the stepfather. Weeks later a new exhibit opens—"The Trapper"—featuring a life-size model of a frontiersman in a beaver hat with lifelike eyes.

"Do you remember what one of the tourists says about the glass eyes of the trapper?" Truman asks, looking up at the stag head.

"'They're so lifelike it looks like someone's trapped inside,'" I say.

"Do you think Darla was right?" Truman asks, bolting down a long swig of bourbon. "Is the ghost of Bridget Feeley killing us in the manner of our college ghost stories?"

"I don't believe it's Bridget Feeley's ghost," I say, "but *someone* deliberately killed Darla and that makes it more likely that Miranda's and Hotch's deaths were deliberate, too."

"It has to be someone who knew us then and hated us for the things we did," Truman says. "I've been wondering if it might be Ben."

"Ben? Our town police chief?"

"He's always been a stickler for justice," Truman says. "Remember *his* ghost story?"

"The one about the sorority girl who vanishes in the tunnels beneath the campus during pledge week?"

"Remember what happens to all the sisters of the sorority afterward?"

What I remember is that each of them is haunted by the banging of pipes in their room and drawn, one by one, down into the tunnels, where they die horrible, gruesome deaths. It's what I'd been thinking about when I looked down the basement stairs earlier in Main.

"Remember what Moss said about that story?"

"'The man who thinks all around him are corrupt should look to himself,'" I say.

"Ben thought we were all corrupt and then after Moss died, he blamed the rest of us. This could be his way of getting his revenge on us."

I shake my head. "Ben believes in justice but not in taking it into his own hands. If he decided we should be punished for what happened he would turn us in. He has the evidence he needs—Laine's locket found in the ice cave with the bones."

"Laine could claim that she lost it earlier," Truman says. "We went down with Ben into that cave senior year."

I pick up the broken frame, pointing at Laine in the photograph. "This proves that she was wearing the locket on the night of the Luminaria." Truman looks at the flash of gold at Laine's throat—evidence she was wearing her locket only moments before Bridget Feeley went missing. "Besides," I say, "if Ben were on a murderous rampage the person he would kill first would be Laine because she was the one he disapproved of the most."

"What makes you think he hasn't?"

Chilton is standing in the doorway, her coat on, icicles in her hair—the picture of an avenging ice spirit.

"What are you saying?" I ask.

"I think Truman has a point about Ben. Of all of us who were there at the end, who was angriest about what happened?"

"Ben," Truman says. "He didn't want to go along with the plan. He only did it to placate you, Nell." He glances at me but looks away quickly.

"Ben has no interest in *placating* me anymore," I say.

"Exactly," Chilton says. "And now that the bones have been found he's afraid it will all come out. He knew it would bring Laine back. He could have waited for her to drive into town—the police have access to traffic cameras—and pulled her over and killed her."

"It would explain why she said she was coming and then didn't," Truman says.

I look from Truman to Chilton and realize that after all these years they've both been holding out the hope that Laine would return to them. Maybe I have, too. "There are a lot more likely explanations," I say gently. "And I can't see Ben killing anyone. He'd want us to face justice."

"But then he would, too," Chilton says. "Of all of us he has the most to lose. How long would he remain chief of police if it came out what we did and that he kept the secret? Surely he'd lose any chance of running for the county legislature. You don't really know what he's capable of." Chilton's voice is sharp and accusatory. "And it would be just like him to use our own stories against us." She looks around the room. "Remember what he said? He thought our stories were self-indulgent because we cast ourselves as the innocent victims."

"'You can't even take responsibility in your fiction,'" Truman quotes in a dead-on impersonation of Ben's most self-righteous tone. "He told Miranda she cast herself as the great writer because that's what she saw herself as."

"He told Darla that she wanted to vanish like the character in her story so she didn't have to take responsibility for her actions," Chilton says. "Do you know what he said about my story?"

What I remember is that Chilton's story had been the most chilling. In it a woman in her forties answers a phone call and hears a hysterical girl crying *Mom!* The voice on the phone explains through gasps and tears that she's been kidnapped and is being held for ransom. Her mother has to wire money to this number or her kidnappers will kill her. Because her daughter is out of the country, the mother believes the caller and wires the money. I remember that what Chilton got so well was the debilitating fear the mother was plunged into. Even Moss grudgingly admitted that it was impressive for one so young to capture the voice of a middle-aged woman and mother.

*Chilton was born middle-aged,* Laine, piqued at Chilton's story getting Moss's approval, had whispered to me. But even Laine was jolted by the story's conclusion.

The mother wires the money only to discover that her daughter is fine—the call was a con, a scam. The daughter and her father tease her for falling for it. The mother is embarrassed, but she can't forget the plaintive cry on the telephone line. How had the con artist been able to imitate her daughter's voice so well? The mother is haunted by the voice in her dreams and she becomes anxious and fearful to the point that she alienates her daughter, who becomes troubled and leaves home. Years later, the mother receives a call and hears her daughter's voice calling for her in the same anguished tone. She thinks it's another scam so she hangs up—only it isn't a scam. It's her daughter calling for help but when her mother hangs up she dies at the hands of her abductors. At the end the mother realizes that the first call came from her daughter from the future and that she failed her *both* times: once by becoming overprotective to the point of paranoia, once by ignoring her pleas for help. She sinks into a deep depression and commits suicide, using a phone cord to hang herself.

"That was the best story of them all," I say, "and the character—the mother—wasn't anything like . . ." I pause, realizing that the character is like Chilton now. "She wasn't like you *then*. What could Ben have said—"

"He said," Chilton goes on, her voice hoarse and her eyes glittering in the firelight, "'You think you've been so clever but someday you'll be that mother in the story and you'll wish you hadn't exploited her pain.'"

"Oh," I say, seeing how that would have gotten to Chilton, "I didn't remember—"

"He wrote it in his comments to me. And now—" Chilton passes her phone to me, her hand shaking. There's a text message from an unknown number on the screen that reads, *How does it feel to be the mother in your story now?*

"There's no proof Ben sent this," I say.

"Then where is he?" Chilton asks. "Did you reach him?"

"No," I admit. "But I got Officer Vegas. She says he's on his way." I don't repeat what she said about him vanishing. Surely it was only that his footprints had been blown away by the wind.

"Well, he's certainly taking his time. And why didn't he make sure there was a police officer here to watch the house?"

Her voice is becoming shrill, hysterical. I start to repeat what Ben told me—that the town's police department's resources were stretched thin and the storm was keeping the state police from getting through—but we're interrupted by the ringing of a telephone, its jangling as piercing as Chilton's voice.

"It's the landline in the kitchen," I say.

"That's not coming from the kitchen," Chilton says, going out into the hall. Truman and I both get up to follow her to the foot of the back stairs. "It's coming from upstairs," she says.

"It could be a cell phone set with an old-fashioned ringtone," I say, even though I can tell from the way the sound vibrates through the floorboards that it's not. I remember that jarring vibration from when we had a hall phone upstairs—only that phone was removed during the renovations.

"Maybe it's Darla's. I'll check, if you want to go outside to call Janie and Em—"

"I haven't been able to reach either of them all day," Chilton says, heading up the back stairs. Truman sets off after her and I follow behind.

Although I know Miranda's body has been taken away I can't help but picture her lying there and recall what Ben said about her story.

*All you writers fetishize death when you don't know anything about it.*

*I don't disagree with you, Mr. Breen,* Moss had said, sitting back in his big chair, enjoying the drama his assignment had caused. *But why, may I ask, if you feel this way toward the profession, did you want to take this class?*

Ben had turned red, I recall, and glanced nervously at me. He'd taken the class, I realized then, to be with me.

When Truman and I get to the top of the stairs, Chilton is already halfway down the hall staring at the wall. The ringing is coming from *inside* the wall. It's where Chilton had noticed that the wallpaper was misaligned and, I realize now as I approach, it's where the hall phone was in our college days. I don't recall what the architect decided to do about the alcove at the end of the hall that had held a wall-mounted phone and a narrow wooden bench, like a misericord in an old church, but I see now as I reach Chilton that it must have been hastily plastered over and wallpapered. Truman looks at the wall for a second and then looks at Chilton.

"Do you want me to—"

"Yes," she says, her lips white.

Truman raises his right boot—shitkickers, he'd called them in college—and lands a kick in the middle of a scene of shepherds and shepherdesses frolicking in a meadow. Plywood splinters and plaster crumbles. Chilton is already tearing away the strips of wallpaper with her bare hands, unmindful of her manicure and the plaster dust that coats her hair and Fair Isle sweater. The ringing of the phone grows louder and somehow more urgent, like a baby's cries, but when Chilton has cleared an opening, she stands staring at the phone—the same ancient Bakelite model that had hung in this hallway twenty-five years ago—only something is different. I don't recall so many wires.

As Chilton reaches for the phone, I grab her arm just as her fingertips graze the receiver. A jolt shoots up my arm so sharp it throws me back against the opposite wall. Chilton hits the wall next to me, cradling her arm, tears making tracks in the plaster dust on her face. Sparks fly up from the receiver, now dangling from the coiled cord.

"Damn!" Truman swears under his breath. "If you'd grabbed it—"

"I would have been killed," Chilton says, struggling to her feet, "by a phone cord, just like the character in my story. I'm getting the hell out of here—" She starts down the hall toward the back stairs but then halts outside the tower room. Coming from behind the door is a sound from our past—the staccato beat of a typewriter pounding out a message so urgently it might be coming from a sinking ship.

# CHAPTER TWENTY-SEVEN

*THEN*

BY OUR SENIOR year, when we moved into Wilder Hall, most students had computers but Hugo Moss, a dedicated Luddite, refused to have any in Wilder Hall. *They'll suck the soul out of writing,* he said, *mark my words.*

So, each daily assignment had to be typed on a typewriter. Although the class met only once a week Moss would leave assignments for us scribbled on index cards in our cubbies every day. They ranged from *Write from the point of view of someone who hates the thing you love most* to *Imagine you are a ninety-nine-year-old man on the last day of his life; what is the day you relive?*

"They're like sadistic little fortune cookies," Truman said one morning after Laine read aloud that day's assignment: "'Write two thousand words about a place you've never been from the perspective of its oldest resident.'"

"Why is he always making us write about old people?" Miranda complained. "Doesn't he know no one buys books about old people?"

"It's because *he's* old," Ben said, "and he wants to make us feel as old and washed up as he does."

Despite our complaints, we would all scurry back to our rooms. Once behind our doors there was a race to see whose typewriters would be heard first. It was nearly always Laine's vintage Hermes Baby, on which her grandmother had written WWII dispatches from Paris. The strikes of the pale green keys would come tentatively at first, like drops of rain hitting a tin roof, followed soon by a pounding deluge that shook the rickety vanity table it sat upon and rattled the old floorboards in the tower room. That trembling traveled down the hallway, where it was joined by the smart tap-tap-tap of Chilton's electric Smith Corona, the halting chicken peck of Truman's battered old Remington, and the machine-gun fire of Miranda's IBM Selectric, whose hum vibrated through the whole house. I could feel that hum in my fingertips as I wrote my assignment by hand in a marbled black-and-white composition book, a thrum of nervous energy that electrified the hall until we heard the final ding of Laine's Hermes Baby and the rip of paper yanked out of the carriage, followed by her bare feet pattering down the back stairs and Miranda's pounding in the hall to catch up with her. Sometimes Miranda would try to trick Laine by leaving her Selectric on memory, retyping the assignment she had just done while she headed toward the stairs, but it never worked. The moment Laine heard Miranda's door open she would yank her page out of her typewriter and race to Moss's office. I once heard them collide so hard the banister cracked and someone fell. All our doors opened at once, confirmation that I wasn't the only one listening to the dueling typewriters, but I was closest so I reached the top of the stairs first to see Miranda nursing her ankle on the landing while Laine calmly stepped over her.

"One of them is going to break their neck one day," Chilton said from behind me.

"I don't see why it matters who turns in theirs first," remarked Darla, who composed in violet ink with a fountain pen in a gilt-edged leather journal.

When I turned back to my room, I saw that the only door not open was Ben's. He didn't own a computer and Moss had deemed his handwriting illegible. I'd find him before Latin class at the classics department secretary's desk, typing his assignment while the secretary, an ancient factotum named Irma who was always covered with cat hair and eraser crumbs, brought him hot chocolate and graham crackers.

"I'm going to end up a diabetic from doing these assignments," Ben said as we walked to Latin class.

"I think I'm getting an ulcer," Lance whispered to me at dinner one night. "I hear typing in my sleep."

The assignments would be returned to our cubbies dripping with red ink. Whatever people said later about Moss—and there was plenty to pick apart and criticize—he wasn't lazy. No matter how much we wrote, he read every word and struck out every other. *Repetitious, dead wood, extraneous, ?????, drivel, trite, cliché, hackneyed, revise, revise, revise.*

"How does he have any time for his own work," Dodie asked one day at our cubbies, "when he's always reading ours?"

"I'm not sure he really reads them," Truman said. "I think he just crosses out every other word and scribbles random invectives over them. I suspect he does the same with his own work, which is why his next book is taking so long."

"He works through the night," Laine said. "I can hear him typing."

Laine's room was directly above Moss's study so we took her word for it. I never heard any typing coming from the first floor but I did hear Moss pacing through the Great Hall muttering to himself. He was supposed to be working on his opus, the long-overdue masterpiece that would solidify a reputation based on a slim, poignant bildungsroman of a young man growing up in the Upper Peninsula of Michigan (Hemingway country, Moss called it) and a collection of short stories written after his service in Vietnam and another collection after he completed his MFA at Iowa. He'd gotten the position of writer-in-residence—

Briarwood's first—based on the literary acclaim of his early work and a contract with Knopf for a novel. But that had been ten years ago. Once, when Moss had me into his private study for a conference, I'd seen a stack of manuscript pages beside a manual typewriter (a Royal Quiet Deluxe, the model Hemingway had favored) on his desk. The stack was three times the height of one of the packs we bought in the college store, which held five hundred sheets of paper. Could Moss's novel be fifteen hundred pages long? Perhaps he really did work through the night and didn't sleep. Like Laine.

I could hear Laine in her room late at night, after she sent Truman away, typing or pacing up and down. Since her mother's death she had trouble sleeping, as if she were still keeping a vigil for her mother to come back across the causeway. She had lost, too, the confidence she had always radiated. In its place were little cracks, like the crazing in those old teacups. She snapped at Dodie, bit her fingernails, and struggled to come up with the story that would win Moss's approval. She'd worked so hard to get in his class that I don't think she'd ever really entertained the notion that she wouldn't shine once she was there, the way she shone everywhere else. But Moss, sitting back in his Morris chair by the fire, acted as equally unimpressed by her work as by ours.

"Why do you hate men so much?" he asked after we read a story about a girl whose mother's boyfriend makes a pass at her. I knew the story was based on something that had happened when Laine was in high school, but I was startled that Moss had broken his own commandment of anonymity and that a creative writing teacher would treat the "fictional point of view" as synonymous with the author. Weren't the two supposed to be separate? Laine had laughed nervously, wholly unlike her usually poised self, and muttered that she "didn't, it was the character . . ."

But Moss had scoffed at that and told her not to hide behind a persona.

After that he abandoned all pretense of anonymity and asked us all similar questions. "Why do you hate your father so much?" he asked Lance.

"Why are you so desperate for success?" he asked Miranda.

"Why do you hate yourself so much?" he asked me.

When he was tired of asking us why we hated everybody he told us our stories were derivative. "I've heard it all before," he would say, rattling his glass full of bourbon and ice at us, his eyes as glassy as the ones staring down at us from the stag's head above his chair.

To my blur-girl story he said doppelgängers were the oldest trick in the book and I should read Poe's "William Wilson" to see how it was done. When Lance wrote a story of a boy who gets stuck in the woods in a snowstorm, he accused him of ripping off Jack London. For everything we wrote he came up with an example of a writer who had already done it and done it better.

"*Nihil sub sole novum,*" Ben quoted in Latin. "'Nothing new under the sun.'"

"Not even that phrase, Mr. Breen," Moss informed him. "The Romans stole it from Ecclesiastes."

"So why even write?" Ben asked.

"Beats me," Moss replied.

"He's testing us," Laine said one night as we gathered in her room. "He's breaking down all our preconceived ideas and bad habits so we can write from a fresh perspective."

"I think he's just breaking us down, period," Chilton said, "so we can't write anything—"

"Because *he* can't write anything," Truman finished for her.

"I don't think his problem is not being able to write," I said. "Have you seen that behemoth of a manuscript on his desk?"

"I think it's page after page of 'All work and no play makes Jack a dull boy,'" Truman joked.

"That would be derivative of Stephen King," Ben said.

"It's three drafts of the same book," Laine said. "He told me that every time he finishes a draft he starts over. He's a very exacting writer. When it's done it will be a masterpiece. I've volunteered to type it for him."

We all gaped at Laine. "How will you have time for your own work?" I asked.

"Or anything else?" Truman asked dejectedly. I'd noticed that he never slept in Laine's room anymore.

She shrugged. "Think of what I'll learn typing his manuscript-in-progress. I'll see all the changes he makes. And he said he'd put me in the acknowledgments."

It was the kind of pandering gesture the old Laine would have despised, a desperate act to get her teacher's approval, another crack in the flawless Wilder veneer.

From then on, the only time the typing stopped in Laine's room was when she was downstairs in Moss's study collecting or delivering pages. Often late at night.

One night I woke up from one of my nightmares—this one that I was lost in the ice caves and had been left for dead—parched and freezing. I put on a sweatshirt and headed down to the kitchen to make myself a cup of hot tea and nearly tripped over Lance on the landing. He was sitting in the shadows, cross-legged, head tilted and listening. I saw him before he saw me so I listened, too. A low rumbling rose from below us that I thought at first might be the pipes, but then I made out the rhythm of speech and realized it was Moss. It sounded like he was reciting the Bible or the Odyssey. Perhaps this is what real writers did in their sleep, I thought, recite the great epics. But then I heard beneath the flow of words a steady patter and recognized the muted keystrokes of Moss's Royal Quiet Deluxe.

Did he narrate while typing, I wondered, and why was Lance spellbound by the performance? Did he think he could absorb the Great Man's genius by listening in—

Then I heard a softer murmur and realized there was a second person in the room with him. "Is that Laine?" I asked, sitting down beside Lance.

He held a finger to his lips and nodded. "She's been there since midnight," he said, "taking dictation." Lance looked up at me, his eyes sunken pits in the shadows. "I'm worried about her. Moss reminds me of my stepfather."

"Isn't your stepfather a used car salesman in Mobile—"

"He's a bully," Lance said, "and so is Moss. All these dictums about what *real* writers do and what *real* writers don't do. Substitute *men* and it could be my stepfather talking."

I'd never thought of it like that. The dictums ranged from instructive to random. *Real writers write every day. Real writers have to write or their souls will dry up and fly away. Real writers don't cry when they get harsh criticism. Real writers don't live in the suburbs or work in offices or marry or have children unless there's someone else to take care of them. Real writers don't ask if they're real writers; they just know.* We all wrote them down as if they were passwords for entry into a secret society, but none of them actually told us how to put pen to paper and make something worthwhile or what to do with a book once we wrote it. *Real writers don't worry about getting published or follow trends or go to those conferences to meet agents* (although Moss would go when he was invited as a distinguished guest and his expenses were paid).

"Worry about finding an agent when you've written a book worth publishing," he told Miranda when she pestered him.

"Laine thinks she'll learn from typing for Moss," I told Lance there on the landing.

"And that he'll write a letter of reference to his agent for her," Lance said. "Which is what we all want, isn't it?"

I wondered then if Lance was jealous of Laine.

"I don't think—" I began, but Lance held up his hand for me to be quiet.

Moss's voice had ceased and so had the typing. We both waited for Laine to leave the study but when she didn't, Lance looked up at me, eyebrows raised.

"You should talk to her," Lance said. "Laine thinks she can control everyone but men like Moss always get their way." Then he got up and went to his room. I stayed on the landing for another hour, until I heard the door to Moss's study open, and then I scurried back to my room and listened to Laine come back to her room.

Lance was right that I should talk to her, but what would I say? She'd be angry if she thought I was spying on her. And what did I really know? Moss might have been reading over the typescript for errors. When she got back to her room, she began typing right away. She must be redoing the corrected manuscript or doing her own work, inspired by her time with Moss. And, in fact, the next day there was a new workshop story in our cubbies for us all to read for the next class—anonymous as usual, but I recognized the typescript because the *e* key on the Hermes Baby was cracked. Only when I read it, I had the eerie feeling that *I* had written it. The protagonist of the story, who lived on a tidal island off the coast of Maine, is haunted by a figure on the causeway half glimpsed in the fog. She calls it her blur-girl.

"Didn't you write a story with a blur-girl in it?" Lance asked.

I shrugged. "These ideas," I whispered back, recalling what Laine had said in the *Raven* office, "are all floating around in the mythic sea."

But Lance wasn't persuaded. To him it was another sign that Laine was in trouble. The next day Laine and I saw him walk by the Rose Parlor, dressed carefully in pressed khaki slacks and a pale yellow oxford button-down shirt, his hair combed back, like a boy on school picture day.

"Someone looks like he's been called into the principal's office," Laine remarked.

Two days later Dean Hotchkiss came to Wilder House and interrupted our seminar to announce that the college was assigning Moss a work-study assistant so he could focus on his teaching responsibilities. Bridget Feeley stood behind him, staring resentfully at us as if we were at fault for her getting this extra assignment. She'd be handling Moss's email account, Dean Hotchkiss went on to say, copying reading assignments, placing books on reserve, and doing all Moss's typing. "It's not appropriate," the dean said, his eyes scanning the whole class but landing on Laine, "for a current student to do the work as it creates a suggestion of preference."

Moss shrugged the insinuation off, but Laine turned bright red and charged up to her room as soon as class was over. This time I did go after her. She was pacing in her room, fuming.

"I bet it was Miranda who complained," she said; "she's jealous of Moss's attention to me—or it was Lance. We saw him heading toward the dean's office just a couple of days ago."

"Why would Lance complain?" I asked, not mentioning the conversation we'd had on the landing. "He's hardly jealous of Moss's attention to you; I think he'd like *less* attention from him."

"I wouldn't be so sure," she said slyly. "People like Lance play the meek victim for attention. He sees Moss as a father figure, which would make him jealous of me. There's a reason Moss calls him Oedipus."

I was so taken aback by this outlandish theory that I couldn't think of how to respond. Laine seemed to be losing touch with reality. "Maybe it's for the best," I said finally. "You'll have more time for your work."

She stopped in front of the rickety vanity table and ran her fingers along the pale green keys of the Hermes Baby. "I suppose you're right," she said, smiling at me, a strange glint in her eyes. "As Moss always says: writing well is the best revenge. Anyone who tries to get in my way will be sorry."

# CHAPTER TWENTY-EIGHT

*NOW*

THE SOUND OF typing fills the hallway. Each keystroke sends an ice shard down my spine as if bone-cold fingers were typing on my vertebrae. Truman's face has gone as white as the plaster dusting his jacket, but there's also a spark of hope in his eyes as he heads down the hall. He thinks it's Laine. I, too, wonder if it could be her but recalling the glint in her eyes when she vowed revenge on anyone who crossed her, the thought fills me with dread instead of hope. I turn to Chilton and see she's still staring at the smoldering phone.

"It's a trick, Chill, it has nothing to do with your girls."

"You don't know that for sure," she hisses. "Someone just tried to kill me. Why wouldn't they hurt my girls?"

She takes out her cell phone and pushes past me toward the front stairs—to try her daughters again, I imagine. I hesitate a moment, wondering if I should go with her. But the sound of typing is so insistent it demands my attention. I turn to follow Truman down the hall. He's standing outside the door to the tower room, hand on the knob, as if frozen.

He turns the knob and pushes open the door. The typing grows louder and seems faster as if the writer wants to finish their thought before they're interrupted—

Laine was like that at the end, typing as if she didn't have much time left.

The typing doesn't stop. It's coming from the table under the window where Laine had her desk. But no one is sitting there. A typewriter set upon the table is typing on its own as if by a ghostly writer.

"That's not Laine's typewriter," Truman says, as if *that's* the pertinent fact, not that it's typing on its own.

But he's right. It *is* the pertinent fact. The typewriter is a huge grey monstrosity, not the slim, pale green Hermes Baby Laine used. And the sound, I recognize now, is the rat-a-tat-tat that used to come out of Miranda's room.

"It's Miranda's old IBM Selectric," I say. "Or one like it. Someone set it to type automatically."

The golf ball–size typing ball is pounding away on a bare cylinder. A piece of paper lies on the floor. Truman picks it up and starts to read from it. "'Ten little ravens thought they were so fine; one fell and cracked her head and then there were nine.'"

"Ugh," I say. "It's like the rhyme from that Agatha Christie book."

"I never liked that book," he says. "Someone's fitted it for us—here's the rest of it:

"'Nine little ravens were all set to graduate; one hung herself and then there were eight.'"

"Dodie," I say with a shudder.

"'Eight little ravens thought they were in heaven; one fell down the stairs and then there were seven.'" Truman looks at me but neither of us say Miranda's name. He reads the rest without stopping for comment.

"'Seven little ravens were up to their old tricks; one put a gun to his head and then there were six.'

"'Six little ravens were so happy to be alive; one choked herself and then there were five.'

"'Five little ravens knocked the wall to the floor; one fried herself and then there were four.'

"'Four little ravens practiced taxidermy; one met an angry buck and then there were three.'

"'Three little ravens thought they knew what each was due; one went down, down, down, and then there were two.'

"'Two little ravens thought a deal with the devil would be fun; one played his cursed bass and then there was one.'

"'One little raven took another's place; when she looked in the mirror she had lost her face.'"

I'm reeling from the last line—the girl who looks in the mirror and has no face—as Truman's eyes lift from the page and meet mine. "Well, how fucking clever is that? I guess I'm supposed to be the one who makes a deal with the devil."

Truman's story had been about a guitar player who sells his soul to the devil for an electric guitar that will make him famous and is killed when it electrocutes him.

"Maybe that booby-trapped phone was supposed to take me out. Who'd be better at rigging wires than Ben?"

"But Ben's in the poem," I say. "The one who knew what each was due and goes down, down, down . . . I think I know where Ben—"

Before I can finish, the air is split by a scream.

"Shit," Truman says, dropping the paper and rushing to the door. "That sounds like Lance."

# CHAPTER TWENTY-NINE

*THEN*

MOSS MAY NOT have liked being saddled with a surly work-study assistant but since he was, he set about getting the most use out of her as he could. Not only did he have Bridget take over the typing of his work-in-progress, but he also had her running to the library looking for literary selections he wanted to compare to our poor offerings. We'd find photocopies in our cubbies along with our daily writing assignments. He might never mention them in class or he might grill us on minute details, saving his withering disdain for the unlucky one who hadn't gotten to the reading.

*Real writers do the work,* he'd say, *they read everything.*

We read pulp fiction of the thirties and Latin American surrealists; medieval fables and Russian realists; Greek tragedies and Japanese Noh plays. We read it all and then tried our hands at imitating.

"Why is he having us imitate?" Dodie asked one day, struggling with the rhyme scheme of a villanelle during study hour in the Great Hall. "Isn't he always telling us *not* to be derivative?"

"Maybe he's bombarding us with so many different styles that no one will be able to detect just one in our work," Darla suggested.

"I think he's just torturing us because *someone* complained to the dean about Laine typing for him," Chilton said. "Was it you, Miranda? Maybe if you confess, he'll leave the rest of us alone."

"It wasn't me," Miranda said, her eyes sliding toward Lance. Before she could accuse him or anyone else, feeding Laine's paranoia, I tried to change the subject. "The one who's really getting punished is poor Bridget Feeley. Moss is working her to death."

"Oh, I wouldn't feel sorry for Bridget," Miranda said. "I think she enjoys spying on all of us and seeing how Moss demeans our work."

"Our work?" Laine looked up from her copy of Borges's *Labyrinths,* aghast. "How would she see our work?"

"Who do you think puts them back in our cubbies?" Miranda replied. "I think she reads them first. I bet she even adds a few comments of her own. Moss called a scene I wrote last week jejune, which is a word he said was only used by hacks."

"*I* would know if it wasn't Hugo's handwriting," Laine said, sitting up very straight and glaring at Miranda. "I was his amanuensis, after all."

"Would you, though?" Miranda asked. "You see, Bridget is very good at imitating handwriting. When she worked at *The Raven* she forged Emily's signature on several rejection letters."

"That's a . . . a crime!" Laine sputtered. "I'm going to say something. First to Hugo and then to Dean Hotchkiss."

"I wouldn't if I were you," Miranda said. "*Hugo* won't like you getting his assistant fired. I think he's rather come to depend on her. And I wouldn't want to make an enemy of Bridget Feeley. Remember she's not only read all the dreadful things Moss has said about our work, she had access to all our files when she worked in the dean's office. Do you want all of that getting out?"

"There's nothing in *my* files I'm ashamed of," Chilton said smugly.

"No?" Miranda replied coyly. "You wouldn't mind your SAT scores being made public?

Chilton laughed nervously. "Who would she tell?"

"She's on a lot of those chat rooms," Miranda said.

"Oh, those." Laine waved her hand dismissively. Although we all had school email accounts she barely used email and shared Moss's disdain for it. "The only people who go on those chat rooms are losers."

"There's one where you can be whatever kind of animal you want to be," Dodie said quietly. "I'm a flying squirrel."

Laine gave Dodie a smile as if she'd proved her point for her. "I'm not going to waste my time worrying about that horrible girl," Laine said, getting to her feet. "I'm going to my room to write; that is why we're here, isn't it?"

Although she professed not to be worried about Bridget's interference, Laine stormed into my room later that night waving the corrected assignment she'd gotten back from Moss that day. "Does this look like the way Hugo crosses his *t's*?" she demanded, jabbing her finger at a paper heavily marked in red. "I've been comparing assignments he returned before the Bridge Troll showed up and after and there *is* a difference."

I looked at the two papers she gave me. The first thing I noticed was that she had continued to use the blur-girl in her stories. I didn't say anything about it, though, because I saw right away that Moss had become much more critical of Laine's work since Bridget Feeley took over her typing job. There were the usual charges we'd all gotten used to—*hackneyed, trite, wordy, lazy*—but then some of the comments were more pointedly personal and cruel.

*You can't rely on your money to buy you praise, Miss Bishop* and *Are you trying to capitalize on your own mother's tragic death?*

"Laine," I said cautiously, "if these *are* Moss's comments some of them seem . . ." I searched for a word that wasn't as prissy as *inappropriate*. "Out of line," I came up with, but only because Moss's handwriting was so erratic that *he* didn't seem able to write in a straight line. "Could you ask him in conference?"

"But how?" she wailed. "If I say something doesn't sound like him, he'll think I'm criticizing him. He's very sensitive."

I barely stopped myself from laughing. The great Hugo Moss was many things, but *sensitive* wasn't the word that came to mind. *Prickly,* maybe? *Peevish? Quick to take offense?*

"Why don't you just ask him to clarify some of the worst comments? If he didn't write them, he'll say, won't he?"

Laine looked doubtful. "He may think he's forgotten. I've noticed lately that he's . . . *forgetful?*"

"I've noticed he forgets our names sometimes," I said, thinking over the last few seminars, "but I thought that might just be an act to show us that we're not important to him." I'd also noticed that he confused our stories, especially mine and Laine's, but if I brought that up I'd have to confront Laine about the similarities between them and I was afraid that would send her over the edge.

"He mixed up Hemingway and Faulkner last week," Laine said in a hushed voice as if reporting a crime. "He said it was Hemingway who said, 'Kill all your darlings.'"

"He may have just misspoke—"

"And then when I was typing for him, he sometimes recited the same passage over to me. He forgot the name of the main character of his own novel—the novel he's been writing for ten years!—and he keeps putting the kettle on and forgetting it. He's going to burn the house down."

"I suppose he has a lot on his mind," I said, alarmed at how agitated Laine was becoming. "Doesn't he always say that real writers dwell in the fictive world, not the mundane?"

"I think . . ." Laine paused to take a big breath. "I think he's losing his faculties."

It was such a polite way of saying it. For a moment I pictured Moss wandering through a hedge maze looking for his Briarwood colleagues. Then I shivered as the import of Laine's words came home to me. "Do you mean he has Alzheimer's?" I asked.

"Maybe," Laine said, biting her lip. "But don't tell anyone I said that. It would be awful, wouldn't it?"

"Yes!" I agreed. "That great mind—"

"Yes, that's a shame," Laine agreed hurriedly, "but what about us? What good will it be to have been his students if he's lost it? And Nell, his book . . ." Laine's face creased with pain. "His book's *terrible*. It's like . . . you know that Borges story he had us read? The one about the Chinese spy whose ancestor had written a book that included all the choices a man could make so that it became a great and impenetrable labyrinth?"

"'The Garden of Forking Paths,'" I said, recalling that I'd had to read it three times to make any sense of it.

"Yes! It's like whenever his character has to make a choice, he makes all the choices and the reader's stuck following him through every possibility. At first, I thought it was brilliant—a great experimental work—but reading it feels like being inside a maze and at every turn you split into two and then two again and then—"

I grabbed her hands, which were clenching her T-shirt so hard the fabric was ripping. "I'm afraid," she said, squeezing my hands, "that's what it's like inside Moss's brain. Sometimes when he was dictating to me, he would just stop and stare out the window, only it was night so all he could see was his own reflection. And when he started up again, he would just repeat the last passage he dictated." There were tears in her eyes.

I thought of the long silence Lance and I had heard. "Is that *all* that was happening when you were down there with him?"

She looked confused for a moment and then she realized what I meant. "You thought . . . ? No, never!"

I should have felt relieved but somehow, I didn't. The thought of Laine patiently typing over the same passage was too horrible. It was like she was a girl in a Greek myth locked in the Labyrinth as a sacrifice to the Minotaur.

"Maybe we should talk to someone," I said.

"And if that gets back to Moss?" she asked. "He'll crucify us. He'll know it was me. I won't get a letter from him or an introduction to his agent or a blurb for my first book—"

"Laine," I said, rubbing her hands. "You're a good writer—on your way to becoming a great one. You don't need Moss; you'll make it on your own."

For a moment I thought I'd reassured her. Her face went still and she relaxed her hands in mine, but then she pulled them loose and shook her head. "You don't know that," she said. "Nobody knows what will happen in the future. It's not just about talent; it's about meeting the right people and making the right choices at every turn. We have to keep Moss together until the end of the year. And we can't let anyone know, especially the Bridge Troll. And if she does find out, we have to stop her from telling anyone. She'd love this, you know. It's the perfect roadblock to throw in our way. She'll ruin us all with it."

# CHAPTER THIRTY

*NOW*

TRUMAN BARRELS DOWN the stairs so fast I'm afraid he'll break his neck like Miranda. By the time I catch up with him, he's in the study, kneeling in front of the couch. For a moment, I'm not sure what I'm looking at. The thing lying on the couch looks like it's wearing a Luminaria mask—and then I see the blood and it all falls into place.

Lance's story—the stepfather killed by the taxidermied animals come to life—

"Is he . . . ?"

Truman is bent over the stag's head, struggling to remove it. When he does, there's a bright spurt of blood that splashes Truman's hands, dyeing them red. I rush to his side and try to stanch the bleeding. Lance's eyes are open but sightless, like the glass eyes of the stuffed stag. I can feel hot tears burning my own eyes, mercifully blurring the sight. When I press my hand to Lance's neck I don't feel a pulse.

"It's like the father in his story."

I look behind me and find Chilton standing in the doorway, her hair and shoulders coated with ice. She looks like the ice queen, but then her face crumples and she begins to sob.

"Poor Lance! He didn't deserve this. He wasn't even with us at the end."

I put my arm around her and squeeze her shoulder. Then I hear the kitchen door open and Ruth's voice.

"What's happened?" she cries. I look down the hall and see Ruth coming out of the kitchen with Nina behind her.

"Go back to the kitchen and lock the back door," I bark, surprised that I'm even able to talk, let alone give orders. A moment ago, I felt frozen solid but the thought of Ruth and Nina seeing what's happened to Lance has galvanized me into action.

Ruth nods and ushers Nina back through the kitchen door.

"What good will it do to lock the back door," Chilton asks, "if the killer is inside?"

"We don't know that," I say, raking my eyes over the study. The only place to hide would be behind the long drapes. I stride quickly toward the windows and sweep the drapes aside, startling at the sight of my own reflection. I look like a madwoman.

"Let's get out of here," Truman says, rising to his feet. He looks down at Lance, winces, and then pulls the afghan up over his face.

"We have to check on Ruth and Nina in the kitchen," I say, tamping down the panic rising in my chest. Truman and Chilton file out and I close the door behind me.

Ruth and Nina are sitting at the counter, a tray of steaming mugs in front of them. "I made tea—" Ruth begins, but then, seeing our faces, claps her hand over her mouth.

"Is it Mr. Wiley?" Nina asks, tears streaking down her face. "Has something happened to him?"

Before I can answer, Ruth says, "Did he harm himself? I read his memoir and he wrote about struggling with suicidal thoughts."

Chilton makes a choking sound that I'm afraid might turn into hysterics.

"No," I say quickly. "I'm afraid not. Someone killed him."

Ruth gasps. "Why would anyone harm him? He was so . . . harmless."

"I don't know," I say, "but someone killed him . . . and Darla and Miranda. We have to call the police and—" I look around the room. At least there's no place to hide in the kitchen but there are a lot of gleaming knives. I wonder if we should arm ourselves. "And then we need to lock ourselves in one safe room and stay there until the police arrive."

"I called 911," Ruth says. "They say that there are trees down on both roads leading into the college and they can't get an emergency vehicle through."

"I'll call Ben again."

"I just spoke with Officer Vegas," Ruth says. "She told me that she hasn't been able to reach Ben on his cell phone or police radio for the last hour."

I notice Truman and Chilton exchanging a look as if this confirms Ben's guilt.

"There are lots of dead spots on campus," I say stubbornly. "I'm going to check the rest of the house and lock the doors and windows."

"I'll come with you," Truman says.

"All right. Ruth, Chilton, Nina, you stay here in the kitchen. The back door is locked. Lock the hall door behind us. If you hear anything . . ." My eyes shift to the knife stand to give Ruth and Chilton the message that they should arm themselves, but Chilton is ahead of me.

"You should all know that I have a gun," she says, reaching into her vest pocket and extracting a small revolver, the metal a dark saturated grey.

"What the fuck, Chilton!" Truman swears. "Where'd you get that?"

"I have a carry permit," Chilton says defensively. "I keep it in my car in a locked safe. I got it for when I was driving the girls to soccer games in Hartford. There are some rough neighborhoods." She looks around at our stunned faces and lifts her chin defiantly. "And now I'm glad I have it. I can protect us."

"Or shoot us," Truman says.

"Only if you two try anything," she says, attempting a smile that wobbles into a grimace. She puts the gun back in her vest pocket, sits down at the counter, and raises a mug of tea to her lips as if she's at a meeting of the DAR discussing her Second Amendment rights.

"Okay," I say, not wanting to argue. "Just be careful. We'll knock three times when we come back. Just stay here."

I glance at Truman and together we head out the kitchen door. I hear the snick of the lock behind us. "Wow," Truman says, as we cross the Great Hall, "who knew Chilton would go all Dirty Harry on us? I guess her core wasn't the only thing she worked on during the pandemic."

He's joking because he's afraid, resorting to the same sarcasm and dark humor he hid behind in college.

"I'm not all that surprised. She dotes on those girls of hers and worries more than she lets on." I check the window locks even though it would be easy for someone just to break the glass. At least we'd hear that. The windows are sealed by a layer of ice opaque as wax. It feels like we've been sealed inside Wilder Hall. The question is: Who's sealed inside with us?

Before locking it, I open the front door to look outside, desperate for a breath of fresh air to dispel the claustrophobic dread that has seized me. The glimpse of the outside world is not reassuring. Everything is coated with a glaze of ice and although it's only three in the afternoon the sky is so overcast that it's almost completely dark. It feels as if we're stranded here, cut off from help. I close and lock the door and then open the boot bench.

"I don't think anyone's hiding in there," Truman says. "Unless the killer is a raccoon."

"I'm checking for ice cleats," I say. "Ruth said she left some in here." I find the cleats and leave them on top of the bench, a tiny escape valve that does little to relieve the mounting dread inside me—and head up the front stairs. As Truman follows me I hear a metallic click and turn around. Truman has a switch-blade in his hand.

"Talk about going Dirty Harry, Tru. When did you start carrying a knife?"

"I've played some rough gigs," he says defensively. "I'm just trying to protect us. I'll go first if you're worried I'm the killer."

"I'm not," I say, heading up the stairs.

"Why aren't you?" he asks as I go into Lance's room and check the closet and under the bed. It breaks my heart to see the pile of meditation and self-help books on his nightstand with his reading glasses neatly folded on top.

"Well, for one thing you were with me when Lance was killed," I say, moving on to Darla's room. "And for another, you loved him." I open the closet and stifle a yelp when I see Darla's long black velvet cloak hanging there. Her presence lingers in it, a cloud of clove cigarettes and patchouli oil. When Truman doesn't say anything, I turn and see that his face is wet. I think the tears are for Lance but then he says, "You think it's Laine, don't you?"

I move into the next room—Ruth's—without answering and then into Truman's. Except for a mussed bedspread it doesn't look like anyone is staying here at all. No personal effects, no books or vitamins on the nightstand. It's the room of a transient—someone used to traveling without leaving a trace of himself.

"I just keep thinking about how unhinged she was senior year," I say finally. "I don't think any of us really understood how badly she was damaged by her mother's death."

"She wouldn't talk about it," he says. "Or she'd brush it off by saying, 'My mother was never there for me so what's changed?'"

"I think it shook her worse than she'd admit. She was afraid that she would turn into her mother. She lost a sense of who she was. And then to have Moss crumbling in front of her—"

"She accused me of dating her for her money," Truman says in a small voice.

"She was paranoid," I say. We've come to the tower room, both of us frozen on the threshold, whispering as if we're afraid she's inside listening. "She thought Bridget Feeley was forging Moss's comments. She was half crazy by the end. I can't imagine that twenty-five years holed up in that house in Maine has made her better."

I force myself to fling open the door. The room is empty, the closet door gaping open from the police search. All Miranda's belongings have been removed. The IBM Selectric is still sitting on the table, its manic typing ceased. I approach it warily as if it's a beast crouched to spring.

"Did one of us turn it off?" I ask Truman.

He frowns. "I don't remember. We left in a hurry."

I look down at the power button and see it's in the on position.

"Huh," I say, checking the power cord to see that it's plugged in. Remembering about fingerprints, I pull my fleece cuff over my hand to toggle the switch. Nothing happens.

"How did the killer turn it on and then off?" I ask.

Truman shrugs. "Some kind of remote switch?"

"I guess . . ." Something tugs at my memory, the same sense I had standing at the top of the basement stairs in Main. "The fuse box is in the basement," I say, recalling noticing it when Truman and I were looking for the scotch. There was something else I'd noticed when we were down there. But before I can find my thought the lights go out, plunging the room into darkness. Below us I hear a shout, and another—this one unmistakably male—and then a gunshot.

# CHAPTER THIRTY-ONE

*THEN*

ONCE YOU KNEW what to look for, it was hard not to see what was happening to Hugo Moss. He was still lucid much of the time, he could quote verbatim long passages of literature and would do so often, sometimes the same passage twice in one class period. It was like he was lost in a maze peopled by the authors he had spent his life reading and admiring—and we were trapped there with him, Laine most of all.

She became increasingly paranoid that Bridget was reading our papers and adding her own comments to them. At the same time, she was determined to gain Moss's wandering and unreliable approbation, taking to restlessly walking the campus late at night as if looking for something she'd lost. She got Ben to show us the service tunnels that snaked beneath the campus like the college's nervous system, like she was trying to find a secret door that would give her entrée into the life she wanted. On the fall day, a week before Halloween, when Moss assigned us the ghost story, her face lit up with a strange light.

"He wants us to face our worst fears," she said, "and I know what we have to do."

"Stay in our rooms and write?" Chilton inquired archly.

"You do that if you want, Chill," Laine said, "but I want to go down into the ice caves."

"We've been down in them," Truman said. "They weren't so scary."

Briarwood's geology department had conducted a tour of a few of the smaller ice caves. They were less like caves than shallow recesses in the earth, accessible by stone stairs with rope banisters, and mostly open to the sky. Still, I had found the few moments when the sky was cut off by projecting ledges claustrophobic and unnerving.

"Not the ones the college lets us in," Laine replied. "I want to go down into the one on the western ridge, the one called Merlin's Cave."

"That's off-limits," Ben said. "A couple of sorority pledges from the class of sixty-three went down there during rush week and only one came out, jabbering about bats and ghosts."

"I bet she did in the other one to stave off the competition," Laine said. "Did she make the sorority?"

"She was committed to a mental hospital," Ben said reprovingly, "and the college abolished sororities and banned access to that cave."

"But you've been in it, haven't you?" she asked, unreproved. "Because that's what boys do in the country. Climb down into caves and blow up things. What else is there to do?"

"I have never blown up anything," Ben said stiffly, "but yes," he admitted reluctantly. "I went down into Merlin's Cave once. It was a sort of rite of passage."

"And are the rumors true that there's a cavern like Merlin's Crystal Cave where you can see your future?"

The summer we were in Maine we'd both read Mary Stewart's book about the wizard and his enchanted cave. Laine had loved the idea of finding a place where you could see the future. I had expected Ben, though, to dismiss this fanciful idea as he did all of her mystical notions, but instead he answered seriously. "There is something . . . *strange* about that cave. Maybe

it's the acoustics. My friend Tad thought there might be subterranean gases. The cave lies along a fault line and the rocks
are always cracking and shifting. Some people say that all that
rock changes the magnetic energy from the Poles."

"Jeez, man," Truman said, laughing nervously. "I didn't think
you went in for all that woo-woo stuff."

"Wait," Ben said, coloring at Truman's mockery, "if we really
go down there, you'll feel it. We'll need gear . . . I think we could
borrow it from the spelunking club."

As he'd continued outlining what we needed I realized that
we were going to do it and that Ben, far from having to be persuaded to go, wanted to. There was a glint in his eyes that I'd
rarely seen. He had experienced something down in Merlin's
Cave that had frightened him, and he wanted to face it again.
Or maybe he just enjoyed being the one in charge.

Later that night, he lectured us on what kind of shoes to
wear and what kind of headgear to protect us from falling debris
and bats. At the mention of bats, Chilton and Dodie decided
not to go. We didn't ask Miranda or Darla, and Lance said he
was too claustrophobic. So, it was just Truman, Laine, Ben,
and me climbing up to the ridge after classes the following day.
Ben had brought the spelunking gear—crampons, nylon ropes,
carabiners; Truman brought a joint.

"We're going to need our wits about us," Ben admonished as
we crossed the scrubby pine barrens, the blueberry and huckleberry bushes bright red under the autumn sun.

"I'm always witty," Truman quipped.

"The ancients used drugs to open their minds to see past the
veil of this world," Laine said, taking a long hit off the joint and
passing it to me. "The Oracle of Delphi inhaled fumes from a
crack in the earth; Aztec priests used peyote."

I took the smallest puff I could, not sure I wanted to be high
while underground—pot .made me anxious more often than

not—but Laine kept passing me the joint and going on about opening the doors of perception. By the time we reached the western ridge the bright autumnal colors were pulsating and the voices of my friends were echoing like reverb on an amplifier. My feet felt far away.

"Watch out—" Ben grabbed my arm and yanked me back from a gaping black hole. "Didn't you hear me say, 'Be careful, we're almost there'?"

He sounded so angry my eyes pricked with tears. He'd been short with me since I'd told him I wanted to stay just friends. I shook my head and looked down. Below us, a long black gash leered at me. Cold sulfurous air wafted up into my face like the breath of some subterranean beast. It felt . . . *alive,* like an animal crouched and waiting.

"That's it?" Laine asked. Her hair was falling in front of her face so I couldn't see her expression. Was she disappointed?

"Yeah," I said, trying to keep my voice light. "Kind of a let-down, huh? Just a big stinky hole in the ground. Maybe we should just hang out up here—"

Laine lifted her head and stared at me, her pupils as black as the hole below us. "Are you kidding? It feels like the entrance to the Roman underworld. Like it's *waiting* for us."

"Yeah," Truman said, "waiting to *eat* us."

"You don't have to go," Ben said, affixing one end of the rope around the trunk of a dwarf pine.

"That'll never hold if we have to haul ourselves out of here," Truman said, extinguishing the joint.

"It's not to haul ourselves out," Ben said, "it's to find our way back." He put on his headlamp, clipped his belt to the rope, and told us we should also clip ourselves to the rope. Laine chose a lantern instead of a headlamp and refused to clip herself to the rope. "I'm not going to spoil the mood by latching myself to you all. I want to experience the mysteries of Merlin's Cave and see my future."

Ben shrugged. "Suit yourself, that's your risk. Nell?" He held out a carabiner to me and I gratefully clipped it to my belt. I didn't want to go at all; the thought of getting lost in there was unbearable.

Ben went first, clipping the rope to steel loops fixed into the rockface, which, he explained, had been put there by earlier spelunkers. "Stay close to the wall," he shouted back to us. "There's a steep drop on the other side of the steps." When I looked over, the beam of my headlamp plunged into the dark and died somewhere far below.

"How far down does it go?" I asked, trying not to sound as scared as I was.

"No one knows," Ben said. "And we don't want to find out."

I hugged the wall for the rest of the way down the stairs, which seemed to go on forever before reaching level ground. Ben warned us again to stay near the wall to avoid the crevasse, as he called it, but Laine went over and held the lantern above the hole. "Hullo down there," she called. Her voice came back so clearly, I felt chills, as if a part of Laine had split off and was trapped down in the bottomless pit. Maybe she had the same thought because when she turned back to us her face in the lantern light was pale and haggard. "Lead on, Macduff," she said, but her voice sounded thinner than her echo, as if the echo had stolen some vitality from her.

Ben led us under a stone arch and through a narrow passage where we had to duck down.

"Look! Are those symbols carved by Native Americans?" Laine asked, holding a lantern up to a carving of a circle with lines through it and a semicircle on top that looked a little like horns.

"Maybe," Ben said. "People have been carving stuff down here for centuries. It's hard to know what's original and what's been added."

"I think they're original," Laine said. "I can *feel* it." She continued ahead, Truman following her. I wanted to go on, but Ben held me back, clipping the rope to a metal loop fixed to the wall.

"This will keep it from getting tangled," he told me. "Be careful up ahead, there's a drop—"

"Holy shit!" we heard Truman cry. I hurried forward, the carabiner jingling at my waist, and found Truman and Laine standing in a circular space looking up at the ceiling, which glittered with ice-covered stalactites.

"It's Merlin's Crystal Cave!" Laine said.

"If it's Merlin's Cave, shouldn't he be here?" I asked. "Trapped by the sorceress Vivien?"

"Maybe he is," Laine said, turning around in a slow circle. Her lantern reflected off the stalactites, sending rainbow prisms flying around the cavern like butterflies. It was like being inside a kaleidoscope. "And we just can't see him. Listen . . ."

When the echo of her voice and the jingle of the carabiners died down, we could all hear a low hum, like a furnace or a generator, coming from everywhere at once. I could feel its vibrations in the soles of my feet and tingling in my fingertips and the top of my scalp. After a moment Ben said, "I've heard it's caused by the wind moving through the caverns—"

"That's no wind," Laine said, her eyes flashing in the lantern light. "That's the earth humming. This place is magic—can't you feel it?" She turned without waiting for us to answer and held her lantern up to the far side from where we'd entered. There were two dark openings in the rock.

"Which way are we supposed to go?" I asked Ben.

"To the left, of course," Laine answered for him. "That's how a maze works. Always turn left—"

Ben started to say something but Laine was already going ahead through the left opening. "She shouldn't be going ahead without the rope," Ben said, clipping it onto another bolt in the rockface.

"She won't lose her way if she always takes the left turn," I said, following close behind.

"We don't know that for sure," Ben said, the light from his headlamp strobing across the ice formations. "Remember what I said about the rocks shifting down here. We're walking on a fault line. The terrain could have changed since the last time I was here and there could be a cave-in."

"You mean we could be trapped in here?" I asked, dread seeping into my bones along with the cold from the ice below our feet and the ice melt dripping down the walls. A body sealed in here might be preserved forever.

"Not if we're careful and stay together," Ben said.

We came to several turnings and always took the leftmost path. I could hear Laine's voice ahead of us, marveling at each new wonder—stalactites that looked like crystal chandeliers, a spiral design that might have been carved by ancient Viking explorers, and runes she felt sure were spells cast by Merlin himself.

"We're walking the labyrinth," I heard her say, her voice bouncing off the stone walls like a shuttle flying across a loom, weaving us into the warp and weft of her fancies and desires.

At the next juncture there were three openings in the rock, but the leftward one looked too slim for even Laine and Truman, who had gone on without us, so I pointed to the middle one. When I turned to Ben to see if I'd chosen right, his face, caught in the beam of my headlamp, was stripped bare of everything but fear.

"What is it?" I whispered, afraid the rope had broken and we were lost and trapped below the rock.

"Can't you *feel* it?" he asked. I saw his face was streaked with tears that glittered like the stalactites above our heads and that his eyes were wide, not just with fear, but *terror*. Ben, the most rational and least superstitious person I knew, was terrified of something beyond reason.

"What?" I asked. But then in the silence I heard the hum again. I had never really stopped hearing it, but now I felt an overwhelming sense of fear, not just that we were lost and trapped beneath the earth, which was horrifying enough, but that we were lost and trapped in our lives, that no matter what we chose, which increasingly narrow cleft we squeezed through, everything was already decided for us. Laine would be the great writer, Truman her loyal hanger-on and troubadour, Ben a lawyer who prosecuted the guilty, and I—after these four magical years at Briarwood—would return to the "real world," that place my mother was always lecturing me on, which probably meant a high school teaching job, because, really, how would I ever afford to go to graduate school?

"Guys?" Truman's voice shook me out of my moment of existential dread, which afterward I put down to an anxiety attack brought on by the pot we'd smoked earlier. I turned away from Ben and followed Truman's voice into a large circular cavern. It took me a moment to recognize that it was the cavern we'd first come to—the Crystal Cave. We had come full circle. We had navigated the maze and found the way out.

"Guys?" Truman repeated, his voice warbly and young, all his usual cynicism and sarcasm stripped away by his passage through the labyrinth. "I don't know where Laine is."

"Wasn't she with you?" Ben asked.

"She went on ahead and then I lost track of her. I thought she'd be here when we got to the end."

"Maybe she went out," Ben said, his voice cool, eyes on the rope he was pulling out of its circular orbit. He had recovered and was embarrassed by his earlier, mystifying fear.

"I don't think so," Truman said. "There was a path that was too narrow for me to get through so I chose a different one, but now I'm afraid she took it and she's lost."

"She'd have been an idiot to take that one," Ben said, not looking at me. He'd seen the other path and knew I'd rejected it. "She just went out and is halfway back to Wilder by now. Come on, we don't want to be in here after night falls."

Truman and I looked at each other as Ben went on ahead. "What happens after nightfall?" Truman whispered.

I shook my head. Then I called Laine's name as loud as I could. The echo of my voice was shrill and frightened, but there was no answering *here*. We tried a few more times, Truman and I taking turns. "Ben's right," I said finally. "Laine must have gone out and is back at Wilder already."

We followed the rope out and climbed back into the air, which had never smelled sweeter to me. The sun setting over the ridge was brilliant after the dark of the cave.

"Come on," Ben said, walking away quickly, as if he couldn't wait to put distance between himself and whatever had frightened him in the cave.

What had it been? I wondered. Had he, like me, seen his future spooling out in increasingly tighter circles? I followed him and then glanced back at Truman, who started walking but was looking at the entrance of the cave, unaware of a small cleft in the rock he was about to step into.

"Watch out!" I cried, hurrying back to keep him from falling into the hole. Only I tripped over a crack and nearly fell into the hole myself. A rock dislodged by my foot fell in and we heard the sound it made when it hit the rock far below us.

"Saving me once again from the abyss," he said, even though he was the one holding me back from the edge. His arm was firm and steady around my waist, his breath warm against my wind-chapped face.

He smiled then bent his head down and pressed his lips to mine. I kissed him back and we stood like that, straddling the cloven stone, as if our bodies could bridge what had been shattered eons ago, until I heard a moan coming from the stone below us, from the wind rushing through the broken places, a sound so sad I felt something crack inside me.

I pushed him away and said, "We can't. It would break Laine's heart."

"I'm not sure she has one," he said.

I stared at him, shocked. "But Laine is always feeling things," I said.

"Sure, but does she care about what anyone *else* is feeling?"

"Then break up with her," I said, surprising myself, "and we'll find out if she has a heart."

I turned and started walking. Behind me I heard him call my name, but I put my head down and kept going.

The last sun was striking Mirror Lake as we came down the mountain, turning it into a glowing golden disk. It looked like a portal to another world—a mirror world, I thought, where I could cast off my old identity, dull Ellen, yearning after my best friend's boyfriend, and be whoever I wanted to. How had so much time passed? It felt as if we couldn't have been in the cave so long—or that we'd been gone longer, that when we came down the mountain, we'd find the campus in ruins and all our friends long dead and gone—like in those fairy ballads Dean Haviland had read to us about a traveler who comes out of a fairy mound and finds that a hundred years has passed. Maybe, I thought disloyally, it really is a hundred years in the future and Laine is long dead and Truman and I can be together.

WHEN I GOT back to Wilder, Laine was in Moss's study, curled up under an afghan by the fire, her cheeks pink in the firelight, drinking a glass of Moss's good whiskey.

"There you are," Moss said to us, his eyes bright as Laine's cheeks. "Miss Bishop has been telling me about her adventures."

"We were up there looking for her," Ben said.

"I got lost in the Crystal Cave," Laine said.

"But we passed through there," Truman said.

"No," Laine said, shaking her head. "I don't mean the one we all saw—that was nothing. I found the real Crystal Cave."

"Of course," Ben muttered under his breath. "She'd have to find a better one."

Moss was smiling at Laine. "Apparently, Miss Bishop took the path less traveled and beat you all back here."

I was going to point out we'd been delayed looking for her but then Laine glanced up and I saw her cheeks were pink because they were scraped raw. Her hands were, too, and when she lifted the glass to her mouth, they trembled. Worst were her eyes, which looked haunted, as though she'd seen some terrifying future for herself inside the Crystal Cave.

# CHAPTER THIRTY-TWO

*NOW*

I'M ALREADY MOVING toward the door, groping blindly in the dark, when we hear a second shot.

"Wait!" Truman cries, grabbing me and holding me tightly around the waist. For a moment all I hear are our heartbeats racing each other and then a woman crying in pain.

"That's Chilton," I hiss, "we have to go help her."

"All right." He switches on his phone flashlight, turning his face into a fright mask. "But let me go first."

I turn my phone flashlight on as I fumble down the back stairs behind Truman. When we reach the kitchen door, I remember that it's locked. I listen at the door and hear Chilton sobbing "I'm sorry, I'm sorry" over and over again as if she's pleading for her life. Then I hear a deeper voice—Ben's.

"Careful," Truman says, but I ignore him and pound on the door.

"Ben? Chilton? Open up. It's Nell and Truman. Ruth? Nina? Are you all right? What's happened?"

I hear footsteps and then the lock turning. The door opens a crack revealing a sliver of bloodstained face that for a moment I don't recognize. When she opens the door wider, I see it's Chilton. She's clutching her arm, where blood is seeping through a hole in her sweater.

"I didn't mean to," she sobs. "The lights went out and then

someone was coming up from the basement. I thought it was the killer—"

I push past her, shining my phone flashlight into the kitchen, and feel something slippery underfoot. The room smells like blood. I hear a moan and aim my phone toward it. Ben is lying on the floor, half propped up against the cabinets. I cry out and fall to my knees next to him, trying to see where he's hurt.

"I need light!" I cry. "Get a lantern!"

"It's not . . . as bad as it looks," Ben gasps, his face grimacing with the effort to talk. "It's just . . . my shoulder . . . I'm pretty sure she missed . . . my heart."

"I'm so sorry," Chilton sobs from somewhere behind me.

"I re-returned fire," Ben says. "I think I clipped her arm . . . You should check . . ."

"I'm fine," Chilton says, "it's just a scratch. God, Ben, I'm so sorry. Please be okay. I'll never forgive myself if . . ."

"Me neither," Ben says, trying to smile but wincing instead. His face is suddenly lit up as Truman returns with a lantern and kneels next to us. He's got a wad of dish towels, which he presses against Ben's shoulder. They instantly turn red.

"We have to get the wound washed and stop the bleeding," I say, looking around the now partially lit kitchen, which is when I notice that Ruth and Nina aren't here. "Where's Ruth?" I demand. "And Nina?"

Chilton blinks and looks around as if she, too, has just noticed their absence. "When the lights went out Ruth said something about checking the generator. I think Nina went with her."

"You let them go?" I demand.

"I was going to go with them but then I heard someone coming up the basement steps. I-I thought I was protecting them!"

I look toward the back door and see that it's been left ajar.

"We'll check on them after we've got Ben bandaged up," Truman says. He's leaning over Ben's chest, using his knife to cut away the shirt. "Chilton, can you soak some dishcloths in hot water? Nell, help me turn him over so we can see if there's an exit wound."

Ben cries out when we move him. "Sorry about that, man," Truman says. "But the good news is the bullet went straight through. We just have to clean you up and stop the bleeding."

Truman takes charge in a way that makes me wonder where he got this first-aid experience. He even distracts Ben by asking him questions—or maybe he still suspects Ben of being the killer and is interrogating him.

"So, how'd you end up in the basement?" he asks first.

"I came through the tunnels," Ben says, wincing each time Truman swabs his shoulder. "When I came downstairs . . . in Main . . . I thought about the door to the basement being open before . . . that it might be how the killer got into the building . . . only . . ." Ben's face turns a ghastly white in the lantern light and I see that look of naked fear I'd seen on his face that day in the cave.

"Only that's where your ghost story was set," I say, remembering the story Ben had written in the days after we came out of the cave. He'd set it in the tunnels below the campus instead of the ice caves, and the main character had been a sorority pledge who's abandoned there during a hazing, but her fear of being trapped and alone was the same fear I'd seen on his face that day in the cave. "What happened, Ben?"

"I got lost. Some of the doors were locked and there were signs painted on the walls . . . like the ones in the cave . . . It was like I was being led someplace . . . like a cow to slaughter . . . but when I got to the end, the entrance to Wilder basement was blocked by boxes . . . I knocked them down and I was coming up the stairs when the lights went out . . . I thought I'd been led into a trap, and she was waiting for me at the top of the stairs . . ."

"Who?" Truman asks. "Who did you think was waiting for you?"

"Laine," he says. "I found out on Hotch's computer . . . he tried to blackmail her . . . Look at my phone . . ."

He fumbles for his phone in his pocket, and I help him take it out. When I open it, I find a screenshot of an email. I scan the first few lines and then read it aloud.

"'Greetings, Ms. Bishop, I am so looking forward to your attendance at the Commemoration of the great Hugo Moss. As one of Moss's last students—and certainly his most successful protégé—I know you won't want to miss it. I still remember when I last saw the two of you together, on the night of the Luminaria twenty-five years ago, standing in front of High Tor. You were so *close*! One of your classmates has been reminiscing about that moment as well. I know you'll want to make sure you honor it appropriately. I think a $500,000 donation would be the right way to remember that important night.'"

"What gall!" Chilton says. "He's shaking her down for a contribution by threatening to reveal what happened that night."

"But he wasn't there," Truman says.

"But he was!" I exclaim, suddenly recalling the photograph in Moss's study and what bothered me about it. "He's in the picture—in the reflection of your glasses, Truman. There's Bridget, but also behind her by the stone wall in front of the path down, I thought I noticed something weird about the shadows and now I know what it was. There's a shadow of someone in a robe. Hotch was hiding behind the wall—of course he wanted to *see* Moss's humiliation when Bridget delivered his message. He saw what happened."

"But then, why has he kept quiet about it all these years?" Truman asks.

"Why antagonize your most generous donor?" Chilton asks.

"Unless you need some extra money twenty-five years later," I say.

"Laine wouldn't fall for that," Truman says. "Why would she believe Hotch—"

"Because he says he has someone to back him up," I say. "One of her classmates, he says. *One of us*. She must have thought that one of us was ready to break the pact."

"Exactly," Ben says, looking suddenly more alert. "Remember how serious Laine was about those pacts of hers? She thinks one of us had broken it . . . so she's come back to kill all of us."

# CHAPTER THIRTY-THREE

*THEN*

AFTER THE CAVE adventure, Laine stayed in her room and wrote—or at least typed. We could hear the steady drumbeat of her keys like rain night and day as if we'd entered a monsoon season. We were meant to be working on our final project, the first draft of which was due on the last day of the fall semester so Moss could read them over break and then we could spend the spring semester revising. Laine was determined to produce a masterpiece, something that would pierce through the fog Moss increasingly dwelt in.

"It's like she thinks she'll cure him with the power of her words," Truman muttered disgruntledly in my room, where he came when Laine had banished him. I'd be at my desk, fitted into the eave beneath the window that I'd scratched *Excelsior!* into, scratching away at a story in my notebook. I'd stop, though, and swivel my chair toward him as he sprawled across my bed and poured out his Laine troubles. Sometimes I felt like I'd become his therapist, my notebook resting in my lap and pen poised in my hand. "But what if she can't?" he'd ask. "What if Moss is too far gone by the end of the semester to even read what she's written? I'm afraid it will break her."

Laine's fragility. That was the reason he'd given the day after our one kiss on the mountain, the reason why he couldn't break up with her. "I can't do that to her while she's working on her final project. It wouldn't be fair," he'd said. I couldn't help but agree. Maybe because I didn't want to face Laine's ire before we'd both finished our projects. Maybe because we didn't want to push her over the edge as she became increasingly paranoid.

One day at breakfast she appeared in her pajamas waving a typescript that had been put in our cubbies. "Who wrote this?" she demanded.

"We're not supposed to tell," Miranda said prissily.

"Was it you, Randy?"

Miranda colored and said no. "It's not my style. It's way too violent."

The story was about a girl who's bullied and abused by a mean girl named Blaine and her friends Ashton and Helen. After she's left for dead her ghost takes her gory revenge from the grave. I recognized it right away as Bridget's story—the one she had submitted to get into the Raven Society that I had read in Dean Haviland's office. But of course, I couldn't say that.

"Maybe Moss wrote it," Lance suggested, "to scare us and make us fight among ourselves."

"That's crazy," Chilton said, but without much conviction. I think by that time we'd all come to suspect that our teacher wasn't entirely of sound mind. He'd become increasingly erratic in class, repeating himself, going off on tangents, sometimes just staring into space for long periods of time. The comments on our work had also become strange and unhinged. *Kill all your darlings!* He had scrawled on every page of my last chapter.

The week before break I heard a knock on my door but when no one came in—as Truman always did—I got up and went to the door. I found Truman and Chilton standing there, Truman looking sheepish and Chilton glancing furtively toward Laine's door. I motioned them both in without a word. Instead of sprawling across the bed, Truman sat stiffly on its edge and Chilton sat next to him. I sat at my desk, my hands automatically reaching for my notebook to feel in control.

"We need to talk about Moss," Chilton said in a hushed voice. "We can't let things go on like this. We have to tell someone."

"Laine says—" I began.

"Laine is following him down into his madness," Chilton said. "I've seen her do it before. At Choate she admired our Latin teacher—Domina Middleton—and she about killed herself memorizing the Aeneid. When she gave Laine an A minus, Laine went to the headmaster and said Domina Middleton had acted improperly toward her. The poor woman lost her job."

"That's horrible," I say, wondering why Chilton had never thought to share this anecdote before. "But how does this apply here? Laine doesn't *want* to get Moss fired."

"No, but I'm afraid of what she'll do if Moss doesn't respond well to her book. Have either of you read any of it, by the way?"

Truman and I both shook our heads. "Well, let's hope it's brilliant, but that won't make any difference if Moss doesn't think it is—it might make it worse."

"What do you mean?" Truman asked.

"Men like Moss," Chilton said with an authority born of growing up among rich, powerful men, "don't like to be shown up by twenty-two-year-old girls. Moss knows his abilities and his legacy are slipping. He won't like seeing a girl like Laine surpass him. We have to head this off by talking to someone."

"Dean Haviland—" I began.

"Has swanned off to the Lake District on sabbatical," Chilton finished for me. "Even if she were here, I'm afraid she loves Moss too much to do what's necessary. We have to go to Dean Hotchkiss."

Remembering what Dean Hotchkiss had said to me after the

scholarship meeting—*You have a lot to live up to, Miss Portman. Try not to screw it up*—I wasn't eager to talk to him again. "Are you sure? He's—"

"A self-centered soulless bureaucrat," Chilton replied. "But he has the power to put Moss on leave until they can find a replacement."

"Laine will hate us—" Truman began.

"If that's more important to you than saving her from herself," Chilton said with a withering look, "I'm willing to take the heat. I'll tell Laine it was my idea. I just need one of you to come with me and back me up. Will you do that?"

Truman looked at me pleadingly. He wanted me to let him off the hook, as I'd done night after night as I let him pour out his heart to me without expecting anything in return. As I'd done when I accepted that he couldn't break up with Laine yet. How could I let him down now?

"I'll go with you," I told Chilton. "We'll have to do it during class so there's no chance Laine or Moss will be in Main. Truman, you can say Chilton and I are out arranging"—I scrambled for a plausible excuse—"arranging something special for the Luminaria. Let Moss think we're planning a special honor for him."

Chilton nodded and even gave me a grudging smile as if pleased I was catching on to the art of managing difficult men.

WE WENT THE next day, slipping out of Wilder Hall like spies—or traitors, I felt in my heart—just before class. The weather had turned cold, a heavy grey pall settled over the mountain threatening snow, daylight almost gone at four as we got closer to the solstice. *This is the worst of it,* I told myself, *we'll get through this and things will be better in the spring.* Dean Haviland would come back and take over seminar and coax us all through our revisions. She'd be strict and demanding, but fair and, above all, sane. She might not have the spark of genius like Moss, she might be only a keeper of the flame, but that was what we needed right now.

Beatrice Ann Betelmans looked up from her typewriter as if we were storming the citadel by requesting an unscheduled meeting, but Dean Hotchkiss called from his office, "Is that Miss Prior? Send her in. I was just talking to her father."

He looked a little disappointed when he saw that I was with Chilton, but quickly adjusted, settling himself behind his big oak desk and straightening his Princeton tie.

"I bet Daddy was calling to ask when Briarwood would have a decent lacrosse team. He was disappointed I couldn't continue my winning streak at Choate."

Dean Hotchkiss chuckled and said something about Princeton men and women's sports that I couldn't even begin to parse. Nearly four years in this world and it still felt like another planet. "But," he went on, "I think he's more disappointed that the written arts have seduced you away from your business degree."

"I'm graduating in both," she replied, "as I've explained to my father many times, and I'm going to do the Radcliffe publishing course next summer. That is, if I'm able to finish out senior seminar."

Dean Hotchkiss sat up a little straighter at that. "What do you mean, if you can finish out senior seminar?"

"Well," Chilton said, demurely lowering her eyes, "there's a little problem. I don't want to speak ill of anyone—and we all admire Professor Moss so much—"

"Our shining star!" Hotchkiss said with a forced enthusiasm that made me remember how he had argued against naming the writing center after Moss. "One of our most *popular* professors." He said *popular* as if it were a character flaw. "Of course, we all can't offer our students the perks of connections with the publishing world. But he is our biggest admissions draw and with Miss Bishop's endowment, the writing center will be an even bigger draw."

"Yes," Chilton said, raising her eyes to meet Hotchkiss's. "I'm sure it will be, only I wonder if Hugo Moss is really the right figurehead. You see, he's . . . Nell and I"—she gave me a dagger look, clearly expecting me to chime in—"have noticed that he's not quite himself these days. To be frank, we're afraid that he's losing his faculties."

"Really?" Dean Hotchkiss said, sitting back in his chair. For just a moment, I caught the hint of a smile and it occurred to me that he might welcome our news. He'd been jealous of Hugo Moss and now he would have ammunition against him. "That's quite a serious issue if it's true. What kind of behavior are we talking about?"

"Well," Chilton said, taking a deep breath, "he's lost track of what he was saying several times in class . . ." She once again gave me a sharp look.

"His feedback on our papers seems increasingly . . . well, *harsh*—" I began.

"Ah, so perhaps this is about him being hard on you."

"It's not just me," I said. "He's written some really mean things . . . to everyone, but especially to Laine—"

"Oh, to *Laine*. I see, well, we really can't have the benefactor of the writing center upset. Of course, I'll have to look into that. But tell me, why didn't Miss Bishop come herself to complain?"

"Laine worships Hugo Moss," I said.

"So, she doesn't know you're here," he said, smiling at me as if I'd proved him right about something. "Are you really so ungrateful for the scholarship your friend has given you that you'd come here behind her back?"

"Scholarship?" Chilton echoed.

Which is when I realized Chilton didn't know about the

scholarship. Laine had told me not to mention it. I'd thought she didn't want to take credit or embarrass me but now I saw that it was because she knew it would make Chilton jealous.

"Oh, didn't you know your friend gave Miss Portman a full scholarship? With a stipend! So generous!"

When Chilton didn't respond, Dean Hotchkiss leaned forward. "All right, girls, I'll look into this and have a word with Moss myself. I can speak with Dean Haviland when she returns in the spring and have her start looking for our next writer-in-residence." Then his gaze shifted two inches above our heads as if we'd already gone.

# CHAPTER THIRTY-FOUR

*NOW*

"THAT'S IMPOSSIBLE," TRUMAN says, starting to argue with Ben, but then Ben's eyes flutter closed and stay closed.

"We need to get the generator working and go find Ruth and Nina," I say, getting to my feet. "Chilton, are you well enough to stay with Ben while Tru and I are gone?"

She nods and sits on the floor next to him. She's still cradling the ugly, painful-looking gash in her arm but the bleeding has stopped. As I stand, I notice her gun lying on the floor. I pick it up, put the safety on, and stow it in my coat pocket. "I'm taking your gun, Chill," I say, "you've got Ben's if you need it." I see Truman staring at me. "What? Chilton's not the only one who's taken firearm safety classes. Have you?"

"What?"

"Taken firearms training?"

"No, but I know how to handle a gun if that's what you're asking."

"Good, then you hold this." I hand him the gun then head to the back door. I find a flashlight in a basket by the door and turn it on, catching Truman's haggard, bloodstained face in its beam.

"Nell, we have to talk."

"Now, Tru?" I ask, my voice shaking with the strain of keeping it all together. "I know you find it hard to accept that Laine could be doing all this but we have to face it and make sure

she hasn't hurt Ruth and Nina. You can't think the killer is Ben
when Ben is lying in there wounded."

"That doesn't actually prove anything—" he begins, but seeing the look on my face, he switches gears. "Okay, whatever,
Ben's not a threat anymore, which leaves, well, you and me."

"And Chilton?" I ask. "She did shoot Ben."

"Yeah, but if it was Chilton, why didn't she shoot both of us
when we came in? She could have said it was an accident like
shooting Ben. And Chilton has too much to lose. You're right
about her doting on those girls of hers." He says this with a hint
of jealousy in his voice that surprises me and makes me wonder
if he regrets not having children.

"So that leaves you and me," I say, pointedly looking down at
the revolver in his hand.

He immediately turns it around and offers it to me.

"Nah," I say, "I don't think it's you."

"Not for a minute?" he asks.

"Not even for a second." As I say it I realize how true it is.
Even more than Ben or Chilton, I don't have to think about
whether I can trust Truman. I just do. He holds my gaze a second longer and I see something shift in his eyes. The perpetual
wariness melts, leaving a naked look I haven't seen since freshman year.

"I don't think it's you either, Nell. And me thinking it's not
Laine? That's not because I don't think she isn't capable; it's
because I know she'd have come for me first after what I did
to her."

Before I can ask him what he means by that, he turns and
walks out through the back door, the gun tucked close to his
body. I follow him around the side of the house, both of us
staying under the eaves where the snow isn't as deep and the
wall gives us support on the ice. I regret not getting those cleats
first. I scan the tree line as we go, looking for figures lurking

in the darkening shadows, but if anyone is watching, they're well hidden. When we reach the generator, we find it sheathed in ice, but the ice is broken along the seal and it opens easily. Ruth must have already opened it—so why didn't she restart it? And where is she? I shine my phone flashlight on the monitor and read the message: "Stopped—Error Code 1300." I vaguely recall Ruth saying she had the electrician show her how to restart it.

"If Ruth made it out here, she would have known how to restart it," I say.

"Maybe she didn't get a chance," Truman says, pointing to something on the ground. I look down and see a piece of plastic sticking out of a snowdrift where the ice has been shattered. I bend over to retrieve it and feel a sickening lurch in my stomach. It's the stem of Ruth's glasses—I recognize the shape and teal color immediately. Digging deeper, I find the rest of her glasses, trampled in the snow.

"Damn it, Ruth can't see at all without her glasses. She wouldn't go anywhere without them. Unless someone forced her." I dig until my fingers, numb from the snow, graze something square and plastic. I pull out a cell phone, its screen cracked. It still has enough power to show the lock screen wallpaper—a photo of a curly-haired girl holding a small shaggy dog. "This is Nina's phone," I say, my throat constricting at the sight of Nina's smiling face, happier than I've ever seen her. What have we done to you, Nina? I wonder helplessly. It had been my job to keep her safe here at Briarwood and I've thoroughly failed.

"There's something else here," Truman says, pointing to the generator. There's a piece of folded paper taped to the inside of the lid. I reach for it, imagining it will be instructions on how to restart the generator. Ruth would have left instructions inside the lid. But the moment I touch the paper my heart clenches. I recognize the heavy textured weave even before I open it and see the gilt embossed monogram, the lines curling together as tight as the knot forming in my throat. I feel Truman's cheek graze mine as he leans over my shoulder and hear the sharp intake of his breath as he recognizes what I recognize. Laine's monogram and Laine's handwriting. *Nell,* it reads, *we have to talk. You know where to meet me. Come alone.*

"You can't go," Truman says, looking up from the note. "How do you even know where she is?"

But I do know.

I look up at the mountain. It's fully dark now but the cloud cover has broken over the ridge revealing a single light. High Tor lit up like a beacon for me to follow.

# CHAPTER THIRTY-FIVE

*THEN*

CHILTON REFUSED TO talk to me on the walk back from Main.

"I thought you knew," I pleaded. "Laine arranged the scholarship for me because my mother couldn't afford to pay my tuition. I'm sure if you needed a scholarship she would have given you one . . ."

I blathered on until we reached Wilder Hall and Chilton turned on me in front of the arched doorway. "I should have known from the first day that you'd get what you wanted. All that bullshit about the Lady of Shalott and your *curse* and 'Let me take the tiniest room so no one thinks I'm a threat.' Well, you've gotten what you wanted—Laine all to yourself. You can have her. Good luck cleaning up the mess after Moss rips her book apart. And good luck with her when she learns that you've been trying to steal her boyfriend."

With that she turned on her heel and flung open the doors, leaving them wide open. I could hear voices from the rear of the house—seminar breaking up—and Chilton greeting everyone, hinting at a big surprise on Luminaria, and Moss laughing his big booming laugh.

"What—a sacrifice perhaps? Like in the old days? Are you going to slaughter me along with the old year?" And then Laine's voice, sweet and high: "That *is* what the druids would do—sacrifice the Raven King at the winter solstice."

I went upstairs before anyone could see me. Would Chilton tell Laine that I had gone to Dean Hotchkiss to complain about Moss? And what would Hotchkiss tell Moss when he talked to him? He'd never say it was Chilton Prior who complained to him. Far easier to throw me to the lions.

I spent the next three days in excruciating anxiety, barely able to focus on the last pages of my senior thesis, waiting for Hotchkiss to talk to Moss and wondering what the outcome would be. I listened to every footfall outside my door to see if Chilton would go to Laine and tell her we'd been to see the dean. I braced myself for Laine to come pound on my door demanding why I'd gone against her wishes. But no one stirred outside in the hall. Even Truman ceased his midnight visits.

We were all holed up in our rooms working, once again the sound of typing deafening. I added to it myself, typing all the scribbled pages I'd produced over the last months. Typing it, I felt as if I were translating some ancient text that had been found in the desert written by a people who had long since vanished from the earth. The girl who had come to an elite college, in my mostly autobiographical novel, and worried about fitting in seemed so hopelessly naive I could barely stand to follow her progress. *Get out!* I wanted to scream at her, as if she were the hapless victim in a slasher movie. *Get out now while you can!*

But it was too late to change it now. I typed it all up and delivered the manuscript to the table outside Moss's study the morning of the Luminaria. I saw that Miranda, Chilton, Dodie, and Ben had already delivered theirs. Lance came up behind me, clad in plaid pajamas, hair sticking straight up, cradling an untidy pile of papers as if it were a teddy bear. Darla flounced down after him, skeletal in a silk kimono, clasping a lavender box. She placed it carefully on top of the pile, closed her eyes, and made some mysterious hand gestures over it.

"Do you think she's cursing everyone else's manuscript?"

Truman asked, coming up behind me. He was in the same jeans, Nirvana T-shirt, and denim jacket he'd been wearing for the last three days and had grown a scruffy beard. He smelled like cigarettes and stale coffee.

"She's probably just turned them all into gibberish," I said.

"Mine won't have far to go," he said, tossing a rubber-banded stack onto the pile. "Anyone have any lighter fluid? We might as well torch the whole lot as expect anything good to come out of Moss reading them."

"Speak for yourself." Laine walked in from the Great Hall in her long black cashmere coat and riding boots, carrying with her the cold winter air and a whiff of Shalimar. Where had she been? I hadn't heard her go out this morning. She carried a worn canvas-and-leather satchel out of which she produced a hefty manuscript tied with twine. She placed it on top of the pile and then turned around, smiling. "There, that's done. Does anyone want to have breakfast at the Nook? English muffins on me."

IT WAS LIKE the old Laine had come back. Hair washed and gleaming, radiant in a pale yellow cashmere sweater and some great-aunt's pearls, she held court in the Nook, laughing and making plans for the Luminaria.

"Chilton, you said you and Nell were working on a surprise the other day. What was it?"

I stared at Chilton in a panic, sure that now she would expose our perfidy here in front of everyone, but she only smiled. "I found us some robes in the drama department and Nell here"—she turned to me with a barbed smile—"has been making solstice crowns. Or at least she said she would. Have you forgotten, Nell?"

Laine turned to me, beaming. I noticed, though, a hectic gleam to her eyes. "Crowns? For us to wear? How perfect!"

"Yes, well, I've gotten a bit behind, what with finishing up my senior thesis."

"That's all right," Laine said, smiling beneficently, "we'll finish them together. What do we need?"

"Holly," I said automatically. "Juniper, spruce, pine, bittersweet—"

I might have gone on listing winter botanicals if Dodie hadn't blurted out, "I know where there's a big patch behind Klement Hall. We can all go gather some."

"What a perfect way to spend our last day together," Laine said.

"Our last day together?" Truman and I echoed at the same time.

"Until after break," Laine said, her smile slipping. "'Gather ye rosebuds while ye may,'" she quoted, "or in this case, your holly berries and pine cones."

And so, we spent that day, the shortest one of the year—although it felt like the longest to me—foraging through the woody groves of the campus for holly, juniper, pine boughs, witch hazel, and bittersweet. Truman helpfully produced a switchblade and Ben a pocketknife. We brought back armfuls of fragrant greens into Wilder Hall and dumped them on the long table in the Great Hall. Dodie remembered that there was a reel of gardening wire in the botany department greenhouse and ran to get it. She seemed infected with Laine's manic energy—we all did. Darla put some kind of Gregorian chants on the stereo, and Lance and Miranda disappeared into the kitchen to make glogg.

Moss's door remained closed, the piles of manuscripts gone from the table.

"Do you think he's already reading them?" Lance asked when he brought in a steaming punch bowl.

"Emily Dawes said he read straight through the break her year and returned drafts by New Year's Day," Miranda said authoritatively. "I delivered mine first this morning so he's probably reading mine now."

"He promised to do mine first," Laine said, twisting a bittersweet vine into her crown. "He's going to give me notes before I leave tomorrow so I can work on it over break. He said he'd write the letter to his agent as soon as he finished reading it so I could submit my manuscript right away."

"Already?" Darla asked. "Won't you need the rest of the year to finish revising it?"

"I don't think it will need much in the way of revision," Laine said with confidence. "Sometimes you just know when something is right."

She hummed while she added a finishing touch to her crown, her eyes unfocused, as if she were gazing into her future and she had already moved on without us. When she went to the far side of the hall to arrange some pine boughs on the mantel, I followed her.

"You're leaving tomorrow?" I asked. "I thought we were going to the city for a few days."

"Oh," she said, twisting a piece of holly around a juniper branch. "Didn't I tell you there was a change of plans? I have to go straight back to Maine to work on Moss's notes. You don't mind, do you? We can go to the city in the spring. I'll have to go anyhow to meet Moss's agent then."

She looked up from the juniper branch, but she didn't seem to see me. Her gaze had drifted a few inches over my head. I turned and saw that Moss had appeared in the doorway.

"Miss Bishop," he said in a booming voice, "come to my study, please. I'd like to discuss your brilliant novel."

Laine's face lit up brighter than the Christmas lights.

"Thank Gawd," Chilton said as Laine left without looking back. "She'd have been hell to live with if he didn't like it."

"Of course he liked it," Miranda said spitefully. "She's Laine

Wilder Bishop. She could have finger-painted it and he'd have said it was brilliant."

"That's not fair," Dodie said. "We didn't even put our names on our final projects. How would he even know which one was Laine's?"

Darla sniggered. "Oh please, we all know whose is whose. Yours is about mushroom people, Dodie. Truman's sounds like a Raymond Chandler wannabe. Laine's got that blur-girl in it—"

"That's Nell's," Ben said.

I shrugged, uncomfortable with the whole topic. "We both have blur-girls . . . They're sort of an archetype . . . like from . . ."

"The mythic sea?" Chilton and Ben said at the same time.

I excused myself then. As I walked toward the back stairs, I saw the study door open and Laine come out clutching an envelope in her hands. The agent letter, I imagined, that she'd worked so hard to get. She rushed up the stairs, so immersed in the vision of her bright future that she didn't notice me in the hallway. At least she'd be happy now, I thought as I went to my room to change. As Chilton had said, she'd have been hell to live with if Moss hadn't liked her book.

I didn't see her again until four o'clock, at the door to Moss's study, our usual hour for seminar and today the appointed time to gather for a celebratory glass of sherry before our departure for the Luminaria. Her face looked shiny and bright as if she'd just scrubbed it.

"Hey," I said, "is everything all right?"

She shrugged. "I just broke up with Truman and he said some mean things." I must have looked shocked because she added, "It was only a matter of time. I need to focus on my book and he doesn't understand that. Now you can have him."

"Laine—" I began.

"Don't pretend, Nell. Do you think I don't hear him go into your room every night? Please. I hope you'll both be very happy."

With that she turned and went into the study. I followed, mute and dumbfounded, and found everyone waiting, wearing the green robes Chilton had unearthed from the drama department and the holly and spruce crowns we had made. Chilton and Dodie had crafted a special one for Moss, woven from spruce and holly but also quilted with moss to celebrate his name and fitted with candles like the Saint Lucia's wreaths that Dodie had copied from a childhood Christmas doll.

"Ah, I see you've decided to burn me alive," Moss quipped jovially. "An effigy won't do for you lot, eh?"

We all laughed too loudly at the joke and gulped down our tiny glasses of sweet sherry. Laine sat stiffly on the chesterfield, her eyes as glassy as the stuffed stag's above the mantel. What had Truman said to her, I wondered, to spoil the pleasure of Moss's approval? Had he, I fretted, said anything about me? When I looked toward her she wouldn't meet my eye.

"Don't you want to wait until after I've read your offerings?" he asked, running with the joke like a dog with a bone. "Ha! I see it now, you've gathered to slay the old Raven King and crown the new. Don't forget," he said, extracting a key from his pants pocket, "I hold the only key to the tower. You can't get rid of me so easily."

Then he stood up and held out his arms like a child waiting to be dressed while Chilton and Dodie helped him into his robe. "Who will crown me?" he demanded, his eyes roving over us and landing on Laine. "Ah, a bishop to crown the king, that seems fitting."

Laine, a frozen smile pasted on her face, approached with the holly crown and stood on tiptoe to put it on Moss's head. Then we were all scrambling to follow Moss down the long narrow hall, through the Great Hall decked in greenery, where someone had set out kerosene lanterns for each of us to take. When we'd lit the lanterns and the candles on Moss's crown,

Moss flung open the doors and strode outside. The air was cold and full of silvery sparks of fine snow as if the atmosphere were charged with electricity. We marched two by two behind Moss to the bowl below the mountains. Mirror Lake was covered by a glaze of ice reflecting the sinking sun as if a fire were stoked beneath its surface. A small group of students and faculty had gathered by a bonfire, sipping Styrofoam cups of cider and hot cocoa. Truman had brought a goatskin flask of glogg, which we passed among us. A murmur rose to greet us and I felt the jealous eyes of other students upon us. We were the anointed ones, the ones chosen for the famous senior seminar. I remembered watching our counterparts in years past climb the mountain first and waiting to see the beacon lit to begin the general procession. Sometimes it took longer than an hour and there were whispers of some strange rite the Raven Society performed. I used to wonder what it felt like to *belong,* but as we began to climb the snaking path I felt thin and insubstantial, as if we were merely a reflection cast up from the frozen lake. Maybe that was the point, to make a mark and vanish, leaving only the best part of ourselves behind. When I looked down, I saw our procession reflected in the frozen lake below us, like a comet's tail, and felt, at last, as if I did truly belong to something even if that something was already burning itself out.

Then I saw Bridget Feeley, in a red duffle coat and fuzzy earmuffs, coming up the trail behind us, a folded note grasped in her mittened hand. Her eyes met mine and she held up the note, signaling me to slow down. It was for Moss, I somehow knew, from Dean Hotchkiss. He had waited until now to deliver the fateful blow and entrusted the message to a *student* to humiliate him. This was his revenge, I realized, for having to kowtow to Moss because he was the famous writer who drew students and alumni donations to Briarwood. What would the note say? Would he name me as the person who had complained?

I had to know.

I tried to catch Truman's eye but he was trying to keep up with Laine, who was trying to keep up with Moss. When I stopped walking Miranda hissed at me to keep moving or get out of the way. I stepped aside and let her and Lance pass; Darla and Ben came after them.

"What's wrong?" Ben asked.

"Nothing, I just—" Before I could answer Bridget reached us.

"I wanted you to tell Professor Moss to slow down so I could deliver this," she said, waving the crumpled note in my face.

"How was I to know that?" I snapped back. "Anyway, I don't think Moss would stop. He's always the one to light the beacon in High Tor. Why don't you give it to me and I'll bring it to him?"

"Dean Hotchkiss said to deliver it straight to Professor Moss," she said, slipping the note protectively into her pocket. She sidled past me and Ben, hugging the rockface as if she were afraid I might push her over.

"What's up?" Ben hissed. "Why do you care about that note?"

"I don't. I just don't want anything to ruin the day."

I hurried behind Bridget, who was making good time now that we'd reached the ridge. She was heading straight for High Tor where Moss and the others had paused outside the tower, standing in a semicircle on the flagstone apron. What were they waiting for? If only they would just go inside and shut the tower door behind them.

"Moss wants to take a picture," Laine called to us, "before the light dies. Hurry! I've relit the candles in his crown but they'll go out again soon." Her cheeks were flushed, the rose and violet sky reflected in her face. When she saw Bridget, though, her eyes narrowed. She held out a camera. "You can take the picture, Bridge," she said, shoving the camera toward her. "Truman, show her how."

"I know how to use a camera," Bridget said, taking her mittened hands out of her pockets. I watched for the note, hoping it might fall out and get snatched away by the wind, but she shoved it back in along with her mittens. Her hands looked raw and chapped in the cold air as she grasped the boxy camera. Laine motioned for me to stand on the other side of Moss and for Ben to stand on the other side of me. "Kneel down in front of me, Dodie, you're the shortest. Darla and Lance can kneel on either side. Tru, squeeze in between Chilton and Miranda."

When we were arranged to Laine's liking, Bridget snapped the picture.

"One more," Laine said, "just in case."

But Bridget was already handing back the camera with one hand and the note to Moss with the other. "Dean Hotchkiss told me to give this to you," she said to him.

Moss looked at the note in Bridget's hand as if he wasn't sure what it was. The flush of good spirits that had buoyed him out of Wilder Hall and up the mountain had subsided and now he looked tired and sweaty and confused. I felt a pang of sympathy for him. I reached out to intercept the note but I was too late; Moss already had it. I dropped my hand awkwardly and noticed Laine staring at me while Moss fumbled the note open.

"What's this?" he roared, his eyes raking us over one by one. "Someone has *complained*? Someone has called my fitness to teach into question?"

"I've heard Laine talking with the others," Miranda said suddenly. "Complaining about your comments and suggesting you weren't as sharp as you used to be."

I heard Laine gasp and then, so quickly her hand was a blur, she slapped Miranda across the face, the sound sharp in the still, cold air.

"You bitch!" Miranda cried, cradling her face. "Wait until I tell Dean Hotchkiss. You all saw—"

She turned in a circle, her eyes skimming over each of us,

dismissing me and Chilton and Dodie and Truman. "Oh, of course you four will stick with your precious Laine and you"— her eyes landed on Ben—"you'll go along with whatever Nell wants in the hope she'll finally go to bed with you." She turned to Lance and Darla. "What about you two? Whose side are you on?"

"Please don't make me pick sides—" Lance pleaded.

But Miranda cut him off. "You already chose your side when you went to Dean Hotchkiss to complain about Laine typing for Moss."

Lance's mouth gaped open but nothing came out. Miranda turned to Laine. "I know you thought it was me, but it wasn't and we all saw Lance go into the dean's office that day."

"I was only trying to help!" Lance cried, turning to Laine: "I was afraid you were being taken advantage of."

"Not everyone is so easy to take advantage of," Laine told Lance in an icy voice.

Miranda smiled at the wounded look on Lance's face and then turned to Darla. "And you, are you going to stay here with Laine after the way she's made fun of you all year for your eating disorder?"

"As if *you* didn't," Darla snapped back and then narrowed her eyes at the rest of us. "As if you all didn't. I'm not picking sides; I'm done with *everyone* here. I'm just going. Are you coming, Lance?"

Lance looked around the group, his eyes wide and glassy as those of a deer caught in the headlights. I could tell he was about to cry. I knew I should say something to him, but I felt frozen to the spot, as if I were still posing for our group picture. "I guess I'm not on anyone's team," he said sadly, turning to leave with Darla.

Miranda smiled smugly at the tumult she had created and turned to join Darla and Lance, but as she passed Moss she stopped.

"Why do you think Laine was so anxious to get that letter to your agent now?" she asked him, her voice low and insinuating. "I heard her saying she wanted to make sure she got the letter while you were still able to write one." Then she turned on her heel and followed Darla and Lance to the path down the mountain, where they all vanished behind the stone rampart.

"Is that true, Miss Bishop?" Moss asked, his voice thin and reedy in the wind. "Is that all you wanted from me?" He sounded suddenly more wounded than angry.

I stepped forward. "Professor Moss—" I began, my eyes meeting Laine's. Hers widened as she realized what had happened. I could tell by the look of betrayal on her face that she guessed I was the one who had gone behind her back and complained. "It wasn't Laine. It was me. I went to Dean Hotchkiss."

Moss wheeled on me, his great head swinging like a bull's after it's been stunned, the candles on his crown sputtering and spraying wax. A drop of hot wax rolled down and hit him in the eye. He cried out in pain. Partially blinded, he raised his hand to bat it away. Laine stepped forward to help him. At her touch he flung out his hand and struck her cheek. When she cried out, he spat at her. "You talentless hack. You'll never amount to anything. I can still take back that letter."

Laine's face in the red glare of the setting sun seemed to break. Moss, still half blind from the hot wax, lumbered toward her and she, whether from rage or fear or shame or some lethal brew of all three, placed both her hands on his chest and *pushed*.

The push sent him stumbling backward and then he went down, like a tree felled by a single stroke of an ax, straight back. His head hit the flagstone with a crack that echoed across the ridge. A tremor passed through him, a convulsion I felt in the soles of my feet as if the ground beneath me trembled. And then he lay still.

# CHAPTER THIRTY-SIX

*NOW*

TRUMAN ARGUES WITH me as we make our way back around the house to the front entrance. "You can't go alone."

"I have to or she might kill Ruth and Nina."

"How do you know she'll let them go even if you follow her rules?"

"I don't," I say, going in the front door and getting the cleats from the boot bench. "But at least it gives Ruth and Nina a chance, and I don't think Laine wants to kill them. They've done nothing to hurt her; it's me she wants."

"She won't stop with you," Truman says, squatting down next to me as I strap on the cleats.

"I'll tell her Ben and Chilton shot each other, which is true, and that you got hit in the cross fire. I'll say you're all dead. Hopefully it'll buy you enough time to keep safe in the house until the police come." I find a lantern on the foyer table and see it's full. I open the little drawer and rummage around for a box of matches.

"Stop it!" Truman cries, grabbing my hand as I strike a match. "Why are you so set on sacrificing yourself?"

"Because this is all my fault," I say, shaking his hand away before the match can burn both of us. "I let this happen. I betrayed Laine. I'm the reason she was so hurt and angry that she struck out at Moss and pushed him. I went behind her back and ruined everything she was working for. If it wasn't for what I did, she would never have become a recluse. When Hotch told her that one of us was willing to back up his accusation, she must have thought it was me. I have to be the one who ends this."

I strike another match but my hand is shaking so hard I can't light the wick. Truman lays his hand on mine to steady it. "It's my fault, too," he says. "That day—the day of the Luminaria— Laine and I fought. I said some things I shouldn't have. I've always thought that when she pushed Moss, it was me she wanted to push."

I stare at him in the glare of the lantern. His face looks naked and exposed. I shake my head. "It was me she was angry at. She realized that I'd complained to Dean Hotchkiss about Moss."

When he still looks unconvinced, I add, "She told me she had broken up with you and that you said some mean things in response but that's not what she was really angry about. She'd guessed . . ." I pause, not sure I can confess this last part but then I realize I might never get another chance to. "She'd guessed how I felt about you and was angry at me for that, too. So, you see, it was doubly my fault. Nothing you said to her could have made her as angry as my betraying her."

He opens his mouth to speak but nothing comes out. My revelations have clearly shocked him, which is what I intended. I use the moment to turn. Before I do he presses something hard and cold in my hand. Chilton's gun.

AS I WALK toward Mirror Lake, holding my lantern high, a full moon rises behind me in the east, casting my shadow onto the silvered ice. I don't need the lantern to see in the moonlight but I want Laine to see me and see that I'm alone as she asked. Stepping onto Mirror Lake feels like presenting myself on an altar for sacrifice. Above me the lit window of High Tor gazes down on me like a jaundiced eye. If Laine is looking out that window she'll see me crossing the lake alone. The whole zig-zag path up the mountain will be visible to her from the tower where we hid Moss's body twenty-five years ago.

# CHAPTER THIRTY-SEVEN

*THEN*

"WHAT ARE WE going to do with him?" Laine cried as soon as we determined he was dead.

"We'll just say it was an accident," Chilton answered.

"It wasn't an accident," Bridget said. "Laine pushed him."

Laine wheeled on her. I think we'd all forgotten Bridget was there. "It was your fault for bringing that message. I'll tell everyone that he yelled at you, and you were the one who pushed him."

Bridget's eyes widened and then, as Laine stepped toward her, she bolted like a scared rabbit. Instead of heading to the path down the mountain, though, she ran west, across the pine barrens toward the ice caves.

"Go after her!" Laine barked at no one in particular, but of course it was Dodie, so used to following Laine's orders, who moved first. She took after Bridget across the ridge, following the deer trails that wound in among the low pine shrubs like a maze.

"Don't just stand there," Laine said, turning back to the rest of us. "Ben and Truman, get Moss inside the tower!"

"I will not!" Ben said, placing himself in between Laine and Moss's body as if he were guarding it. "We have to call the police—"

"Are you sure you want to be questioned by the police, Ben? Who are they more likely to suspect of pushing a big man like

Hugo Moss? Little me or a fit young man like yourself? And I wonder who they will be more inclined to believe. And if you're arrested what will happen to your dreams of becoming a lawyer?"

Ben stared at Laine, his face turning as red as the blood on the flagstones, then he shifted his gaze to me, the pleading look in his eyes asking me who I'd choose—him or Laine. I wanted to tell him that I'd stand up for him—I'd never let Laine falsely accuse him—but then the thought of being questioned by the police scared me. I'd seen how things went for Laine when she came in contact with authority. It was never her who had to face the consequences. When Ben saw that I wasn't going to defend him I saw something die in his eyes. Laine saw it, too.

"Good. Now wash that up," she added, pointing toward the blood on the flagstone. Then she grabbed Truman's flask and poured the rest of the glogg over the blood. "There," she said as if her gesture had solved everything. She seemed seized with a mania like a maenad in a Greek play. When she knelt beside Moss's body, I thought for one crazy moment that she was going to rend his clothing, but she only reached into his pocket and took out the key to the tower. "When you've got Moss inside lock the door and tell everyone that Moss went looking for Bridget when she ran off and he took the only key to the tower. We'll go take care of her and make sure she doesn't say anything." She started off across the ridge, glancing back at me and Chilton. "Are you coming?" she asked.

Chilton nodded and glanced at me. "Please," she whispered. "I don't want to deal with her on my own."

It was the first time Chilton had ever said *please* to me and it shocked me into following.

We threaded our way single file along the narrow trails toward the ridge where the figures of Dodie and Bridget were dark silhouettes against the violet scrim of western sky like cut-out puppets in a pantomime, but then Dodie drew nearer to

Bridget, reached out her arm to grab her flapping hood, and lunged forward, the force of her momentum pushing Bridget forward into a stumble—

And then Bridget vanished as completely as if she *had* been a puppet snatched under the stage by the puppeteer. Only, the sharp crack reverberating over the ridge told a different story. When Laine, Chilton, and I reached Dodie, we found her crouched on the edge of a chasm. It was the cave we'd explored earlier in the year—Merlin's Cave.

"What the hell happened?" Laine demanded.

"She-she-she *fell!*" Dodie cried. "I didn't push her."

"You idiot!" Laine cried. "I told you to stop her, not *kill* her."

Dodie shrank further into herself and began to rock back and forth.

"Are we sure she's dead, though?" Chilton asked, peering down into the cavern.

"I don't know, Chill," Laine replied venomously, "why don't you go down and check. You've taken everything else into your own hands lately."

Chilton stared at Laine and then at me. "I didn't tell her—" I began, but Chilton only clucked her tongue and began climbing down into the cave. I held my lantern up so she'd see where she was going but she was soon swallowed by the darkness. "Careful," I warned, "there's a steep drop over the side of the steps." As I peered into the void, I considered following her— and never coming back. Being swallowed up by the earth felt like a better option than standing there in the cold with Laine, who seemed to be exuding her own personal chill.

"So, what didn't you tell me?" Laine asked after a moment.

There didn't seem to be much point in hiding it any longer, not with Moss dead.

"Chilton and I went to see Dean Hotchkiss to complain about Moss's behavior. We did it for *you,* Laine. The way he was treating you . . . well, you saw how he acted tonight and the things he said to you. You know he wouldn't have said those things if he wasn't jealous of your talent and aware he was losing all of his. He was coming at you like a madman. No one would blame you for pushing him back. We'll say it was self-defense."

"We'll say nothing at all," she said, her voice so cold it made me shiver. Before I could respond Chilton emerged from the cave, her face so white she might have been one of those albino creatures that spend their whole lives underground.

"Is she . . . ?" I began.

"Her head was cracked open like an egg," she said.

Dodie began to wail.

"Shut up!" Laine barked. "We have enough problems without you going into hysterics, Dorothy Ann. Chilton, take her back to Wilder and keep her quiet. Give her one of those sleeping pills you got from your mother. Don't let her talk to anyone. Nell and I will go back to High Tor and tell Security that Bridget ran off because Moss spoke harshly to her, and he went to look for her. We'll wait until later tonight when everyone from the Luminaria has gone and then we'll carry Moss's body out here—someplace where it will be visible in the morning. When they find it, everyone will think he fell while looking for Bridget. He'll die a hero's death, which would have made him happy."

"And what about Bridget?" I asked, looking down into the dark gash in the earth, the cold air rising up out of it seeping into my bones.

"What about her?" Laine asked. "If they find her everyone will assume she fell and cracked her head open. If they don't, they'll assume the same thing. She'll become one of the legends of Briarwood, another girl who was lost in the ice caves. She'll be better remembered than she ever would have been otherwise."

## CHAPTER THIRTY-EIGHT

*NOW*

WHEN I REACH the top of the ridge I stop for a moment, struggling to catch my breath. It's always colder on the ridge, the reservoirs of ice inside the caves exuding an arctic chill, but tonight it feels as if that air is filling my lungs with ice water instead of oxygen.

The door to the tower is closed but when I try it, I find it's unlocked. I remember Moss boasting that he had the only key, but it had been easy enough for Laine to take it from his pocket once he was dead. But even if she'd kept it, the locks were changed years ago. How did she get a key? As I open the door, I remember the particular dank mineral odor of the stones. Looking up the spiral stairs that lead to the beacon light on top feels like looking up from the bottom of a well. A muffled moan fills the stone shaft and for a moment I think the sound has come from someplace deep inside me, but then I realize it's coming from above and that it must be Nina or Ruth, gagged and crying out to be saved.

"I'm here," I shout. "You can let them go, Laine. I've done what you asked me to do. I'm alone."

I wait and hear only the echo of my own voice—*alone-alone-alone*—as if mocking me. I take out Chilton's gun and hold it tight to my side as I start up the stairs.

The moment I set a foot on the wrought iron staircase I realize how unsafe it is. The whole structure groans and trembles, straining at the rivets drilled into the stone wall. An engineer deemed it unsafe ten years ago.

How do I know Laine is even still here? What if her plan is to let the whole structure come down, plummeting Ruth and Nina and me to the stone floor and crushing us?

"Laine?" I say experimentally, as I take another step.

No answer.

I keep going up—there's really no other option—and I keep talking because otherwise I'll have to hear the voices in my head. "I can understand how angry it made you when Hotch threatened to blackmail you. I want you to know I had nothing to do with that. I've kept our secret all these years—"

The stairs lurch suddenly, tearing a bolt out of the wall. I hear it hit the floor far below me with a percussive clang that reminds me of the *crack* that came out of the cave twenty-five years ago.

"I've tried to honor your legacy," I go on, gripping the rusted banister. "Your Writers House endowment has done so much good over the years for students like Nina. I know you don't want to hurt her—or Ruth, who's worked tirelessly for the program. Let them go and I'll take responsibility for what's happened now—for Miranda, Hotch, Darla, Lance . . ." I pause a moment and then add Ben and Chilton and Truman, too. "Their deaths are all my fault. I'll say I did it. I'll write a confession and then jump from the tower if you'll only let Ruth and Nina go."

I've come to the last turn of the stairs. A few more steps and my head will clear the opening to the platform. I try to peer through the perforated grate to see where Laine is, but the light from the lantern casts a crazy web of shadows that I can't see through.

*Out flew the web and floated wide . . .*

The old lines sound in my head in Laine's sweet voice that

first day she found me in Rowan Hall. I thought she had released me from my solitary curse but what she'd really done was
ensnare me in a web of her making—

Or maybe it was always of my own making.

I take the final steps and come up onto the platform. For a
moment the glare of the lantern blinds me and then, as I shade
my eyes, my vision seems to double. I see two figures bound to
chairs and gagged—Nina, apparently unconscious, and Ruth,
wide-eyed and terrified. I turn around and survey the top floor
of the tower, but there's no one else here. Ruth moans and
shakes the chair, making the whole inner skeleton of the stairs
and platform tremble. I rush to her first, imagining how painful
the ropes are on her older joints. I put the gun in my pocket and
remove her gag.

"Thank God!" she cries out. "My arms! I can't feel them anymore."

I reach behind her, Ruth slumping heavily against me as I
untie the knots. They come undone easily enough, though, as
if Laine had been rushed when she tied them—or maybe she'd
felt sorry for Ruth and tied them loosely. I feel Ruth's hands
clutching my coat as if hanging on to me for dear life.

"Do you know where Laine went?" I ask, kneeling to untie
her legs.

"To hell, I imagine, after you pushed her in the cave twenty-
five years ago," Ruth says.

I sit back on my heels and stare up at Ruth, only this woman
suddenly looks nothing like the Ruth I know. Maybe it's because
she's not wearing her glasses or because her bangs are pushed
away from her face, revealing a nasty scar along the hairline, or
because the expression of smug disdain is one I've never seen
on Ruth's face. Or maybe it's the gun in her hand—Chilton's
gun, I realize, feeling in my empty pocket—that clicks the final
piece into place. Suddenly, I recognize Bridget Feeley.

# CHAPTER THIRTY-NINE

*THEN*

ON OUR WAY back to High Tor from the cave it started to snow. When I looked up at the falling flakes, I saw a flare streak through the sky. It looked like a comet, like one of the ill-fated omens I'd read about in Roman history, but then Laine said, "It's an emergency flare to alert the town that someone's gone missing on the mountain. They must have believed Ben and Truman when they said Moss went looking for Bridget."

Despite her words, I half hoped that when we got back to High Tor, we'd find a crowd gathered around Moss's body, our crime (and I *did* already think of it as *our* crime) revealed, the jig up. Maybe I already suspected what covering it up would do to each of us—or maybe I just wanted to see Laine face the consequences of her actions without a safety net to catch her for once. But instead, the flagstone apron where Moss had lain was now full of students, teachers, and staff along with two local police officers organizing a search. I looked anxiously for the bloodstain that Laine had hastily camouflaged with spilled wine, but the flagstones were already covered by a few inches of snow. Truman was telling the story Laine had made up to Dean Hotchkiss while Ben stood a few feet away, shivering in his sweatshirt, glaring at Truman but not contradicting him.

"Moss barked at the girl," Truman was saying, "and she ran off. Moss felt bad and headed after her and a few of us went with him—oh, here's Laine and Nell now," he added. "Any luck, girls?"

"No," Laine said before I could answer. "We searched the southern slope and then Moss said he was going to search the western ridge where the ice caves are but he wanted us to go back for reinforcements and warmer clothes and flashlights. We tried to convince him to come with us but you know how Professor Moss is." She smiled at Dean Hotchkiss. "He's very stubborn."

"I've had some word that he's been behaving erratically lately," he said.

Laine bit her lip and looked embarrassed, then she stepped closer to Dean Hotchkiss, glancing side to side as if to check to make sure no one else would overhear, but when she spoke her voice was loud and clear. "Frankly, yes, Dean Hotchkiss. That's true. Chilton and Nell told me they'd been to see you, which I think was very brave of them." She gave me such an admiring glance I almost felt relieved before remembering that it was all an act. "I was too afraid of tarnishing his reputation but now he's gone off half-cocked. Will you send out searchers for him and poor Bridget? I'm so afraid they'll both freeze to death or break their necks in those treacherous caves." Laine glanced from Hotchkiss to me but I couldn't meet her eyes.

"I'm going to join the searchers," I said, seeing Miss Higgins arriving on the ridge, already equipped with orange neon vests, flashlights, and walkie-talkies. Her eye fell on me accusingly, as if she'd known I was no good from the moment I allowed Laine's influence to get me a better place in the registration line.

As I turned to walk toward the search groups forming around her, Ben joined me. "We have to talk," he said. "We can still stop this."

Making sure no one was close enough to hear, I hissed, "Bridget is dead. It will fall on poor Dodie if we don't go along with this and it all comes out." When he didn't respond I added, "You went along with dragging Moss into the tower. It's too late to go back now."

I joined a group with Kara and Jocelyn, who looked surprised I was with them and not my Raven Society friends. We searched until the snow started coming down too hard and our leader received a crackly message on her walkie-talkie that the search was being called off; it was too dangerous to proceed.

I watched Kara and Jocelyn heading back to their dorm, wishing I could go with them and spend the rest of the night drinking hot cocoa and conjugating irregular Latin verbs, but I made my way back to Wilder Hall, half expecting to find the police there. Instead, I was greeted by Laine at the front door demanding where I'd gone off to.

"We have to go up the back path to the tower and move Moss's body out onto the ridge before it stops snowing. He has to be there long enough for the snow to cover him and conceal our footprints."

"There's a problem," Ben said, coming up behind her. "A medical examiner will be able to tell that the body's been moved."

Laine clucked her tongue. "In *this* backwater? No one will examine his body because it will be obvious how he died."

Ben started to say something else but Laine wheeled on him. "If you want to be a cop so much, sign up for the police academy—oh, but they probably won't take you if you've been arrested for aiding and abetting a murder. So shut up and help, Breen, or go home to your janitor dad. That's the only job you'll get if this all comes out."

Ben looked from Laine to me, his eyes clearly asking, *Is this what you've sacrificed everything for?* I turned away. "Laine's right," I said, "there's no point arguing about it. We don't have any good choices here."

"When have we ever?" he asked. But he went with us, him and Truman, and me and Laine and Chilton and even Dodie, groggy from the sleeping pill Chilton had given her, because Laine insisted. "We all have to go," she said, "because we're all in this together."

Up on the mountain, the snow was coming down so hard we couldn't see each other's faces, which was just as well. I didn't think any of us would ever want to look at the others again. When we got to the tower, Laine unlocked the door. Moss was inside, lying on the stone floor, one of the green Luminaria robes beneath him and one over him. Ben and Truman must have taken their robes off to afford him this bit of respect and it touched me to think of them doing this together despite their dislike of each other.

Maybe, I thought, as we stood in a circle around the dead body of our former teacher, this terrible thing would bring us all together. Laine must have thought the same thing because she reached out and took my hand and Truman's. Dodie took my other hand and Ben's and he and Chilton completed the circle. "We have to make a pact," Laine said. "We have to swear never to tell anyone about what happened here tonight."

"What if it comes out?" Chilton asked. "What if they find Bridget's body?"

"If they find her body and it comes out, we'll all return to Briarwood and face it together. Whatever happens to one of us happens to all of us. Agreed?"

Laine pinned each of us with her gaze until everyone said yes. Then she bent down and grabbed a corner of the robe. We each took hold and carried him out of the tower. As we trekked across the pine barrens in silence, the weight of Moss's body seeming to grow heavier with every step, I felt the weight of our lies grow heavy as iron chains. When we laid him down on the crest of a cliff facing west the wind tore the blanket off and I saw with a shock how frail and slight his body had become. I had always thought of Moss as a big man but death had shrunk him. How could this scarecrow have been so heavy to carry? As I stood up, though, I could still feel his weight pulling on my arms and shoulders and I guessed that I would always feel it.

"I need to talk to you," Laine said as the others started heading back across the pine barrens. It gave me a little pang, the old feeling of being chosen by her.

"I'm not going to say anything," I said. "You don't have to worry about me. We'll leave this in our past—"

"As if it's ever possible to walk away from the past," Laine said, clucking her tongue. "I'm not worried you'll say anything," she added, scanning the ground with her flashlight. "Look, I think this is the cave Bridget fell in. I just want to look again to make sure."

"I'm not going down there," I said.

"I wasn't going to ask you to," she said, looking back at me. "You know, you could have stood up for yourself at any time. I would have respected you more for it."

I started to laugh, but the sound that came out of me was more a strangled cry.

"Don't pretend, though, that you haven't gotten plenty out of our arrangement."

"Our arrangement?" I echoed.

"Our *friendship*, then. At least I thought that's what it was, but maybe for you, it's always been about what I could give you—entrée into the right classes, summers in Maine, a scholarship. Of course I enjoyed your company, and I have to admit I'm really going to miss you."

"Miss me?" Apparently, I'd been reduced to an echo. Soon I'd be like the Greek nymph with nothing left of me but my voice dwelling in the ice cave with Bridget Feeley's decaying corpse.

"I think it's better if we part ways here. We'll just be a re-minder to each other of these last painful moments and I'll have to focus on my book."

"You mean to go on with it still?" I asked, finding my own voice again. "Without Moss's notes?"

"I don't think his notes would have been much good any-way," she says. "Although I'll *say* they were *invaluable* in my acknowledgments. And he already gave me the letter for his agent. It's really quite flattering." She turned to me, a smile on her face so wide it seemed to stretch into a snarl. Then her eyes flashed as if she were furious with me. I was so startled that I took a step backward, where I teetered on the edge of the cave. Laine stepped closer—to pull me back, I thought—and I reached my hand out to grab on to her. But instead of pulling me, she placed her hand on my shoulder and pushed. I grabbed the lapel of her coat, and she stumbled toward me, losing her balance. As she fell into the cave, I tried to pull her back, but I wasn't fast enough.

And then I heard the crack from below, its echo spreading across the ridge.

# CHAPTER FORTY

*NOW*

I SEEM TO hear the echo of that crack as I stare into the scarred face of the woman standing before me. Her features swim and blur in the glare of the lantern light. For a moment she's the blur-girl of my nightmares, then she's the ghost girl I ran into in the fog, and the girl who sat behind her row of pencils at registration. The girl who was always there but I never really saw all that well—because her face was always half covered by glasses and bangs? Or because I never really looked at her too closely because I was afraid I would see myself in her—an outsider looking in through the bars of the college gates? Of course, I think almost triumphantly, Bridget Feeley has been my blur-girl all along.

"I thought you were dead," I say. "You fell in the cave. Chilton said your head was cracked open . . ." *Like an egg.*

"I guess Chilton didn't check carefully enough. Although it's true my head was cracked open." She touches the scar along her hairline. I remember once glimpsing a bit of the scar and thinking that something awful must have happened to Ruth—*Ruth!* I think of her with a pang as if the woman in front of me has murdered her.

"But how . . . ?" I don't know where to begin, what question to ask first.

She smiles at my confusion so benignly that I see Ruth—*my*

*Ruth!*—for a second and I want to hug her. I must actually lean closer because she jabs the gun muzzle into my sternum so hard I stumble backward and sit down in the chair she was in.

"How did I survive after you all left me for dead?" she asks. "I guess I had a hard skull. It certainly wasn't any thanks to you or your friends, who abandoned me. I don't know how long I lay there, semiconscious, bleeding out, freezing to death, until I came to, hearing voices. Yours, I think, was the first I heard and for a second, I thought you had come back for me. That you weren't as bad as the rest. But then I made out what you were saying—'I'm not going down there'—and I realized you were just like the others. I heard you talking with Laine—she was giving you the brush-off, which would have made me laugh if I wasn't lying there dying. Your dear friend whom you'd kowtowed to since freshman year giving you the heave-ho—and then you gave it back to her, didn't you?"

Bridget—she looks nothing like Ruth now—leans forward and peers into my face. "You'd finally had enough. You pushed her, didn't you?"

"She pushed me!" I cry. "And I pulled back. I tried to keep her from falling . . ."

She clucks her tongue. "That's the problem with you, Ellen, you don't have the power of your convictions. You always second-guess yourself. Pushing Laine was the right thing to do. She was a monster! And you did a good job of it! Talk about cracking like an egg! Bam!" She claps her hands and I jump at the sharp sound—or maybe at the realization that Bridget Feeley was alive listening to us, that she had seen me at my absolute worst. And most of all, that for the last five years, the witness to my crimes has been sitting at my side. "She hit the rock like a sledgehammer! I might have stayed there feeling sorry for myself if you hadn't sent Laine down to join me. *That* gave me an idea and, even better, a plan, and plans have always energized me. When I heard you coming down to find her, I knew what I had to do. Laine and I had both landed on a ledge over a steep drop. I shoved Laine into the pit so you'd never find her—luckily you were too busy calling her name to hear her thump to the bottom. I knew from reading Laine's story about the cave that it went far back so I knew I had some time. And as I said, I had a plan. I hid behind a rock until you passed by, then climbed out of the cave and made my way back to Wilder. All your friends were passed out—none of them even worried that you and Laine hadn't come back yet—so I was able to slip up the back stairs and into Laine's room, which she never locked. None of you locked your rooms. I used to have quite the time exploring when you were in seminar."

"Were we that interesting to you?" I ask.

"You think I was pathetic, don't you? It's what you all thought then. Poor Bridget Feeley, the ugly Bridge Troll with no life of her own, spying on the talented literati of the Raven Society. But you were the ones who were pathetic, scratching away at your feeble stories and carping at each other's work, hanging on to every word of a senile old man. I was studying you all, like an anthropologist studies a primitive tribe. I even had some thought of writing my own book skewering the lot of you. But then I didn't have to. When I got to Laine's room, I saw I had everything I needed—a letter from Moss to his agent recommending a bright new voice and her brilliant debut novel—*The Intended*. There was also, by the way, a letter to you, explaining that she'd heard you and Truman talking above Merlin's Cave and about your wanting him to break up with her. She'd ended with a note saying she needed to talk with you, but she must have changed her mind. I left that for you in the generator—a nice touch, if I say so myself. You see, she knew you had betrayed her. No wonder she was ready to cut ties with you."

I picture Laine turning to me as we stood above the cave, the way her face seemed to crack.

"So you see," Bridget says, "*you* broke her. I just swept up the pieces."

"So, you took the letter—"

"And the cash she had so conveniently taken out of the bank that day for Christmas break, and her suitcase, which was already packed, and her car—"

"In the middle of a snowstorm?"

She sniffs and for a moment looks like Ruth coming in on a snow day. "What's a little snow when you're beginning a new life? Of course, I didn't know yet how far I'd get. If you had gone to the police and told them that you'd pushed Laine into the cave—and that Dodie had pushed me—the jig would have been up! But I already had a feeling you weren't going to do any of that. So I drove to Maine. I knew where the house was from all her personal information I'd filed and typed."

"Weren't you . . . hurt? And bleeding?"

"Oh yes, thank you for remembering. I wrapped one of Laine's nice Hermès scarves around the cut and stopped at an urgent care outside of Worcester. They stitched me up and charged Laine's insurance and believed me when I said I'd had a car accident in the snow and cracked my head on the windshield."

"Why didn't you stay and tell everyone what we did?" I ask. "You could have had your revenge then."

"And then what? Go back to being 'Bridget Feeley, victim'? Is that what you would have chosen when you had the chance to become *Laine Bishop*? Isn't that what you always wanted? Wasn't she your blur-girl?"

Before I can answer—and really, how would I?—we both hear Nina moan.

"Oh dear, she's coming to. I didn't want to give her too much sedative—what? I'm not a monster! But if she comes to and sees me holding a gun on you I'll have to kill her, so we'd better be going. Come on." She waves the gun at me. "I can continue my story on the way there. Go on down first—and remember, if you try anything I'll come back here and kill the girl."

I get to my feet, but before I go to the stairs, I take off my coat and drape it over Nina.

"You're going to be sorry you did that," Ruth says. "We still have a bit of a walk and it's rather nippy out there."

"You've made it clear you intend to kill me," I say. "Nina might as well have a chance to survive."

I start down the iron staircase, its frame trembling under our feet. One good shake and I could bring it down, I think, but then it would bring Nina down as well. I'll have to wait for a chance outside.

When I open the door at the bottom, the icy wind slaps my face. Outside the moon is high in the sky, turning the pine barrens into a frozen sea. I'd be clearly visible, I think, as Bridget pokes me in the back with the gun and steers me onto a narrow path between the stunted shrubs, if I tried to run.

"Go on," I say, "what did you do when you got to Laine's house?"

Bridget laughs, her voice as brittle as the ice cracking under our feet. "I'm glad you're enjoying the story. I have to admit I've always wanted to tell it. It would make a good book, wouldn't it? Like *Mr. Ripley,* which I read while I was hiding out on the causeway. It was even easier for me. No one ever came to that house."

*Isn't it wonderful not seeing anyone,* Laine had said that summer.

"And *you* made it easy for me because you never told anyone that Laine was dead."

"I didn't think she was dead!" I cry. "When I saw her things and her car were gone the next morning, I thought she must have climbed out of the cave and left before I got back to Wilder that night."

"I suppose it was easier to think that than living with the guilt of killing your best friend. And convenient for me, as was the fact that Laine had already arranged for food and liquor delivery. I did get a little tired of sardines and saltines and I don't drink so the gin went down the drain, but I didn't want to arouse suspicion by changing anything. And it was easy enough to use Laine's email—she had bought a brand-new iBook, by the way; so much for that cute little typewriter—and open an online banking account and submit the manuscript with Moss's letter. When I did need to go into the village I just wore an Hermès scarf and big sunglasses. No one batted an eye. Honestly, I don't think Laine ever talked to the locals. I hired a new caretaker who would be discreet and set about managing the Wilder money. You can thank me for preserving the estate to fund the endowment. Those women had no idea how to get a proper return on their investments! Even before the money started rolling in from *The Intended,* I'd restored the Wilder fortune and fixed that crumbling seawall. I made quite a nice hideout for myself."

"So, why'd you leave it?" I ask. We've come out of the pine scrub onto the western ridge. A bank of fog is rising from the valley below, lapping over the ridge like frothed milk. The moonlight paints the ice silver, a dark gash in the rock the only place untouched by its light.

"After a few years I got bored! Those bottles of gin started looking attractive. I could see myself going the way of the Wilder women. So, I began playing around with some alternative identities I could pose under. It's really not that hard. All you need to do is find a dead person who's died far enough from home that their death wasn't registered in their hometown and who didn't have any family. You'd be surprised how many loners there are.

I was a caterer named Bettina for a couple of years in Bangor—close enough to keep tabs on the house on the causeway. Then I found Ruth in the obituaries in Saco, Maine. She was a good ten years older than me but it was easy to add the years with a little hair dye and a few extra pounds. No one really looks at older women anyway. I decided she needed a new life and job at the local community college. It was fun to be on a campus again and learn all the new technologies and see what could be done with them. As you know, I aced all the civil service exams."

"You were always smarter than the rest of us," I say. We've reached the entrance to the cave, where, I knew all along, we were headed. I can feel that cold sulfurous air wafting up against my face. I picture the deep, bottomless pit and the jagged rocks below, where I will land in a moment if I don't stop Bridget.

"Certainly smarter than you, Nell. Five years and you never recognized me! You were so busy trying to atone for what you'd done—as if it were ever possible for what you did—you never really saw me."

"You're right," I say. "I'm sorry. But why risk it—why did you come back to Briarwood?" I'm playing for time, hoping to keep her boasting of her prowess long enough for help to arrive—Truman or the police. She's stopped close enough behind me to make a dash away impossible but not close enough for me to get the gun from her.

"Actually, it was Hotch. I began to notice some anomalies in the financial reports Laine received and I thought I should keep a better eye on things."

I turn and meet her eye. "You knew he was embezzling? Why didn't you raise the issue as Laine?"

She smiles but not as smugly. "You've caught me," she says, almost sheepishly. "This place—" She waves her gun across the icy moonlit landscape and I know she isn't really talking about the pine barrens; she's talking about Briarwood. "It gets its hooks in you and pulls you back. When I left, I swore I'd never come back, but the minute I stepped foot on campus I felt it again—that *magic*."

In the moonlight, hair blown back and without her glasses, her face is naked and open. It's the first time, I realize, that I've ever really seen her, and the person I see is myself—the girl who stared at the gates of Briarwood College on the brochure cover and dreamed of being the person to step through them. Only when I got here, they were closed to me, and instead of coming to feel like I belonged I felt like I'd had to become a different person to be here.

"So why ruin that now?" I ask, no longer just playing for time but genuinely curious.

"Hotch again, the greedy idiot; he threatened to blackmail Laine. I could have just exposed the embezzling then but I was afraid that if he made too much noise about Laine the authorities might pay a visit to Maine and uncover the lack of a real person up there—although I go as often as my busy schedule here allows to keep things up. Then he got the idea of this little commemoration and I thought, what fun to have you all back here—all of you who sneered at me and made me feel like a freak and then left me for dead in that cave."

She jabs her gun toward the opening and I tense myself to spring for it but she quickly snatches it back and holds it tight against her waist. "The first thing I did was send the incriminating evidence, anonymously, of course, to Miranda Gardner. Let Hotch get a taste of his own medicine when she started blackmailing him, as I knew she would. Then, I thought I'd like to have some fun with the rest of you. I'd made copies of the ghost stories you wrote and set up some pranks, like the dead crow in Miranda's bed, publishing Darla's story online, the phone inside the wall set to electrocute whoever touched it first, the Selectric programmed to type the Raven poem, and some locked doors and cryptic symbols for Ben to follow in the tunnels—I'd rather hoped he'd get stuck down there, reliving his sorority girl story until he put a bullet in his head. Is that what happened?" she asks eagerly.

She asks with so much relish that I'm tempted for a moment to tell her that her plans failed, but then she'll try to kill them when she's done with me. "No," I say. "Ben came up from the basement and Chilton tried to shoot him but he shot her first and then Truman and Ben shot each other."

"Ah, not quite what I planned but a fitting end for all of them. A bit like the end of that Agatha Christie novel."

"Poisoning Darla and spearing Lance with that stag's head were a little more than pranks—what did either of them do to deserve such horrible deaths?"

"Don't talk to *me* about horrible deaths!" she snarls, abandoning all semblance of calm and reason. "They weren't innocent. I know it was Darla who switched her story submission with mine and ruined my chances of getting into the senior seminar. And Lance was the one who complained about Laine typing Moss's manuscripts and got me assigned to work for him. I should have been in the seminar in the first place instead of being sent to *work* for Moss."

I could point out that she'd seemed to enjoy working for Moss and that Darla hadn't switched the submissions, but I don't want her angry; I want her smug. I've noticed that when she's pleased with herself, she splays open her right hand—the one that holds the gun.

"You must have had to act quickly when Nina fell in the cave and saw the bones in the pit," I say, wincing with the realization that those bones must belong to Laine.

"I did!" she says, as proud as when she told me she'd fixed the Xerox machine herself. "It made me regret not moving them, but when I looked for them a few years ago, rubble had fallen into the pit and covered them up. The rocks must have shifted since then—those caves have never been stable—and uncovered them. It was bad luck that girl fell in just the wrong place and then aimed her phone light down into the pit on Laine's skull. I knew that as soon as the police found out that the bones were Laine's they'd look more closely into her cyber trail and the house in Maine. Fortunately, I've taken precautions with that, but they rather require a fall guy and you, I'm afraid, are well set up for that."

"Me? How does that work?" I ask, not rising to the bait. She's gone back to looking smug. She's so wrapped up in her speech—her coup de grâce, I believe she must see it as—that she doesn't seem to notice me discreetly inching my feet slowly away from the cave and toward her.

"Once they know that Laine is dead, they'll need another suspect and they'll go through Laine's cyber trail. What they'll find is that many of the communications from Laine have come from your work computer—camouflaged, of course, but rather shabbily. When they go to the house in Maine, they'll find your DNA and a few of your possessions—some scarves you've lost over the years, some coffee cups with your lipstick prints, a few books . . . you know, the ones you put on the free pile that get snatched up so quickly. You see, I've been keeping you as a failsafe all along."

"Do you really think that will be enough to convince the police"—I almost say *Ben*—"that *I* took Laine's identity and killed all my classmates?"

"Well, there's also the confession you've left on your computer desktop, explaining that you can't live with the lies anymore and that you know it will all come out now that the bones have been found—that you killed Laine and took her identity."

"And why, exactly, did I have to kill all my classmates?"

"You've blamed them all these years for making you go along with covering up Moss's death," she says.

"That's a little weak," I can't help pointing out, "as motives go."

She smiles, seemingly unoffended. "I agree, but that's what happens in *The Intended*—the narrator's alter ego, her blur-girl, kills all her classmates—which you will also reveal, finally, to be your book. You see, when I went back to Laine's room, I found the letter Moss wrote to his agent. Only it wasn't for *her* book; it was for yours."

She smiles at the surprise on my face. "Didn't you wonder why Laine stole your book? Moss had confused them!" She laughs and splays her hand again. "Isn't that rich? Imagine Laine's dismay! But being Laine Bishop, she'd figured out a way to solve the problem. She'd taken both manuscripts from Moss's study—hers and yours. She was already planning to steal your book. In fact, now that I know she tried to push you I bet she thought her plan would work best if you were dead. Of course, she needn't have bothered. I knew you'd be too afraid to say anything." She smiles triumphantly at this revelation and splays her hand open.

I reach for the gun, quickly enough that she is unprepared and loses her grip on it. My hands are so numb from the cold, though, that I don't manage to grasp it. It falls to the ground and slides toward the black chasm of the ice cave. I lunge for it, scraping my knees on the ribbed surface of the rock. *Chatter marks*, I remember Ben telling us, crescent-shaped marks made by the retreating glacier. I dig my fingers in them now to drag myself closer to the gun. I've just grazed it with my fingertips when Bridget grabs my ankle. I kick her away, then reach for the gun, but end up pushing it. It skitters across the slick ice and falls into the cave. Behind me I hear a low growl and I imagine Bridget turned into a mountain lion—her final transformation. I don't turn to see. Instead, I slide forward on the ice, letting the curve of the rockface and the slick of the ice take me into the cave.

CHAPTER FORTY-ONE

THEN

December 21, 1996

Dear Cyril

It's rare these days that a student's work moves me so much that I feel compelled to recommend it to you but when you read Miss Bishop's novel <u>The Intended</u> I think you'll see why I am writing.

"A bildungsroman!" I hear you say. "Have you lost the plot, Hugo? What could be special about that?"

But what is special about <u>The Intended</u> is how this young woman captures the essence of the insecurity and fluctuating identity of youth. Do you remember, Cyril? Those days when anything was possible and the future loomed uncertain and portentous as a specter? From the first scene in which our narrator imagines herself arriving at the college gates to be greeted by a facsimile of herself—the true intended for her place at the college—what she calls the blur-girl, to the final scenes in which she kills her rival to take her place at the table—you will be entranced. True, as in any freshman effort, there are echoes of the masters—Poe and James (both M. R. and Henry) and Brontë (Emily, of course, with her inimitable "I am Heathcliff!"), with a dash of Highsmith's Ripley, but the voice that emerges is wholly her own. A voice which, dare I say, is intended for a large audience.

Miss Bishop will be happy to send you the ms. posthaste after the holidays at your request.

Love to Betsey and the children.

Yrs, HM

# CHAPTER FORTY-TWO

*NOW*

I HIT THE stone steps and roll down them. It's painful but at least I've avoided the drop into the pit. When I get to the bottom I feel for the gun but I can't find it. There are any number of crevasses and hollows it could have fallen into. I look for my phone, then remember it's in the pocket of my coat, which is with Nina. When I searched for Laine's body after she'd fallen, I hadn't been able to find her or Bridget. I'd kept going through the cave, convinced Laine had crawled into some nook to die. Now I know Laine had already been dead and Bridget was hiding from me, waiting for me to go farther into the caves so she could climb out. I could have gotten lost and died here that night, but I hadn't—and if I'm careful I won't now.

I'm searching for the metal bolts that Ben had used to guide our rope twenty-five years ago. I find one and then the next one, focusing on them to keep blind panic from rising up in me the deeper I go. When the echoes change I know that I'm in the domed cavern—what we had called the Crystal Cave until Laine told us there was a better one. There's no light to reflect off the stalactites but there is a purplish aura kindling in the dark and tiny sparks of light, some phosphorescence in the mineral deposits that fills the cave with an eerie glow in the darkness.

"Do you feel it, Nell?" I startle at Bridget's voice not far behind me. Then I hear a metallic click and I realize she's either found Chilton's gun or she had one of her own.

The shot blasts through the cave, the echo deafening. I feel the bullet speed past me as I hurtle through an opening in the rock, groping with my hands to find my way. The rock wall is vibrating with the impact of the bullet. Could those vibrations cause a cave-in? I wonder, remembering what Ben said about the cave being unstable because it was on a fault line. The ground beneath my feet seems to be trembling, but that might just be from our feet pounding the ground as Bridget pursues me. I keep going, blind in the dark cave save for an occasional disorienting flash of violet or emerald light.

"Have you come to the narrow pass yet?" Bridget asks, her voice a whisper on the air. "Oh yes, I read all about the cave in Laine's story, one she didn't share with the rest of you. Do you think you can still fit through it? No offense, but you're not quite as slim as you were at twenty-two."

I nearly laugh. Bridget in the guise of Ruth has been bringing me treats for the last five years—scones and muffins she baked, cakes and cookies left over from departmental parties, as if she's been fattening me up. I am certainly *not* as slim as I was in college, and I recall that the leftmost passage was a tight squeeze even back then. I could take the middle opening and circle back behind her. Surprise her and take the gun. I picture us going around in circles for eternity. Or I could climb out and make a run for it. Will I even be able to tell when I've reached the place where there are three choices? If I take one of the right passages by mistake, who knows where it will lead? I might end up buried alive in a dead-end passage.

The thought arouses such a stab of claustrophobia that I suddenly can't breathe. Panic itches at my scalp, spreading cold, clammy sweat down my spine. Whatever happens, I have to keep taking the leftmost turn.

I grope along the walls, clinging to the left side of each passage, each opening narrower and narrower, each one tighter than I recall. It's not just the spread of my hips, I realize; rocks have fallen in the course of twenty-five years. Any one of these passages might have been sealed off. I come to one that is nearly blocked by a big round rock. It's loose, though, so I roll it a few inches away and squeeze through, crawling on my hands and knees, ice freezing my ungloved hands, the walls scraping against my cheeks—

As Laine's had been scraped when she came back to Wilder House and told us she'd taken "the path less traveled." I'd taken it, too, twenty-five years ago, thinking it was the way she'd go because it was how she'd gone before. She'd told Moss that she'd found the real Crystal Cave and I'd seen right away what she meant.

As I do now. The narrow passage opens up suddenly into a round cavern full of blinding light. It had so dazzled me last time that I thought I'd died and been blasted into the afterlife. I *could* have died. There's a sheer drop at the end of the narrow passage that falls ten feet onto jagged rocks. The light comes from a hole at the top of the cavern—an oculus. The full moon is shining through it tonight, turning the ice-covered crystals into a blazing kaleidoscope of refracted light. The sight that last time had made me weep—for Laine, who I believed was dead; for myself, because I suddenly knew that no matter how much pain and trouble she had brought into my life, she had also brought me this—a place so magical and beautiful I would doubt for all the years following that it had been real.

Shivering from the cold, I slither forward onto a projecting ledge and lower myself down to the floor using the cracks in the walls as handholds, wedging my feet in between two stalagmites. Some of them have joined with their parent stalactites on the ceiling to form columns that ring the circular space like the colonnade of a Greek temple. I step behind one just in time for it to block a bullet.

The column shatters in a spray of ice and limestone that splatters my face.

"Please don't make me wreck the whole place," Bridget calls from her perch on the ledge. "Think of all the future generations of Briarwood students who have yet to have the excitement of discovering the Crystal Cave and seeing their future here."

I dart quickly behind the next column, which explodes the second after I'm behind it, so I leap behind the next one. "Tell me, how did you feel when you got that first email from Laine after Christmas break and you realized she was still alive? You must have been so afraid that she would tell someone what you did!"

"Why didn't *you* tell?" I cry, careless of revealing my position. "You could have ruined me back then. Ruined all of us."

"I *did* ruin you all," she says, her voice thick with venom. "I've seen the way you try to atone for what you did to me. How you live in that little cottage like a penitent nun. But it's never been enough, has it? You should be glad I'm here to end it all finally."

The column I'm standing behind suddenly explodes into a pillar of salt. A stalactite loosened by the shot's vibrations crashes inches from me, nearly impaling my foot. I crouch down behind the remains of the pillar.

"And now when you die in here and everyone reads your suicide confession they will know what you did. Bridget Feeley will have justice and I can live out my life as Ruth in peace. I deserve that after what you all did to me."

She slides down from the ledge onto the cavern floor and walks straight toward me with her gun raised and pointed. "And don't worry about lying here for eternity. Your trusty, dependable assistant will find your body after she gets free from the tower and follows you here."

I stand up quickly, launching the stalactite like a missile as I rise. It hits Bridget in the chest hard enough that she doubles over, but she still has hold of the gun. I use the remaining base of the pillar as a stepping stone to propel myself up to a ledge and out through a cleft in the wall. The passage curves sharply right and leads back toward the narrow passage I went through to enter the Crystal Cave. This is what I discovered the last time I was here—the Crystal Cave doesn't lead to a "path less traveled," it's a dead end, or rather, a cul-de-sac. The back exit leads around to the narrow passage. I squeeze through it into the main passage, barely getting past the large silvery rock. As I do, I hear Bridget behind me, shouting my name, and then I hear a gunshot just as I make it through the tight squeeze. It's so loud in the confined space that its vibrations shake loose the rocks above the cleft and shower my head with pebbles. The big round rock moves to and fro—all it needs is a push—

It rolls in front of the passage and settles there firmly. There remains only a tiny chink through which I hear Bridget's howl when she understands what I've done.

"No!" she screams. "You can't leave me here! Not again! You can't do that to me. When they read your confession, they'll think you murdered me."

"I'll come back," I say as the roof begins to cave in. And then I'm running through drifts of dirt and falling pebbles, her cries following me like the echoing pleas of someone who died a long time ago.

## CHAPTER FORTY-THREE

*NOW*

BEFORE I CAN go back for Bridget I have to get Nina and take her down to safety before she freezes to death. I make my way across the pine barrens, my feet so numb I can barely feel them. The temperature has dropped into the single digits and the wind feels like a scythe scraping across my face. I am terrified I'll find Nina dead of hypothermia in the tower—one more victim of what we did twenty-five years ago—because that is where the blame lies. Whatever Bridget became, she became it because of what we—I—did to her. We ignored and mocked her for three and a half years and then left her for dead in that icy cavern. And even when she came back, I failed to see her, right in front of me for five years. Miranda, Hotch, Darla, Lance—their deaths are on me. I just hope there's not one more on my head.

When I come up to the top platform of the tower I see Nina slumped in the chair, her lips blue in the moonlight. I rush to her and shake her, chafing her cold hands in mine, trying to bring life back into her. After what feels like an agonizing stretch of time she stirs and opens her eyes, confused.

"Dean Portman? What happened? Ruth told me we had to come up here to help you but then . . ." She sits up suddenly and looks around the room anxiously. "She gave me some hot cocoa to drink, to keep me warm, but it tasted funny so when she wasn't looking, I spilled the rest out . . ." She begins to shake so hard she can't talk.

"It's okay, Nina," I tell her as I struggle with the ropes binding her. "I'm going to bring you someplace safe and warm." When I get the ropes off, I help her to stand. I notice then a flash of light from outside. I look out the window and see that the bowl at the foot of the mountain is full of flashing lights. Ambulances and police cars are parked on the lawn, their lights reflecting off Mirror Lake. Help has arrived at last.

When we come out of the tower the flashing lights below us turn the air into a river of light to carry us down. The Luminaria in reverse. We are headed to the tower reflected in Mirror Lake. Maybe, I think, as I feel hands grasping me and hear voices burbling around me, I have finally come home to the mirror world below the lake where the girl I cast away twenty-five years ago is waiting to pull me under and drown me so she can take back her rightful place.

WHEN I SURFACE, I am in a hospital room and Truman is sitting by my side. He's a little blurry around the edges, as if I'm looking at his reflection.

"Welcome back," he says hoarsely, as if I've been on a long journey.

"Ben and Chilton?" I croak.

"Both fine," he tells me. "Ben's down the hall and Chilton's husband and daughters came to bring her back to Connecticut for better treatment. You, by the way, had hypothermia and frostbite. You lost a pinky toe, but the doctors say you'll walk just—"

"And Nina?"

"Fine, too, thanks to you."

"And Bridget?" I ask last.

His face wavers as if he really is a reflection in water. "Bridget?" he echoes. "She's dead."

I try to nod, understanding that they must have found her too late, and then I sink back into the mirror lake.

When I come to again, Truman is still there, and Ben is sitting beside him in a wheelchair. His arm and shoulder are bandaged. His face is uncharacteristically stubbled while Truman's is unusually clean-shaven. It's like they've switched places, I think, and then I recall how it was Bridget who changed places with Laine. I try to explain to Ben and Truman but they look at each other as if I'm mad. "You're saying that your assistant, Ruth, was Bridget Feeley?" Ben asks.

"Yes!" I cry. "I know it sounds amazing but it's true. If you look on Ruth's computer—" They exchange another incredulous look.

"My colleagues have been going through Ruth's computer—and yours." Ben looks embarrassed and then I remember what Bridget said about using my computer to send the messages from Laine and the confession she planted.

"She set me up," I begin, so agitated that a nurse comes in to check my blood pressure. She admonishes Ben and Truman not to upset me. But it's a little too late for that. "Does everyone think that I was the one embezzling from the endowment? That I killed Miranda and Hotch and Darla and Lance?"

"No one believes that," Truman says.

"But that is the way it looks," Ben concedes.

"It's her revenge—Bridget's revenge," I say. "Did you at least find her in the cave?"

Truman gazes at me, then says, "There was a cave-in after you got out. There's nothing there but rubble."

"You mean her body wasn't found?" I ask.

"No," Ben says. "But we have determined that the bones

that Nina found belong to Laine Bishop. There's no trace of Bridget Feeley from then—"

"Or now," I finish for him.

I spend a restless night haunted by images of Bridget rising from the cave, coming to seek vengeance on me.

*Anyone who dies in the caves comes back to avenge their death.*

Bridget made sure of her revenge before she died. I know how meticulous Ruth was. If she wanted to make it look like I was an embezzler and a murderer she would have done so thoroughly. I wake in the morning with the grim thought that it serves me right, having become dependent on Ruth's efficiency, to be undone by it in the end. This is the punishment I deserve for leaving Bridget in the cave to die.

Although I'm told that I can be discharged it takes most of the day to complete the paperwork. The whole time I expect the police to arrive to arrest me. When Truman comes to collect me in a taxi, it's dusk. Only as we head back to my house, driving past houses with Christmas lights and cheery wreaths, do I realize it's Christmas Eve. There's a basket of Greek Christmas cookies on the doorstep with a note from Photini and her mother welcoming me home. Inside, my house is full of flowers—a tasteful bouquet of white lilies and freesia from Chilton with a note telling me to "keep my chin up," and a burst of purple, pink, and orange anemones from Kendra with a note that just says *Peace*. There's more food from the Acropolis and my cat, Earl, looks fat and happy. "That girl from the diner let me in," Truman explains. "I hope you don't mind that I stayed here. Chilton invited me to come spend Christmas, but I figured I'd just be in the way and . . ." He hesitates, and then adds, "I didn't want to leave until you came out of the hospital."

"Thank you," I say, stroking Earl. The place looks both cleaner and more lived in than it has for the last decade.

"I can get a hotel room now," he begins, but I stop him by stepping closer, swaying on my bandaged foot, and laying a hand on his chest. When I look up at him his face still has that shimmer I saw when I came to in the hospital. I felt then that I was looking at a face reflected in a mirror but now it feels as if I'm looking through time at the boy I first saw on the registration line in Wilder Hall. From the way he's looking at me I can almost believe that he's seeing the girl I was then.

"You can stay," I tell him.

And he does.

BEN COMES TO the house the next morning to tell us that Nina has given a statement that Bridget drugged her and then forced you at gunpoint into the tower. She hadn't apparently said anything else that she had overheard. "She backs up your story," he says. "We still have to investigate the evidence on your computer that ties you to the embezzling, but we should be able to clear you."

"*Should*, man?" Truman asks. "You know Nell is innocent."

I tense for a flare-up but instead Ben smiles. "Yeah, I do, *man*, and I'm working to make sure everyone else does."

To my amazement Truman smiles back.

Then Ben turns back to me. "We've gone through Ruth's apartment but so far there's nothing directly linking her to Bridget Feeley. We did find, though, a file on her home computer labeled 'A Confession,' which seems almost too good to be true. While it doesn't go into the specifics of these murders, it's close enough in spirit that along with the fact that Ruth Morris is missing and Bridget Feeley's bones were never found, the DA seems inclined not to charge you."

"That's weird," Truman says, "that Ruth would be so careful about not leaving anything that would identify her as Bridget Feeley but then leave a confession."

"Criminals aren't as smart as everyone thinks they are," Ben says. "But they are egotists, and they usually want *someone* to think they're geniuses. And this confession, if it *was* written by Bridget Feeley, it makes it clear how much she hated us—*all* of us."

I expect him to say something about how she had been right—we were terrible people back then and we did terrible things and we're still awful people who don't have a right to be happy. But instead of this judgmental screed—which I'm able to generate in my own head without any help from Ben—he says, "In my experience, the person who thinks that everyone else is the villain ought to look long and hard at himself before he starts accusing other people."

Then he looks from me to Truman to Earl, who's sitting in Truman's lap, wishes us all a happy Christmas, and leaves.

"Wow," I say, turning to Truman, "do you think Ben has *evolved*?"

I expect Truman to make a joke at Ben's expense but instead he nods gravely. "It was shooting Chilton," he says, "that weighed heavily on him. He kept saying, 'I could have killed her.' So yeah, I think he has evolved. And if he can"—he looks up at me, that grave expression shading toward something like hope as he reaches for my hand—"maybe it's not too late for the rest of us."

WE DON'T LEAVE the house for the rest of the weekend. On Monday, even though the college is closed, I go in. I leave Truman searching online for property to buy in the Catskills—something with a barn where he can build his own recording studio. We haven't talked about what will come next for us—or even if there is an *us*—but it's clear we both want to be close enough geographically to find out.

I leave my car for him in case he wants to check out a listing and walk to campus—slowly because of the bandages on my right foot, the missing toe creating an imbalance. The campus is looking its most picturesque. The iron gates look festive, trimmed with snow, and Mirror Lake is a brilliant silver disk in the bright sunshine. It's hard to believe that four people—five, including Bridget—died here just a week ago. I stop for a moment by the lake, feeling an ache for Lance and Darla and even Miranda. They were each flawed but they didn't deserve to die. It doesn't seem right that they're gone and I'm here.

I swipe my ID card to get into Main. The click of the electronic lock echoes in the empty building as I push in and I catch myself thinking, Ruth will probably be here. Ben told me that Hotch's office has been searched and cleared and is no longer a crime scene. When I finally opened my laptop last night, I had a slew of emails from the provost and the CFO of the college informing me that all of President Hotchkiss's files and all of mine related to the finances of Writers House had been confiscated for an internal audit. As I walk slowly up the central staircase, I prepare myself for a scene of chaos. When I reach the fourth floor, I hear a crooning voice coming from down the hall—Ella Fitzgerald singing "Summertime," the same song Laine had played out her dorm window the first day of freshman year.

*Whoever dies in the caves comes back to avenge their death.*

But then I hear the soft voice of a radio announcer asking for donations and I recognize our local NPR station. When I arrive at the outer office—Ruth's domain—I find Kendra Martin in sweatpants and a bright orange sweater cross-legged on the floor sorting files. When she sees me, she unfolds her legs and leaps nimbly to her feet and hugs me.

"Thank God!" she says. "I was afraid you wouldn't want to come back after what you went through and I need your help."

"What are you doing?" I ask. "Weren't you going home to Pittsburgh for the holidays?"

"Pfft." She puffs up her cheeks and blows out a puff of

air. "I got tired of my aunties trying to fix me up with a 'nice girl.' And someone has to hire the new writer-in-residence." She brandishes the bright orange folder she showed me before break, the one with the candidates she was recommending for the position.

"Kendra," I say, hating to extinguish the spark of enthusiasm in her eyes, "I'm not even sure Writers House will open in the spring, or that there's still funding for it after the money Hotch siphoned off and now that—" I swallow, bracing myself to say her name. "Now that we know Laine Bishop is dead, we don't know how that will affect the endowment for Writers House."

Kendra's eyebrows shoot up. "Didn't you hear?"

"Hear what?" I ask, afraid of what new discovery there's been.

"The CFO checked the wording of the original bequest. In the event of Elaine Bishop's death all decisions regarding hiring fall to Ellen Portman. And he says that there's plenty of money in the trust to support the bequest," Kendra says. "That book of Laine's just sells and sells."

I sink down in the chair behind the desk—Ruth's chair—and stare up at Kendra. That Laine left such a responsibility to me nearly undoes me. At some point before she became unhinged by her mother's death and the toxic pressure of Moss's seminar, she did think of me as a friend. For the first time since I learned that she was dead I feel a space opening up inside of me to grieve for her—but not now. Now there's business to take care of.

"Does that mean I can select the director of Writers House as well?"

"I guess so. I thought you might want it—"

"Would you do it?" I ask.

She grins. "And you and I can pick who we want for writer-in-residence?"

"Pending the approval of the hiring committee," I say primly before breaking into a grin. "But essentially, yes."

"Then my answer is yes," she says, holding out her hand.

I take it, grateful for its warmth. I notice that Kendra is studying me. "Go ahead," I say, "ask me whatever is on your mind."

I think she's going to ask me what it was like to face down the ice cave killer or whether I believe the legends, or even whether it was me all along who was the real killer, but instead she asks, "Do you ever miss it? Writing, I mean. You got into Moss's famous seminar. You must have been serious about writing. Why did you give it up?"

I start to say what I usually say, a line borrowed long ago from Dean Haviland—*Some people have the Promethean spark; some of us are keepers of the flame*—but then I remember sitting in this office with Dean Haviland at the end of my senior year. When she took over for Moss, she had offered to guide us all through our senior projects, but mine, the novel I had written, had vanished from Moss's study and I didn't have a copy. Instead, she offered to help me expand an essay I'd written on the Lady of Shalott for her called "The Woman in the Mirror: Doubles in Victorian Literature" with a view toward submitting it as a writing sample to Ph.D. programs. At the end of the semester, she had called me into her office to tell me I'd been given a full scholarship to the Syracuse University doctorate program, an offer I suspected she'd helped facilitate.

"Unless you still want to pursue writing?" she had asked. "I recognized your story when I judged for the Raven Society and I thought it was the best out of all of them."

I'd felt a flush of pleasure at her praise, but then a queasy sense of guilt that I knew then would always accompany any success in writing—a sense I didn't deserve it.

"I'm not sure I have the stomach for it," I told her.

"No"—she nodded—"it's not a profession for the faint of heart. I think it destroyed Hugo in the end . . . I should have seen that . . ." Her eyes had filled with tears and she looked frail and uncertain. "I'm so sorry I wasn't here," she said. "I'll never forgive myself."

I think now about seeing the book I had written published and winning awards and accolades under someone else's name. I should have felt angry, outraged, jealous, but instead I felt as I had when I wrote it—that it never really belonged to me.

"I do miss it sometimes," I tell Kendra, "but when I wrote I felt as if I left myself and, in the end, I'd rather *keep* myself."

Kendra nods, a shadow flitting across her face that tells me she knows what I'm talking about. *As a real writer would,* I hear Moss say in my head.

The shadow lifts and she says, "Oh! I almost forgot. Nina Lawson put in a work-study application to work in this office. What do you think?"

"I think I'm glad she's up for coming back in the spring after what she went through. Yes, by all means, yes!"

I leave in better spirits than I arrived, even though I can hear, as I pass Mirror Lake, Bridget's voice telling me that none of it is enough to make up for what I did. *That doesn't mean I shouldn't try,* I answer back as I start on the path up Briarwood. The climb is hard on my injured foot and I can feel the cold touching the dead spots on my fingers and toes where the frost bit in deep. I fear that there are places in my body that will never feel warm—or much of anything—again. I fear that the legend is true and I'll see Bridget rising up from her rocky crypt in my nightmares for the rest of my life. And I fear that the last line of "A Confession," which I remember well from the night I sat in Dean Haviland's office reading Bridget's story about a girl who takes revenge for the ill treatment she received, will come true. *My true revenge,* the story had ended, *will be to leave my victims always looking over their shoulders for me.*

As I come to the top of the ridge and face the setting sun, I know that what I fear most of all is that when I look in the mirror, I'll see *her,* the blur-girl, the one intended for my life, and I'll have to answer to her for how I'm living it.

# ACKNOWLEDGMENTS

Thank you to my agent, Robin Rue, and her assistant, Beth Miller, of Writers House for their ongoing support and encouragement. Thank you to Liz Stein for her steady editorial hand and to everyone at William Morrow for all their hard work—Ariana Sinclair, Mallory McCurdy, and Kelly Cronin.

I am beyond grateful to my friends who patiently listen to my plotting and gnashing of teeth—thank you, Roberta Andersen, Alisa Kwitney, Nina Shengold, and Ethel Wesdorp, and a special thanks to Nancy Johnson, who answered dozens of questions about what a dean does on long walks through the woods.

Thank you to my family—Lee Slonimsky, Maggie Vicknair, Nora Slonimsky, and Jeremy Levine—for always making me feel at home in this world.

I began this book before the pandemic of 2020 and put it aside for a little while until I could better visualize what the world was going to look like in the coming years. During that time, I began zooming with a few college friends. The few grew to many and the weekly Zoom sessions were welcome companionship through trying times. It also reminded me of how powerful those ties we make in college are so that when I returned to this book it was with a fresh appreciation for the friends I made there. Thank you to the Vassar Zoom Group—Andrea Massar, Arielle Curtin, John Bodinger de Uriarte, Connie

Crawford, Gary Feinberg, Howard Lutz, Fran Rosenberg, Josh Blum, James Brophy, Ken Franklin, Judith Kristl, Lisa Wager, Mitchell Merling, Michael Weekly, Shari Norton, and Scott Silverman—for bringing light to dark times; to you I dedicate this book.

# READ MORE BY CAROL GOODMAN

## Two-time Mary Higgins Clark Award Winner

**THE DISINVITED GUEST**

**THE STRANGER BEHIND YOU**

**THE SEA OF LOST GIRLS**

**THE NIGHT VISITORS**

**THE OTHER MOTHER**

**THE WIDOW'S HOUSE**